KEEPER

Ingrid Seymour

PenDreams • BIRMINGHAM

Published by PenDreams

Cover design by Ingrid Seymour

Manufactured in the United States of America
Copyright © 2013 by Ingrid Seymour

ISBN-13: 978-0-9910934-1-0

To Isabella and Alexander
You make life shine

ಹ Chapter 1 ೞ
Greg

Greg Papilio wanted many things, and most of what his heart desired hinged on his impending metamorphosis.

Today, though, all he wanted was to pass the trig test that lay in front of him. But, to his mounting horror, it didn't look like that was going to happen. He stared at the page. This final was kicking his butt. He hadn't even managed to get past the first few questions. A drop of sweat slid off his forehead and splattered onto the paper, forming a gray circle. He wiped a hand across his brow and looked at his watch. Only thirty minutes left?

What?! That was it? Where had the last couple of hours gone?!

His mind was hazy, his vision blurry. Greg shook his head, trying to dispel the dream-like state that clouded his thoughts. Suddenly, he felt as if piranha teeth were biting the back of his neck. A shiver made his skin prickle. He straightened with a jolt and put a hand to the base of his neck. His fingers tentatively traveled down each vertebrae. Something bumpy and oozing blistered under his touch.

Oh, shit!

Not exam jitters. How stupid he was to confuse the symptoms with nerves. He had to get out of here. Now.

"Are you done, Mr. Papilio?" the teacher asked when Greg stood up to leave.

He shook his head. "No . . . no, I think I'm sick," he croaked out in a hoarse voice. Greg crumpled up his exam, stuffed it in his pocket and wobbled out of the classroom under the disapproving stare of the teacher and the whispers of his classmates.

He staggered out to the school parking lot. Holding a hand to his roiling stomach, he started walking the short two blocks home. The backpack grew heavier on his back as he weakened. His head pounded and his joints felt as if they would come unglued.

Please, let me make it home. Please.

The sun scorched the pavement. Cicadas made a racket in the nearby trees. Greg felt as if they were inside his cranium, their calls echoing between his temples. With each step, his feet sent a jolt of pain through him. They dragged, hurting like hell, as if someone had smashed his toes with a hammer. Sheer will carried him to his front yard. He slid the backpack off his shoulders and let it dangle. He dragged it by one strap and stumbled toward the porch, legs weakening, every ounce of strength slipping away. Moisture slid down his forehead in rivulets, a grimy mixture of sweat and New Orleans humidity.

His stomach lurched and a loud burp escaped his half-opened mouth. Even through the pain, he winced at the smell. His breath was foul, like meat left out to spoil. Greg abandoned the backpack on the plush lawn. He staggered forward, covering the remaining distance. His shoulder slammed against the front door, sending excruciating pain across his back, through the telltale swelling at the base of his neck.

Opening the door took all he had left in him. The key shook in his hand and the keyhole danced from left to right as he tried to make the connection. After several attempts, he unlocked the door, shouldered it and closed it behind him, and took a few steps toward the bathroom. A violent twist in his gut brought him short. A moan broke from the back of his throat. The awful pain oscillated, drawing back for an instant, then hitting him again—even more viciously than before. Clutching his middle, he fell to his knees, then pitched forward. Part of his body hit the tiled foyer, while his face thankfully landed on the hall's sage rug. The scented powder his mom used for vacuuming traveled up his nostrils and made his stomach convulse. Greg had never felt this sick before in his life. He lay there for several minutes, struggling to take deep breaths.

Something's wrong. They never said it would hurt like this.

If his parents didn't hurry up and get home, he was going to die. A few more minutes and his insides wouldn't only feel like a slushie, they would *be* a slushie.

A wet, sucking sound distracted him. Greg swallowed thickly.

What the hell?

He tried to move, but felt stuck to the rug. Desperately, he fought to open his eyes to see what was happening. As he labored to lift one eyelid, he imagined himself as a mushy vegetable, trampled by feet in a busy kitchen.

With a loud pop, his eyes sprang open. He tried to look around, and his eyeballs made a noise as they swiveled back and forth inside his head. Ignoring the sound, he tried to focus, but everything was blurry. A thick gel . . . *what is that?* . . . obstructed his vision. He stared at something that was supposed to be his hand, except it looked like a shapeless chunk of ground meat. The sight of it drove Greg into a panic.

Something is *wrong. Oh god, I don't wanna die!*

The door opened. "For Pete's sake, Greg," his mom said. "You left your backpack out in the yard and the door's unlocked." Her words came to Greg muffled, as if wads of cotton plugged his ears.

"Oh my," she said, kneeling in front of his blurry eyes. "Greg, honey? Aw, poor baby."

Poor baby?! He was disintegrating on the floor and all she could come up with was "poor baby"? Greg made out his mother's long legs and impossibly high stiletto heels. She crouched by his side for a minute. He tried to speak, to ask for help, but only gurgles came out.

"It's okay, honey. It'll be over before you know it." She patted his head gingerly. "I'll have to wait for your dad to move you. You're too heavy. Oh, I'm so proud of you, baby. Don't worry. I just know you'll be a Companion." She stood and walked away. Greg heard the *tap, tap, tap* of her heels as she headed for the kitchen.

He listened intently and couldn't believe it when he heard the refrigerator open and close, followed by the unmistakable sound of a soda can opening. She was drinking a Coke while he lay dying on the floor! The radio came on, and she began to sing along, howling, "girls just wanna have fun," at the top of her lungs.

Dad! But his father wouldn't be home for another hour, and that would be too late, too late. *Please, don't let me become a vegetable. Pleeease,* he pleaded with every ounce of his being.

He was dimly aware of his mother rattling pots and dishes in the kitchen. Was she actually *cooking*? Maybe she was planning to make meatballs out of him if things went awry with his metamorphosis. It was spaghetti night, after all. His father's favorite.

ஐ Chapter 2 ∞
Sam

Sam hid a bread roll behind her back and looked around to see if anyone had noticed. They hadn't. She and the other volunteers had taken care of the long line, serving everyone limp green beans, Swiss meatballs and instant mash potatoes—sadly one of the best meals the soup kitchen had to offer.

She walked to her messenger bag at the back of the small serving area and put the bread behind the comic books. She slung the bag over her shoulder and walked into the dining hall. Every table and chair was occupied. There was a big crowd today, too many hungry bellies. A few quiet conversations went on at different tables, but most people just hunched over their plates and ate. A little hand went up in the air and waved her over. Sam smiled, her chest filling with fondness at the sight of Jacob's little round face and lively blue eyes.

Darn cute kid. I could eat him up. She winked at Jacob and couldn't help but smile.

"Hi, Sam," he said when she reached his table.

She mussed his dirty blond hair. "Hey, rocky. How are you? Like those meatballs?"

Jacob smiled at his already empty plate and nodded. A simple meal made him happy, even when everything else was screwed up for him.

"I got you an extra buttered roll." Sam knelt next to him, pulled the piece of bread out of her bag and handed it to him under the table. No one noticed. Not even his father who sat next to him staring into space and chewing his food languidly as he always did. The man hunched over his plate from his considerable height. He had to be well over six foot six. Hard to believe Jacob was his son. The kid was eight, but he was scrawny and was no taller than a six-year-old, likely due to the lack of good nutrition.

Jacob bit the roll in half. His cheeks puffed out. He swiped the other half across the plate, wiping what little meatball gravy remained, and devoured that too, truly enjoying himself.

"I got you something else," Sam said when he finished chewing.

"What is it?" Jacob asked, eyes wide with excitement.

Sam pulled out the comic books and spread them like a fan for Jacob to see.

"Batman!" Jacob exclaimed, his high-pitched voice carrying across the room. A few heads turned his way, then went back to their business.

"I thought you'd like them."

On her way here, Sam had stopped at a comic book store and bought them for the boy. She'd been pleasantly surprised when she found out he could actually read. So many of the people here, even the adults, weren't that privileged. His mother had taught him . . . before she abandoned him. At least she'd done something worthwhile for the kid.

"Do I like them? I love them." He hugged them to his chest. His clear blue eyes wavered and, for a moment, it looked as if he might cry.

Sam didn't want him to cry. She wanted him to smile, to be happy. "Here," she said for a distraction and unhooked his backpack from the back of his chair. "I got a few other things."

She concealed Jacob's backpack with her body and transferred a package from her messenger bag to his pack. She didn't trust some of the adults not to steal it from him. She'd seen some of them do worse. Sam had stuffed the package with nuts, protein bars, a jar of peanut butter, a package of granola and several Snickers bars. She'd thought about slipping in some money as well, but she didn't know what Jacob's father might do with it. Buy booze? Drugs? And what after that? Beat the kid? Not that the man looked like an addict, he looked more . . . disconnected from reality than anything else, but you never know.

"What's in it?" Jacob asked.

"Look later, okay?" Sam whispered. "When you and your dad are alone, got it?"

"Got it," Jacob answered like an obedient little soldier.

He was such a sweet kid. It broke her heart she couldn't do more for him now and that she *wouldn't* be able to do more for him later. This was only their third time here, and people came and went all the time. Sam had tried to ask his father a few casual questions, but that hadn't gone well. Afterward, she thought of calling somebody, a social worker or something, but what if she caused the kid to be separated from his father. He really seemed to love him, even if the man was as detached as an unplugged toaster.

"Jacob's a great kid," she'd told him, hoping to break the ice.

The boy's father stared at the table. "They cut this tree down too early," he'd said, tracing a knot in the wood with his finger. "Sapiens always do that."

The what? "Um, I don't mean to intrude but . . . Jacob says you don't have a place to stay. Maybe I can—"

His eyes snapped to Sam's. They were now alert and full of distrust. Their sharp blue color transfixed her. His brow was strong and his cheekbones high. Sam supposed he was the kind of man that women around her mother's age might find attractive. Suddenly he seemed so different, so out of place.

"What do you want with my boy?" he demanded.

Sam got flustered. "Well, I was just . . . I was thinking he . . . maybe you two could . . ."

As she struggled to make sense, he went back to caressing the wood, his eyes vacant and her presence forgotten. "It must have been a pretty tree, colorful leaves in the fall." He had petted the table like a beloved dog, and he was doing the same now while his little son paged a comic book with delight.

"Thank you. They're awesome," Jacob said.

The world was upside down if a precious kid like this had to live such a rough life. She stayed at his side until they left, helping him read the words that gave him trouble. As a farewell, she mussed his hair again and said a little prayer for his wellbeing.

* * *

"Hello?" Sam called out, closing the back door behind her. Her voice echoed through the kitchen. No answer. Same as always. She didn't know why she kept pretending someone cared enough to be here. She walked to the dining table and found the usual: A ten dollar bill under the salt and pepper shaker. Sam stuffed the money in her pocket. This week, her savings amounted to fifty dollars. Her parents were loose with their cash, but not so much with their affection.

She looked in the fridge for something to cook. Cooking cleared her mind. Cooking made her happy.

The Sub-Zero refrigerator hummed, making the loneliness and silence even more palpable. Sam swallowed the thick knot forming in her throat. Her emotions had been hard to control lately. They surged at unexpected moments, choking her. The feelings of desolation, the sense that she didn't belong, had been growing stronger ever since school had let out last week. It'd been bad before, but with her only friend, Brooke, gone to New York for the break, it was worse.

She blinked at the light inside the expansive fridge and tried to focus on dinner. It was hard to invoke her usual indifference, but she managed. There were enough ingredients to make a salad: Lettuce, tomatoes, cucumbers. She could boil an egg, cut up some ham and make a chef salad. She patted her belly. Her waist line could use something healthy. But what was the fun in preparing rabbit food? Unless she got creative with the salad dressing. She pondered making something from scratch, even if that would send her pants size in the wrong direction.

Suddenly, her butt buzzed. She started and reached into her back pocket, drawing out her phone. The display read: Bureau of Doom. Her mom calling from the office.

What the . . . ?

What was her mom? A freakin' psychic or something? Did she know—from behind the mahogany desk of the Gibson & Gibson law firm—that Sam was thinking about making salad dressing at three hundred calories a teaspoon? That her hips were in terrible danger of doubling in width? She closed the fridge and reclined against the island.

"Hey," Sam answered curtly, falling into her usual, childish hostility.

"Samantha, your Dad and I have to meet clients over dinner tonight," her mother said without preamble.

"Ah-hum."

"We'll probably be late, so you don't need to wait for us. Okay, baby?"

Baby? Sam shook her head, irritated. Barbara Gibson never called her daughter baby. "Sure, fine."

"And Samantha, don't open the door for anyone. We love you, honey. Sleep tight." The last few words were hurried, and then the receiver went dead.

In disgust, Sam tossed the phone on the counter. It hit the sleek surface and slid a few inches. Impulsively, she pulled out a large metal spoon from the ceramic utensil holder by the stove and thought of ninja-chopping the phone with it. After a few deep breaths, she decided it wasn't worth the hassle and set the spoon down.

There must have been someone in the room with her. That was the only reason her mom had sounded like the perfect Stepford Mother, because cold-blooded trial lawyers don't say, "We love you, honey. Sleep tight." At least, not this one.

Her parents were probably going out for Friday night cocktails, not a business meeting. But it wasn't the lie that bothered Sam. The problem was their phony attitude when others were present. Why the act when they didn't really care? No matter that she was a good student, stayed out of trouble, and did everything they . . . Sam cut off the train of thought. It was a waste of time. Her parents thought of her as nothing but an unwanted chore. Plain and simple. No use trying to find other reasons.

She fought the stinging sensation in her eyes. Only two more years, and she would be out of here, gone to culinary school, on her own, starting a new life. The idea dissipated the sadness a little, but some of it lingered. Well, only one thing could get her out this bad mood: A triple-cheese grilled sandwich.

She dug out the ingredients from the fridge. Bread, butter, Cheddar, Swiss and Gouda. Not an award-winning recipe to impress them at Le Cordon Bleu, but—when it came to comfort foods—it was one of her favorites. She dropped butter in a skillet and turned on the burner. The warmth and dancing, blue flame set her mind at ease, immediately releasing her frown and shoulder tension. Guiltlessly, she spread butter on the bread and layered cheese on top. A smile appeared on her lips. She placed the sandwich on the skillet and pressed it with a spatula, flipping it a few times until it turned golden-brown and the cheese went gooey in the middle.

Sam paired her buttery creation with creamy, whole milk. She filled the tallest glass to the rim. Standing over the granite island, she bit into her sandwich. Her eyes closed in ecstasy. Her taste buds reveled in the rich, gooey taste.

Mmm!

She guzzled the milk and devoured the rest of the sandwich in the same fashion. When she was done, she contemplated the dirty dishes and bread crumbs left in what—pre-grilled cheese yumminess binge—had been a spotless kitchen. Like any respectable cook, she hated the cleaning part. A dogged, adolescent stubbornness reared its head. The gluttonous evidence would annoy her mother. It always did, which was perhaps even more satisfying than the pigging-out itself.

Sadly, Sam's eating habits were the only thing that aroused semi-appropriate parental behavior from her mom. She insisted all those rich foods weren't healthy, and even had the nerve to suggest a diet of tofu and leafy vegetables. Really? Sam was going to be a chef, for God's sake! How clueless could her mother be? Maybe if health were her mom's real concern, Sam would be grateful for the advice. However, comments such as, "one day you'll blow up like a puffer fish," made it clear that her image was the real issue. Her mother didn't want a chubby for a daughter, because—*gasp!*—what would her friends and clients think?

Two more years and I'll be out of here. There's more to life than this. There has to be. She wouldn't go on feeling like she didn't belong for much longer. She would re-invent herself. Get new friends. A boyfriend, even.

But for now . . . she sighed, staring at the dirty dishes. Her bratty side lost the battle. Sam cleaned the kitchen and left it the way she'd found it. In the media room, she turned on the TV and scrolled through her favorite channels. Nothing worth watching. After a huge sigh, she picked up the phone and dialed Brooke's cell.

"Hey, Sam," Brooke's excited voice boomed through the receiver, accompanied by loud music.

"How's New York?" Sam yelled.

"Oh, it's great. I love it! Right now, we're at the M&M store in Times Square. They have a huge tube filled with M&M's. It goes all the way up to the ceiling!" Sam could almost see it herself, and smiled in spite of her sour mood. "How's everything there?"

"The same. Really waiting for summer school to start." She knew it sounded pathetic, but it was the truth. She wasn't enjoying her time off. School had ended just last week, but she was already desperate for something to do.

"Sam, you have to go out and do something," Brooke said.

Sam blew an exasperated puff of air. Easy for her to say. They didn't have giant tubes full of M&M's in West Lafayette, Indiana. What was she going to do? That's why she had signed up for summer school tutoring (yeah, piling up the pathetic) but no one had called her yet.

"Hold on," Brooke said. The music became louder. Her voice faded in the background, but Sam could still hear her. "Okay, Jenny. I just need to pay for this." Sam imagined her friend waving a stuffed M&M toy—little gloved hands hanging at its sides—while Brooke's cool Aunt Jenny told her to hurry. "I've got to go, Sam. We need to find a place to eat dinner before the show."

"Oh yeah, tonight's *The Lion King*, right?" Sam tried to sound upbeat.

"Yeah, I can't wait!" Brooke was brimming with excitement, and rushed to get off the phone. Who could blame her? "Sorry, Sam. I'll call you later, okay?"

"Sure." Sam wouldn't hold her breath, and, if Brooke didn't call, she wouldn't hold it against her. Someone deserved to have some fun.

Sam hung up the receiver. She felt even worse than before. Why did she have to whine to Brooke? Sam sensed the shroud of depression falling over her again, a heavy weight in her stomach that made her entire life seem hopeless. Her outlook narrowed, as if she couldn't see past her nose anymore and nothing outside her safe cocoon was worth any effort. She tried to push the darkness away, but it hung close.

Only work could keep her mind occupied. There was only so much she could cook. She really needed someone to call for lessons. Besides, tutoring wasn't only good for her mood, it was also good for her savings account, and her dreams of becoming as independent as possible once she got to college.

After a refreshing shower, Sam surfed the web on her phone. Nothing there lifted her spirits either; quite the opposite. She tried to think of the worthiness of her work at the soup kitchen, but all she could focus on was little Jacob's unfair situation. She found nothing to cheer her up. No use.

Finally, she crawled into bed with a book and abandoned her worries inside the fluffy layers of her blossom-scented linens. With a sigh, she opened the novel at the place marked by her Snoopy bookmark. She had good fiction to provide respite tonight, taking her into a world where friends didn't forget to invite you to New York and parents didn't pretend to care by leaving cash on the table.

Two hours later, quite suspended inside a world of gratifying fiction, Sam was jolted back to reality by the sound of a door opening and closing. Lifting her dried-out eyes from the page, she set the book down and listened.

Her parents usually stayed out later than this, so her mind was already conjuring images of hooded men tiptoeing on her mother's expensive rugs. Her feet hit the plush, padded carpet. She inched to the door and cracked it open. Sticking her head out into the hall, she looked right and left. Only a night light shone, highlighting the runner rug that led toward the master bedroom. She quietly closed her door behind her.

Straining to see in the dark hall, Sam stepped out and collided against something unexpected. She yelled and jumped backward, flapping her arms like a frightened hen and crashing into her bedroom door. It flew open. Light from her lamp sliced the hall in two. Sam's mother stood in the spotlight, looking back with squinting, bloodshot eyes, unnerved by Sam's sudden and dramatic reaction.

"Have you lost your mind?" her mother's speech was slurred. Cocktails, no doubt. Other than the red eyes and a little drawl, however, she looked sober. It took inordinate amounts of vodka to melt her glacial core.

"Um, I wasn't expecting you guys home this early," Sam said.

Her mother blinked once, then headed toward her room and, from the corner of her mouth, said, "Go to bed."

"Where's Dad?"

A raging tornado, her mother spun, face contorted into a mask of fury. On the verge of exploding into a verbal lashing, she seemed to bite her tongue, maybe hard enough to draw tears to her cold, gray eyes.

"*He* stayed with the client," she answered. "*I* developed a headache." Each word was exacting and bitter. Sam looked down at the floor, unable to hold her mother's hateful gaze. Something told her not to push the woman's buttons tonight. After a tense moment, her mom walked off and slammed her bedroom door.

Sam blinked, feeling as if she'd taken a bath in a cup of bitter espresso. She'd never before seen pain in her mother's Darth Vader's gaze. If the woman's icy interior had cracked, it meant something major was up. Sam knew she'd better find out, because it could mean life was about to get a lot worse.

✆ *Chapter 3* ☙
Greg

One second, Greg was dead to all. The next, he opened his eyes to an unpolished and battered new world. He stared at the popcorn ceiling of his bedroom. *Weird.* He didn't remember it being so dirty, or in such bad shape. The glow-in-the-dark stars he'd attached what felt like a million years ago were partially detached. A hairline fracture ran from the top of one wall to another. A layer of dust clung to the light bulb overhead. Curious, how he had never noticed those things before.

Greg convinced himself to peel his eyes away from the ceiling. The light on the night table was on. Oddly, he sensed its warmth, and it made him feel like a roasted chicken at the grocery store. He squinted into the intense brightness. All of his senses seemed to be in overdrive. Even his nose twitched at the strong smell of perfume. The sweet scent guided him to a slumped figure on his desk chair: Mom, sleeping peacefully.

So she hadn't cooked him for dinner, after all. Instead, she'd nursed him back to health. He must have been delirious with fever. Totally delusional.

With a jolt, he sat up, remembering what had happened. When he saw the length of his body, he gasped. His feet extended past the end of the twin-size bed. He'd grown an entire foot, and that wasn't all. His legs looked nothing like the skinny twigs he was used to seeing. They were thick and muscular. Dumbfounded, Greg looked down at his chest and marveled at his chiseled pecs and abs. They flexed and relaxed with ease. His body had never looked this good before. His parents had assured him this would happen, but only seeing was believing. He stared and stared.

"Oh, baby, you're awake!" Mom rushed to his side, sat at the edge of the bed and locked him in a viselike hug.

Going crimson from head to toe, Greg pawed at the sheets and pulled them up to his waist. He was dressed in nothing but a pair of boxer shorts, which were now way too tight for comfort. She grabbed his shoulders and held him at arm's length. Pride filled her bright blue eyes.

"Mom, what . . . ?" he started to ask, but the sound of his own voice stopped him. He brought a hand to his throat. The new, deep tone was familiar, but certainly not his own.

Excited, Mom hurried to the door. "Nick, Nick . . . Greg's awake. Hurry!"

She rushed back to his side and returned to beaming like an adoring lioness over a brand new cub. Dad appeared in the doorway. He looked pale, with dark circles under his eyes. Greg suddenly saw how exhausted both his parents looked. Mom's hair was in disarray, and she wore a pair of Dad's pajama pants along with one of Greg's favorite t-shirts. It was short on her and showed her navel. Self-consciously, she tugged on the garment.

"Don't be mad. You won't need it anymore," she said.

Greg frowned, annoyed at the fact that he would need a whole new wardrobe. He hadn't thought of that.

"Oh, my baby," Mom said, "I'm so proud of you."

"Everything . . . went okay?" Greg asked, trying to ignore his new, velvety voice. Apprehension writhed in his chest as he waited for the answer. He'd always known these changes would happen, but that didn't make him less anxious.

Dad sat on the other side of the bed. His expression was stern, but Greg thought a hint of pride showed in his eyes. "Yes. So far, everything's gone as it should, but the final step hasn't occurred yet."

Greg nodded, wishing to be done with it, desperate to find out his caste once and for all. Just one more step and he would know. Ever since he could remember, he'd wondered what his destiny would be. He'd always known that he wouldn't be the same scrawny kid forever, that one day he'd be tall, fit and handsome like Dad. But his caste, his fate in life, that had always been a mystery, an obsessive question ever-present in the back of his mind.

"Erica," Dad said, "why don't you fetch a mirror?"

While she was gone, Greg stared at his hands. They were large and strong, like Dad's. A burning sensation at the back of his neck made him shrug involuntarily. He took a hand to the spot and felt a collection of bumps and protuberances.

"My mark . . . ?" Greg asked, just to make sure.

"It's still illegible," Dad confirmed.

Greg knew this. His mark would stay blurry until the final step. The physical transformation was taxing enough. A Morphid's mind wouldn't change—and reveal their mark—until the body had time to rest.

"But don't worry about it. It'll be alright." Dad tried to soothe him, but his voice wavered a little.

"You don't sound so sure," Greg said.

Dad blinked a couple of times. "Oh, don't mind me. You know I worry too much." He gave a weak smile.

Mom reentered the room, sat and extended the mirror his way. With a slight nod, Dad encouraged him to take it. Suddenly apprehensive, Greg snatched the mirror into his lap, averting his eyes.

"There's nothing to be afraid of, honey," Mom said. "You're quite the handsome devil. You look just like your father when I first met him." She winked at her husband.

Even now, the idea still seemed ludicrous, considering how plain Greg had always been. If he had a dollar for every time he heard things like, "maybe you're adopted, dude," or "your real folks abandoned you under a bridge, 'cause you must have been a fugly baby," he would be a freakin' multi-millionare. No one could believe two extremely attractive people like his parents had produced a homely-looking kid like him.

With trepidation, Greg lifted the mirror and took a look. His breath caught at the sight of his familiar, yet drastically evolved features. He saw the same nose, mouth, blue eyes, and black hair, except everything was somehow . . . perfect. The blue in his irises sparkled. His once-dull hair had luster, gleaming blue-black like an anime character's mane. His nose, previously big for his face, was now a plastic surgeon's dream. His lips were full, and a little too red for his taste.

Annoyed with the length of his eyelashes, Greg blinked slowly. "Ugh, what's wrong with my eyelashes?" He pinched and tugged at them with a thumb and index finger.

"Nothing's wrong. They just grew, like the rest of you," Mom said.

"They look fake." He almost said they were girlish, but he wasn't about to voice such a disturbing thought.

"I can't believe you've come of age. My baby's a man!" Mom exclaimed, smiling from ear to ear.

"How long was I out?" Greg asked.

Dad rubbed his forehead and stood to pace alongside the bed. "Nine days," he said.

"Nine? I thought it was supposed to take at least two weeks?"

Dad gave a simple nod.

"That doesn't mean anything bad, does it?" Greg asked, panic rising in his chest.

Mom put a hand on his. "No, honey. Of course it doesn't."

Greg pulled his hand away. "Dad?"

"Try not to worry about that right now. Relax. You've been through an intense process. And even if it went fast, well, everything appears to be okay."

"Everything appears okay?" Greg's breathing became rapid. "Everything appears okay?!" he asked again, his new voice now rising an octave.

"You did fine, baby," Mom reassured him, pushing a lock of platinum blond hair behind her ear. "We watched you closely. Every minute. We were a bit worried at first, since everything was going so fast, but when you started shedding, it was obvious you were perfect. When things don't go right—which rarely happens—Morphids don't make it this far. You're fine." She smiled reassuringly, which did nothing but intensify Greg's fear.

"Dad?" Greg pressed again. Mom was always too positive, too cheery about everything. He needed Dad's realistic perspective.

"Oh, Nick, see what you've done? Now, he's worried," Mom said. "Your father thinks the speed means you won't share our caste, but that's just crazy. The odds are in our favor. You *will* be a Companion," she said emphatically.

They'd had this conversation a thousand times before. Mom had always insisted that Greg would become a Companion. It was what she wanted, so she always refused to consider any other possibility. Dad, on the other hand, had always been more conservative. No one's caste was guaranteed—not even if all family members had shared the same one for generations. It had nothing to do with bloodlines, and everything to do with fate. Fate, the stubborn ruler of their kind, the hidden entity behind everything that happened to anyone. Greg peered up at his dad, expecting some sort of explanation. He got only a blank stare.

So Dad didn't think he would be a Companion. Greg felt the idea sink in. He'd never told his parents this—he hadn't wanted to hurt their feelings—but Greg didn't *want* to be a Companion. They were the most common Morphid caste. It was like being a housecat when he could be a panther. He wanted to be different; special.

As he contemplated the possibility of a different caste, a little smile graced his lips. *Not a Companion. What, then?* He thought of his parents' identical marks between their shoulder blades: A gray wolf, a Companion for life. Circular and approximately four inches in diameter, each Morphid's mark proclaimed their caste, and looked to the casual observer like elaborate scarification tattoos. If he didn't get a gray wolf, what would he get?

When he was little, he'd wanted to be a Companion like his parents. At seven years old, he had even tried to draw a gray wolf on his back with a felt-tip marker. It came out looking like a clumsy smudge. As he grew older, the idea lost its appeal. Companions were just like Humans. They had no special abilities of any kind. The only thing their castes gave them was a compulsion for someone they'd never met. He didn't want that. He loathed the idea of being chained to somebody. He didn't want to "support the growth of the population." Even if Companions were the only ones who truly fell in love and had a fated soul mate, their role was . . . well . . . boring.

He wanted to be a *Singular*—a Morphid without attachments to anyone. Not just that, he wanted a cool caste, like a Sorcerer or a Shifter, both these casts could wield magic, the former to do all kinds of tricks, the latter to alter his appearance into almost anything. Even something simpler would be okay, too. Like Dad's friend, Marcus. He was a Seeker, and could help anyone find anything they'd lost. He made tons of money, finding all sorts of things for people—even missing children.

Besides, if Greg morphed into a Companion, where would he find his pre-destined partner? In his seventeen years of life, he'd never met a Morphid girl—other than a distant cousin he'd met in Florida ten years ago, when they vacationed in Disney World. He and his family didn't go advertising they weren't human. Clearly, the others—if there were others—didn't either. If he told his friends, they'd think he'd lost his mind. He could only imagine their faces if he told them his ancestors came from a long-lost realm called Nymphalia.

Hell, even Greg thought that was bogus half the time. Now, his own metamorphosis proved it all, and his parents' teachings about their kind—passed down from generation to generation—suddenly took a whole new meaning.

"He'll be a Companion like us. You'll see," Mom said adamantly.

Perhaps if they were discussing whether he would become a janitor or a rocket scientist, this conversation might be productive. Being Morphids as they were, it was mere speculation.

"Fate will determine his caste, not his lineage," Dad finished in a quiet voice.

Looking dissatisfied, Mom stood and started pacing. "I know that, Nick. I don't need a lecture. Is it so wrong for me to wish happiness for my son? It's the most common caste. Odds are Greg will be one, too. His destiny will be to love and be loved."

"I want to be a Singular," Greg burst out, unable to stand this argument any longer. He had never dared utter those words in front of his parents, but saying them out loud seemed to solidify his wish.

Mom put a hand over her mouth. "You don't know what you're saying, Greg," she murmured, horrified.

"It would be better," he said, his voice now growing hoarse. "If I'm a Singular, I could stay here, finish high school, go to college. I wouldn't get the sudden urge to leave."

"As much as I'd like for you to stay with us, I want much more for you. I want you to be happy," Mom said.

"Erica, he actually has a point," Dad said, sounding as if he'd thought about this before.

"Mom, a Companion caste might send me across the world to find my *Integral*. Clearly, New Orleans isn't some huge Morphid Mecca. Besides Marcus, I've never met any others here. Who the hell knows where I'd end up?"

"Language," Dad commanded.

Greg ignored him, feeling heat rising from his chest. "But maybe Fate's considerate and thoughtful, and tomorrow at six in the evening, my caste and its damn new instincts will urge me to drive to the convenience store. And tah-dah, I'll find my stupid Integral buying a packet of gum, right here in our own backyard. Yeah, not likely . . ."

Greg was filled with stubborn irritation at his lack of power over his own destiny. No amount of denial, on his parents' part or his, would make a difference. His path was already chosen. Still, it felt good to finally speak his mind.

"Companions aren't the only ones who have Integrals," Mom reminded him. "Would you like to morph into one of *those* castes instead?"

Greg sulked. She had to bring *that* up. "It's not like it's up to me, anyway," he said, wishing to end this useless conversation.

"I know, but you shouldn't wish to be alone; or worse, be a servant. That would be awful," she whispered, rubbing her arms as if she'd gone cold. "I just can't believe you would . . . give up love." Mom shook her head, incredulously.

She'd always believed that sharing a link for any other reason besides love was a terrible thing. Greg imagined it *would* be, which was precisely the reason why he wanted to be a Singular, so he wouldn't have to share a link with anyone at all—not for love, not for servitude.

"Erica, this prejudice of yours is tiring," Dad said.

"It's not a prejudice," Mom said, but it was obvious she didn't mean it.

"A Morphid would never see his Integral as a burden or an enemy. You know that. He could be a protector or a guide, even. If he's called to serve another, he will do so gladly."

"But what kind of life is that?"

"One of fulfillment."

"Maybe."

"No, not maybe, Erica. Just a different kind than ours. You know it's true."

"Do we?" she asked.

So much of their knowledge about their own kind seemed to be just a concept. Tales handed down by his grandparents' grandparents and further back. For all they knew, Morphids were at the brink of extinction, and here they were, arguing over nothing. It didn't help that his parents had detached themselves from the Morphid community, going into hiding from what they perceived as overly controlling leaders. They couldn't even reach out to anyone if they had questions or needed help.

"Is it so bad I want our son to be as happy and loved as I am?" Mom asked, near tears.

"Greg will find his Integral—if he has one—and no matter what, he'll be happy. Okay?" Dad said in a reassuring voice.

The fact that he didn't say "happy *and* loved" wasn't wasted on Greg. Suddenly, he felt a squirming apprehension in his gut. No love. Ever. His parents loved each other unconditionally, and they were extremely happy, weren't they? Being a Companion wasn't that bad—not at all. Greg shook his head. What did he know about love, anyway? He'd gone without it this long. He'd tried to like human girls, but they weren't even of the same species. It would be like a parrot fancying a chipmunk. He'd felt nothing, just an empty space that begged to be filled.

Greg's head throbbed with anger. Why was he angry? Hadn't he decided love and "making babies to sustain the population" wasn't for him? Was it because, even after his body had morphed, he still had zero say in his own life? All of a sudden, Greg wanted to hurt somebody. Mom drew the short straw.

"You know what, Mom?" he interrupted the debate in progress. "If I do have an Integral, I hope the compulsion sends me to Tibet. I'll send you a postcard . . . maybe."

A ringing started in his ears. Dizzy and disoriented, Greg slumped back against the headboard. His tongue felt heavy and dry as sandpaper, and his vision blurred. "Screw it," he mumbled. "I don't want that. I'd much rather be a Singular."

"There's no need to be so hurtful," Mom said, but he was beyond caring.

Unable to keep his head up any longer, Greg held it between his hands. "I'd rather . . ." His breathing was labored and the ringing in his ears and blurring in his eyes became more disturbing.

"Son," Dad said, "I think it's time."

Greg fought to keep his eyes open. He didn't want to be brainwashed, and struggled against the fog that weighed down on his thoughts.

"It's no use, Greg," Mom pleaded. "Don't hurt yourself fighting it."

Greg fought to stay awake, but it was useless. The final transformation would happen whether he wanted it or not. After a few excruciating moments, he slid down the headboard and passed out, his mind at the mercy of Fate's molding fingers.

৪০ *Chapter 4* ৪৪
Sam

Sam shook her head in defeat. Coming to the mall by herself had been a terrible idea. Everywhere, people were talking, smiling, holding hands, laughing and carrying shopping bags. All of them so happy, so together. It wasn't fair.

Not even the pretty blue tank top she'd bought could lift her spirits. After all, she couldn't show it to anyone. She slung her shopping bag over her shoulder and stood to free up the table. It was almost six, and the food court was rapidly filling up with cheerful families, friends and couples looking for a fast dinner.

She slurped her milkshake—which could use a little cinnamon—and walked away without looking back at the eager faces that snatched up the space she'd vacated. Why couldn't she have what they had? She shuffled toward the exit. As she went, she returned the blank stares of the androgynous mannequins inside the store windows. After a minute, her milkshake stopped flowing. Aggravated, she swirled the straw and sucked as hard as she could. A large, cold gulp suddenly flooded her throat. She halted, pressing two fingers to her forehead.

Brain freeze!

Sam clenched her teeth and squeezed her eyelids shut. When she opened her eyes, the first thing she saw were a couple of preppy-looking girls, walking by and staring with snobbish looks on their thin faces.

"Weirdo," one of them mouthed.

Sam whirled to face the window display to her left, doing her best to appear both normal and indifferent to their scrutiny—even though it was eating away at her insides. She found herself staring at ostentatious jewelry, lying on top of blue velvet. The girls continued on, whispering in each other's ears and hanging around each other's shoulders. Sam watched their reflection in the glass, itching to wring their little necks. *Why did there have to be such mean people in the world?*

"Idiots," Sam said under her breath.

"That's for sure," a rich, melodious voice came from behind her.

She gave a little yelp and spun around, almost bumping her nose against someone's chest. Startled, she backed against the window display. Her gaze traveled upward and settled on the face of a complete stranger, a man or boy—Sam couldn't decide which—dressed in jeans and a simple black t-shirt. He just stood there, examining her with penetrating black eyes. Sam's skin crawled with some sort of recognition. Did she know him? She struggled to place him, but nothing came to her. Clearly, her brain hadn't thawed out yet.

"Hello," he said, the tone as deep as that of a baritone opera singer.

She glanced around. There were crowds of people everywhere, coming in and out of stores. Sam reminded herself not to panic. He didn't seem threatening. On the contrary, his words were kind and his features calm and inviting—not to mention extremely handsome. Something about his face made her want to pick up a pencil and start sketching. That was weird enough because, in her entire life, she'd never felt compelled to draw anything, much less some random guy. But who wouldn't want to draw him? His angular face, sculpted nose, full lips, but most striking of all, the combination of longish blond hair and deep black eyes. Such perfection would be enough to drive any artist to the canvas. Though he would have been sublime if he'd had dark hair instead, she thought. She'd always favored dark hair. His t-shirt and designer jeans looked brand new, and he wore them awkwardly, like he'd just stepped out of a dressing room.

"What's your name?" he asked with a warm smile. And oh God, if he didn't have an English accent.

"Samantha."

She blinked. Had she just told a stranger her name? Just like that? She groaned at her stupidity. She'd been so busy drinking in his every detail, drooling like a Saint Bernard, that she didn't realize her mouth had grown a mind of its own.

"Pleased to meet you, Samantha." He leaned closer, extending a hand in her direction. Was he bowing?

No. . . that would be absurd! The guy was so tall, he had to practically stoop to reach her. He was of medium build and very elegant. Sam distrustfully stared at his hand. She looked around. Was this someone's idea of a joke? Why would a guy like this talk to her? Stuff like this happened all the time to Brooke, not her. Random guys never talked to Sam. Not any guys really, and certainly not ones who looked like this.

Boys and Sam just didn't . . . jive. But strangely, a lot was jiving right now, at least on her end. And it wasn't just that he was absolutely, undeniably, drop-dead yummilicious—like triple fudge brownies. Sure, there was that, but there was something else, too. Some undercurrent she'd never felt for any member of the opposite sex. An aura that was new and familiar all at the same time. A feeling that he was someone she could relate, to or belong with; the strangest and most illogical sensation ever.

He was talking again, brushing golden hair off his forehead. Sam struggled to capture his words, feeling like a total airhead. She didn't lose her wits over cute boys, and she'd always been proud of that.

"For the past few months, I've dreamed of nothing but making your acquaintance." A gentle smile stretched across his lips, and his eyes seemed to grow watery for a second, like he was about to cry.

Sam blinked and let his words sink in. When she understood what he was saying, her heart took a tumble. Of course it was too good to be true. This wasn't some random cute guy who'd felt compelled to talk to her. This was a prankster, or a loony, or worst of all . . . a creep.

Okay, maybe now was the time to freak out. She tried, waited for alarms in her head to start blaring and flashing "Danger" in huge, red letters.

And . . . nothing. No panic. All she felt were nerves, the giddy type. She stared, bewildered, unable to peel her eyes off him, lost in his magnetic allure. She'd never seen him before, yet it felt as if she knew him somehow. He was what one would call unforgettable, with haunting, black eyes that could dismantle a girl with one glance.

Sam swallowed the huge knot in her throat, thinking what an impressionable idiot she was—the perfect victim for a handsome serial killer. She twisted her shopping bag in her hand. Time to get out of here. This was too weird to lead to any good outcome.

"Uh . . . well, I . . . I have to go," she said, putting her thumb up and pointing in the general direction of the parking lot. She gave him a sheepish smile and walked away. After five steps, she glanced back over her shoulder. He was following her.

Sam whirled around. "What are you doing?!"

He smiled with pride, the way someone might smile at their kid for standing up for themselves.

"Well . . . ?" Sam waited for him to say something. "Are you some sort of stalker?" she pressed. "Because if you are, I'll start screaming, and the mall cops will be on you like white on rice." Sam tried to sound convincing, but she felt ridiculous.

He simply pointed at a bench. "Would you sit with me?" His calm tone made her feel like a lunatic. But lunatics stayed alive, she reminded herself. Only compliant fools ended up in landfills.

"No! Why should I? I don't even know you."

"Well, we can fix that. If you sit with me, of course." Without making contact, he reached an arm around her shoulder and herded her toward the bench.

Without knowing why, Sam lost her anger and complied. She should have been running out the door or calling out for help, but the truth was . . . she was smitten. Besides, what would be the harm of sitting there for just a minute? It had to be safer staying inside the mall, with witnesses all around. Going out to a lonely parking lot was less sensible, she reasoned.

When they sat, Sam scooted to one end of the bench. He turned to face her, letting his dark eyes examine her from head to toe. Sam hugged her stomach, feeling self-conscious.

"Are you doing all right?" he asked, the way one might ask an old friend.

"So what's this about?" Sam snapped, irritated with herself for going along.

"I want to know everything about you, Samantha," he said with a fascinated look.

Chills ran down her spine. He offered her a sweet, innocent smile, and her dread vanished. *Man, he's smooth.* Why wasn't she at home, reading a book under her safe comforter? Instead, she was right here, being seduced by Smooth Operator.

"Are you for real?" Sam asked, shaking her head. "Who are you? Someone put you up to this, right?"

"My name is Ashby."

"What do you want, *Ashby*?" Sam pronounced the name with mockery. She'd never heard such a name. It had to be made up.

He grinned and was about to answer when the mean, preppy girls walked by again. Apparently, they were making the rounds, and it hadn't taken them long to come back. Their eyes danced incredulously from Sam to Ashby. They were practically gaping. Involuntarily, Sam's mouth twisted into a cocky smile. As she gave them the once-over, a strong arm wrapped around her waist and pulled her in. Suddenly, she was right next to Ashby, the length of her body tight against his. She stiffened and felt the color drain from her face. Still, she couldn't help but notice the two girls blanching with envy.

"They're positively jealous," Ashby said, laughing.

Taken aback by his cocky charade, she pushed away, trying to hide her smile of satisfaction.

"Are you always this . . . grave?" Ashby asked, composing his face into an exaggerated mask of propriety and concern.

"That's none of your business," Sam snapped. "I should go."

"No." He put a hand on her forearm, his fingers gentle and warm. Ashby composed his expression, erasing all traces of humor. "Can you not guess who I might be?" His eyes searched hers, full of hope.

Sam squirmed. What kind of weird question was that? "Mm, no," she snapped. "I have no clue."

"C'mon," he said with a wink, as if she were playing a joke on *him,* not the other way around.

Irritation got the best of her. "Okay, I'll give it a try. Right now, I'm thinking you might be a stalker or a serial killer. Best case scenario, you've just escaped the insane asylum."

Ashby's face fell. First, his gaze filled with incredulity and hurt, but slowly a sort of understanding made his eyes widen. "Wait, you don't know you're . . ." he trailed off. He sounded as if he'd made some sort of big discovery about her.

She grew defensive. "I'm what?" she demanded.

He ran a hand through his hair, silky blond strands sliding between long fingers. "You . . ." he winced, suddenly at a loss for words. After a heavy sigh, he looked back into her eyes. "I—I came here to meet *you.* Now, it seems, I must also warn you." His voice was quiet, conspiratorial. "You won't believe what I'm about to say, but . . . a lot will change for you, hopefully soon. When it begins, you'll feel you've lost control over your life, but you mustn't be afraid."

Sam's skin crawled and her shoulders shivered involuntarily. "Ha, ha, very funny," she managed. "C'mon, tell me, who put you up to this?" She tried to sound unimpressed, but a feeling of foreboding began to crawl over her.

Ashby blinked with patient understanding. His long lashes moved through the air like gentle butterfly wings. They were almost too long. His dark eyes examined her face with tenderness.

"I know you think this is a joke. It's a reasonable reaction. I don't expect you to believe me, but just remember me when it begins. More importantly, remember that," Ashby seized her hand and looked at her with fire behind his eyes, "everything will be all right. I promise."

His words seemed so sincere that Sam almost believed him. Almost. She pulled her hand out of Ashby's grip and looked away.

"You're a great actor, you know?" she said, feeling hurt. Who had the time and interest to play such a stupid joke on her? Sam could think of no one. She didn't have any enemies. You had to be noticed and important to have enemies, and she was practically invisible at school. Heck, even at home. So who would bother? It didn't make any sense.

"I'm telling you the truth," he said, "I wish I could tell you more, but I shouldn't even be here. Samantha—"

"Sam, call me Sam." She had no idea why she'd given him her full name. She hated it.

"We're wasting our time together," Ashby said.

"No kidding. Look, it was nice meeting you, *Ashbee*," she dragged the syllables out, then flinched, realizing how immature she sounded.

"Sam, please, I'll have to go soon." He sighed and let his eyes wander upward, as if he were waiting for something to drop on his head.

Surreptitiously, Sam looked up, too—to see what was there. She felt stupid for doing so, but she couldn't help it. Maybe Ashby was just wrong in the head. It wouldn't be the first time something like this had happened to her. She was a weirdo magnet. Homeless people would always come to her with wild stories when she worked at the soup kitchen. The other volunteers always marveled at it and complimented her on her patience since their nonsensical stories were more far-fetched than unicorns on Mars. Sam scrutinized Ashby as his eyes wandered all around. He didn't look crazy. He just looked . . . worried.

Oh, give it up, Sam.

No one could ever think he was insane. His profile was too riveting, his eyebrows too perfect. Heck, the sum of all his parts were too perfect. Maybe they'd call him eccentric, but that was all. Beautiful people are just lucky like that. As she examined his face, a self-conscious blush rose to her cheeks. The first time she felt attracted to someone, and he turned out like this.

Ashby returned his tortured gaze to her. A strange feeling of longing filled her. His strong jaw set firmly and his thick eyebrows furrowed in an anxious expression. Those black eyes had lost their initial twinkle and now seemed haunted. Suddenly, in her roller coaster of emotions for the guy, she felt sorry for him and thought that it might be best to indulge him.

"Listen, it's okay. I consider myself warned," Sam said.

Ashby's worry lines relaxed and some of his previous warmth returned.

"I wish I could tell you more, but that would be a mistake."
He was speaking quickly now, but his words were choked.
Fervently, he seized both her hands again. "I'll come back as soon as
I can." He lifted her hand and kissed her fingers gently. Sam was
petrified by this total stranger's gesture. Still, even though she knew
"stranger" was the right word, a small part of her felt as if she knew
him already.

"Please remember, there's a reason for what is about to
happen, and soon everything will be as it should." He paused and
looked around again. "I need to go."

Sam found herself clinging to Ashby's hand, as if to stop him
from leaving. He smiled tenderly and deposited her hand on her lap
with utmost delicacy, as if she were made out of glass. He stood and
looked down at her with something like anxious frustration. He
didn't want to leave. He opened his mouth and closed it again, then
abruptly turned and walked into the crowd.

She looked down at her hand, then back in Ashby's direction.
Her eyes danced through the crowd, but she couldn't spot him. He'd
vanished in the short instant she took her eyes away from him. For a
few seconds, Sam sat on the bench rooted to the spot. Finally, she
shook her head. Loud music, voices and laughter regained their
normal volume. Nervously, she peered all around her, waiting from
someone to jump out from behind a plant to tell her she'd been
duped. When no one did, she got up and wobbled off on gummy
legs. She walked away, forgetting her unfinished milkshake and
shopping bag, feeling as if the world had been turned on its head.

℘ Chapter 5 ℘
Ashby

As soon as he materialized in his bedroom, Ashby knew he was in trouble. Violet eyes glared at him, and a shrill voice pierced his ears like a thousand tiny needles.

"What on Earth were you thinking, you stupid child?"

Ashby objected to being called a child *and* stupid, but thought better of saying anything. Regent Danata looked blue with rage, as if she'd not taken a breath for the last ten minutes. Veins pulsed furiously at each of her temples. Displays of temper were nothing new, but this bluish tint certainly was. One of her fists shook in front of Ashby's face. Stiff as a board, he kept his nose away. Little could be done when she got this way, except take it like a man.

"This is the stupidest, most inconsiderate thing . . . you've ever done . . . in your life!" Her words were like hammer blows, and with each breath her right eye twitched.

Ashby's eyes darted around his bedroom until he spotted Perry. The young *Sorcerer* was practically hiding by the large windows, behind one of the velvet curtains, his back terribly close to the bare stone walls common throughout the castle. Portos, Perry's mentor and the Regent's High Sorcerer, was there too, clutching the lapels of his tweed jacket and standing by the door, ready to run in case Danata's wrath boiled over.

Well, Perry had been right—the castle had measures in place to alert them to security breaches. He'd warned Ashby not to go, had also reminded him that only certified Sorcerers were allowed to perform magic—especially a transportation spell—on current or future council members. Ashby had insisted, tired of waiting, desperate to finally meet his Integral. Though the truth was, it hadn't really taken that much convincing. Perry had agreed after little insistence, and he'd magically transported Ashby to Indiana for his own selfish reasons—namely, learning those special spells. *I shouldn't have to feel so guilty about it. Perry knew the risks.* But still.

Poor Portos, on the other hand, his only crime was being Perry's mentor. The old man hadn't known of Ashby's plans. He shouldn't have to suffer the repercussions. Except he was the High Sorcerer, and claiming ignorance of his pupil's behavior wouldn't help him; not with Danata. Now that Ashby thought about it, Portos had probably been the one with the unfortunate task of informing the Regent of the breach, after one of *his* spells detected the use of magic within the castle walls.

"What if something had happened to you in that godforsaken place?" Danata continued, "We might have been unable to help you. If only God had given you a single gram of common sense." She held a pale finger up. "You, of all people, received the worst of the lot in terms of prudence."

Ashby rolled his eyes. If only he had a gold coin for every time she'd said that.

"And you!" She swiveled and pointed her accusing finger at Perry, her green silk dress and black hair billowing with the force of her movements. "Don't think I have forgotten about you. Soon you'll wish you'd morphed into a mere Companion instead of a Sorcerer."

"With all due respect, Mother," Ashby intervened. "Perry was following my orders."

"Is that so? Then he'll suffer the consequences for both his lack of restraint and his inability to discern a stupid order from a sound one."

Perry and Portos kept their eyes averted, but Ashby defied his mother by walking right up to her. She glared back, her narrow face impervious, her long neck stiff and stately.

"The punishment should come to me alone," Ashby said in a clear tone. "As a member of my retinue, Perry would be breaking the law if he disobeyed my orders. I made that very clear to him when he first refused." It was a lie, of course. Perry had never refused. He'd simply warned Ashby of the dangers, then done as he was told, eager to learn new spells that Portos wouldn't teach him yet.

Opening and closing her mouth, Danata seemed ready to quash his explanation, but said nothing. She couldn't argue with his reasoning. The young Sorcerer was under his command, and had been since Ashby came of age two months ago. As the future Regent, he was entitled to a retinue of skilled, young advisers as soon as he morphed. By tradition, such an entourage was assigned to future rulers to forge good relationships between would-be Morphid leaders and would-be council members.

His mother hated to lose a battle, no matter how small, and was beside herself with fury. Ashby began to fear the punishment she might be devising inside her head at that very moment. He needed to distract her.

"Um, I met her, Mother," he blurted out. "I had to go. You know this."

Sam's image returned to Ashby's mind, and suddenly he didn't care if his mother sentenced him to walk across the Sahara desert as punishment for his disobedience. It had been worth meeting her, no matter the consequences.

"She's everything I thought she would be," he added dreamily.

The fear that he would be forced to be without Sam, for who knew how much longer, suddenly assailed him. Walking to the nearest chair, he sank down, oblivious to what his mother may do to him. The sound of a clock ticking filled the silence. It was past midnight on this side of the world. Ashby looked around his room, trying to imagine what Sam might be doing in her home and the things she might have in her room. Surely, her possessions were nothing like the array of ostentatious objects fastidiously arranged here: Louis XVI chairs, leather sofas, suits of armor, damask cushions of all shapes and sizes, jewel-studded stands, exotic plants in every corner, sculptures and paintings, massive four-poster beds, the old and the new combined in impossible harmony. What would she think of this place with its old stone walls, underground dungeons and many turrets? Would she like it? Or hate it?

His life was so different from hers. Would she like England and its impossible weather? Would she miss her home too terribly when she came here? Yes, it was different, but the same sun and the same moon shone in the sky. The land gave its fruits and the wind blew the leaves just the same. It couldn't be that bad. She could learn to love it, if she didn't right away.

In the two months since he found out his Integral was in the United States, Ashby had been trying to learn as much as possible about these differences, wishing he had paid more attention to his international studies earlier on. If only he could know more about the world Sam called home. If only his mother hadn't kept him so sheltered his whole life.

He looked up and, under the new light, saw that his mother's anger had been replaced by curiosity. Surely, she wanted to know about Sam—her future daughter-in-law—almost as much as he did. Still, she'd forbidden him to visit her and ordered him to wait for her to be ready to morph. So he supposed she could hardly start asking the questions that must be burning on her tongue. His mother was too proud.

"She's fine. She seemed like a great girl," Ashby said, hoping to change the subject.

The Regent's stern expression returned. "You two disobeyed me in more ways than one." She looked from Ashby to Perry. "You used magic, breaking our laws in the process, *and* went against my explicit orders to wait."

Perry had also "borrowed" material from Portos's library to learn the conjuration to transport Ashby to the correct geographical coordinates, but Ashby wasn't about to add to his list of offenses. Not if Portos hadn't. The old man squirmed uncomfortably and gave Ashby a wary, defeated look. Clearly, he wasn't going to tell on himself, though Ashby had the feeling the Sorcerer's library would be locked after this. But Ashby was beyond caring about the rules and his mother's orders, even if she was the Regent. Being away from Sam was painful. Every day that went by was agony. And of course Danata knew nothing of that pain and anguish. She was a Singular—not linked to anybody, full only of herself.

"I had to find her, Mother," Ashby said. "Not seeing her was driving me crazy."

"You were instructed to wait until the connection between you grew stronger, until she came of age."

"I don't understand why I have to wait," Ashby said in frustration.

"We've been over this already. Do I need to explain again?

"To hell with the law. You're the Regent. You can make allowances for your son."

"*Do not* let anyone hear you say that!" Danata barked. "The law is clear, and to be of any use, it needs to apply to everyone, regardless of their birthright. Contacting Morphids outside our known channels is strictly forbidden. It endangers our kind. If the Council finds out about your *escapade,* they won't be lenient, even if you're my son—especially because you're my son. Luckily, Portos detected the breach before anyone else."

"Samantha, her name is Samantha in case you're wondering, is not a dissident," Ashby said with sarcasm, furious that his own mother didn't care about his suffering or happiness. His mother always assumed anyone not found in the Morphid census was a dissident by default—which is what she'd decided about Sam as soon as he pinpointed her location to Indiana, a place where there were no registered Morphids.

"And you know that how?"

"She doesn't even seem to know about our kind. I believe she thinks she's human."

Danata's eyebrows went up. "Is that so?"

He nodded.

Her eyes tightened and danced from side to side as she puzzled out the idea. "What makes you so sure? She could be lying."

Sam's honest face appeared in Ashby's mind's eyes. "She was not. And even if she were, it won't matter once she morphs."

Danata was slow to answer. Her thoughts seemed to wonder elsewhere. "Regardless," she said, after shaking herself back into the moment, "there are proper ways to deal with this sort of situation, and you *must* follow them."

"But it could be months before she morphs! In the meantime, an official inquisitor could determine whether there has been foul play or not."

"A minor cannot be questioned by any officials. You know that well."

"She. Is. Not. A. Criminal. She's my Companion," Ashby yelled.

His harsh words seemed to slap Danata on the face, leaving behind a shocked and astonished expression. She stood mute, looking back in disbelief. He'd never talked to her this way. Guilt tried to claw its way into Ashby's chest, but he closed himself to it.

She couldn't continue this nonsensical line of reasoning. True, the official census had failed to identify any Morphids living in Indiana, but that didn't automatically make Sam a dissident. Danata shouldn't immediately assume that Sam had gone against the Regency and its policies. She shouldn't refuse to let Ashby meet his Integral, forbidding all means of getting information, such as an inquisitor or a private investigator. The whole affair was ridiculous. Sam was too young. She couldn't be a dissident, couldn't be blamed for something her parents had probably done thirty years ago when many Morphids had gone into hiding, concealing their identities—not only from humans, but from their own kind.

Of course, it didn't help that the entire subject was a sore one with his mother. It had been Morphid laws instituted by a young Danata, when she first came into the Regency, what had sparked dissidence in the first place. Laws like the census itself, which required every Morphid to register with the Council, had caused objection in many circles and even sent people into hiding. They accused the new Regent of wanting to institute a police state. "Big Brother," George Orwell's style. It was ridiculous. His mother had only wanted to take stock of their dwindling numbers, in an effort to find out why Morphids were a dying species.

His mother had to understand that Sam wasn't a criminal. Ever since his mark revealed Ashby as a Companion, however, his mother had distanced herself from him, as if disappointed. As a Singular, Danata had never been tethered to another Morphid. When she needed a mate, she found someone suitable and got what she wanted out of him: Namely, a successor to the Regency. Ashby never knew who his father was, and often wondered about his fate, but the topic had always been off limits. Danata was completely independent, free to govern the Morphid council without *interference*, as she called it. But she knew better. Discord was never an issue between Companions. Ashby would be just as capable as she to lead their kind. Having Sam at his side would only make him stronger.

Danata turned her back on Ashby, straightened and clenched her fists. As she answered, he wished he could see her expression.

"All the more reason to follow the rules," she said in a chilling voice. "We don't want to risk a scandal. There are many who would seize the opportunity to challenge your leadership. I do this for your own good, *son*."

"Let me go back and stay with her until she comes of age," Ashby practically begged.

"No," she said plainly.

Ashby tugged at his hair in frustration and growled. "It's not fair, Mother."

"I know." Her tone was suddenly one of understanding. She unclenched her fist, faced him, and slowly walked to him. She stopped only a few paces away.

Ashby stiffened and looked up into her violet eyes with suspicion. She put a hand on his forearm and moved her long fingers back and forth, caressing him. She smiled kindly, an uncharacteristic gesture, and one to which Ashby was unaccustomed. He guessed she loved him in her own way, but her attempts were always controlling, and only came when she had a vested interest. Real empathy was something Ashby never thought her capable of.

Everything had been so much simpler before he came of age. No impulses or longing to find his Integral, no tugs or urges that nearly drove him mad. His mother just couldn't understand, couldn't begin to comprehend the deep need brought by being linked to somebody else. If he at least knew how much longer it would take for Sam to morph, maybe . . . maybe he could wait.

Ashby stood and walked away. "I will do as you say . . . " *for now.*

The Regent opened her mouth and seemed on the verge of saying something, but stopped. Instead, she merely inclined her head in acknowledgment. Ideas were already forming inside her head—Ashby could tell by the sudden, liquid quality of her gaze. It frightened him to even imagine what she was planning.

"A punishment must be chosen, Portos," she said, turning to her High Sorcerer.

"Mother, decide on *my* punishment and leave Perry out of this. I've already told you he was following orders." *Time to distract her again.* "Besides, nothing happened to me. I'm fine and most importantly, I have met Samantha. Actually, *Sam* is what she prefers."

"Sam?!" she asked with distaste. "Samantha is hideous enough. *Sam* is simply horrendous. It's a boy's name. Americans are just so . . . crass."

So far, so good. If Ashby kept this conversation off track, there would be no more mention of punishments. His mother would have made an example of him if there had been others involved, but only Portos and Perry knew of his disobedience. She might let it go.

"Yes, she goes by Sam, and I don't think it's horrendous. I rather like it."

"Oh, of course you do," Danata said, waving one hand with a scoff.

"Is she well, Ashby?" Portos spoke for the first time, sensing the danger had passed.

"Yes." Ashby's face lit up with a smile as he remembered Sam standing by the jewelry store.

After Perry transported Ashby, and he appeared next to a gigantic flower pot inside the mall, his first sight was Sam herself. Unlikely as it might have been, Perry's very first attempt at such complicated magic had been one hundred percent successful. After a huge effort divining Sam's exact location, learning how to actually transport Ashby to those coordinates had taken even more work and research. Perry had to learn how to visualize the location in order to deliver Ashby to a safe location and not inside an innocent bystander. That wouldn't have been pretty.

Understandably, the young sorcerer was apprehensive, and warned Ashby that a mistake at any stage of the process could land him hundreds of miles away from Sam; or, worse, lost in another dimension—without any possibility of return. But Ashby had been too desperate to care, and after all, Perry jumped at the chance to learn something worthwhile, a welcome break from the nonsense Portos called an "age-appropriate education."

When Ashby had materialized at the mall, people had obliviously walked right past him, engrossed in conversation, looking in their shopping bags, or simply staring off into nothingness. He had known Sam as soon as he laid eyes on her. The magnetic pull between Integrals was impossible to ignore. No one noticed how he doted on the lonely girl by the window, or how he almost fell to his knees at the mere sight of her. He might have even gone on staring forever, if his time hadn't been limited.

Rousing himself, he had then noticed two girls looking at his Integral in a contemptuous manner. Sam had seemed clearly bothered by them, so he approached, hoping to gain her trust by commiserating. Once he realized how little she knew about herself, it had taken all his restraint to keep from giving everything away. He had wanted to tell her the truth, but worried it would scare her. The best he could offer was a warning of the changes to come, hoping that a gradual understanding of her situation would be better than a sudden landslide of unexpected knowledge.

"What did you tell her?" Portos asked as if guessing his thoughts.

When he had probed Portos about a visit to his Integral, the High Sorcerer had warned him against it, pointing out that revealing too much about himself and his connections to the Regency could put Sam at risk.

"I didn't tell her anything." Ashby kicked off his sneakers.

"What exactly *did* you share with her?" His mother demanded.

"Only that her life will change soon."

"What else?" asked Portos.

"Nothing else."

"What else?" the Regent insisted.

"Nothing else, Mother. That's all I told her. She didn't believe me, anyway. She thought I was a lunatic. I told you. I don't think she knows about our kind."

"Oh, just grand," the Regent said sarcastically. She turned to Portos and asked, "Any harm done, do you think?"

"I don't think so, but I will check," Portos assured her.

"You do that. And inform *me* right away. Tell no one else. I won't have my son or others interfering in matters that concern the welfare and future of the Council. Understood?"

Portos inclined his head, keeping his eyes on Ashby. "I will not share any details with *anyone.*" The High Sorcerer nodded his agreement and accepted the reprimand graciously.

Ashby, on the other hand, disregarded his mother's threat. "You'll not keep me in the dark about Sam. Will you, Mother? I'll go mad if I can't at least have news about her."

The Regent ignored him and continued to address Portos.

"I'll see you in an hour for an update on any harm Ashby's half-witted actions may have caused. As for you," the Regent turned to face her son. "If you ever do something like this again, you'll sorely regret it. You *are* my son, but I am the Regent. I won't have my authority challenged, even by my successor. Is that clear?"

"Yes, my Regent," Ashby responded, inclining his head the same way Portos had.

Smarter. He just had to be smarter about visiting Sam without being discovered. If his mother was going to keep him in the dark regardless, he didn't have much incentive to play the obedient son.

"And take off those ridiculous clothes," she said, pointing at his jeans and t-shirt. "I've never seen anything more disgraceful in my entire life."

Ashby looked at his cheap clothes and had to agree with his mother this once. The pants fit him the wrong way, especially around his bottom. The *relaxed fit* was decidedly not for him. He had always preferred more sophisticated attire, as opposed to this shabby ones. But he'd wanted to fit in, which he'd accomplished. At any rate, the clothes were coming off, and he would be happy to never wear them again.

Ashby decided his path. He would see Sam once more. Soon. No matter what his mother said. Regent or not.

✂ Chapter 6 ☙
Sam

Sam arrived home, feeling like she'd been hit by a bus.

How could I forget my shopping bag?! How could I have been so awestruck by some random guy? Some lunatic?

She parked her blue Toyota Prius, in the driveway and got out, feeling extremely angry for letting that crazy guy get to her. She unlocked the back door and walked into the kitchen. Flipping on the light switch, Sam looked toward the table, expecting to find dinner money once again under the salt shaker. Nothing. The house seemed quiet, but the lack of cash meant at least one of her parents was here.

Her stomach rumbled. Half a milkshake was not even close to a satisfactory supper. She opened the fridge and stuck her head inside, leaning lazily on the door. Just what she was afraid of. There was a boxed lunch with her name on it. The usual leftover crap from some lunch meeting at her parent's law bureau. Some sort of wheat wrap filled to the brim with bean sprouts and cold, grilled vegetables. *Yuk*! Whatever happened to real food? Gooey lasagna, grilled steak and creamy potatoes, even just plain old mac and cheese.

She took the wrap and buried it deep inside the garbage can. The last thing she wanted was a lecture on not eating her dinner, or a reproach from her mother about the trouble she'd gone through to bring her something to eat. After a moment trying to decide on her gastronomic inclinations, Sam filled a large bowl with vanilla ice cream and crumbled Oreo cookies on top. Ashby had sent her into a carb-loading kind of mood. As usual, if her mom caught her with the triple-scoop beauty, Sam would say it was dessert—not the main course.

Quietly, she walked upstairs, her bowl of ice cream in one hand. When she reached the landing, she checked her parents' bedroom. A light shone through the slightly open door. Normally, she would have continued on to her room, trying to pass unnoticed. Even the stack of library books on her night table was much friendlier than the blank looks her parents usually gave her. But, unsettled by her run-in with that crazy guy at the mall, Sam wanted to make sure she wasn't alone in the big house.

Without knowing why, she tiptoed toward the master bedroom, taking a moment to gingerly deposit her bowl on a console table off to the side. When she reached the door, she stopped and listened. All was quiet until the rustle of paper broke the silence.

They brought their work home. Sam lost all interest in secrecy and detective work. She turned to leave, but changed her mind. After all, they'd thought of her and brought her dinner. The least she could do was thank them, even if she hadn't eaten it.

After a quick knock, Sam walked right in. "Hey, I wanted to thank you for dinner."

At first glance, all she saw was an empty room. Then she spotted her mother kneeling on the floor. She was leafing through a sheaf of documents, the doors to the antique cabinet in the corner wide open in front of her. Her mother gasped and looked back at

Sam with murderous eyes. Trying to recompose herself, she stuffed the papers back into the cabinet. Only the subtle trembling of her hand gave her anxiety away.

Sam didn't know what to say. For a moment, she stood frozen, watching papers spill out onto the floor as her mother tried to shove them into the cramped. Barbara Gibson was not the type of woman who got flustered easily. She was a trial lawyer who ate prosecutors, witnesses and the odd judge for a snack. She could chew nails and spit bullets. Whatever was in that cabinet had to be major to upset her so deeply. Seeing her this way was unsettling. Sam let her eyes peruse the cabinet's contents, hoping for some clue of what was going on. For a split second, she almost offered to help pick up the mess, but something told her that'd be a bad idea.

"Sorry, Mom," Sam apologized. "I'll let you work. I didn't mean to bother you." She backed up and closed the door behind her, grabbed her bowl of soupy ice cream and hurried into her room. She was sitting on the bed, distractedly slurping ice cream when a knock on the door startled her.

"Come in," she said, after hiding her bowl behind her tall stack of library books.

For a few seconds, no one came in. Sam started to get up, thinking the door was locked, but before she got a foot on the floor, the knob turned and her mother walked in, glaring. Her eyes were red. Sam fumbled with her old teddy bear, feeling extremely awkward.

"Haven't I taught you it's rude to barge into people's room?" her mom said in a subdued but shaky voice.

"I said I was sorry." Sam stared at a bald spot on her bear's fur.

"Your father went on a business trip," she snapped as she turned to leave. "He's not sure how long he'll be gone. He said he'll call you."

Call me? He went on business trips all the time and never called. Sam frowned. "O-kay?" she said. It sounded like a question.

"Oh! One more thing," she whirled and faced Sam again, "don't leave dirty dishes up here."

"I won't," Sam said, biting her tongue. She wanted to say something else, something with some snark, but she knew that it wasn't a good time to poke the beast.

After her mother left, Sam tried to read a little, but it was no use. She was too distracted, coming up with scenarios that could explain what was going on. She set the book down and retrieved her dirty ice cream bowl from its hiding place. In the kitchen, she rinsed it, dried it and even put it back. *A model daughter.* She went back upstairs and considered going to bed, but it was only seven thirty. She changed into her shorts and tank top pajamas, trying to ignore how pathetic that was, telling herself she was just getting comfortable.

A movie, she decided. *A new one.* She was sprawled on her bed, browsing through the new releases when her cell phone vibrated.

"Hey, what are you doing?" Brooke asked.

It was good to hear a friendly voice. "Trying to find something to watch. How are things in New York?"

"A little bit boring. Jenny had to go back to work, so I was cooped up in the apartment all day today. We just finished dinner. How about you?"

"Mostly boring too, though . . ." she dragged the word, remembering her weird day.

"Do tell!" Sam could imagine her friend making herself comfortable.

Sam explained about Ashby, emphasizing how batty he was and leaving out the part about how the bizarre conversation had affected her.

"He sounds crazy!" Brooke agreed. "But if he was hot, we can overlook that. Was he hot?"

Sam laughed. "Pure eye candy," she answered, feeling a twinge of shame for using the cheesy phrase.

"Sugar coma of the eye?" Brooke asked. They both laughed. That was Brooke's favorite way to describe guys she found irresistible. "Well, did you get his number?" her friend asked, still laughing, though Sam could tell she wasn't joking.

"No way! The guy was bananas. I wouldn't be surprised if he was some sort of charming, extremely-good-looking serial killer. They'd probably find my body in a junkyard or something."

"Well, at least then you could say you went on a date before you died," Brooke teased.

Sam bristled. "Hey, that's uncalled for."

"I know. By the way, Reed called me. He's back from chess camp, and he's wondering if you wanna go out."

"Man, he doesn't give up, does he?"

"Maybe you two should go to a movie or something. Just so you both can get it out of your systems."

"I have nothing to get out of my system. *I* don't want to go out with *him*. You know that."

"I meant you can have your first date and get *that* out of your system," Brooke clarified.

"You're the one who's obsessed with me going on a date. Maybe you're the one who needs to get it out of her system, not me."

"Fair enough," Brooke admitted. "I'd just like to go on a double date with my BFF before we are . . . let's say . . . forty?"

"Whatever!" In spite of herself, Sam laughed. Brooke always had a way of lifting her spirits.

"So, anything else going on?" Brooke asked.

Sam considered telling her about her mom, but she didn't want to spoil her good mood already. They could talk about that another day.

"No, nothing else, really," Sam said.

"So, what movie are you going to watch?" Brooke asked.

"Umm, let's see," Sam picked up the remote and scrolled down the list, rattling off names. Brooke shot several of them down with gagging sounds and grunts. They were narrowing down to a few when the creaky step in the stairwell moaned. Sam listened for a second, then threw the remote on her pillow and walked to the door, phone pressed to her ear.

"I'd pick that last one," Brooke said, after a short moment of silence.

"Yeah," Sam whispered distractedly into the receiver. She cracked the door open and peered into the dark hallway.

"Why are you whispering?"

Is someone coming or going? Sam wasn't sure. After a moment, she decided someone was *going,* since nobody appeared at the top of the steps. The door to her parents' bedroom was closed, and the light was off. She walked into the hallway and leaned over the railing to look down into the foyer. No signs of life.

"You still there?" Brooke asked.

Sam tiptoed back into her bedroom and crept to the window. "Yeah, I'm here," she said.

"What are you up to?"

"I thought I heard someone sneaking up the stairs."

"You mean like a vampire or a werewolf?" Brooke joked.

"No, just my mom."

"Close enough. Why would she be sneaking around?"

Sam held the curtain to one side and peered out. Her mother's car pulled out onto the street.

"It's a long story. I'll tell you later."

"Okay," Brooke's voice was uncertain. "Is everything all right?"

"Dunno. We'll talk tomorrow. I'll call you." Sam pressed the "end" button before Brooke could protest.

She ran downstairs and opened the garage door. It was empty. Sam paused for a second, and, without warning, a sneaky idea took hold in her mind. She tried to dispel the sudden urge to spy on her mother. Closing her eyes, she tried to convince herself it wasn't right to invade people's privacy, but that just made the itch worse. She had to scratch it or she'd go mad.

From a shelf, she retrieved her father's toolbox, found a small flathead screwdriver and made her way back upstairs. Already, her heart sped and palms sweated. She took a steadying breath, and, barely making a sound, she climbed the ample staircase toward the bedrooms. There was no need for stealth, but she couldn't help it. She felt sly and clandestine. So not her, but whatever.

No one's here, she reassured herself. *Chill out.*

Right now she had the chance to satiate her curiosity—if she could muster the courage and stop shaking like a wet puppy. A little prying shouldn't be such a big deal. It wasn't like she was stealing her mother's cash. She was only going to see what was inside the cabinet, and then she would leave everything exactly the way she'd found it. No one would be the wiser. She was only this nervous because her mom was scary—super-villain scary, to be clear. If she discovered Sam sticking her nose where it didn't belong, she'd probably turn her to stone with one look.

Well, she isn't here to find out, is she? Sam thought, trying to embolden herself.

She stood at the master bedroom door. *This is stupid. I don't need to do this!* She would find out whatever was going on sooner or later. But as she remembered her mother's strange behavior, all hesitation leaked out of her mind. She turned the knob and gave the door a push. The hinges creaked just a little. A shadow moved, scaring her, but it was only the door opening and letting light in from the hall. She breathed deeply, telling herself there was no reason to be nervous. *I'm alone. I'm alone.* Goose bumps rippled through her body in waves.

Sam turned on a small bedside lamp and squinted, focusing on the cherry cabinet—the one she had never cared about before. There were enough papers around the house, all full of legal jargon that she couldn't understand, so the inconspicuous cabinet had never seemed important.

Trembling, she knelt in the same place she had seen her mom. She placed the screwdriver on the carpeted floor and wiped sweaty hands on her bare legs. Closing her eyes, she listened intently for the garage door. Silence. If her mother came back and found her snooping, Sam would be grounded for life—or worse. Her mom could probably even think of a way to sue her for breach of trust or something.

She shook her head and, with a firm hand, placed the tip of the screwdriver under one of the old cabinet door hinges. A simple pin held them together. She tapped the screwdriver handle upward with the heel of her hand, and little by little, the pin inched out. Quickly, she repeated the same procedure on the second and third hinges. Once the three metal pins were out, Sam gently jiggled the door until it came away.

It was even easier than she'd imagined. Just like that, she was staring into several piles of documents. All the junk inside made Sam want to give up. The cabinet was ready to reveal its secrets, though, so she decided to finish the dirty deed.

With one door removed, the second invitingly swung open. Systematically, she went through the different piles of paper, trying to disrupt them as little as possible. Most of the documents were meaningless, but soon she noticed a manila envelope jutting out from the middle of a large stack. Its edge didn't align with the rest of the papers.

She pulled it out and opened it. Hesitantly, she started reading. Two words jumped off the page and all but bit her on the face. *"Irreconcilable Differences"*. Her father had filed for divorce! Sam closed the envelope and put it back where she found it. She stared blankly into the cabinet while an enormous sadness settled in her chest. Ironically, she wasn't sad because of the news. She was sad because she wasn't really surprised. She had expected this for a while now. She had just never imagined her mother being so upset about it. She had to have known. The only surprising thing was that it took her dad this long to do it.

Idly thumbing through the divorce papers, Sam actually felt disappointed with her findings. She'd expected something juicier, like money laundering, bribes from a drug cartel, something . . . not this. Well, it wasn't as if Sam's life would change all that much. She doubted her dad would want visitation rights. Although it was wrong to just assume she would stay with her mom. Maybe they'd just draw straws to decide who would keep her.

Disgusted, she moved to replace the unhinged door when something else caught her attention: A brown leather folder, lying at the very bottom of the largest pile. For some reason, Sam had the distinct feeling she'd seen it before. She reached a shaky hand toward it. When she pulled it out, a terrible urge to put it back came over her. Against her better judgment, she undid the leather strap that held it closed.

As she read the old document, the pages shook in her hand and a crazy rhythm hammered her chest. Like a rain gauge, her eyes filled up with tears until they spilled over her cheeks and fell onto the words that finally explained her entire life all too clearly. She sat there, completely still, before moving a muscle.

After several minutes, Sam came back to life. Mechanically, she put everything back in place. When she left, it was as if she'd never been there. Just as planned. She went into her bedroom, placed the screwdriver next to her books and stared at it for a very long time. A simple tool, one in a set of twelve, all with bright red, ergonomic handles. An expensive set that had helped Sam find out the cheapest, most tasteless piece of news.

She wasn't their kid. Gibson & Gibson had adopted her when she was two years old.

After some time, Sam crawled under the blankets, suddenly cold. She closed her eyes and quietly wept. There were tears, but they didn't register. Just like she couldn't feel her nails or her hair growing, she couldn't feel the tears leaving her eyes. What *did* register, however, were two thoughts. Or maybe it was one, except it was double-edged.

One, Gibson & Gibson—it was amazing how quickly she became unable to think of them as "Mom and Dad"—had always had a reason for not loving her. Two, her biological parents had given her away. In the end, both facts led to the same conclusion.

She was unwanted.

Sam felt lost. Adrift. In an instant, the precious little bit of self-image she'd cultivated was snatched away. She was left with an empty void, an enormous desolation that immediately stole her sense of direction. She wanted to run away, but had nowhere to go. All she had were questions. One of them stood out as the most important.

Who are my real parents?

℘ Chapter 7 ℨ
Greg

Greg was alone in his room. He sat up slowly, his body unable to fulfill his urgent desire to escape. A fog clouded his brain as if it'd been burning hot and someone had dropped a bucket of ice water on it. Heavy steam rose, obscuring all but the most basic thoughts.

He peeled his tongue from the roof of his mouth. He was absolutely parched. Throwing his feet to one side of the bed, he set them heavily on the floor. He wiggled his toes and stared in disbelief. His feet had grown three sizes, at least! They looked as if they belonged to someone else.

Feeling clumsy, still unaccustomed to his new size, Greg wrapped a sheet around his waist, stood and wobbled on his large extremities. Strangely, he didn't feel tall; rather, everything in the room looked smaller. It felt as if his head would hit the ceiling. Stumbling, he headed for the bathroom and had to duck under the door frame. He had to be well over six feet! Days ago, he'd been barely five nine.

He approached the mirror over the sink and was again shocked by his new look, by how much he resembled his father. He felt stupid to be surprised; for once, people would finally believe he wasn't the homely kid adopted by the nice, gorgeous couple. He examined his chest and arms. His biceps bulged and looked as if he'd been pumping iron with some infomercial exercise guru. He wondered if the new musculature would help on the basketball court. He couldn't wait to give it a try.

So this is how Dad always keeps in shape? Morphid genes? Maybe if I worked out on top of it, I could be the next Mr. Universe. The thought amused him for a split second, then reality struck. He didn't look like himself. No one would recognize him, or believe this was some uncanny growth spurt over summer break. No one! Not his neighbors, or teachers, or even his friends. The thought made him sad. He knew he couldn't tell them the truth about how he'd turned into some pretty, supermodel dude (he just knew this was how his average-looking friends would see it.) They wouldn't believe him anyway, because, to the world, going into stasis inside a cocoon and hopping right out brand-spanking new wasn't normal. It was creepy, like out of a horror or Sci-Fi movie.

Feeling glum, he turned on the water and splashed some on his face. His mental fog lifted slowly, which only caused his thoughts to multiply, rushing in like gasoline through a fuel injector. Suddenly, his new appearance was less important. The room revolved, and Greg gripped the sink, overpowered by an onslaught of weird, unfamiliar ideas. His mind was on fire.

-Get dressed!

He blinked, backed out of the bathroom and sat at the edge of his bed, breathing heavily.

-A map. Get a map.

"Greg?" Mom appeared and hesitated at the threshold.

His head still spinning, Greg lifted a pleading gaze toward her, silently asking: "What's wrong with me?" She smiled back, obliviously proud of what she thought he'd become.

-On top of the fridge. Hurry!

Greg gripped the edge of the bed. Every new thought was more urgent and ardent than the last. He felt the urge to run downstairs and pull out the road atlas that rested on top of the refrigerator, but his body was stiff with opposition. It was like he now had two minds: the human mind Greg knew himself as; and the new, Morphid mind that was filling his head with strange thoughts and urges. His breathing grew ragged as the two natures battled inside him. His Morphid side's commands were plain and simple, but Greg had no idea of their purpose.

"It will get clearer, son," Mom said. "I'll go fetch Dad. Don't move."

He couldn't move even if he wanted to. The weight of his convoluted mind paralyzed him. Part of him wanted to run, but he remained perched on the bed, clutching the mattress with white-knuckle strength. More thoughts spurted out, setting his mind ablaze.

-C'mon. No time to waste. Move. Now!

He could hear his parents running up the stairs. Dad walked in first, dragging his wife by the hand. He smiled and echoed her words. "It'll get clearer, Greg. Just try to calm down."

-Calm down? I can't calm down! I have to get dressed and find a map. His brand new self won this round. Greg said nothing and rushed to his dresser. Behind him, Mom gasped. He ignored her and yanked the top drawer open. Empty.

"Where are my clothes?" he demanded, looking back at his perplexed parents. "What? What is it? Why are you looking at me like that? Where are my clothes? I need to get dressed. Now!"

They didn't respond. Instead, they stood there, speechless, looking as if they'd just found out a meteor was going to hit the earth in the next second. His mother clung to her husband as if searching for protection from the imminent cataclysm. Slowly, Dad pushed her aside and walked toward Greg.

"Would you let me . . . see your mark?" he asked gently.

Greg had forgotten all about the mark, but the look of uncertainty in Dad's eyes brought it all home. An anxious panic seized him; once he knew his caste, there was no going back.

"No," Greg said with sudden dread, taking a step back as tension tightened his entire body.

"Son, please."

Greg's gaze shifted from one apprehensive parent to another. It was stupid to refuse. Whether he showed them or not, the mark wasn't going anywhere. It was there to stay, like the sharper blue of his eyes and the creepy length of his lashes. He unclenched his now-huge fists and allowed Dad to walk behind him. Greg waited with a lump in his throat for Dad to say something, but all he heard was a tremulous inhale.

"What . . . is it?" Mom asked, looking as if she'd rather let that meteor hit than hear the answer.

"It's a . . . I don't know. It looks like wings," Dad murmured.

"What caste?" Greg asked, tasting his panic. His parents had never mentioned any castes marked by wings, but that didn't necessarily mean anything bad. A least he wasn't a Companion. He was glad he wasn't a Companion.

"Wings? What kind of wings?" Mom asked in a shaky tone.

"Maybe . . . like angel wings," Dad said doubtfully.

"Dad. What. Caste?" Greg repeated, punctuating each word.

"I—I don't know." Dad sounded at a loss. He walked around, faced Greg and put a hand on his shoulder. Greg blinked. Dad was now a few inches shorter than him. Looking down at him felt wrong and gave him a slight feeling of vertigo.

Bowing his head slightly, Dad said, "It's a mark I've . . . never seen or heard of before."

Mom put a hand on her mouth as a single sob escaped her lips. A strange heaviness and dread settled in Greg's gut. Right away, he felt the fear of what he had become, fear of what the mark meant, of the erratic thoughts and urges filling his head. After all that, he still had no idea what his destiny was. A rapid pounding filled his chest. The room spun. Greg put a hand on Dad's arm. Just as the panic almost drove him to his knees, it abruptly stopped.

"I have no time for this," he blurted out, the words taking shape before he realized they were coming out. His Morphid side was back in action. "I need my clothes."

"They're too small now," Dad said. "We thought we would take you shopping for some new ones." He smiled sadly, watching the future he'd imagined for his son disintegrate. "You can go in my closet and find what you need," he finished, in complete understanding of his son's urgency.

Greg lumbered out of his bedroom, clumsy and unaccustomed to his oversized limbs. He found his way to his parents' closet, feeling disoriented. Clothes hung from white plastic hangers in neat, color coordinated rows. Greg dropped the sheet he wore around his waist and snatched what was closest at hand: A pair of khaki pants and a white, button-up shirt. They were pressed and starched, just back from the cleaners.

He threw the shirt on and stuffed his bulging arms through the long sleeves. After pulling on the slacks, he buttoned and zipped everything. Standing in the closet, he gaped at himself in the body-length mirror. Everything was tight and a couple inches too short. Part of his mind rebelled at the sight. He looked dorky as hell.

-It doesn't matter, the new part of him said.

Yeah, not important, he answered himself. Greg shook his head.

Shoes, he needed shoes. He found a pair of leather loafers, but after trying and failing to stuff his feet inside of them, he settled for a pair of sandals.

Now I really look retarded. Dress pants and sandals?

With one sandal on his foot and another in his hand, he walked past his wide-eyed parents, and staggered downstairs to the kitchen. Going straight for the tall fridge, he easily reached out and retrieved the road atlas that sat on top of it. He threw the old, dusty thing on the kitchen table and stared at it, bewildered. After a long moment, he scratched his head. He started to open it, but . . . to where? The force that had driven him to find the atlas was gone. Hopping on one foot, he slipped the other sandal on. He squinted at the atlas as if it held the key to a door he never wanted to open. He took a step back.

"It'll come to you," Dad said from behind, startling Greg. He whirled and faced his parents. They looked wary, especially Mom, who tightly held a fistful of her t-shirt.

"What's happening to me?" Greg asked, pressing the heels of his hands to his temples. "I'm going crazy."

"Don't fight it, son," Dad said.

"Maybe he should," Mom blurted out.

"Erica!" The shock and reproach in Dad's voice was close to outrage.

"We don't know where this is going to take him, Nick!" She seemed on the verge of tears. "His caste . . . we don't—"

"You know he can't fight it."

"He sure looks like he's trying," she said, pointing at Greg.

Shaking on the spot, Greg felt the renewed urge to open the road atlas to look for . . . for who knows what? He had no idea.

"If he fights it, he may go mad," Dad argued. "Is that what you want?"

"It would be better than losing him. We don't even know what he is."

"How can you say that? He's our son!"

His parents continued their argument, completely ignoring him. Greg caught their words like random flashes of light that both enlightened and blinded him. What they said made sense for one instant and the next, it sounded as convoluted as the theory of relativity.

"What would you have him do, then?"

"Why couldn't he just be one of us?"

"It wouldn't be much different. He would still have to leave to find his Integral."

"But for what? Danger? Slavery? What?!" His mom sounded almost hysterical.

"There are other—"

Why didn't they just . . . "Shut up!" Greg screamed, falling to his knees and covering his ears as if to crush the madness raving inside his head.

This is what it feels like to be possessed, he thought. Maybe what they needed was a priest. Holy water would fix him, a crucifix and maybe some incense, too. Whatever had taken hold of his mind was fierce. He needed it out. His eyes squinted shut and tears rolled down the sides of his face as he fought the intruder chattering in his mind. A hand grasped his shoulder. He recoiled.

"Honey," Mom said, a new, gentle tone in her voice. "Don't fight it. It's okay. It's who you are."

Greg looked up. Mom looked pained, but weary acceptance filled her eyes. She hugged him, and his resolve melted away. It was too much. He was too weak to fight the call in his mind. He stood shakily, took a deep breath, and just listened. Like a bolt of lightning, it hit him.

-Turn the pages.

He flipped the atlas open.

-Keep going.

Greg obeyed and turned the pages until he knew to stop.

There: Indiana. He leaned forward and waited for the next command. Nothing else came. He looked to his parents, confused. His impulses had been so clear and demanding just a second ago, and now he felt as empty as a bubble floating in midair.

"Give it time," Dad said. "It takes practice, and it's never really perfect or foolproof."

"Indiana," Mom said, peering over Greg's shoulder to look at the map. The name sounded hopeful on her lips. At least Indiana was in the States, not across the world. "Do you think his Integral is in Indiana?" she asked Dad.

"I don't know. Maybe . . . maybe it's something else. We don't even know what his caste would have him do."

"But what else could it be?"

Silence.

Greg pulled out a chair and sat, feeling as if he'd just hiked Mount Everest. His hands shook, and his breathing was ragged. He felt completely sapped of energy. Suddenly, he realized he hadn't eaten in nine days. Greg gave his parents a dramatic look, and took a deep breath.

"I'm hungry." His stomach growled in agreement. He gave Mom his practiced starving puppy look. The tension in the room dissolved, and they all laughed, even if a little hysterically.

"I'll make you breakfast," Mom said, glad to have something to do.

Four slices of toast, three eggs, six pieces of bacon, and a tall glass of OJ later, Greg felt almost like his old self. There were no crazy ideas firing inside his head, and his hands were steady. Maybe food was all he needed to keep the Jekyll and Hyde turmoil at bay.

"Feel better?" Dad asked.

Greg nodded. They sat across from him at the small kitchen table.

"Any idea what's in Indiana yet?" Dad asked.

Greg shook his head.

"It'll come to you when the time is right."

"Is it always so confusing?"

"I wouldn't call it *confusing*. I'd call it . . . incomplete," Dad said.

Yes. That was it. The message wasn't confusing. Just incomplete. He'd known exactly what he needed to do. The message was plain and strong. Get the road atlas. Flip the page. Stop. He just didn't know the rest of the message, or why he must do these things.

"Was it the same for you guys?" Greg asked.

They nodded.

"Hard to think these messed up *calls* helped you find each other," Greg said, unable to spare them his bitterness.

"The *calls* are foolproof," Mom said.

"So if I'm not a Companion . . ." Greg said. He felt like he should be happy, but not knowing his own caste was spoiling it for him. "Any idea of what I am?"

His parents exchanged nervous glances.

"No, not really," Dad said. "There are rare castes, ones that only come every few generations when there's great need— sometimes new castes, to fulfill a need never seen before."

Greg swallowed. "And you think that's what this is?"

"Maybe, son. I—I really don't know." Dad shook his head.

"Great, just great!" Greg buried his face in his hands. If he knew his caste, he could at least guess what or who was in Indiana. But he had nothing to go by.

"I guess I have an Integral, after all." Dread overtook him. What if his Integral turned out to be a mafia boss who was in need of a hired thug?

"We don't know if you have an Integral or not, baby," Mom said in a sad tone. "Anything could be in Indiana. Oh, I don't like this. It isn't fair for you to have a life without love."

"We can't judge his life based on our experience, Erica. Our purpose was to find and share love, but Greg's isn't. He won't have the same feelings and needs we do. The desire to love and be loved aren't in his nature. There's no reason to worry about him suffering over that."

"That's a cruel thing to say," she argued.

"It is what it is."

"How can you be so sure, Nick? Yes, other castes aren't supposed to feel love the way we do, but what do we know? Just what others say and—"

Greg couldn't take it anymore. "Quit talking about me like I'm not here," he snapped. In all the times he'd wished not to be a Companion, the idea of a life without love never sounded so depressing. Was this the reason he'd never felt anything for any of the girls he'd ever met? Was he incapable of feeling love for anyone? Sadness washed over him as he realized that even if he could never fall in love, he could still feel the pain of an existence without affection. He'd thought that wouldn't be part of the package, but maybe he'd been wrong.

"I'm sorry," Mom said, lowering her eyes. "I shouldn't say those things. I just . . . want the best for you. It's difficult to see my only son all grown up, with his own destiny ahead of him. Your father's right. I'm just being selfish. Love is for Companions. What you have is something different." She smiled sadly.

But if that was true, why did he feel as if something had been stolen from him? If loving wasn't in his nature, why did he feel empty? He kept the question to himself.

A pang of urgency hit Greg square in the chest. He immediately recognized the feeling, growing familiar with the way these "calls" felt. His focus shifted inward. His scalp felt crawly.

-Indiana.

Mechanically, Greg pulled the road atlas closer, sliding his plate out of the way. He swept his eyes over the Hoosier State, concentrating on the middle of the page, where a spider web of highways radiated outward. Greg had never liked math, but geography, well, that was different. He had always loved it. As soon as he laid eyes on the city, a slew of trivia flooded out of his human side's memory. He was looking at Indianapolis, the largest metropolitan area in Indiana. It was also the state capital, located in Marion County and . . .

-Not important.

The thoughts disappeared as if a hand had dusted them from the surface of his mind. Indianapolis wasn't relevant, he needed to look west. With mounting determination, Greg carefully scanned the city names: Lebanon, Frankfort, Lafayette . . .

"West," he said, his own voice startling him. It had come out involuntarily.

"West what, honey?" Mom asked in a tone as fragile as crystal.

"West of Lafayette."

"You mean West Lafayette?" Dad asked.

Greg looked up.

"Yes!" he blurted out. "Yes," he repeated, but the second time his voice was barely a whisper. The chair slid back with a screech as he stood.

"I have to go there," he announced. "Sam needs me."

Wait . . . who the heck is Sam? He was getting annoyed with the two brains stuffed inside his skull. One was completely insane, and the other too dumbfounded to be of any use.

"An Integral!" Mom exclaimed in a sob.

"Does he need you right away?" Dad asked. "Is he okay?"

"Yes. I think he . . . he is, for now?" Greg said, doubtful of his own words. Something wasn't right, but he couldn't tell what. "I'll pack a few things and go. I have some time, but not much." He had no idea how he knew this, but he did.

"Nick," Mom pleaded, putting a hand on her husband's arm. Wide-eyed, Dad stared at the salt shaker. He looked like his mind was racing ten thousand miles per hour.

"I can get a job there," he said after a moment. "Purdue University is in West Lafayette. If Greg's move is permanent, we can go with him." His father was a professor at Tulane. He could probably get a recommendation from someone.

"I can't wait, Dad." Greg's voice carried more conviction than it ever had in his entire life, even while his old self felt scared to death.

"I know, I know," Dad nodded in resignation. He stood and searched in his pocket. "Here. If driving is an option, you can take my car. It'll be cheaper." He fished a set of keys from his pocket.

Greg allowed the thought to sink in for a moment, waiting for his Morphid side to howl in protest. Nothing. "Yes, driving is an option," he said simply, taking the keys. Somehow he knew he had enough time to drive up there. No need to fly.

When the trance-like sensation passed, he abruptly felt the need to do a celebratory dance.

The car is mine! All mine! His Dr. Jekyll side chanted inside his mind. Somehow, he managed not to shake his ass in celebration, and stayed put, frowning, thinking he'd officially stepped into Bizarro world. While one part of him—the new part—understood that taking Dad's car was the most practical solution, the other part couldn't help but think how he'd never even been allowed to drive to the Quick Mart without supervision. Now he was going to drive to Indiana all by himself.

"Here's some cash," Dad pulled out a handful of twenty dollar bills. "Oh, and my credit card. You may need it." Blinking in amazement, Greg took the American Express card.

Oh, my God! I can get my iPod chock full of music. He blinked. Well, no question where that thought had come from: The stupid and inconsiderate side. His parents weren't rich. They weren't poor either, but their budget was tight enough. He wouldn't use their card unless it was an absolute emergency.

In the meantime, his Morphid side informed him that he wouldn't need music any more than he'd need love. He calmly filed the thought away. Maybe his brain was finally completing its transformation. Acceptance of what he must do came by degrees. Maybe that small human voice that still lingered in a corner of his brain and made him regret not ever being able to experience love would extinguish soon. Greg felt a sudden twinge of sadness, and immediately knew this emotion didn't belong to the adult Morphid he'd become. This sadness and regret were all too human.

He would go—would find Sam, whoever he was—and leave the life he'd always known behind.

ඊ Chapter 8 ౭
Ashby

Ashby looked around the large ornate table, fervently wishing he could be anywhere else. He was starting to hate this ancient room and didn't see the point of attending these Council meetings if he wasn't allowed to say anything. "You're simply there to observe and learn, Ashby. The main lesson you need is keeping your mouth shut when your opinion isn't relevant," his mother always told him. He scoffed inwardly. He wasn't useless. There was plenty he could do to help, if they would let him. But he was only allowed to be a figurehead; and a recluse one, at that. He rarely went outside the castle, even to the nearby towns. He only attended events sanctioned by his mother and not even his studies provided an excuse to let him out into the world. For that, he had many tutors with knowledge of every possible Human and Morphid subject.

Portos smiled benevolently at him from across the table. The old man understood him, and had even intervened for him from time to time, making suggestions to the Regent on ways Ashby could help the Council. His mother had always shot all the ideas down, of course.

Sir August Dabworth sat next to Portos, reading his notes over round spectacles; gray, bushy eyebrows arched high, forehead wrinkled in concentration. He wore his customary sneer, a facial seal all his relatives seemed to possess, like a proud emblem of their elevated aristocracy—one they enjoyed in both Morphid *and* Human circles. Ashby smirked, remembering how mad his mother got every time Sir Dabworth reminded her that he had been knighted by the Queen of England.

"As if filthy human titles matter to us," Danata always sneered. She hated the man, Ashby guessed, but what could she do about it? Fate decided who the members of the Council would be, not the Regent. And Sir Dabworth, just like everyone else here, bore the Council staff on his back as part of his caste. But, for Sir Dabworth, it wasn't just the Council staff. He had a *Dual* mark, which made him a Morphid with two castes—much like Ashby, except the man's second caste was a *skilled* one. Something Ashby wished he possessed, if for no other reason than to prevent his mother from ordering him to sit quietly. If he, like Sir Dabworth, were more than a mere Companion and had special powers, he could do so much more for his people. The old man was a powerful *Actuary.* He could, after a mere glance at a set of data, infer a million different permutations, patterns and possibilities. His skill was most useful to the Council, all the way from finance issues to seating arrangements at official celebrations.

Ashby shook his head, thinking of Sam and feeling ashamed. If he were anything other than a Companion, he wouldn't have her. The mere idea made his stomach cramp. He turned his attention to Florence Finely, who sat to the right of Sir Dabworth. She was the youngest member of the Council, a pouty-lipped redhead with emerald green eyes and a beauty mark on her right cheekbone. Finely was also a Dual, bearing the Council staff and, of all things, the sword of the *Warrior* caste, a Morphid breed that was almost extinct and possessed astounding fighting skills, be it with weaponry or hand-to-hand combat. Ashby tried to picture the mark on her back, recalling images from an old textbook. He imagined the circle, a trait all marks shared, with a jeweled sword in the middle and a small staff on top of the outlining circumference. She was one of his mother's favorites, often used as a bodyguard due to her keen senses. Florence caught him staring and winked at him. Ashby gave her a disapproving frown.

Singulars! They could be so infuriatingly inappropriate, just like Perry. Finely smiled wickedly, pursing her pouty lips as though she were about to blow him a kiss. Ashby looked away—doing his best not to look scandalized by her guile—and turned his eyes on Cora Warelow, the famous *Seer.* Warelow was yet another powerful Dual, a woman of sixty with smooth gray hair and warm brown eyes; much like Sam's, Ashby thought. She smiled amiably at Ashby and waved with one finger—the same way she used to wave at him when he was a preschooler. He returned her greeting in kind.

Horace and Julius Lywood sat at the end of the table, talking to each other in hushed tones. They were brothers, simple Council members with no Dual castes, under-appreciated by Danata due to their lack of special powers—which made no sense to Ashby, since she had no powers herself. He supposed having the mark of Regent, a crown, made her feel justified in her arrogance, especially since she was a Singular and her crown was accompanied by a staff, indicating she had full power.

Margaret Obryen and Victor Redwood's chairs sat empty, but they were on speaker phone, attending the meeting long distance as they took care of Council business abroad. Ashby looked from the high-tech sound station in the middle of the table to the lions carved on the backs of the few empty chairs to the ancient coat of arms on the wall and he had to smirk. The contrast often struck him as ridiculous.

The conference room door opened and Regent Danata walked in, followed by Veridan. The Regent took her seat at the head of the table, while her Succeeding Sorcerer—Veridan would take Portos' position in any contingency (Ashby shivered at the thought)—sat to her left. Danata offered the group a stern look and set the meeting in motion without preamble.

The council meeting began with a dry financial report from Sir Dabworth. He reported the status of the Council coffers, giving detailed account of all investments and their gains or losses. They included stocks, real estate, investments in private businesses and more. He petitioned a vote to make some changes on a few overseas holdings, based on new information. Approval was obtained without a fuss. Ashby yawned under his hand several times during his report, wishing they'd move to other topics.

"Very well, August," Regent Danata said, content with their financial status. "I assume these new investments will benefit the Arise Program."

Ashby straightened, far more interested on this subject.

"They should," Sir Dabworth said. "The program's funds should grow by at least 10% in the next year. This should allow for the inclusion of at least two hundred more families."

The Arise Program was near and dear to Ashby's heart. Two thousand Companions and their families had already benefited from the funds offered. With the world's Morphid population in decline, Arise had been his mother's way to encourage Morphid families to have more children. Companions who signed up for the program received monetary benefits for having a third child, benefits that ranged from increased pensions for the parents to college tuition for all their children. Since its inception twenty years ago, more than four hundred families had joined. It wasn't much, but it meant many new Morphids who wouldn't have been born otherwise. The Council discussed particulars of the program for a few minutes, weighing the pros and cons of sponsoring Morphid families in third world countries, something that—not surprisingly—Regent Danata was opposed to.

"Mother, the same funds go much further in developing countries. I have some ideas for charitable events that could help raise separate funds for some of these areas," Ashby spoke up, impatient with his mother's lack of foresight.

Danata's eyes swiveled his way, so slowly he could almost hear them grind in their sockets. "When I'm in need of ideas, I will make sure to contact you, Ashby."

He clenched his fists and struggled not to spit at Veridan's smirking face. Florence Finely gave him "poor baby" eyes, and Seer Warelow shook her head at the Regent. She always disapproved of the way Danata treated her son, but was never brave enough to speak up in his favor. Ashby felt like stomping out of there in a rage, but he sank back in his high-back chair and simmered.

My time will come. My time will come, he repeated the same mantra over and over in his head.

After hearing more reports, the Regent turned to the Lywood brothers with a disdainful expression. "You said there were two matters you wanted to bring to the Council's attention. Please make it quick, I have another commitment after this." She looked at her wrist watch with arched eyebrows.

Horace Lywood cleared his throat, looking a little flustered. His brother gave him an encouraging look. "Yes, Regent Danata. Two strange matters have been brought to our attention, troubling phenomena we feel the Council needs to investigate."

Danata tapped her fingers on the desk, unimpressed so far.

"Uh," Horace looked at the file in front of him, fingers dancing over the pages nervously. "The first deals with a personal dispute between two Companion males."

"A personal dispute? I fail to see why that should interest the Council, Horace," the Regent said.

"Well, they were fighting over . . . the same female, Regent. They both claimed to be fated to her."

Portos raised his eyebrows. "But that is unheard of. Are you sure there isn't some sort of error in this report?"

Veridan pointedly rolled his eyes, making it obvious how he felt about the High Sorcerer. It was common knowledge that he thought Portos was a bumbling idiot, too passive and aged for his role. Ashby seethed. Maybe Portos was slow to process and sometimes act, but when he did, he was always decisive, precise and compassionate. Traits that Ashby hoped Perry would develop before his time came to become High Sorcerer.

"We have corroborated the facts twice," Horace said, "but this occurred in a remote town in Iceland, so we would like to see for ourselves."

"It sounds like an utter waste of time," Veridan said, inspecting his fingernails nonchalantly and looking at everyone down his aquiline nose. His slicked back, dark hair shone, reflecting the light and showing the inordinate amounts of hair product that he used.

"I agree," Danata said.

Despite his fuming at his mother and Veridan, Ashby was inclined to agree. There had to be some sort of mistake. *Not that anyone asked me*, he thought.

Julius spoke up. "We wouldn't worry, except we've heard rumors of similar incidents occurring elsewhere. This just happens to be the first documented instance, which is why we decided to share it with the Council, and why we think we should confirm or disprove in person."

Similar incidents happening elsewhere? In that case, maybe it wasn't such a waste of time. Portos and Danata exchanged a meaningful look. The High Sorcerer nodded lightly.

Danata sighed. "Very well, open a full investigation and report back. I feel certain it will turn out to be a mistake, but it's better to be safe, I suppose. Anything else?"

"Y-yes," Horace said, looking even more doubtful than before. "We have also received three independent reports from our eyes and ears in New York city. They alert us of an extremely high number of homeless Morphids in the metro area."

Danata scoffed. "Homeless? Don't we already have enough to worry about? Do we have to also concern ourselves with the lazy and unwashed?"

Even Sir Dabworth looked appalled at the comment. He aligned his already aligned notes, staring down at the pages in consternation.

"Uh, yes Regent," Horace said. "The homeless have never been a concern before; beyond what every member of the Council finds charitable, of course. However, the numbers, in the city of New York in particular, have increased rapidly in the last year, especially in the last three months. It seems they are . . . migrating there, congregating as if for some special reason. Many have arrived from different cities, even creating a problem for the human authorities."

Regent Danata sighed tiredly. But the more Ashby thought about it, the more he found both problems rather disturbing, and the less he shared his mother's indifference. One of these issues in isolation wouldn't be cause for concern, but two strange phenomena like this . . . that should give her pause. Morphids were a strange race, shaped by Fate and its peculiar whims. It wouldn't be the first time that mysterious events like this marked the beginning of momentous changes.

"I'd like to aid the Lywoods in this research, Mother," Ashby said. "There may be something noteworthy in all this."

Regent Danata scowled back at Ashby as if he were a pesky Chihuahua that wouldn't stop yapping at her heels.

"Of course you'd want to concern yourself with such issues," she said, shaking her head. "I'd rather you volunteer to help August research the Council's investments, but I suppose you would yawn through that."

Veridan let out a choked laugh, then disguised his mockery by faking a cough and looking at the ceiling. Trembling, Ashby stood and pushed the chair so hard that it hit the wall behind him. He looked down at his mother with ill-contained rage. The Regent stared back, unperturbed by her son's anger. Everyone else looked at Ashby with pity in their eyes.

"I suppose I would," he said between clenched teeth. What was he here? Nothing but a joke. He saw no reason to stick around.

Not in the Council meeting, nor in the castle. Indiana began to look like greener pastures, and a plan began to develop in his mind. "Since you have *everything* under control, I think I will take myself elsewhere." And with that, he left the conference room, a new plan for disobedience throbbing in his temples.

ℰ Chapter 9 ℂ
Sam

Sam jumped out of bed and seized her ringing cell phone. It read, "Bureau of Doom." She flinched. It was too early to talk to her mother . . . or was it? She suddenly realized it was actually past noon. She'd spent the night crying in silence. Of course, she wasn't ready to talk to her after what she'd found out. No matter the time.

"Hello."

"Hi, Sam." It was her fath . . . no, it was James.

"Hi." They couldn't even lie properly. He was supposed to be out of town on a business trip, not at the bureau. An awkward silence ensued, but Sam didn't plan to make this easy for either of them.

"Er, your mother wants me to . . . talk to you."

Sam huffed.

"Have you had lunch yet?" he asked in a business-like tone.

So, I'm just another one of his clients. Her immediate instinct was to answer, "yes", but that would be letting him off the hook. Besides, if this was her mom's plan—Barbara's plan—there would be no way out of it. Sooner or later, she'd have to have this conversation with James.

"No, I haven't had lunch yet," Sam answered.

"All right, I'll pick you up in ten minutes." James sounded like he was about to hang up, but then seemed to opt for a little diplomacy. "Where would you like to eat?"

An impish smile rose in Sam's lips. "The Dragon."

James hated Chinese food. It gave him heartburn. Maliciously, she wished for the power to make all the world's antacids disappear.

"Hmm, why don't we go for some light Italian instead?"

"Nope, I'm in the mood for Chinese today," Sam said, trying to sound much more chipper than she felt. "Lo Mein noodles is what I'm having. What about you?" she added, hoping James's stomach was already twisting in protest.

"Maybe some soup," he grumbled. "Pick you up in ten."

Sam didn't wait by the curb as she normally would have, and when her cell phone rang she ignored it. Instead, she watched James get out of the car and stomp to the front door, fuming like a locomotive. One second before he slipped the key in the lock, Sam swung the door open.

"Hey, you're already here. Sorry, I was in the bathroom." She bounded toward the car, leaving the door ajar behind her.

James mumbled something unintelligible, locked the door, then joined Sam, who was already sitting comfortably in the passenger seat.

"This is great!" she enthused, finding it too easy not to use the word *Dad*. "We should do it more often, don't you think?" James half-smiled and nodded, looking as if he'd rather eat live scorpions. He loosened his silk tie and ran a hand through his salt and pepper hair.

They didn't speak on the way to the restaurant. Instead, Sam played with the radio, switching from one station to another, singing along whether she knew the lyrics or not. James gripped the wheel tightly and said nothing, biting his tongue with courtroom slyness.

At the restaurant, Sam piled food high on her plate while James settled for bowls of steamed rice and egg drop soup. She slurped her lo mein noodles, raving about how good they were and all the different spices she could taste.

Halfway through the meal, James set his spoon down and said, "Well, there's no point in dancing around the issue. You're not a child anymore, and I think you can handle the news. Your mother and I are getting a divorce." Sam could tell he was trying to keep a serious face, but a small, crooked smile betrayed his undeniable happiness. She waited for more explanation, but none came.

"Is that it?" she asked.

"Yes. That's what your mother wanted me to tell you."

What?! No fake apologies or empty promises?

Sam pushed her plate aside. Ironically, she was now experiencing the heartburn James should have gotten. "I think I'm done."

"Well, in that case, we should go. I have business to take care of at the office."

They left the restaurant in a hurry. It was the fastest lunch Sam had ever had. When they got home, she got out of the car and stormed toward the house with no intention of looking back. However, when James called out her name, she stopped and peered over her shoulder. The passenger window slid all the way down. Reluctantly, she turned and looked back where James sat, looking apologetic.

"If you . . . need anything, you should call me," he said, eyes shifting from side to side unable to look at her directly.

He feels guilty. That was unexpected and somehow hard to believe. He was probably already regretting the offer, and planning to change his phone number as soon as possible.

"Don't worry," Sam said, "I won't bother you." She walked away, feeling a little guilty herself. Maybe his remorse was real, but it was too little, too late, and it couldn't make up for all the times he hadn't been there when it would have counted. His offer meant nothing, especially since it came the day he was walking out of her life.

The key trembled in her hand, but she managed to open the door. Her small purse dropped to the floor as she buried her face into her hands. She cried bitter tears for a long while, her back leaning against the closed door. She was worth no more than a cold-hearted business transaction. It hurt. It deeply hurt.

* * *

Barbara arrived home early that afternoon. Sam was caught off guard, rummaging through the pantry trying to find a bag of instant noodles for dinner. She was so despondent that she had stooped to the worst culinary crime imaginable.

"Oh, hi," Sam said when she saw Barbara standing by the kitchen table with a self-satisfied grin on her face. Hiding the package of noodles behind her back, Sam closed the pantry door.

"You saw your father today." It wasn't a question, so Sam said nothing. "He's a . . ." Barbara paused and seemed to rethink her words. "He's despicable, isn't he?"

"Uh . . ." Sam was at a loss for words. "I—I suppose it's for the best?"

Barbara's grin snapped into a glare, her brow wrinkling until she resembled a Shar Pei dog. "For the best?! You think it's 'for the best' he cheated on your mother and destroyed your home?"

Sam almost choked on her own saliva. A lot was wrong with what Barbara had just said, but she focused on the only piece of real information.

"He cheated on you?" she asked, surprised, although not very much.

"He didn't tell you?!" The all-too-common anger charged Barbara's voice.

Sam wanted to run to her room and avoid the imminent neutron explosion. The dust bunnies under her bed would be fantastic company right about now. But she was trapped.

"Um, no, he didn't happen to mention anything about . . . cheating," Sam said reluctantly.

And there it was: The red face, the bulging eyes, the protruding vein in her neck. Textbook.

"The bastard," Barbara yelled, throwing her arms up in the air. "I'm gonna kill him!"

Sam knew it would be a slow and painful death.

"What exactly did he tell you?"

"Just that you were getting a divorce."

"Anything else?"

Sam shook her head.

"You mean he didn't say you'll be spending the rest of the summer with him?"

"What?"

"The vermin's been keeping an apartment with his *girlfriend* for almost a year. You're supposed to . . . no," Barbara corrected herself, "you *are* going to spend the rest of the summer and *all* holidays with him."

Barbara wanted to punish James for his philandering by forcing him to keep Sam, by imposing the daughter on the girlfriend. Something bled inside of Sam, and she felt the cut at her core. Pain upon pain. And as if Barbara's disdain weren't enough, James hadn't bothered to mention it. He had no interest in spending time together and playing the paternal role. Sam was just an instrument they could use to dampen each other's fun. Her feelings meant nothing to them, and although now she knew the reason for all their indifference, it didn't make the pain easier to bear.

A crunching sound filled the kitchen, and Sam suddenly realized she was pulverizing the bag of instant noodles. Slowly lifting her hand, she slammed the small package onto the countertop, exploding dry pieces of pasta all over the granite surface and the hardwood floor.

"I. Am. Not. Your. Toy!" The fury and hatred she felt surprised her. She'd never spoken to Barbara like this, but any shred of respect she'd felt obligated to show was gone now.

The kitchen was totally silent as a tense look passed between them. Finally, Sam walked past toward her room. Barbara stayed frozen on the spot, too stunned to say anything. Something inside of Sam broke with a tremendous shatter. She could feel the pieces falling to the pit of her stomach as she climbed the steps. In her room, she collapsed on the bed, feeling her broken insides rattle.

The tears finally came, after a few minutes of incredulity. They came forcefully, with no sign of ever stopping. She went through a full box of Kleenex. When that ran out, she used toilet paper and chapped her nose, but hardly even noticed. After what seemed like hours, her bed was a cotton field sprinkled with wads of tissue.

Curled up in a ball, Sam forgot herself.

* * *

Sam spent the next two days in bed, with no one to care or even notice. She felt like an empty shell. Books, tissues and empty bags of buttery popcorn lay strewn around her. Empty glasses sat on her night table and dresser, cloudy with the remains of dried milk.

Her hair looked like an eagle's nest, and she was still wearing the same pajamas from two nights ago. She rolled over in bed to face the window and watched the sun poke shyly through the sheer curtains. The book she'd been reading rested on the pillow. A huge sigh escaped her at the sight of it. Vaguely, she wondered what would happen to the heroine, then realized she didn't actually care.

Sam closed her eyes and tried to force herself back to sleep, but her body refused, aching from having been in bed too long already. Stubbornly, she managed to will herself back into slumber by picturing a blank sheet of paper. Her efforts were rewarded by an all-too-real dream invading her fitful sleep.

Her short legs slid off her messy bed. A candy wrapper fluttered to the floor, chanting about extra pounds around her waist. Sam pinched an inch of her belly and shrugged indifferently. She walked over the piles of junk and into the bathroom, where she drew a hot bubble bath with kiwi and strawberry body wash. The mirror clouded up with steam. She wiped it with a bony hand and looked at her reflection. Her face was gaunt, like a skeleton's, but she didn't feel scared. It was just weird; she'd been fat a minute ago, and now she was skin and bones. Oh, well. Vaguely, she wondered about the nutritional value of popcorn. She would have to try peanut butter sandwiches next time she spent two days brooding in bed.

Shaving cream and a razor in hand, she climbed into the tub. It was important to shave her legs. A girl had to keep her dignity, even in times like this.

Goose bumps crawled from her toes to the tips of her ears as she lowered herself into the luscious bubbles. She squirted foam on one hand, lathered one leg with a thick coat, then proceeded to shave. As the pink razor traveled from her ankle to her knee, apple-scented lather accumulated into globs and dropped into the tub. When she finished one leg and moved to the other, she noticed the lather changing color to a shade of pink, which quickly intensified to match the magenta handle of her disposable razor.

With mild interest, Sam picked up the shaving cream bottle and read the label. It said nothing about color changes. Shrugging, she went back to the task. After a few more strokes, she froze as the light pink color deepened to a bright red. Her legs, the water, her hands were crimson with . . . *with what?* She dropped the razor and lifted her hands to eye level. Red rivulets ran down from her wrists to the crook of her elbows and dribbled in slow motion into the tub.

Drip, drip, drip. There was no sound, but the metallic patter of red droplets hitting the bathwater. She screamed in realization, and watched the blood flow faster, as if spurred on by her hysteria. It poured into the water until the lower half of her body was obscured by the tainted liquid.

In the next second, Sam woke from her nightmare, screaming at the top of her lungs. She jumped out of bed and tried to stifle her shrieks with the sheets. Cold sweat dripped down her back. Finally, the pristine whiteness of her comforter grounded her enough to rein in the overwhelming fear and come back to reality. She collapsed on the floor and sobbed, unnerved by how eerily real the dream had been.

After a long time, she mustered enough courage to walk into the bathroom. The tub was empty, and its surface as white and immaculate as ever. She huffed in a weak attempt to laugh at the stupid dream. There was no way that shaving her legs could ever go so wrong. She shuddered and sat on the edge of the bed. The nightmare had shaken her badly, and its suggestive meaning reared its ugly head, taunting her.

She shook herself, trying to think of something else. Her mind filled with dark, mocking shapes. *No.* Thinking was no good, she had to *do* something. She set into action.

In minutes, she picked up all the garbage and books, made her bed, combed her hair and brushed her teeth. After a few controlled breaths, she built up enough courage for a shower. The idea of a bath wouldn't appeal to her for another decade.

She was bending over carefully shaving one leg—she wasn't going to let a stupid nightmare stop her from having smooth legs, she refused to—when her phone rang on top of the toilet tank. Blindly, she pulled the curtain and reached for it. It was Barbara. As soon as Sam answered, she went into a tirade about James. It had taken much convincing—Barbara actually used those words—but James had finally capitulated and agreed to let Sam stay with him.

"I don't want to stay with him," Sam protested.

"It's not about what you want."

"Then what? About making James pay?"

There was silence for a few seconds, then Sam realized her mistake.

"Don't you dare start calling *me Barbara*," she warned.

Sam's upper lip curled in anger and toxic fumes seemed to spew from her ears. She knew what name she'd *really* like to call her, but an instinct of self-preservation kept her from making that mistake.

"Pack your bags. *James*," mockery marked Barbara's voice, "expects you at his place by five o'clock. I e-mailed you the address. Pack enough clothes, toiletries and anything else you might need."

Even the pretense of parenthood and caring were over. Only the cool water splashing on her back kept Sam from boiling over. She had never felt so infuriatingly helpless in her entire life. A puppet, that was all she was to them. That was all she'd ever been, she suddenly realized. Never a daughter, just a prop they could use or forget at their convenience.

"I'll see you when school starts." Barbara hung up.

The phone beeped, signaling the connection had dropped. Sam held it in one hand and the razor in the other, two instruments fully capable of hurting her. She stared at her wrists and the blue-green veins running through them, pulsing with her unwanted, worthless life. Nobody cared about her. Nobody.

Her hands shook, but her eyes grew glassy, staring with detached interest. A terrible nothingness settled in the pit of her stomach, and everything that had been important in life seemed to shrink. Her excellent grades, her love for reading, volunteering at the soup kitchen, her friendship with Brooke, her dreams of going away to culinary school. All the things she loved and had always made life at the Gibsons' bearable, now seemed mere trifles.

What's the point? There was no point!

Her hands shook violently now. The sound of water running and going down the drain filled her head with its hypnotic gurgle. Maybe she was still dreaming? If she was, she knew exactly what she needed to do next. With her foot, she flipped the stopper to allow the tub to fill up. Mechanically, she pulled the shower curtain open and set the phone down. She was lowering herself into the water when the phone rang again.

She ignored it. One, two, three, four times. It stopped, and went to voice mail. Sam lifted the razor and placed it on her opposite wrist. A tear slid down her cold, wet face. She didn't have to be their puppet anymore.

For once and for all, she would set them *and* herself free.

ℰ Chapter 10 ℭ
Sam

A phone rang. Its echoes stretched away in the distance. Sam sat in the tub, a pink razor pressed to her wrist, tepid water up to her waist. Her face was slack with indifference. A sliding motion would be all it would take and all would be over. Easy. Fairly painless. Then her awful parents, and everything else, would fade from her mind.

Her cell phone—which rested on top of the toilet tank—rang again, louder and more insistently it seemed, as if it knew what she was about to do. A final, ear-splitting ring. Sam snapped out of her trance, dropping the razor into the water. She hugged her legs, in shock at how close she'd been. And for what? For whom? For people that didn't love her or want her.

"H-hello."

Someone spoke right away, interrupting her "hello" before she could even get it out.

"I need to speak to Sam, please!" The deep, smooth voice sounded desperate.

At the sound of the person on the other end, Sam's horror began to melt away. Her rapid breathing slowed down, and her heart quickly regained its normal rhythm.

"This . . . this is Sam." She shut off the water running into the tub to better listen, but only static came over the receiver.

"Hello?" Sam asked.

"I . . . I thought you'd be a guy," the person sounded confused.

"Well, my name is Samantha, but everyone calls me Sam. Who is this?" The caller's voice had a familiar ring to it, rich and musical, but Sam couldn't place it. She glanced at the number displayed, but could only tell that it was from an out-of-town area code.

"Yeah, sorry. I'm Greg. Gregory actually," he gave a nervous chuckle, "but everyone calls *me* Greg. Are you all right?" The question was normal enough, but Greg sounded so full of concern, and suddenly intimate, that it took her aback. It was as if he knew something wasn't right. A wave of shame swept through her.

"Excuse me?" Sam asked. The appropriate answer should have been, "Doing all right, and you?" but the intimacy in his voice made Sam defensive.

"Well . . . um . . . Mr. Wright gave me a list of tutors I could call, and you were at the top," Greg said.

"Do I know you from school?" Sam thought hard, trying to remember anyone named Greg. She stepped out of the tub and dried herself, holding the phone awkwardly between her ear and shoulder.

"No. I—I'm new. I just moved from New Orleans. I'm making up trig this summer, and Mr. Wright recommended a tutor. You aren't all booked already, are you?" he asked hopefully.

"No, you're the first one to call, actually."

"Great! Can we start today?" He seemed in a hurry.

"Hmm . . ." She wanted to say yes, but didn't want to seem eager. Greg was probably anxious to get started so he could pass the class. She, on the other hand, just needed company. Badly. No need to divulge how pathetic her life was.

"Any time will work for me," Greg said a bit more casually.

"All right, sure. Today's fine."

"Awesome! Where do you want to meet?"

"It's up to you, really. You'll be the one paying."

"Well, in that case . . ." There was a smile in his voice. "I'm new in town. I only know a few places. The school will be a bore, but since I'm already here . . . this first time, anyway."

"That works for me. Do you want to get together now?" *Get me away from this place.* She had to pack and be at James's by five, but she didn't care. She'd be damned if she was going to play nice.

"Sure, now would be great! I mean, take your time. Short notice and all."

"I should be there in twenty . . . at most. Let's meet at the library."

Sam had never gotten dressed so quickly. Even though it was hot outside, she slipped into a pair of jeans. She had only managed to shave half of one leg, so shorts were totally out of the question. After shrugging into a white top, she grabbed her purse and trig textbook. She was halfway out the door before she remembered to put on shoes.

Ten minutes later, she parked in her usual spot and speed-walked toward the school's front entrance, a desperate and inexplicable urgency bouncing in her chest. She hurried down the hallway leading to the library, but before she reached the door, she slowed down and composed herself. *Calm down.* Why was her heart racing, anyway? Probably because she was still alive. Great reason to be giddy any day, right? And this guy, Greg, had saved her, even if he didn't know it.

When she walked into the library, she didn't have to search. There was but one person sitting in the open reading area, and her gaze immediately locked with his. He stood and walked briskly toward her. Sam couldn't help but notice his height, and the awkward way he moved, like his body was too big for him. As if he were a magnet, Sam felt drawn to him, but managed to stay put by the door. When he reached her, Greg stopped abruptly. Sam could have been another girl visiting the library, but something in his eyes said he *knew* she was the person he'd been waiting for.

She looked at his face and felt a measure of recognition. She'd never met him before, but she had met someone *like* him. The memory of Ashby rushed back into her mind as she examined Greg's fair face. There was something similar in their features, an unlikely resemblance in their strong, masculine faces that somehow put them in the same mental category, in spite of their marked differences. They were both tall, fit, and extremely gorgeous.

"Sam!" Greg exclaimed with something like relief. "You're all right."

Great. Yes, like Ashby, here was another guy, strange and erratic, who said off-the-wall things. Yet also a guy whose presence immediately made her feel safe and. . . hopeful, for the first time in a while.

℅ *Chapter 11* ℆
Greg

The weight of the world rolled off Greg's shoulders as soon as he laid eyes on Sam. She was in one piece, or at least appeared so. He had driven here sensing an impending tragedy, somehow knowing that reaching his Integral in time was a matter of life or death.

Greg cleared his throat. "So, you made it." He tried to sound casual as he carefully examined her from head to toe, making sure she was alright.

She didn't say anything, but also looked him up and down, surely wondering about his ridiculous clothes—another pair of Dad's too-short chinos and a button-up shirt. After a moment, she rubbed her arms and looked back toward the door.

Probably figuring out an escape plan, you idiot. Greg kicked himself mentally for his over-the-top concern. "Uh, sorry, you're Sam, right?" He didn't need to ask. His blood was singing with awareness, his built-in GPS flashing a bright, "you have reached your destination," message.

"Yeah."

"And you're all right?" It was half question, half statement.

Her eyes filled with uneasiness and a crease crossed her brow.

Damn. Try again.

"Uh, Mr. Wright said, 'Call Sam, my best tutor.'" Greg tried to sound like the jolly old man, but failed. He winced, a crooked grimace on his lips. He was trying too hard. "He . . . he thought you must have the chickenpox or something. Said you haven't been around."

"No chickenpox. I'm fine," Sam laughed, breaking the tension and graciously ignoring his social ineptitude. "Not a single pockmark. Skin's clear." She put one arm out. "See?"

Obeying a strong protective instinct, he took hold of Sam's wrist and examined it. As they touched, a strange current of energy snapped between them, making Sam pull her hand back with a yelp.

"What the heck?" She rubbed her wrist.

"Uh . . . static electricity . . . I guess," Greg said sheepishly, shaking his hand and feeling his whole body, even the tips of his ears, tingle. He shook to dissipate the odd sensation. "Ready to start?" he rushed the question, before the awkwardness sent her running out the door.

"I . . . guess." She didn't sound sure at all, but walked toward the table where he'd been sitting and chose the chair across from his.

Greg took a seat, unable to take his eyes off her, try as he might. Sam cleared her throat and checked her watch.

"Trigonometry!" he exclaimed, drawing the word out as if he'd just unearthed a long-forgotten memory. Opening the textbook, he thumbed aimlessly through the pages.

"Well, what'd you need help with?" she asked, keeping her gaze fixed on the table.

"Uh, here. This is what Mr. Wright said they covered on Monday, I think. I start class tomorrow, so I need to go over that and all the stuff from Tuesday. Plus today's material."

"Okay," Sam said, opening her book to the same page and immediately lunging into a detailed explanation of the first problem.

Greg's math brain was down, though. His thoughts went as far away from the subject as possible. *She's a teenager and . . . a girl,* Greg thought as he watched her explain. He'd expected a guy, but boy, had he been wrong!

"Does that make sense?" Sam pointed at the equation with her yellow pencil.

"Uh, I think so."

She raised an eyebrow.

"Well, not really." Greg hadn't been paying attention in the least. He had been busy imagining what Sam would look like once she morphed. By human standards, she wasn't what anyone would call pretty, but with his Morphid's eyes, he could see the dormant beauty within her—like a lush garden, seen through a foggy window.

After a second and even third explanation for most of the problems, Sam's impression of Greg's mathematical skills had to suck. True, he was no Pythagoras, but he wasn't that bad either. He bit the inside of his cheek, trying to concentrate, but it seemed impossible with Sam so close.

His fascination with her wasn't the only distraction. Ever since he'd left home, a battle had been raging inside Greg's head. His Morphid and human sides were still wrestling for control, sending him mixed signals, even though his parents said his pre-metamorphosis self would slowly die out. In truth, it only seemed to be worsening. And, at this particular moment, the turmoil had tripled.

-You have to tell her why you're here.

No way, stupid. She'll freak out! She hadn't said anything to acknowledge their Morphid heritage. It was only sensible to play it cool today.

As she explained a particularly difficult problem for the third time, her hands traced the page. Almost hypnotized, Greg's gaze wandered slowly from the tips of her fingers to her face. As she spoke, her nose twitched a little. It made him smile. Her lips moved, but he didn't really hear the words. He was too mesmerized by the narrow curve of her lower lip, which glistened with a shade of pink gloss. He swallowed, feeling his palms go clammy under the table.

-What the hell?! Why are you staring at her like that? That's wrong.

But she's so . . . beautiful.

-No. Stop thinking that way, his Morphid side shot back. *She's not beautiful. She needs your protection.*

Greg shook his head, frustrated.

"Is something wrong?" Sam looked a bit uneasy.

"No, no. I . . . I'm fine. Just a little tired, I guess. Didn't sleep one bit last night."

"How come?"

"Oh, I was driving. Just got in from New Orleans this morning. I hope I don't smell too bad." He wrinkled his nose and offered a wry smile.

She ignored his joke. "New Orleans?"

"Mm-hmm. I drove about thirteen hours nonstop to get here." Greg exhaled, tired just to remember the feat.

"Did your parents relocate?"

"Um, something like that." Greg didn't know what else to say. He could hardly explain what brought him here, even if his Morphid side thought he should spill his guts. She seemed freaked out enough already. Jumping into the "by the way, you're my Integral" speech was *so* not the right idea.

Sam narrowed her honey-colored eyes and looked put out by his evasive response, so he added, "I'll tell you one day when we know each other better." He gave her a meaningful look, hoping she would pick up the hint that he was her Integral. Instead, she just gave him a shy smile and flicked a strand of long, brown hair behind her ear. It was a quick, habitual motion, but, as she tilted her head to accompany the maneuver, Greg understood—for the first time—what femininity was all about. His heart hammered inside his chest.

"Oh, man," he mumbled, as his Morphid and human sides began yelling—one in disapproval, the other in encouragement.

"Something wrong?" Sam asked.

He shook his head.

"Um, maybe we should continue tomorrow," she said, looking at him with a frown.

"O-okay," Greg said a bit disappointed.

"Greg, you're obviously exhausted. Go home and get some sleep."

"Yeah, home." Greg rubbed his eyes to hide his sarcasm.

"The lessons won't stick if you're too tired to concentrate. We can catch up later."

"I guess you're right. A nap would be nice." No need to tell her that until his parents made it up here, home would be his car. "Tomorrow, then? Same time?"

Sam nodded, and Greg thought he saw a fleeting smile on her lips. Or maybe it was just wishful thinking. They walked outside together without saying a word. He accompanied Sam to her car and gave her another meaningful look, hoping she would ask what a handsome Morphid like him was doing in Indiana. Nothing.

As she drove away, no sense of dread assaulted him. She was safe now, and somehow he knew that if she needed him again, his instincts would give him a fair warning. Kicking a pebble, Greg walked to his car. He'd parked under the shade of a huge oak tree, away from the school, where he'd be safe sleeping in the back seat without being discovered or roasting to death. Stepping inside, Greg was grateful that Mom had thought of packing a pillow. Resting his head, he closed his eyes and relished the comfort and blissful quiet inside his head.

His stomach growled, but sleep was his most immediate physiological need. Food could wait. It'd been a long, desperate ride from New Orleans, almost a thousand miles, stopping only to refuel. He got to the school before it opened and bit his fingernails, waiting to enter the classroom where the next clue would be.

Enroll in Mr. Wright's trigonometry class at West Lafayette High School, his brain had ordered soon after he left home. During a quick call to his parents, Dad had assured him that he'd contact the school and find some way to enroll him. If everything happened for a reason, Greg's struggles with math were no accident.

To his relief, the school officials signed him up, on the condition that his parents completed the required paperwork as soon as possible. Dad must have some connections through the University, he thought. His parents had immediately purchased plane tickets for the next day, making Greg wish he'd known the situation better before his frantic, thirteen-hour journey. They could have just flown together, sparing his butt all those hours in the car.

Greg's breathing was slow and deep now. For the first time in the last couple of days, he relaxed. He'd found Sam. Better yet, his sense of calm meant she was out of danger. He sighed, remembering her face and her sad, amber eyes. As he drifted off to sleep, his heart swelled with a strange fondness. His Morphid mind tried to shut the emotion away, but even as he slipped into nothingness, he knew he wouldn't let the intruder in. Something was incomplete about his transformation. The side of him that should be gone had taken root instead, while his new self fought to pull it out.

-This is wrong. Unnatural. You shouldn't feel that way about her. Get out.

Nope, you're not getting rid of me. Not now.

Not after meeting her.

ଞ Chapter 12 ଓ
Sam

The Sam who arrived home was an entirely different person than the one who had left earlier that afternoon. At ease, with a pleasant feeling of harmony in her chest, she now realized that all her troubles, which had seemed staggering before Greg's call, now looked insignificant. As she parked, she wondered how this odd boy could have lifted her spirits so much, especially after all that epic awkwardness.

How can a good-looking boy like that be so socially challenged? She wondered.

Again, she felt like someone was playing a joke on her, just like the day she met Ashby. Something told her there was a link between the two, but she decided to ignore the eerie gut feeling. Better to just relish the fact that her self-pity was gone—even if it didn't make sense why.

Walking toward the front door, she pulled out her cell phone to check the time. Five twenty-two. How was that possible? Had they been studying that long? It certainly didn't feel like it. She should have gotten to James' place by now, and she hadn't even packed. Then again, she wasn't in a hurry. None at all.

She stepped into the foyer, threw her backpack on the floor next to the coat rack and headed for the kitchen. A proper meal hadn't crossed her lips in several days. Now, her soaring spirits had ignited her appetite.

The refrigerator contained very little to work with, but enough to make something tasty. After beating two eggs in a small pan and mixing in some milk, she sprinkled sugar and cinnamon and whisked it with a fork. Licking her lips, she dipped a slice of white bread in the mixture and let it get nice and soggy. When she placed it on the skillet, hot oil jumped and sizzled, making her smile in delight. The last time she had eaten French toast was one morning at Brooke's house, after a slumber party. Sam had cooked the special treat for her friend, and it had been finger-licking delicious. She jigged to the pantry and pulled out a bottle of honey.

"What are you doing here?" The voice behind her was like the screech of an angry bat.

Sam cringed, but faced Barbara calmly, fighting to put on a smile.

"I'm making French toast," she said. "Would you like some?" She walked toward the stove and placed the honey on the counter next to an empty plate.

"Don't play dumb," Barbara said. "You know you're supposed to be at your father's."

"I had to tutor and didn't have time to pack." She grabbed a spatula and flipped the piece of bread over. It had browned nicely and looked delicious. "Sure you don't want some?" Sam tried again.

"No, I don't want your stupid French toast. I want you to pack your clothes, and . . ." she trailed off.

"And leave?" Sam finished for her, surprised by her own composure. "What difference does it make *when* I leave? We don't even see each other as it is. I always stay out of your hair and never bother you. Why do you hate me so much?" The question came out before she could stop it, but only because she'd wanted to ask it for so long.

"Spare me the melodrama," Barbara said, unfazed by her daughter's demands. "I gave you an order. You're going to your father's right away. It's not open for discussion."

"I'm not your pawn, you know. It's not my fault James did this. You guys never . . ."

"I don't need psychoanalysis from you," Barbara said with disdain. "I'm your mother, and you'll do as I say. Now!" She pointed a finger, indicating the stairs.

"A mother isn't the same as a *good* mother." The words serenely glided out of Sam's mouth. She was beyond anger, and well beyond caring what Barbara might think. Now that she knew the truth about Barbara's "motherhood," she finally felt empowered to speak her mind.

"How dare you?! If you knew the half of it, you'd bite your ungrateful tongue."

"And what is it that I need to know . . . *Barbara*?"

Barbara's face twisted into a grimace of cold hatred.

"I knew one day I'd regret bringing you into my life." Barbara was out for blood now, but Sam felt invulnerable, protected by an outer shell that hadn't been there just hours ago. How crazy she had been to expect love from this woman. She was nothing but an empty shell.

"Well, I'm sorry you feel that way." Calmly, Sam turned off the stove and moved her French toast onto the plate. She squeezed a ton of honey on top, cut a piece with a fork, speared it and stuffed it into her mouth. "Mmm," she moaned, closing her eyes.

Barbara just stared, disconcerted by Sam's new self-assurance.

"Don't worry." Sam licked the fork distractedly. "I'll be out of your hair tomorrow for the summer, and out of your life sooner than you think." Sam didn't know what made her say that part, but it felt true enough. She took her plate and walked past Barbara who, for the first time, seemed to have lost her ability to throw verbal barbs.

"If I were you," Sam said, stopping by the foot of the stairs, "I wouldn't be in such a hurry to end up all alone."

Half-expecting Barbara to chase her, venom spewing from her mouth, Sam stopped halfway up the stairs when she heard . . . a sob? Was Barbara crying?! For a moment, Sam hesitated. She hadn't meant to make her cry. Heck, was that even possible? Sam turned, ready to apologize but her guilt was short-lived.

"You had better watch your words from now on, if you expect me to pay for your fancy culinary school." She looked over her shoulder to see Barbara smiling with spiteful pleasure.

Sam's fist tightened around her fork. "That's what makes you such a successful lawyer. You love to hit below the belt. Keep your money. I don't want it."

She hurried upstairs, away from all the ugliness, locked her door, finished the rest of her dinner, then sat by the windowsill to think. Surprisingly, she didn't think of all she'd lost. She knew she'd figure out a way to go to culinary school. Instead, she closed her eyes and pictured Greg. His awkwardness aside, something about him made things click. As she recalled each and every one of his perfect features, her breath caught. How was it possible to remember the flawless shape of his eyebrows or the exact angle of his nose? She couldn't even remember if Drew Puckett was a blonde or a brunette, and he was the hottest guy in school.

Butterflies unsettled her stomach with exciting emotions, emotions that left her strangely embarrassed and frightened, as if they were an anomaly or something she shouldn't feel.

Is this how it's supposed to feel when you like somebody? She had no reference point. She'd never gone this giddy over a guy. Amazing how she'd managed to do that while tutoring and pretending not to notice the way he was looking at her. Was this normal? And if it was, why did it feel so strangely . . . wrong?

Help from an expert was in order. She picked up the phone and dialed.

* * *

"Hey, Sammy," Brooke greeted her happily.

"Hi, Brooke. How's it going?"

"Kinda boring the last few days. How 'bout you?"

"Not boring. That's for sure."

"Spill, girl. Got nothin' but time."

"Okay. For one, my adoptive parents are getting a divorce." It was unfair to spring it on her like that, but Sam wanted to get to the real topic of interest as quickly as possible.

"Wait . . . what? Back up, Sammy. Is this a joke?"

"Nope. Barbara and James are getting a divorce, and they aren't really my parents. They adopted me when I was two."

Brooke was mute.

"Hello?"

"I'm here," Brooke said uncertainly. "Are you all right? This is a heck of a lot, even for me to digest. How are *you* taking it?"

"I'm fine . . . *now*."

"How did you find out? Did they just spring that on you along with the divorce news? 'Cause if they did, they're worse than I thought."

"No, no . . . it's a long story."

"I told you I've got time. You sure you're fine?"

"I wasn't, until this afternoon. I . . . met somebody."

"Ah-hum." Brooke sounded cautious.

"His name's Greg." Sam felt her cheeks heat up like carnival lights just by saying his name.

"You mean you met a *guy*? One you actually *like?* Who is this Adonis, this god, and where did you meet him?" Sure enough, as soon as there was the mention of a boy, Brooke seemed to forget all about the adoption/divorce business.

"At school."

"Huh?" Brooke sounded confused, and Sam chuckled, enjoying throwing her for a loop.

"You don't like any of the guys at school. The only Greg I know is Greg Romani and he's too young for you . . . unless . . ." Brooke let the word hang in the air teasingly.

"It's not *that* Greg!" Sam protested. "He's a baby." She shuddered at the thought. "There's a new transfer student taking trig over the summer. He called me 'cause he needed a tutor."

"Oh, my gosh! This is so cool. Tell me what he looks like. Better yet, send me a picture."

"I don't have a picture. I just met him." That was just the kind of thing Brooke would do, take a picture of someone she had just met.

"Well, take one A.S.A.P. and send it," Brooke ordered. "How hot is he? Is he *Sugar Coma of the Eye*?" she sang her favorite expression, but then huffed in frustration.

"What?"

"I just had a thought, how come you meet all these hot guys while I'm up here? A stranger at the mall, a new student, what's next? Are you just making them up to make me jealous?"

"Oh, they're real," Sam said, reassuring herself as much as Brooke that she hadn't imagined the whole thing.

"So tell me more," Brooke urged.

"Well, I wanted to ask you . . . when you like a guy . . ." Sam didn't know how to continue.

"Yesss?"

"Do you ever feel as if . . . you shouldn't like him?"

"You sure we're not talking about the Romani kid?"

"I'm being serious, Brooke." That was the problem with Brooke. Sometimes, it was hard to reel her back to reality.

"Okay. Um, I guess if I knew he was dating somebody, I might feel guilty. This Greg's got a girlfriend?"

"No, I . . . I don't think so. He just moved here."

"Well then what? Does he look like Quasimodo or something?"

"No, he is . . . he's unlike anyone I've ever met . . . except for Ashby."

"Wait. Ashby? The crazy guy from the mall?"

"Mm-hum."

"What do you mean?"

"Well, it's just they seem so . . . similar. Like brothers. No. More like the same breed or something," Sam said with a nervous laugh. It sounded crazy, but it made sense in her head.

Brooke laughed. "What are they? Dogs?" And after a pause in which Sam didn't laugh, "Look, it's great that you met somebody, but I don't know, Sammy. Here you are, talking about a couple of guys you barely know, when some really serious stuff's going on in your life. Guys are one of my favorite topics of conversation. You know that, but I think you're using them to avoid talking about what's really bothering you."

"I see your point. If we'd talked this morning, the conversation would have gone a lot different. But then I met Greg, and as crazy as that sounds, he changed everything. I feel . . . safe from everything, even from all my parents' crap. It's hard to explain."

"Well, if he's hot enough, I may let him be my guardian angel and eternal keeper, too," Brooke laughed, trying to lighten the mood.

Sam's lungs stopped working momentarily.

Keeper? Keeper?!

If her brain was a marionette and somebody was controlling the strings, then they were pulling a cord every time Sam thought of the word.

"We can take turns," Brooke joked.

"No, you can't have him!" Sam snapped back.

Ugh, what the hell made me say that?! I'm going crazy.

"Ooohhh," Brooke teased. "If you're gonna be that way . . . fine then."

After that, they both giggled and left it at that. They talked lightheartedly for another twenty minutes, but after hanging up, Sam was left with an uneasy feeling. Brooke liked being silly most of the time, with her "life's too short to take it seriously" philosophy. But her comment about Sam's avoidance of the real issues kind of hit home. Could she be in denial about the situation with her parents? Was her imagination getting carried away with these two boys in an effort to distract herself? She didn't think so, but wasn't that why they called it being in denial?

Sam pressed her palm against her forehead. If she thought about it anymore, she would get a headache. Instead, she found a suitcase and started packing. As she rummaged through her closet, her thoughts lazily wandered back to Greg, his sparkling blue eyes and his midnight, glossy hair. She imagined how silky it would feel to the touch.

ಇ Chapter 13 ೞ
Greg

Greg woke up in a cold sweat. The feeling of peace he'd had when he lay down to sleep was gone, replaced now by the same anxiety that had driven him cross-country to Indiana. He sat up as if propelled by a spring and tried to look out of the car windows, but they were foggy in the morning mist.

A cold prickle at the base of his neck made him shudder. He opened the door and hopped out. It was daylight already, but just barely. He'd slept for the rest of the afternoon and through the night. He looked around with the distinct feeling that someone was watching him, but the parking lot was deserted except for his car.

No. Nobody was watching him . . . but maybe they were watching *her*. Jumbled thoughts and emotions ran through him. Greg tried to relax. There had to be a way to interpret his surge of instincts, but he didn't yet know how. He was learning, just not quickly enough. He'd almost been too late yesterday. Something told him that if his phone call had reached Sam a minute later, he would have lost her. The mere thought made his heart ache. Breathing deeply and purposefully, he concentrated.

Closing his eyes, he relaxed his shoulders and let his hands drop loosely at his sides. After a few more deep breaths, his eyes sprang open, a large, yellow-and-green logo burned into his mind's eye. He recognized the symbol immediately. A gas station.

Blood pumping, Greg got into the car and switched on the ignition. Soon, he found himself driving aimlessly through town. There were several gas stations nearby, but none with that yellow-and-green logo. He was about to stop and ask when he spotted it.

Greg pulled in and parked in front of the adjoining convenience store. A confident feeling washed over him. This was the right place. He stepped out, his eyes darting around, looking for trouble in every corner. His nose registered the smell of gasoline and burnt motor oil. He heard the slow traffic running down the adjacent road. All of his senses were fine-tuned and on red alert. He didn't know what he was looking for, but his gut told him he was in the right place. He walked around, trying to act natural. It was still early, and everything was serene.

Inside the convenience store, a middle-aged woman slumped over the counter. When Greg walked in, she straightened and blinked.

"Good morning," she said, sounding more lucid than she looked. "Up early, huh?"

"'Morning." Greg walked toward the back, opened a freezer and pulled out a bottle of milk. Breakfast wasn't a bad idea.

"We've got hot, fresh donuts over here, if you're interested," the lady at the counter said.

Greg surveyed a set of shelves and found something more to his liking: Pop-Tarts. While his body procured breakfast, his mind rifled through a slew of images that desperately needed sorting. Crackling red lighting, a huge ball of fire, a dark figure. The snatches of information were frustrating, too slippery to be of any use.

"This summer's just brutal, isn't it? My geraniums are looking dreadful these days," the cashier said as she scanned Greg's items. "It's four ninety-eight."

He pulled out a five dollar bill while the cashier continued chattering, undeterred. She looked like a child behind the counter. She couldn't be more than five feet tall.

"Thank you, Miriam," Greg said, grabbing his food and change.

The cashier's face lit up as she self-consciously touched her name tag. She grinned.

"You're not from around here, are ya?" Miriam asked.

He shook his head and twisted the cap off of his milk bottle.

"A handsome boy like you, I would have noticed." She winked. Greg felt uncomfortable, but he could tell Miriam was harmless enough.

"My parents are relocating. I'll be going to school here." He took a swig of milk. "Hey, Miriam, if I hang out in my car and study, you won't call the cops on me, will you?" He flashed her a smile.

She frowned, her guard immediately up. So much for trying to rely on his good looks.

"I don't mean any trouble," he added quickly, "I just . . . don't know where else to wait. Uh, my parents are flying in today, and . . ." Greg's shoulders drooped. He was terrible at this. She probably suspected foul play involving her cash register.

Miriam chuckled, amused at his discomfort. "You can wait as long as you want. I don't know what you're up to, but I don't think it's anything bad. Deal's off if I see any funny business. Okay?" she added, raising her eyebrows.

"I'll just be studying," Greg said, walking outside before she changed her mind.

Two hours later, Greg was still waiting. He'd gone back inside to buy a pack of gum, and now he sat looking out the rearview mirror, blowing bubbles to kill the boredom. Traffic had picked up, and several people stopped to fill up their tanks or get breakfast. Still, there was no sign of anything suspicious.

Greg was almost out of his mind with boredom when he noticed a blue Toyota Prius pull in. He recognized Sam's ride from the day before, and immediately got out of his car. Greg rushed in her direction, looking all around for the source of the danger he now sensed looming over her. Sam set the nozzle to fill automatically and stepped to the side. As the gallons ticked by, she looked around distractedly. Slowly, her eyes wandered and met Greg's approaching figure, surprise registering on her face as she recognized him.

"What are you doing here?" she asked.

Stopping only two steps away, Greg towered over her and looked around frantically. Sam stepped toward her door, clearly taken aback. No doubt she would change her mind about tutoring him, his human side pointed out. But he had no time to dwell on these matters because, his Morphid nature kicked into high gear. Across the street, a dark figure caught his eye. His first instinct was to grab Sam and drive her to safety. He snatched the nozzle away from the gas tank. Locked open, the nozzle gushed gasoline across the pavement as he dropped the hose.

Sam was somewhere between terrified and furious. "What in the hell are you doing?!"

Gripping her firmly by the arms, Greg tried to shove her inside the car, but she fought back, eyes wide with panic.

"Get in, get away from here, quick," he ordered.

"No! Get your hands off me." She looked more hurt than horrified. She had liked Greg, and had never imagined she'd see a monster in his eyes. He hated to do this, but there wasn't time to explain.

"Get in, it's too dangerous," he repeated, straining to push her in, but it was like trying to put a feral cat in a pet carrier. She held on to the door frame, her panic mounting.

"Are you crazy?" she shouted.

"Do it, unless you want to meet that guy." He pointed toward the man who was now practically running toward them, murder stamped on his face, a hand extended in their direction as if to reach out and strangle them as he crossed the street.

Sam saw the man and hesitated, her grip on the door frame slackening only slightly. "What are you talking about?"

"Hey! What's going on?" Miriam yelled, sticking her head out through the doorway. Greg could only imagine how the situation looked from her angle. She must have shut off the gas pump from inside, because the nozzle was now still, inert within a small lake of fuel.

His eyes flicked toward their would-be attacker, now in the parking lot. It was too late to get away in the car. Opting not to fight Sam, he let her go.

"Run," he said. "Hide!"

Sam just sat there dumbfounded still braced against her driver's side door. With a jolt, Greg's instincts blared a powerful alarm through his brain.

"Duck," he yelled, pushing Sam down and out of the way. Just as she dropped to her knees, a crackling ball of red energy passed through the driver's side window, flying only inches over Sam's head. Amazingly, the glass remained intact.

"What the hell was that?" Sam shrieked, eyes wild with terror.

Continuing downward, the electrified red thing hit the asphalt right where the gasoline had spilled, igniting it on contact.

"Shit!" Greg exclaimed, grabbing Sam by the arm and pulling her away from the car. They'd only taken a few steps toward the convenience store when, behind them, flames from the spilled gasoline came to life with a *whoosh.*

"Call 911," Greg yelled at Miriam who stood open-mouthed, staring through the glass door as if she were at the movie theater, engrossed in the latest action flick. Miriam blinked and nodded, hurrying back behind the counter.

"Hide in my car," Greg ordered Sam, pointing at it. She tripped and fell. Greg was about to help her get up when his body urged him to turn. He whirled without a moment's hesitation and found their attacker calmly standing just a few yards away. Greg crouched defensively and found himself staring into a dark, cold gaze. Unimpressed, the man smirked, twisting his lips, a deep chuckle reverberating in his throat.

"And you are . . . ?" he asked in a heavy English accent.

Greg said nothing and simply stared back, wary of the man's next move. The flames by Sam's car were spreading, serving as a raging, orange backdrop to the threatening figure before him. Greg gestured with his hand behind his back for Sam to retreat. He sensed her cautiously moving back.

"Well? Where are your manners, my dear boy?" the man sneered.

"Cut the crap," Greg snapped, his mind racing. He looked at the man's hands, wondering if he had shot that red electricity out of them. This man was a Morphid. No doubt about it. The beauty and grace were always a dead giveaway. But not just a Morphid; a Sorcerer, too.

The man straightened the cuff of one sleeve and sighed. "Another uncouth Morphid raised amongst the unwashed human throngs. How unpleasant." He wore a perfectly tailored black suit, a pristine white shirt and a silver tie. He looked like he belonged in an executive meeting, not blasting fireballs across a rundown service station. The man was slender, with an aquiline nose and jet black hair that gleamed under the sunlight. Fastidiously, he removed a nonexistent piece of lint from his lapel.

"This will be more disagreeable than I anticipated," he said, unexpectedly lifting a hand and releasing a bright bolt of energy that hit Greg square in the chest.

Greg heard Sam cry out as he threw his arms up in a belated defensive gesture. An uncomfortable prickling sensation spread down his torso. He looked down in terror, expecting to find a gaping hole through his ribs, but he was unharmed. He shook his head, confused, panic ringing in his ears.

The Sorcerer's eyes widened. "A . . . a *Keeper*? No, impossible!" he said in a whisper.

Keeper?! The word struck a chord in Greg's mind.

"Well, isn't this unexpected?" The man looked shaken, but soon regain his composure. He took a few casual steps to one side.

Sidestepping with him, Greg followed his every move, mind racing again. How was he still standing? Why wasn't he lying dead on his back with a smoking hole on his chest? Judging by the Sorcerer's reaction, he'd intended to kill Greg, not tickle him.

"You best get out of here, mister! I've called the police," Miriam threatened from behind the glass door.

The Sorcerer scowled at the clerk, and she shrank back into the store with a little yelp. Furtively, Greg glanced toward Sam. She'd made it to his car, but she was still standing by the door, transfixed. He shot her a meaningful look, and she slowly went for the door handle.

-Do something, before things get out of hand, Greg's Morphid instincts cried out.

This man was here to kill, without a second thought. He had to act or he and Sam would end up like two pieces of charcoal, either by the Sorcerer's magic or the explosion from the gas pump. Greg could already feel the heat of the tall flames on his face. Making up his mind, he charged forward.

"Stop," the Sorcerer ordered, holding a hand up. He took two steps back, fear now in his eyes. Taken aback by this reaction, Greg slowed, wondering if he could get the reason for the attack out of him. "What do you want?" Greg demanded, casting a fearful glance toward the fire. Was there still time for this?

The man composed himself and tried to look collected. "Simple. I want *her* dead." He pointed a finger at Sam.

"Why?" Greg growled.

The man smirked, primped up his tie, then slid a hand behind it as if to smooth the shirt underneath. His fingers stopped, fumbling with something through the gap between two buttons. Greg frowned in suspicion.

"You're a bit clueless, aren't you?" the man asked with a grin. "What's your name?"

"You say you're here to kill her? There's no room for stupid introductions."

"There's no need for such . . . coarseness. *My* name is Veridan," he said with a slight tilt of his head.

Enough of this. Greg charged. The Sorcerer, Veridan, held his hand out, lips moving silently, but at a frantic speed. Suddenly, a red cloud burst into view around the man's hand. Greg didn't hesitate this time. The magic hadn't hurt him before. He hoped it wouldn't this time, either.

Removing his other hand from under his shirt, Veridan dipped it into the crackling, red haze, pulled out a long tendril of energy and unleashed it. Without thinking, Greg planted his feet and stretched out his hands, wrists together, as if he were catching a ball. Fire-red electricity crashed into his palms and tightened into a wild mass between his fingers. It was somehow contained, yet furiously thrashing in his hands, like a captive bird of prey. The Sorcerer staggered backward, astonished.

With a sudden jerk of his arms, Greg threw the globe of energy back at its creator. The orb flew straight into Veridan's still-outstretched hand. For an instant, he gaped as his magic popped and sparked in pathetic, tiny flares of red. Veridan shook his arm to dismiss the spell, but it didn't budge. His eyes widened in panic. Before the Sorcerer could fight off the sticky ball, Greg closed the distance and caught hold of the man's lapel, grabbing the side of his neck with his other hand and driving him back.

"Why do you want to hurt her?" he asked, as Veridan started howling and shrinking away from Greg's touch.

A burning smell made Greg realize just what was happening. Horrified, he pulled his hand away from Veridan's neck and saw the charred imprint of his fingers. Gasping and holding his wound, Veridan staggered back. Police sirens whined in the distance. With a murderous glare at Greg, the Sorcerer rolled to his feet and began sprinting away.

"Hey," Greg yelled, giving chase.

He followed him across the street and into an alley. When Veridan was only a few paces away, Greg reached out to grab hold of his trailing jacket, but his fingers snatched only air. Swirling like an idiot, Greg looked in all directions. Nothing. He'd vanished into thin air. Cursing under his breath, Greg rushed back to the gas station. As he crossed the street, he found the flames lapping the sky. They had engulfed the gas pump and the narrow roof above it.

Greg redoubled his step, fearing the worst, then staggered backward as the gas pump exploded, rocking the earth under his feet. He fell to the ground with a painful thud. His face flared hot. Struggling back up, he squinted through the blaze.

"Sam!"

He saw his car through roaring flames and thick smoke. A piece of metal flashing had landed on the trunk of his car. He had to get to her. Running straight into the flames without a second thought, Greg found his body pulsing with cooling energy. He passed through the fire, a forearm in front of his eyes. Scorching flames reached for his exposed skin but didn't burn him. They didn't burn!

He reached his car. Sam had climbed inside. Greg pulled on the blistering handle and wrapped the fearful girl with his large arms. Carrying her like an infant, he ran into the store, just as fire trucks and police cars arrived at the scene. He herded a petrified Miriam through the back door. Spent, he collapsed on the ground.

Miriam waited only to catch her breath before starting in on a frantic rant that wouldn't stop for hours.

ℰᴏ Chapter 14 ℭℛ
Sam

"Who do you want us to call?" the officer at the police station asked.

Not Barbara, thought Sam, but she didn't say it out loud. If she did, that would surely be the first thing they'd do.

"James Gibson," she said, writing the bureau's number on a yellow pad.

"The lawyer?"

Sam nodded. Her parents had billboards all over town, with James standing behind Barbara, arms crossed over their chest, stern looks on their faces. The toughest lawyers in town.

"Oh, great," the officer grumbled, walking toward the phone at his desk. Maybe he'd dealt with them before. Sam knew it couldn't have been fun.

Greg was being held in someone's office while Sam sat in the receiving area. Through the glass door, he appeared calm . . . way too calm, considering what had happened. She narrowed her eyes in suspicion. Clearly, he knew what was going on, and he owed her an explanation. A very good one. He turned to look at her with his impossibly blue eyes. Her breath caught and her anger dissipated. Even now, his look was comforting and protective.

"Look, I'm not crazy. I know what I saw," Miriam the cashier repeated for the *hundredth* time. She had insisted on coming to the police station after the police had dismissed her story as crazy. "The boy tried to kidnap the girl, but a wizard or something came out of nowhere shootin' death rays outta of his hands. She saw it, too." She pointed a chubby finger in Sam's direction.

Feigning distraction, Sam looked the other way, trying to hide her embarrassment as best she could. Poor woman. She was the only one telling the truth, and all she'd gained was a place in the Looney Tunes category.

Just remembering what had happened made Sam's palms sweat. Tension tightened her shoulders as she ran clammy hands along the lengths of her thighs over and over again. She swallowed and squeezed her eyes shut. The charred remains of her car rose behind her eyelids.

Why?!

Maybe if one of the lowlifes Barbara and James had landed in jail had attacked her, in the hopes of exacting some twisted revenge, she could understand. At least that would have made sense. Instead, there had been flying red *things* that blew up gas stations. Things that would surely make her question her sanity if it weren't for poor Miriam, insisting on the same story.

Then there was Greg and the way he'd come out of nowhere to protect her. It had been courageous and amazing and . . . well, weird. She glanced over his way again.

"Where is he?" an apprehensive voice demanded.

Sam's head swiveled toward the entrance.

A middle-aged woman—tall, slender and beautiful—stepped through the door, followed by a gawking young officer tripping over his own shoes. Sam would have never imagined anxiety could sound so melodious and look so stunning.

The woman scanned the room. Three officers rose from behind their desks. "How may I help you?" they all asked in unison.

"He's right this way," the young officer sputtered to the disappointment of the others.

He led the woman toward Greg. She was undoubtedly his mother. They had the same piercing blue eyes and unearthly beauty. A moment later, and to the dismay of all males present, an equally striking man followed in step. Like deflated balloons, all the officers sat back down.

Sam stared wide-eyed, craning her neck. Greg's mom hugged him, and his father put a heavy hand on his shoulder. They looked relieved. The scene struck Sam like something out of a sentimental movie, and a pang of jealousy hit her. It wouldn't be anything like this with her parents. It had never been.

Greg's mother stepped out of the office and demanded to see the person in charge. Two officers hurried to help her. She went back inside and sat next to Greg, listening intently as her son explained. Greg talked, gesticulating and shaking his head at times. At some point, he gave a slight nod in Sam's direction. As curious eyes turned her way, Sam slid down the cheap, plastic chair and picked at her fingernails.

"Your parents are on their way," the officer in charge of Sam said from over the counter.

My parents? Both?

Sam sank lower, wishing she could melt into the chair. Of course Barbara was coming, too. She wouldn't miss the opportunity to humiliate her, not after last night. If only Sam had been able to speak to Greg, they could have gotten their stories straight. For her part, Sam had left out all the stuff about electric rays, magic or whatever, and explained how a crazy man had attacked her, and how Greg had rescued her. They believed her easily enough.

A few minutes later, the *clop-clop* of high heels announced Barbara's arrival. Like a laser beam, her eyes homed in on Sam as soon as she walked in. She looked furious to say the least. Jerking her poisonous gaze away, she strode to the first available officer.

"What are the charges?" she asked in her most professional voice.

Unbelievable! She thinks I'm a criminal.

James followed his wife, but stayed behind, as if unsure what to do. Sam tried not to listen, but Barbara's voice seemed somehow amplified. Words like *damages* and *witnesses* acquired a worse connotation when spoken in the woman's dry tone. Sam busied herself looking at the tile floor.

"Are you okay?" James walked over and sat in the chair next to Sam.

The question took her by surprise. There seemed to be legitimate concern in it.

"I'm fine," Sam nodded.

"Are you sure?" Unlike Barbara, James sounded seriously concerned.

"You mean you called us just to come pick her up?" Barbara said, pointing a stiff finger toward Sam.

"No, ma'am. We called you because your child was attacked by a stranger, and had it not been for the intervention of that boy over there, she might've been seriously injured, kidnapped, or even killed. There was an explosion. It's all over the news."

"That's ridiculous," she scoffed. "Who would want to kidnap *her*, plain old looking thing that she is?" Sam looked up, just in time to see the officer rub his forehead in exasperation.

Seeing that there was no fight to pick here—they'd called her as a mother, not a lawyer—Barbara changed her tone. "We'll keep abreast and take the necessary measures to keep her safe. If there's nothing else . . ."

"You see why I had to leave?" James said, looking at Barbara with a grimace. "She has this . . . ability to poison even the good things in life."

Sam looked at James, bewildered. He'd never talked to her like that.

"Listen," James said, staring at his hands, "I want you to know you're welcome at my place. I understand if you'd rather stay home for a few days, but . . ." He looked up and gave her an apologetic smile. "I just wasn't sure at first, but I've thought it through. Especially considering all this."

"Thank you." The words almost choked her. She swallowed hard to let the knot in her throat pass. She wondered what made James change his mind. Were a few days away from Barbara enough to remove the poison from his blood?

"Well, thank you," Barbara said, extending her business card. "In case you need to get in touch with me." The way she offered it suggested that dialing her number would cost the caller a limb. She whirled and began walking toward the door.

Out of nowhere, Miriam stepped into Barbara's path, an urgent look on her face. "Are you this girl's mother?"

"Ms. Grove," called out the harried officer who had been questioning her, "that won't be necessary."

Barbara looked down at the woman as if she carried a deadly disease and quickly tried to circumvent her. Determined not to be ignored, the little woman side-stepped with Barbara.

"You'd better not let that child out of your sight if you don't want something terrible to happen to her," Miriam said. A warning like that might have worked on most mothers, but it had zero effect on Barbara Gibson.

"I won't," she said, summoning one of her best courtroom grins. Quickly, she walked around the plump woman and headed out the door without waiting for Sam and James to follow.

"She was almost killed by a ball of red lighting," Miriam yelled into Barbara's back.

Barbara stopped, but didn't turn around. She seemed to be considering Miriam's words. However, her pause was brief. Resuming her crisp step, she exited the police station, probably glad to get away from yet another lunatic, just like the ones who plagued her courtroom.

James stood, but Sam remained seated, reluctant to go anywhere. She cast an anxious glance toward Greg, who gave her a reassuring nod. She waved half-heartedly and stood up. Just looking at Greg gave her courage to go outside and face Barbara's wrath. When they exited the police station, Sam squinted in the bright sunlight. Barbara wasn't in sight.

"We drove separately," James said, seeing Sam's puzzlement.

"Oh."

"Do you want to talk about what happened?" James asked.

Sam shook her head. There was only one person to whom she could talk about this, and that was Greg.

"Are you sure? They told me what happened on the phone. It must have been terrifying. Did you recognize the man?"

She shook her head again.

"I can find someone who might be able to help, if you want someone else to talk to. There are people who can help you process these things, he said as they got into his car."

Wow, what was up with him? Freud paled in comparison. "I'm fine. I promise. I think it was just one of those random attacks you hear about."

"All right. Well, if you change your mind, let me know."

Good. He would let it go.

"However," he added, before turning the key in the ignition.

Well, it couldn't be that easy. It never was.

"For the next few days, I don't think you should go anywhere alone. At least until the police find out more." Sam could tell James was uncomfortable trying to fill the paternal role.

"That pretty much means I can't go anywhere," Sam complained. Who was going to take her places? Him? Barbara? Not that she could go anywhere with her car burned to a crisp.

"We'll work something out. Rose can help," he added the last bit gingerly.

"Rose?" Did he have a new secretary?

"Uh . . . you know." He looked at Sam as if she were being dense.

"Oh." *The girlfriend!* "Well, I . . . I wouldn't want to . . ."

"She's a nice person, Sam. I think you'll like her. Please give her a chance." A hint of command was in his voice, but he quickly went back to his more conciliatory tone. "She's been wanting to meet you for a while."

"Really?"

James nodded. "Will you give her a chance? Be nice to her?"

"Uh, sure. No problem." Thinking for a moment, Sam realized she really had nothing against the woman. It wasn't as if she'd broken up a real home or anything.

He smiled and started the car. "Great. Let's get out of here. We can drive by the house to get your things, then head over to my place. Sound good?"

"Oh, no!" Sam exclaimed.

"What?"

"I had everything in the car. All my stuff . . . it burned." She'd been so focused on everything else that she hadn't even realized it. That morning, she'd been on her way to James's when she stopped to get gas. She'd wanted to catch him before he left for work. That way she wouldn't have to cut Greg's lesson short. At least that's what she'd been telling herself, denying the fact that she just couldn't wait to see him again. Her suitcase had been in the back of the Prius, packed with her clothes, books, even her wallet had been in the car . . . so much. Sadness washed over her. He shoulders slumped forward.

James gave her a sympathetic glance. "It's okay, Sam. It's just stuff. What's important is that nothing happened to you."

Sam nodded. She knew that, but it was still hard to lose all her favorite things.

"We'll go by the house and get some extra things. Whatever else you need, we can replace it," James said, voice full of understanding and something close to tenderness.

Sam sighed and smiled sadly. Maybe this wouldn't be so bad after all. Maybe James deserved a second chance, and things would be better if she stayed with him for a while—perhaps even permanently. Sam shook her head. She was getting ahead of herself, and that could land her in a world of hurt.

After going by the house and helping her pack, James drove them to his new apartment. When they arrived, Sam got out and hurried to the trunk to get her backpack, while James carried the big suitcase.

"Oof," she winced when she hoisted the backpack on her shoulder.

"Is it too heavy? I can carry it," James offered.

"No, no, it's fine." Sam rubbed the back of her neck. What a day!

The apartment building was new and modern, and while they made their way toward James' unit, he told her about the pool, tennis courts, gym and other amenities. When they reached the front door, James pulled out a ring of keys and jiggled them in the lock, as if to announce their presence. As the door swung open, he called out, "We're home," but he didn't need to. Rose was already standing there, waiting with a slightly anxious look on her face.

Sam forced a smile that felt more like a grimace. How could she trust this new person? For all she knew, James's taste in women hadn't improved with time. He'd picked Barbara, hadn't he?

"Hi, Sam," Rose said. Her voice was hesitant, almost shy, but it was welcoming.

"Hello."

James stood frozen, watching them for a few seconds. Then he escaped with Sam's suitcase through a hall on the right.

"C'mon in," Rose said, guiding Sam toward the living room. "I can't image the day you've had. James told me what happened. That's horrible. Are you okay?"

Sam didn't know what to say, so she just shrugged.

"Um, are you thirsty?" Rose asked, and Sam was glad for the woman's tact. "I have soda pop, tea, coffee . . ."

"Coke?" Sam was actually hungry, but she felt weird asking this stranger for food. A Coke would hold her for a while.

"Diet?"

"No. Regular, definitely regular . . . please."

Sam breathed a sigh of relief and slumped on the couch, closing her eyes. What an unbelievably crazy day. After a few minutes, she opened her eyes and looked around. The place didn't look anything like she'd expected. There were books lying around and a couple of chenille throws draped over the sofa and armchair. Half-burnt red candles rested on beds of spent wax, and chew toys lay at the foot of the brick fireplace.

There was a lot of color on the walls. Pictures, unmatched frames, contemporary art—a far cry from Barbara's black-and-white prints and muted, classy décor. This was Rose's place, Sam realized.

"Here you go." Rose walked in, depositing a tray on the coffee table. A sandwich, a bag of chips, and a dish of cookies sat next to her Coke.

"In case you're hungry," Rose shrugged with a hopeful smile.

"Oh, wow. I am . . . actually. Thank you," Sam said in a surprised and grateful tone.

Rose sat down in the armchair to Sam's right. She jumped slightly as something squeaked and reached behind her to pull out a plastic toy in the shape of a double stacked hamburger. With an apologetic grin, she squeezed the toy, making it squeak again, then threw it toward the fireplace, next to the others.

Ravenously, Sam took a bite of her sandwich, while Rose watched with satisfaction. It was past one and all she'd had to eat today was a glass of milk. The Coke burned as it washed the sandwich down. She bit a cookie in half, then quickly composed herself, remembering her manners. Rose chuckled good-naturedly.

"You have a dog?" Sam asked.

"Yes. But he won't bother you," Rose added hastily.

"I know . . . I like dogs," Sam added matter-of-factly.

"But I thought you . . . didn't." The last word was but a whisper. Obviously, Rose felt this was something she shouldn't bring up. She was treating Sam as if she was breakable.

"James said that?"

Rose nodded, looking at Sam curiously.

"Where would he get that idea?" Sam said dismissively, but she knew who would make up something like that in order to keep a *filthy animal* out of her pristine house. "I like dogs *and* cats just fine," Sam said.

"Oh! Great." Rose seemed relieved. "Wassily is a great dog. I think you'll like each other."

Wassily? Sam didn't want to ask.

"He paints, you know." Rose said, getting up and walking toward the far wall. "He did all the paintings on this wall."

"The dog did those?!" Sam got up to get a closer look.

They stood side by side, admiring the paintings. There were about ten of them, each one an explosion of abstract colors. They were quite messy—no surprise, since each one was rendered in pawprints. Sam smiled and then, without knowing why, she started laughing. The last thing she wanted was to offend Rose, but the paintings were funny and . . . cute. To her relief, Rose laughed with her. This was probably the very reason she hung her dog's paintings. They had the ability to fill the heart with silly joy.

"Wassily . . ." Sam snorted. "I get it, as in Kandinsky, right?" Rose nodded. They were still laughing when James came into the living room. He walked up to Rose and put an arm around her.

"Ah, you've showed her Wassily's masterpieces?" A smile curved his lips too, and it struck Sam as odd. She didn't remember ever actually seeing him happy.

"I guess we should show Sam her room," Rose said, looking up at James. "She may need some rest and privacy." James nodded while gazing into Rose's eyes. It was strange to see him this way, and a little awkward, too. She was unaccustomed to seeing such displays of affection.

"It's this way," James said, leading her.

The room was much smaller than hers, but that wasn't what bothered her. It was its . . . plainness, in stark contrast to the rest of the apartment's vibrant colors. The walls were a boring off-white color and, from the smell of it, they had been painted recently. Clearly, they weren't trying to make her feel too comfortable. She tried not to feel disappointed—after all she was only staying until the end of the summer.

"I didn't know what color you'd like on the walls, so I repainted," Rose said, walking to the window to open the curtains. "If you like, we can pick a new color, and we can paint together. We want you to make the room your own," she said, standing next to James and giving him a meaningful look.

"Yes," James added, clearing his throat. "Rose . . . uh . . . we want you to feel at home."

It sounded rehearsed, Sam thought, but sincere nonetheless. It seemed Rose was the positive influence and the reason for James brightening mood.

"Thank you," Sam managed. She blinked and looked away. "It's really nice," she added, trying to sound casual, but swallowing a lump in her throat.

"We'll leave you for now," Rose said.

"I have to go back to work or . . ." James didn't finish his sentence, but Sam could just imagine. She wondered how much longer he would stay at the bureau. She doubted it'd be long.

"See you at dinner time." Rose leaned in and kissed him on the cheek, then turned to Sam. "I'll be out here if you need anything. Come and meet Wassily when you're ready." She smiled warmly and closed the door.

This had to be the strangest day in her entire life. Barbara's claws had lost their grip on her, James was happy, and she'd almost been killed by some kind of wizard at a gas station. In one quick motion, Sam pulled the phone from her back pocket. She flipped through the recent calls until she found the right number. She called without hesitation.

"Hello, Sam," Greg answered.

"We need to talk."

ℰ Chapter 15 ଓ
Ashby

"Hey," Ashby called out, sprinting after a figure hurrying down the winding, stone corridor. He caught up quickly and grabbed the man by the arm. "I was calling you . . ." He stopped short when Veridan turned around to face him.

"What do you want?" Veridan snapped, without even the forced respect he normally showed. Ashby was the next Regent, whether the Sorcerer liked it or not.

"Ugh, are you all right?" He released Veridan's arm and took a step back. Black as tar, half of the Sorcerer's neck looked like it had roasted over a fire pit. An acrid scent tweaked Ashby's nose. One side of his shirt and jacket were black and in burned tatters.

"Do I look all right to you?" The Sorcerer's lip curled up slightly, but then his eyes filled with strained pleasantry. "May I be excused to tend to my injuries . . . unless you need me for something *pressing?*"

"No, it's not important. Go on," Ashby dismissed him.

He'd only wanted to ask about his tailor. Veridan was extremely well dressed and always boasted that his tailor was the most talented *Fitter*—a Morphid with a special talent to make any designs fit perfectly. Better yet, the tailor's shop was within driving distance of the castle. Next time he saw Sam, he wanted to make a good impression. Jeans and a t-shirt had been appropriate for their first meeting at a mall, but Ashby was used to more elegance than that.

It had been stupid to ask Veridan, anyway. The man was too full of himself. The oh-so-wonderful, self-proclaimed Morphid Ambassador to Humans, who spent much of his time delving undercover into their world, mingling with high society and political figureheads—not to mention celebrities. Trusted by Regent Danata, even when no one—including Ashby—could understand why.

"How insufferable," Ashby said as he walked into Perry's room.

"What did she do now?" Perry asked, not looking up from his book. He lay comfortably on a large, four-poster bed, reclined on at least a dozen damask pillows.

"No, not my mother. Veridan."

"Oh, him." Perry grimaced.

A year ago, when Perry morphed into a Sorcerer, he was given a choice between Veridan and Portos for his tutelage. He'd chosen the latter without hesitation. Veridan had taken offense, and ever since, had treated Perry with utter contempt.

Ashby sat on a stiff Louis XVI chair and crossed his legs. "Not a pretty sight." Ashby put a hand on his neck, remembering the Sorcerer's nasty burn.

Reclining on one elbow, Perry set his book on the night table and gave Ashby his full attention. "What was it?"

"Well, the skin on half of his neck was burnt to a crisp."

A broad smile spread on Perry's face. "Really?"

"Maybe one of his spells went wrong." Ashby knew the difference between a burn caused by fire and one caused by magic. This was definitely the latter.

"I hate to admit it, but the bloke's too good to have one of his own spells go that wrong. Hmm." Perry rubbed his chin.

"Yeah, I don't know anyone who could get the best of him, except maybe Portos."

They looked at each other and shook their heads. There was no way in the world Portos would do that. Diplomacy was the old man's main weapon, not magic—even if many believed he was the greatest Sorcerer alive.

"I've got to find out what happened. Come on!" Perry hopped off the bed and skidded over the wood floor with socked feet and a big laugh. Ashby smiled and followed him out the door.

🕉 Chapter 16 ᙗ
Veridan

Staggering into his bedroom, Veridan threw the door open. He viciously kicked it closed behind him. His neck burned like the damned must burn in hell. A tremor ran down his spine, making his legs shake and almost give way. He grabbed the bed's footboard for balance and took a deep, halting breath. It was becoming hard to swallow, even breathe. He loosened his tie with great difficulty, but it didn't help.

He lurched toward the armoire in the far left corner. Collapsing to his knees in front of it, he fumbled for his talisman. His hands shook and his teeth chattered like he was in the middle of a blizzard. He was burning, yet felt cold.

It took him a long, excruciating minute to undo two shirt buttons and pull out the heavy pendant that hung from his neck. He cradled the object in both hands, afraid to let it drop from his trembling fingers. The talisman was made of pure silver, round with a coin-sized onyx set in the middle. An intricate pattern was carved in the outer ring, with lines upon lines crisscrossing each other—lines with no end or beginning, which could store a bit of magic within their confines.

Veridan pressed the amulet, face down, into a recessed spot on the armoire. A hidden drawer clicked open at the bottom. Close to a convulsive seizure, he pulled it open. Several magical items lay inside the thinly cushioned interior. His eyes zeroed in on a small wooden box. He blinked as his vision blurred, and hurried to retrieve the case. He lifted the lid and prayed that his elixir would work.

There were two glass vials inside, both filled with the same murky liquid: A healing potion of his own creation, one he had never needed and had been stored in his armoire for years. Unchallenged for so long, he'd grown complacent, he chastised himself. Now, it might cost him his life.

Veridan removed the stopper. His bottom lip quivered as he touched the bottle to his mouth. A foul smell wafted upward, inundating his nostrils. He swallowed hard against his gag reflex, the rank liquid scorching his throat as he drank.

Clutching his stomach, he crumpled to the floor, quaking from head to toe. Shudders raked him in waves. He lay there, trembling like an infant, until their intensity diminished and his putrid elixir did its miraculous work. After long minutes, he stood, took a deep breath and stripped off his ruined suit. Burned pieces of his shirt fell to the floor. He threw everything on a pile and called for a maid to clean up the mess.

As he dressed in an identical suit, he kicked the secret drawer shut with one foot. Before slipping on his white shirt, he examined his neck. For the most part, his skin had regained its normal color, except for a small spot over his Adam's apple, where the imprint of a thumb could still be seen. He cursed under his breath and continued dressing himself.

What if the potion hadn't worked? He clenched his fist at the thought, the boy's face flashing in front of his eyes. A boy, a snotty boy had almost killed him! Rage boiled inside the darkest depths of his soul. His balled-up fists shook with tension.

Not a boy, after all.

Veridan cracked his neck.

Much more than a boy. Immune to magic. To his knowledge, there was only one caste capable of that. Keepers. A caste almost forgotten after centuries since its last known member died.

A knock at the door pulled him out of his thoughts. He calmly walked across the room and opened the door, now in perfect control. A meek, red-headed girl stood on the other side, hands clasped in front of her. She wore a black and white uniform with an apron.

"You called, sir," she said.

"Clean up that mess and dispose of the suit." He pointed to the pile of clothes. With not another word, he left his room and took the hall to the right, headed to the north gardens exit.

Outside, the sun hung high in the sky. It was a brisk 15 degrees Celsius and the chilly air felt good on his flushed neck and face. Veridan walked down the path, gravel crunching with every step. As he rounded a tall hedge, a hunched figure startled him; easy to do at the moment, considering his raw nerves. But it was only Bernard, the castle idiot. Veridan's lip curled in disgust at the sight of the man, who obliviously stared off into space.

He pressed forward and, at the end of the garden, slipped behind a thick hedge that grew close to the castle's west wall. Behind the hedge was a door, locked to all except Veridan and his talisman. After pressing the onyx against the thick, wooden door, he disappeared behind it.

Danata wasn't going to like the news. Not at all.

ಸಲ Chapter 17 ಲ
Ashby

Ashby and Perry rushed down the castle's long halls, just like they used to do in their childhood. As they passed the severe housekeeper—Mrs. Garrot—she gave them a disapproving look, but little else. As Perry skidded to a halt before turning the corner toward Veridan's room, Ashby collided into the young Sorcerer's back. They laughed and shushed each other between chuckles and shoves. After a moment, they quieted down and listened. They heard nothing. Casually, they stepped out into the hall. The narrow passage led to an exit into the north gardens, so it would be perfectly normal for them to be walking in that direction.

They passed in front of Veridan's door once, but didn't hear or see anything. Before reaching the garden exit, they turned back and retraced their steps.

"Are we just going to walk back and forth?" Ashby whispered.

"Well, do you have a better idea?"

Ashby didn't, actually, but he didn't have to admit that, since right at that moment, Veridan's door opened. A young maid stepped out, a crumpled suit draped over her arm. She started at the sight of them and stared at her shoes, avoiding Ashby's gaze at all costs.

"Hi, Xasdia," Perry greeted the girl with a crooked smile. She turned crimson.

Ashby didn't remember seeing her before, but Perry's tone suggested he knew all about the young lady. She was a pretty girl of about seventeen with red, curly hair and green eyes. Perry leaned a shoulder on the stone wall and let his eyes travel down the length of her body. "I didn't know you worked on this wing of the castle."

"Sometimes . . . *sir*," Xasdia mumbled.

"Oh, there's no need for that." Perry waved his hand, though Xasdia didn't seem so sure about doing away with the formalities. She shot a quick look at Ashby, then buried her chin deeper into her chest.

"Don't worry about him. He's just *the future regent*. A blockhead, if you ask me," Perry laughed, quite amused with himself.

The girl looked positively discomposed.

"Never mind *him*, Xasdia," Ashby interrupted. "He's just a wanna-be Sorcerer."

"I . . . I . . . have to go," Xasdia blurted out. "It's not my place—"

Ashby pushed Perry aside and led the girl away from the still open door. "Don't worry. It's fine. We just . . . want to know if Veridan is all right. He seemed to be hurt before. Did he look okay to you?"

"Um, yes. I think," Xasdia said, still seeming to find Ashby's shoes the most interesting thing in the world.

"You didn't notice anything wrong with his neck?"

Xasdia looked confused and shook her head.

"I guess not," Ashby said, feeling disappointed. "Is he in there?" He hooked at finger toward Veridan's bedroom, where the door stood half-open.

"No, sir."

"Do you know where he went?"

"No, sir. I was called to get his clothes. He left just a minute ago."

"Such a shame," Ashby fingered the jacket's collar and noticed a label that read, "Karos Out*Fitters*." A smile stretched his lips. "Thank you." He gave Xasdia a gentle wave of dismissal, and she walked away in a hurry.

When Ashby turned back toward Perry, he instead found an empty hall. He cautiously eyed Veridan's door, which was now barely open.

"Perry," he hissed as he pushed the door with one finger. The hinges creaked ever so slightly. Chills of anticipation ran down his back. He'd never been in Veridan's room, and since he and Perry had been little kids, they'd joked that it must look like a torture chamber. He stepped inside and let his eyes adjust to the gloomy interior. He searched for Perry among the shadows. Where was he?

"Perry," he whispered again.

"Shh, over here."

Ashby walked along the wall, feeling an ominous dread slide down his spine. He couldn't understand the sensation at the sight of such an unremarkable room. A bed, a desk, an armoire . . . nothing scary about any of it—just austere, quite in contrast with the man he knew and what he'd imagine. Almost boring. He tiptoed in the direction of Perry's voice, toward a narrow door in the far corner of the room. He looked over his shoulder toward the entrance, the door cracked just enough to let a sliver of light in. His heart shuddered. What if Veridan found them in his private quarters?

As he stepped through the narrow doorway, he found himself inside a small closet. What he saw there wasn't boring at all. It fulfilled his darkest expectations of Veridan's lair. Mouth gaping, he inched closer to Perry although the young sorcerer would be no protection against the forces at work there.

"What is that?" Ashby's voice wavered with emerging panic.

"I don't know," Perry said in a bewildered breath. The horror in his voice made Ashby's skin crawl.

In front of them floated a black, viscous cloud, bobbing up and down like a boat at sea. The shapeless blob was the size of a man's torso, and it vibrated at regular intervals, taking a different shape every few seconds. It gurgled like a pit of hot petroleum, bubbles bursting and leaving behind mouth-like openings. One yawned and snapped closed, letting out a tenuous, despairing mewl.

"Did you see that?" Perry asked.

Ashby nodded. "Did you hear it?"

"Mm-mmm."

The blob lost its shape again, but Ashby could still see the orifice that had formed in its center.

"He's far more powerful than we suspected." Perry whispered to himself, tearing his eyes from the blob. "How can he keep all of this going without being here? Not even Portos could . . ." He walked around the room, examining everything else.

Ashby stayed rooted to the spot, eyes glued to the black mass. It kept changing, and with each shift, the shapes solidified, as if Ashby's imagination were feeding them, telling them exactly what he didn't want to see and showing it to him anyway. The blob took a new shape, and a black, mangled hand reached out toward him. He stepped back and stared, unblinking, heart frozen. The hand opened and closed with a quick snap. A sensation of dread and loss filled his chest, and he staggered, feeling as if something had been cut away from him.

"Let's get out of here," Ashby said breathlessly, one hand pressed to his forehead. He took a step back toward the door. "Hey, don't touch that," he cautioned as Perry reached for an uncovered jar. Something that looked like it had once been alive floated inside, releasing a noxious plume of vapor into the air.

Ashby gave one last look around. Did his mother know all these things were inside the castle? She had always preferred Veridan over Portos, and their secrecy had given the Council cause for concern before. Everyone had suspected that, through the years, Veridan had helped Danata fulfill some grim but necessary tasks. Still, Ashby didn't want to believe she would condone whatever experiments the Sorcerer was carrying out right under her nose.

They stepped out of the alcove. Perry shut the door and murmured a spell over the knob. A click signaled the door locking.

"We shouldn't have gone in there," Ashby said as they walked out into the garden.

Perry ignored his comment. "There were three human brains in those jars."

The sun was shining, but Ashby found it hard to believe. His soul felt so grave after seeing such blackness, it seemed impossible there could be light anywhere. He rubbed the back of his neck, willing his head to clear.

"Are you all right?" Perry asked as Ashby sat on a bench and stared at the gravel underfoot.

"Do you know what any of those things were?"

Perry nodded and sat next to Ashby. "Some of them, but I've only read about them. Portos never even talks about the obscure, much less teaches it."

"You think my mother knows Veridan . . . ?" He didn't finish the sentence.

Perry's answer was a huff.

"Yeah. That was a stupid question," Ashby said. Of course. She had to know.

The sound of dragging steps made them look up. Haggard as ever, Bernard, Ashby's uncle, approached. Arms wrapped tightly around his chest, the man walked as though he were freezing. His eyes stared into the distance, and it wasn't until he was a few steps away that he noticed their presence. Stopping, he looked from Ashby to Perry.

"Hello, Uncle Bernard," Ashby said respectfully. He'd always felt sorry for him.

The man shivered and hugged himself tighter. He gave a sideways glance toward the hedges, then nodded slightly to acknowledge the greeting.

"It's cold," Uncle Bernard said in a raspy voice. He wobbled to a bench across from them and laboriously lowered himself onto it.

Out of the corner of his eye, Perry gave Ashby an uncomfortable look. Uncle Bernard always liked company, but no one could figure out why. The poor man hardly ever said a word.

"You should go inside and have a cup of tea," Ashby suggested.

But Uncle Bernard's eyes were distant, looking into the hedges again. It was as if he'd already forgotten he had company.

His hair had more gray than any man of fifty should, and today, the circles around his eyes were more pronounced than usual. Why didn't anybody ever remember Uncle Bernard? Ashby had ordered several servants to keep an eye on him, make sure he took a bath and ate three square meals a day. But here he was again, wandering the gardens alone, looking gaunt and weak.

"He scurries away when we aren't looking," the servants always said. Ashby couldn't reproach them too harshly. Uncle Bernard was easy to lose track of, always so quiet, sitting in dark corners for hours at a time, still as a statue. Then—when you remembered to look again—he was gone.

"Come with me, Uncle." Compliant as always, Uncle Bernard followed. Ashby delivered him to the castle's bustling kitchen, where he ordered hot broth for him.

"Make sure he eats it," he instructed one of the maids.

"He looks worse," said Perry when they left.

"I know."

"That must have been some wicked bond he shared with your aunt," Perry commented. "Don't get mad, but he makes me glad I'm a Singular."

Ashby had heard his aunt and uncle's story many times from some of the older staff members. They all said they'd never seen another set of Companions as connected as Roanna and Bernard. Their link was so strong, they'd both morphed prematurely and at the same time. They found each other immediately and were married within days. Sadly, it was that link's very strength that had left Bernard in his current state when Roanna died.

Ashby thought of Sam then, so far away, with no knowledge of who or what she was. What if harm came to her before they could be together? Would he lose his sanity like his uncle? Ashby pushed the grim thought away, feeling sick to his stomach. She would be safe. She'd been safe this long, after all.

"Yep," Perry continued, oblivious to Ashby's quiet. "Just glad there's no pair for me."

Ashy snapped out of it and forced a smile. "I see that doesn't stop you from sampling every flower in the garden. I suppose Xasdia is your latest carnation?"

"Very perceptive," Perry chuckled. "Hey, where are you going?" He asked when Ashby took a turn down a separate hall.

"Veridan's tailor," he said. "Now I have his name, and I'm getting a new suit. I want to make a good impression next time I see Sam."

"What are you talking about?" Perry asked in a hushed but urgent whisper. "You're not going back there!"

"I am."

"Well, I won't help you this time. Your mother's furious, and Portos threatened to fuse my legs together if I do it again."

"No one has to know, Perry," Ashby said, winking as he walked away backwards.

"You'll be the death of me," Perry called out in a stage whisper, looking around nervously. "Besides, I advise against a suit. Too pretentious."

Ashby turned and hurried out, ignoring Perry's suggestion. He was tired of always doing everything his mother and everyone else said. He wasn't a child anymore.

ಖ Chapter 18 ೞ
Greg

"I'd rather not discuss what happened over the phone, Sam," Greg said, tightly pressing the phone to his ear as if that would bring her closer to him. "Maybe we can talk after our lesson." He rode in the back of his parent's rented sedan.

"Our lesson?!" Sam asked in disbelief. "Are you outta your mind? I don't think I even want to know you anymore, much less tutor you."

"Sam, you . . . you don't mean that." The certainty and intimate tone in his voice were too strong, he realized. But he felt so linked to her, so sure of her feelings and reactions, that it was hard not to just blurt things out.

Sam fell silent. Biting his lip, he reminded himself that she hadn't morphed yet and had no way of knowing where all his weirdness was coming from. She had no idea what Morphids even were, as far as he could tell, much less that she was one.

"Um, Sam? Are you still there?"

"I'm here," she sulked. "Look, I can't get away for a lesson today. After this morning, James doesn't want me to go anywhere alone. Besides I don't have a car anymore."

"Well, I could come there," Greg suggested, wishing he could sound less eager. "My car's a little messed up, but it still runs. Uh, who's James anyway?" He felt fiercely protective at the mention of another guy.

"I'll tell you later today."

In spite of her evasive answer, a smile stretched over his lips. He would see her again today!

"Mom, let me borrow your pen."

She dug inside her giant purse and produced a pen. Greg scribbled Sam's address in the palm of his hand.

"Is she all right?" Mom asked after he disconnected the call.

"I think so. I'll feel better once I see her." Man, I don't know how I'm gonna explain what she saw. She's demanding answers." His mom smiled knowingly, and Greg felt a pang of guilt. His parents were still in the dark about Veridan—they thought he'd used his powers against an everyday, crazy assailant not a magic-wielding, Morphid one.

Greg looked out the car window at the buildings rushing by, considering the best way to break the news to Sam—first so she would believe him, then to keep her from having a panic attack when she did. Based on her reaction today, he'd concluded that she had no idea what she was. Telling her, "oh, by the way, you're not human," wasn't going to be easy. He guessed this morning's events would help, at least partly. She now had proof that he wasn't just a typical teenager, or messed up in the head. Even he couldn't believe half of what he'd done, like throwing off a magical attack. Not only that, but running unharmed through huge flames to rescue Sam. Greg tried to conjure the same power again, but nothing happened. It seemed his magic only worked when Sam's life depended on it.

He might be able to explain all about himself, but what about Veridan, where he'd come from? And why he wanted her dead? She would assume he knew something, but these were all questions he had himself. Greg squeezed his eyes shut. A Sorcerer wanted his Integral dead. He dug stiff fingers on his thighs. The knowledge made his new instincts roil.

To top it all off, there was the matter of the police. Luckily, he and Sam had been on the same wavelength, and gave the officers similar stories. If they hadn't, he might be sitting in a jail cell, rather than looking for a place to stay.

Mom pointed at an apartment building. "Oh, we just passed it." She folded the map. They *so* should have paid for the GPS upgrade. Greg and his parents were directionally challenged, and always had been. Dad turned the car around in an empty lot.

Shifting her attention back to Greg, Mom returned to his question. "We'd be happy to talk to her, if it would help."

"You have a plane to catch."

"We could phone her."

"Maybe . . ."

Dad parked by the apartment complex's front office. "This is it."

They all got out of the car and looked around.

"What do you think?" Dad asked.

"Well, it looks better than the last one." Mom didn't sound convinced.

"It looks great to me," Greg offered. The other place had seemed fine too, but Mom had shut down that option on first sight, saying it was too dingy. They hadn't even gotten out of the car to check it out. Greg didn't want to be a burden on them, but Mom hadn't even listened when he said he'd be happy there.

"Let's see if we can check out one of the units," Dad said, walking toward the front office.

Inside, they met a friendly, stout guy who was the complex manager. He chattered happily and jingled his keys as he showed them around. "The place was built in the seventies, but the units have been properly maintained. The one I'm about to show you was upgraded in the last . . . oh, I don't know . . . six years or so."

Greg's mom shot them a look that seemed to ask, "And that's good?"

"It's really private, since it sits in the back corner," the manager pointed out.

They all exchanged glances. That actually *was* a good thing. They needed to conceal the fact that Greg, a minor by human standards, would be living here alone—the fewer prying eyes, the better. Greg still worried that his parents might reverse their decision to let him live on his own. It'd been hard to convince them not to drop everything in New Orleans to come here with him. But they both had good jobs and a good life there. It wasn't fair for them to lose it all for his sake. He was infinitely grateful to whoever managed to get Miriam out of the police station before his parents had a chance to hear her rants. If they knew there was a murderous Sorcerer involved, they'd never go back home—even if there was nothing they could do to help. The farther away from here, the safer they would be.

The manager showed them into unit 204. They stepped into a plain and dated assembly of muted tones: tan carpet, off-white walls, taupe countertops. The walls looked like they'd been painted a hundred times over. The carpet appeared clean, but was certainly not new, and the kitchen and bathroom were the size of closets.

Perfect! Greg immediately loved it.

He couldn't say why, but he got a good feeling about the apartment. It was quiet, cozy, and simple. *My very own place*. He'd fantasized about having his own place countless times.

"It's rather small for three people," the complex manager said, shooting them a pitiful glance. "Are you sure you don't want to look at a two-bedroom unit?"

Greg shook his head.

Mom put on a regretful face and lied, "We can't really afford anything bigger, right now. We need the place because my son has started summer school. But until we can sell our house in New Orleans and move up here permanently, only one of us will be staying with Greg. So we'll manage just fine."

"Yes," Dad added, "that's why we'll take the month-to-month lease. A contract would make it harder to find a bigger place once we all move up here."

"Well, it sounds like you guys have everything figured out," the manager said.

"What do you think, honey?" Mom asked Greg, sounding uncertain.

"It's great. I like it."

"We'll take it, then," Dad said, before Mom could find something wrong with the place.

After signing the lease, his parents drove him to the police station where his car was still parked. In a few hours, they'd managed to save him from jail, straighten out the school paperwork, and rent an apartment. Now, it was time for them to drive back to Indianapolis to catch the flight home.

"Here," Mom said, handing him an envelope. "Buy a few things for your new place. The suitcase I brought you has your sleeping bag, towels and extra clothes, but you'll need things for the kitchen and living room. We'll arrange for a bed to be delivered in the next couple of days. Also get you clothes that fit."

"I don't need anything else, Mom." He pushed the envelope back. "You've already spent enough money."

"We're just trying to imagine you've gone off to college a few years early," Dad joked. "We broke your college fund open."

Greg smiled bleakly. "Well, I'll get a job for whatever else I need, which won't be much."

"Use the money for food, then," Mom said, stuffing the envelope into his pants pocket. "I don't want you surviving on Pop-Tarts alone. You need meat and vegetables."

She wrapped him in a tight hug before he could say anything else. Greg rested his cheek on her head. "I'll be all right, Mom." He squeezed her in turn. He still wasn't used to being taller than his parents. Hugging Mom felt different, but was still as comforting as ever. Greg extended a hand toward Dad, and he took it. They shook for an instant before Dad pulled him in for a tight bear hug.

"Take care, son."

"I will."

"I wish we could help more," Dad said, pulling back to look him in the eye.

"You're already paying for . . ."

"Nonsense," Dad cut him off. "That's the least we can do. It's nothing."

It was hard for Greg to believe he would be on his own now. No rules to follow but his own. It was scary and exciting at the same time. It was the Morphid way. He was an adult.

"Sometimes I wish . . . we were more like humans." Dad was struggling to say this, but seemed determined to get it all out. "I wish we didn't have to let you go, but this is your path. We're proud of you, son."

Dad took a step back, releasing Greg and wrapping an arm around his wife. Greg clenched his teeth and blinked while Mom buried her face in Dad's chest.

"I'll . . . miss you," Greg said, fighting back tears.

"We'll miss you too, son," Dad said. And with that they got in the car and drove away.

Greg stood in the parking lot for a few seconds before he realized it was a bad idea after what had happened this morning. He got in the car and started the engine. As soon as he remembered Sam was waiting for him, his heart felt lighter, and he let that feeling take over. He didn't want to dwell on the possibility that he might not see his parents for a long time . . . or ever. Shifting his attention completely to Sam was just what he needed at the moment. But first, he would find a store and buy some new clothes.

ℰ Chapter 19 ℭ
Greg

Wearing new jeans, t-shirt and tennis shoes, Greg found Sam's apartment without difficulty, and practically lunged for the doorbell as soon as he spotted the right apartment unit. A happy-looking lady in her mid-twenties answered the door.

"Ah, you must be Greg, the hero," she said, extending her hand with a smile. He briefly shook it. "Come in. I'm Rose. Sam's waiting for you."

He followed her into the living room and liked the place immediately. It had a relaxed, inviting feel to it—not stuffy or too formal.

"Please sit down. I'll let Sam know you're here." Rose turned just to find Sam already standing behind her. "There you are. Well, your student's here." Greg thought he saw Rose wink at Sam as she left. "Oh, and dinner'll be ready in an hour. You're welcome to stay if you want *and* your parents don't mind, Greg."

"Thank you, Mrs. Rose," Greg said.

"Rose will do," she said with a shudder, "Mrs. Rose makes me think of my mother."

"Your mom's nice," Greg said after Rose left.

"She's not my mom," Sam corrected him. "I just met her."

Huh? This was confusing, to say the least. Although, now that he thought about it, Rose did seem too young to be Sam's mother.

"We'll save that for later," Sam said, noticing his confusion. "Right now, you're the one who's got some explaining to do."

"Right." Greg dropped his backpack on the floor. No trig today, then. He would have rather discussed geometry, chemistry, calculus, anything but this.

"Is there anywhere else we can talk?" he asked in a whisper.

Sam was about to reply when Rose came back in, carrying a tray with two soft drinks and a plate of cookies. "The weather's nice. Why don't you kids study outside? They have picnic tables around the corner. I'm sure some fresh air would help you relax after the day you've had, Sam."

Crap! She heard.

Greg winced. Good thing she wasn't Sam's mom, or she'd make sure they didn't go anywhere after catching a glimpse of his secrecy.

"Yes, that'll be nice," Sam said.

"Here. Take this." Rose pushed the tray in their path as they headed for the door. They both grabbed their drinks and a handful of cookies.

Outside, Sam set her unopened soda can on the picnic table, stacked the cookies on top, and sat expectantly across from Greg.

Sam looked at him from head to toe. "You look . . . different."

Greg tugged his new t-shirt subconsciously. She had noticed.

"Well?" she said impatiently as he tried to draw out a gulp of cold soda. He hadn't realized how thirsty and hungry he was. A whole cookie went into his mouth while Sam watched with irritation. He reluctantly set his food aside.

"Did she make those cookies?" He licked his lips.

"I don't know."

"They're really good." If Rose had made the cookies, he'd take her up on the dinner offer. His stomach growled.

"Yes, they're really good and I'd love the recipe, but enough about the cookies!" Sam snapped.

"Okay, okay" he said, feeling defensive in the face of her impatience.

"Where do I begin?" he thought out loud.

"How about you tell me who that man was, and what the hell was that red ball of . . . of whatever that was? Why was he trying to hurt me? And how did you . . . ?" she couldn't finish the question.

"You'll find this hard to believe, but I don't know who he is. I'd never seen him before."

"You're right. I don't believe you! Don't get me wrong, I appreciate the help. But this is all just too freaky, and I need answers."

Greg rubbed his neck. "Look, I'll tell you what I know, but . . . fair warning . . . you won't believe that, either."

"Try me. After seeing what I saw this morning, I wouldn't be so sure."

He cleared his throat and decided to just rip off the Band-Aid. "Okay. I'm not human," he said. Sam's eyebrows shot up about ten inches. She looked mad and irritated by the ridiculous notion. Hastily, Greg added, "and in case you don't know, neither are you."

Sam scoffed, rolling her eyes. "That's just absurd and . . ." She trailed off and squeezed her eyes shut, probably remembering murderous balls of energy flying straight for her face. "Wait. What makes you say that about me?" She went with the flow, although the skepticism didn't leave her voice. Clearly, she wasn't ready to outright buy what he told her in spite of what she'd seen.

"Well," he tried to think of what to say. At a loss for words, he turned his back on Sam and pulled down the collar of his t-shirt.

"What is that?" she asked at the sight of his mark.

"Something I didn't have a couple of weeks ago," Greg said.

"So you got a weird tattoo. What does that have to do with anything?"

"It's not a tattoo. Look closely."

Sam moved closer and examined the mark. As she leaned in, Greg felt her breath on his neck. A shiver ran down his spine. He had to clench his teeth not to visibly shudder.

"Okay, so it's one of those . . . scarification things. I've read about them. How do wings on your back prove you're not human?"

"It's not a scarification thing either," he said, letting go of his t-shirt and facing her. "I never got it made. It just appeared when I . . . changed. I'm a Morphid, and Morphids grow marks like this when they become adults. My parents have them too, although theirs are different."

Sam squinted, exhaled and sat back down. "You're an adult?" She smirked. "Now you've really lost me. I'd believe *everything* up to that point."

Greg glowered at her.

"Okay, okay, I'll play along a little longer. So how did you . . . *Morphids* get there and why?"

"Well, there are legends that say we came from another realm called Nymphalia, but no one really knows if they're true.

From what most people can tell, we've always been here. I know, I know, it sounds crazy. I didn't quite really believe it myself, until a few weeks ago."

Sam tried to restrain a chuckle, but failed.

"Sorry." She cleared her throat and asked, "So if Morphids have always been here, how come no one knows about it?"

"We keep it a secret. Um, things work a little differently for us and our population has never been large." *As in, we don't all get to procreate,* Greg thought, but no way was he getting into that conversation right now. He continued, "In the past, any time humans found out about us, they thought we were witches or demons or whatever was the latest fashionable enemy. As you can imagine, that never ended well for us. So we just lay low, pretend to be human and live our lives in peace."

"Is that so?" Sam said with sarcasm.

"Most of us, anyway. I promise I don't know what was up with that guy. All I can tell you is that he was a Sorcerer."

Sam leaned forward, her voice hushed. "Alright, alright . . . so are you also a . . . ?"

"No. I'm not a Sorcerer. When I morphed—"

"When you what?" Sam's eyes went wide. She looked somewhere between incredulous and frightened, like this was all a bad joke that had gone too far.

Greg continued, trying to choose his words carefully. "Remember how I told you that a few weeks ago I changed? Well, what happened is that . . . I morphed."

"What? Like a bug?"

"I guess, but I'd rather not think of it that way."

"And you think I'm . . . I'm . . ." She couldn't bring herself to say it.

"You're going to morph, too." He finished for her.

The desperation and disgust in her voice sounded like she was picturing hideous cockroach legs sprouting out of her abdomen. "Into what?" she managed to ask.

Into the most beautiful creature on earth, one side of him wanted to say. He could see it in her, how magnificent she would be, how perfect. He bit the inside of his cheek, his new side pushing him away from the thought.

What mattered was which mark would decorate her back, what caste she would be, and how it would affect her mind. Both sides of his split personality feared the answer. But that was a harder conversation. Telling her she would morph into a beautiful woman would be a lot easier to digest at first. Reaching for his backpack—which he'd brought outside to keep up the tutoring pretense—he retrieved his cell phone, pulled up the latest picture of himself, and handed it to her.

She examined the image for a moment, then looked up, confused. "Who's this?"

"Me. It was taken a month ago. Look at the date."

Sam lowered her eyes to the phone and frowned. "Sure, that's some amazing growth spurt. What are you on? Steroids?" She handed back the phone, smirking sarcastically.

Greg gave her an unamused stare.

"You're serious?" Sam whispered in a half-question.

His parents had taken the picture at one of his basketball games at school. He was standing by the sideline during a time out. The jersey and shorts hung on his body as if they were draped over a broom stick. His old, unremarkable face held a disapproving frown. Something must have been going wrong in the game, but he couldn't remember what. It seemed like ages ago.

"Let me see that again." Sam snatched the phone from his hand and, this time, she examined the picture in greater detail, looking back and forth between the image and the boy in front of her. Greg shifted in his seat as she scrutinized him.

"It's impossible," she said after a moment, having seen the resemblance he still shared with his old self.

"Tell me about it," Greg said in commiseration. "It's still weird to see myself in the mirror every morning."

"Well, you did change for the better," she said, sliding the phone back across the table.

He took it and peered back, hopeful at the comment, at the fact that she might find him attractive. But when he saw the twinkle of a sarcastic joke in her eyes, he realized how stupid that hope had to be.

Sam grinned crookedly, putting a ton of attitude in her expression. "Okay, so what you're saying is that tomorrow I'm going to look like Barbie?"

"No," Greg said, ignoring the joke. "What I'm saying is that Barbie won't hold a candle to you." There was no twinkle of a joke in *his* eyes when he said this. He made damn sure of that.

It was Sam's turn to squirm. She averted her eyes and smoothed her hair, her cheeks flushed red. Part of Greg writhed at his own words. His Morphid side nagged at him that it was wrong to talk to her this way, that this sacrilege would soon cost him hell.

Sam shook herself visibly, then said, "So, just like Barbie, I'll come with my own logo." She touched to the back of her neck, where her mark would be.

Greg nodded.

"Why? What for?"

"Because Morphids don't only change on the outside, and the mark reveals how we change . . . inside," he added cautiously.

Sam seemed to recoil inwardly. Greg felt her anxiety triple. He'd been aware of it all along, and now it made the hairs in the back of his hands stand up straight. He needed to be careful as her wall of incredulity weakened. Biting his lower lip, he decided to say nothing else until she was ready for more.

After a quiet and awkward moment, she homed in right on the issue. "What do the wings on your back mean?"

"They mean I'm a sort of . . . guardian, *your* guardian, and I've come to realize it's my job to protect you."

"What do you mean *you've come to realize?*"

"Well, my parents had never seen a mark like mine before, so they don't know what I am. That guy, Veridan, he called me a . . . Keeper, and it feels right for some reason."

"Yeah, I heard him. He said he wasn't expecting a *Keeper*," Sam said the last word in a whisper. She pinched the bridge of her nose between two fingers and squeezed her eyes shut.

Again, he let her take the time.

"So I need someone to protect me, because . . . because that guy wants to hurt me?" she asked after some time.

"I think so. It makes sense. That's how things work for Morphids. Fate decides a lot of things for us."

"Fate," Sam echoed, making the word sound like something forbidden and dirty. "But why? Why does he want to hurt me?"

"I don't know. All I know is that when you're in danger, I feel it," Greg put a hand on his chest, "And I know just where to find you. Like when I called you on the phone that first time. My instincts were screaming you needed my help."

Sam's eyes widened in surprise, and maybe anger, as if he'd just quoted a secret page from her diary. Sam lowered her eyes and turned her back on him.

"Or at the gas station," he decided to continue, "I knew I had to be there to protect you, I just didn't know from what. That's why I acted so strangely when I saw you. It's just an instinct, a very strong one."

"Is this what you mean by changing inside?" she asked, still facing away.

He nodded, wishing she would turn around. He wanted to see her eyes, to guess what she may be thinking. She stayed put.

"Yes," he said finally, hoping she wouldn't lose it.

"And after you . . . *changed* . . . you started feeling this . . . pull toward me?"

"Yes. I took my dad's car and drove all the way from New Orleans as fast as I could. I knew to come here, to this town, although I didn't know exactly where to find you. Bonds between *Integrals* are that strong."

"Integrals?" Sam's voice was shaking, barely audible.

As calmly and rationally as possible, Greg explained everything his parents had ever told him. When he finished he waited, hoping all that information didn't push Sam over the brink.

"So you truly don't know that guy?" she asked.

"If you search your heart, you'll know it's true." It was a strange answer, spoken by his Keeper half, but it seemed to have an effect on her.

She sat silent for a long time. Then Greg noticed her shoulders shaking ever so slightly. He got up and stood next to her. Sensing her need for comfort, he put a hand on her shoulder and forced her to face him. She turned, reluctantly. Placing a finger under her chin, he forced their eyes to meet. Her eyelids remained half-shut at first, but eventually she looked him in the eye.

"It'll be all right," he said softly. "I promise I won't let anything happen to you. I . . . don't freak out . . . but I would give my life for you. You should know that."

She shook her head.

Damn it! He was making things worse blurting out stupid crap like that. He had to learn to control himself.

"Things are hard enough already, and now this," Sam said.

"I know something else has been bothering you, I can . . ." He stopped. He wanted to say he could feel what she felt, he could sense her moods, but that would just freak her out even more. "I'm a good listener. You can talk to me about it—whatever it is."

Sam seemed to consider it. "I think . . . I can trust you."

Greg smiled. He wanted to know *everything* about her. He already sensed so much, it was as if her soul spoke to his, but he could only understand a fraction of it. He wanted nothing more but to figure it all out.

She was close, and he wanted to embrace her.

-You can't, his Keeper half screamed in his mind, while a more human Greg longed to fill the emptiness of his arms with her warmth. Still, he fought his desire and took a step back instead.

"I guess we should go back in," Sam said with a sniffle. "I know I'll come up with more questions, but right now, I just . . ."

"I know. It's a lot to take in. We can talk anytime you want."

They walked back to the apartment in silence. When they reached the door, Sam turned the knob, but stopped halfway.

"Thank you," she said. "Thank you for being here."

Before he could respond, Sam opened the door and stepped inside.

"There you are," Rose called from the kitchen. "Dinner's ready. I don't know if you're staying, but I set a place for you, Greg."

He wanted to, but figured he should give Sam some breathing room. "Thank you, but . . ."

"He'd love to stay," Sam said, grabbing his hand and pulling him closer.

Rose looked from Sam back to Greg. He shrugged.

"Great!" Rose exclaimed. "Just make sure you let your parents know. We don't want them to worry," she added, before disappearing into the kitchen.

"Will your parents mind?" Sam asked in a low voice.

Greg shook his head. "No, they've . . . gone back to New Orleans. I'm on my own."

She looked up at him in surprise and concern. "You're staying, then. Definitely staying."

Sam took his hand and pulled him along. He relished the feel of her palm against his and warred with himself not to pull away.

❧ Chapter 20 ☙
Greg

A few days later, Greg was in his small kitchen, frying an egg for a late breakfast, when a prickly feeling at the base of his neck made him stop. He froze, spatula in hand, waiting for a warning to go off inside his head. He had been getting better at reading his Morphid instincts. This time, though, the alarm didn't come. Still, the feeling of uneasiness remained.

He turned off the stove, left the half-cooked egg on the skillet and pulled out his cell phone. Sam answered on the second ring.

"Is everything okay?" he asked.

"Hi, Greg. Good morning. How are you doing? I'm doing just fine, thanks for asking," Sam said in a sarcastic singsong, pointing out his lack of greeting.

"'Morning," he sheepishly said, then went back to his questioning. "Seriously, though. Is everything all right? What are you doing?"

"I'm getting ready to go to the soup kitchen. I volunteer there on the weekends. Why?"

He didn't want to worry her, especially now that the uneasiness had subsided. "Oh, just feeling bored. Can I come with you?"

She didn't buy his forced casual tone. "Should I be worried about something?"

"N-no, I don't think so, but maybe I should come with you. Do you mind?"

"No. Actually, I could use another set of hands."

Twenty minutes later, Greg was waiting for Sam outside the soup kitchen, located in a rundown area of the city that no one—much less a teenage girl—should visit alone. He was definitely glad he'd come. Sam pulled up a few minutes later, parking on the street behind Greg.

"Whose car?" Greg asked.

"Rose's. She doesn't mind if I borrow it, being that mine was char-grilled." She smiled, giving Greg a little pang of joy in the chest.

Sam wore jeans, bright blue sneakers with pink shoelaces and an old, white t-shirt. She pulled her hair up in a tight ponytail. "Ready for some manual labor?"

"Sure, why not?"

They walked into the building through a set of glass doors. Sam strolled between long, white tables surrounded by cheap, plastic chairs. The building was right next to the local homeless shelter, and fed anyone who needed a hot meal. Sam walked toward a serving counter in the back. The place appeared deserted.

"Where's everyone else?" Greg asked.

Sam pushed a swinging door and walked into a small kitchen. "Probably out back, smoking. It's still early. Plenty of time to get ready for the lunch crowd." She got right to work, pulling utensils out of a drawer and setting a tall stockpot on the counter.

She handed him a can opener and pointed to a row of industrial-sized "Hearty Vegetable Soup" cans on a nearby shelf.

"Wipe them down with this," Sam threw him a container of disinfectant wipes.

Greg caught it in midair and started pulling cans down.

"It's a shame we have to serve that," Sam complained as she pulled a large package of disposable bowls from a cabinet. "Canned soup is never good. I've asked if we could cook something ourselves, but it's too expensive. I do spice it up a bit, though." She smiled.

Greg watched her with admiration. "How long have you worked here?" he asked, turning the can opener's handle and slicing the heavy lid.

"Since I was fourteen."

"Is this all they serve? Soup?" Greg asked, looking down at the red liquid and globs of fat floating on the surface.

"No. There's meat and vegetables, too. But today, they're bringing those in from another kitchen across town. Our cook quit last week, and they haven't found a replacement yet. They let me do the soup, since all you have to do is heat it up. I used to help Laraine with it. She was the cook." Sam walked toward the swinging door. "I'll be right back. Let me put these bowls out in the serving area."

While she was gone, Greg opened the other cans. "What do you want me to do with these?" he asked when Sam walked back in.

"Pour them in that pot. Wait, there were only four?" She looked up at the shelf. "I'll have to get more from the storage room."

"I can get 'em," Greg offered. "They're heavy. How many do you need?"

"Two more. Thanks. I'll pour these in the pot and get the rolls out. The storage room is through the door, all the way in the back, on the left."

Greg went out the swinging door and across the dining area. His steps echoed on the linoleum floor. He noticed something move out of the corner of his eye. His head snapped to the side, but it was only someone walking past the glass doors outside. A door in the far left corner had a sign that read, "Storage." He opened it and flipped on the light switch. Fluorescent lamps came on overhead with an electric snap and a hum. He was greeted by tall, metal shelves stocked with huge containers of food: Flour, canned soup and tuna fish, rice, spaghetti and more.

He stepped inside and started looking for the soup. He heard the front door open and looked out through the narrow doorway. All he could see was the far wall, along with a few dining tables. His uneasy feeling from earlier returned, but no alarms sounded. He stepped toward the door to take a look around. Before he reached the threshold, a man appeared there. He was tall, taller than Greg, and dressed in a ragged army coat that hung to his thighs. His hair was thinning and his skin had a dry, sallow appearance. In spite of that, his gray eyes sparkled with a quality specific to Morphids.

"Who are you? I've never seen you around," Army Coat demanded.

Greg felt a slight tingling in his spine. "It's my first time here," he said, a claustrophobic feeling and the need to check on Sam flooding his chest.

"That so?" Army Coat's eyes pierced Greg's. He rubbed gray stubble with his grimy fingers.

"If you excuse me, I need to get back." Greg took a step forward, hoping he'd step aside. He didn't budge.

The man scanned the shelves behind Greg for a quick second. "You're stealing," he said with conviction.

"What?! No, I'm not stealing. That's ridiculous. I—"

But the man didn't let him finish. "I'll show you ridiculous . . . stealing from the poor. You got no shame." Army Coat shoved Greg back into the small room.

Arms pinwheeling, Greg tried to regain his balance. Army Coat stepped in, crouched low, face twisted in anger.

Greg put his hands out. "You need to calm down, sir. You're mistaken. I—"

Army Coat lunged forward, rammed his shoulder into Greg's chest and drove him backward until he slammed into one of the metal shelves, the edge cutting into his back. Boxes of instant oatmeal rained down. Greg grunted and blinked to clear his vision, putting his hands up defensively, but Army Coat wasted no time.

He planted a leg next to Greg, grabbed him by the collar and shoved him sideways. Greg tripped over the man's leg and fell to the floor with a thud that knocked the air out of him. Army Coat dropped on top of Greg, sat on his stomach and pinned his arms with his knees. Greg struggled, bucking, but the man was too large, too heavy.

"Get off me," Greg yelled.

Army Coat put a grimy hand on Greg's face and viciously dug his fingers into Greg's cheeks. Still struggling, Greg opened his mouth, grunting as the tender flesh of his cheeks dug into his own teeth.

"This is the last time you'll ever steal from anybody, boy." Army Coat reached into his pocket and pulled out a small, glass bottle of murky liquid. The man removed the cork with his teeth, spat it out and started lowering the bottle toward Greg's mouth.

Eyes wide with fear, Greg fought frantically to get his arms loose, but it was no use. Army Coat felt like two thousand pounds of bones and meat, and Greg's hands tingled from the lack of circulation. The bottle with its dark contents was only inches from his mouth, still clamped open in a vicious grip. A rancid smell reached Greg's nostrils.

He bucked harder, bending his knees and thrusting upward, trying to throw the man off. Army Coat swayed to one side. Some of the liquid from the bottle spilled onto Greg's neck. His skin sizzled like a drop of water hitting hot oil. Greg screamed. Army Coat saw his chance and tipped the foul liquid into his mouth. The vile acid burned his tongue. The man pressed a hand over Greg's mouth and nose.

"Swallow," Army Coat ordered.

Greg resisted as long as he could, but his mouth was on fire. He reflexively gagged, allowing the liquid to go down his throat. It seared his insides like lava. His neck muscles spasmed violently.

Army Coat jumped off, laughing with delight. "That'll show you, you little thief."

Rolling onto his side, Greg spat the brown muck on the floor. His stomach seized painfully. He got to his knees, coughing and holding his mid-section. Through a haze of agony, he watched Army Coat take a few steps back. Greg felt as if he was morphing again, his insides aching as if they were being ground down into pulp.

Poison! Whatever it was, it was killing him. He coughed again, spraying the floor with tiny droplets of blood.

Army Coat pulled out an envelope from his pocket and ripped it open. He withdrew a slip of paper, read it and raised an eyebrow. Next, he retrieved a bill from the envelope. "Easiest hundred bucks I ever made. Serves you right, you little punk." He pulled both ends and made the bill snap taut. "And now, part two," he said with an evil smile.

Part two?! An icy finger went down Greg's back, freezing each of his vertebrae. Vivid images appeared before his eyes. Sam's terrified face, her bright blue sneakers kicking helplessly, her arms ineffectually trying to fend off her attacker.

Greg grabbed the shelves and pulled himself up to a feeble crouch, his legs trembling beneath him. "Sam," he said hoarsely.

Army Coat had left. He was now strolling past the tables, whistling a happy tune.

Greg took a step forward. A cramp twisted his stomach violently. He fell to his knees, gagging, bright red blood spewing from his lips, leaving trails down his chin. His eyes rolled to the back of his head, and he fell on his face. A danger sign flashed before his eyes, as bright and red as the puddle of blood under his cheek.

ஐ Chapter 21 ଔ
Sam

After Greg left to fetch the soup, Sam turned on Laraine's radio. The old cook had left it behind, as a gift to the next cook. "For good time's sake," she'd said. It was still dialed to the oldies station she liked. A rock 'n roll song by Def Leppard—at least, Sam thought that was the name of the band—was playing. It was a pretty good song, although she couldn't speak to the truth of its lyrics. Love biting and all. She figured it could. She just hoped it never bit her.

Humming the song, Sam started pouring the canned soup in the stockpot. The thing was so tall she had to climb on a stepstool to pour it properly. She was glad Greg wasn't here to witness the trials of a vertically challenged person.

The greasy, reddish liquid sloshed in, tiny droplets jumping and splattering Sam's gloved hands. She dumped one can after the other, watching the cut vegetables and small pieces of beef rush down. A salty, slightly acidic scent filled her nostrils. It really was a shame they had to serve this junk, but it was better than nothing, she supposed. One day, though—when she was making enough money as a chef—she would volunteer as much of her time and skill as possible to cook decent, flavorful meals for people in need. That was a promise.

Halfway through pouring the last can, Sam thought she'd heard something. She stopped and listened. Def Leppard played on, the lead singer really belting it out. Sam shrugged and poured the last of the soup into the pot. Stepping off the stool, she grabbed the pot's handles and lifted it. It was heavier than she'd thought. With a huff, she placed the pot on the stepstool. The last thing she wanted was a greasy lake running down her shirt and across the kitchen floor. They'd never let her do anything again if she couldn't even handle heating up some soup. She decided to wait for Greg to get back. He could put it on the stove with no problem. One simple flex of his beautiful, perfect, grope-worthy biceps and, voilà. She sighed.

Snapping out of her hormone-ridden thoughts, she turned her attention to the rolls. She was laying them on baking trays when a movement caught the corner of her eye.

She looked up. "Help me put the pot on the—"

Not Greg! Sam's heart slammed in her chest. She stared up at the man, wide-eyed and thought she'd seen him eating here before. The grimy army coat was vaguely familiar.

"You're not allowed back here," Sam said, trying for a calm, friendly tone, but failing. Her voice came out high-pitched and frantic, instead.

The man smiled a crooked smile. "Now, for the easiest thousand bucks I'll ever make." And with that, he lunged toward Sam and grabbed her by the shoulders with plate-sized hands, fingers brutishly digging into her skin.

She screamed and instinctively dropped to the floor. The man lost his grip.

"Greg! Help!" Where was he? Had this man hurt him?

Her attacker bent over, grabbing at her again. Sam fell backward and kicked her legs out, as if she were riding a bike. Somewhere she'd read to do that, since your legs are stronger *and* longer than your arms. But the man was huge. He got hold of one of her ankles, then the other.

Sam twisted at the waist, bucking and clawing the floor. The man lost his grip as she spun. She struggled to her feet, turned, and managed one short step away before a thick arm wrapped around her waist, pulling her off her feet. She jerked from side to side, thrashing in a frenzy, and almost slipped out of her attacker's hold.

"Help!" she screamed again, her voice going hoarse at the end.

"Oh, no, you don't." He put his free hand over her mouth. Sam sank her teeth into his skin, drawing blood.

"Argh! You little bitch. You'll pay for that." The man looked around the kitchen. "Well, look at this . . . maybe some soup will keep you quiet . . . *forever*."

Sam's attacker pinned one of her arms against his body and cruelly grabbed her by the hair with his free hand. Half-carrying her to the soup pot she'd left on the stool, he shoved her head down toward the greasy liquid. Screaming at the top of her lungs, she tried to get her arms free, but couldn't. Her head plunged into the thick soup, choking her scream, stuffing it right back into her throat.

She held her breath and fought, kicking and squirming ineffectually. The soup gurgled and sloshed with her struggles. A maddening darkness encompassed her, filling her mouth, her ears, her nostrils. Sam's lungs began to burn from the need to breathe. Her attacker held her under steadily.

Through the panic, a thought came to her. *Stop fighting, and he'll think you're dead.* Already dizzy from the lack of oxygen, she easily went limp. The viscous mask pressing against her face was too much to bear, and she only had enough energy left to pretend for a few seconds.

The man's hold slackened some. Sam fought the pressure in her lungs, the primal urge to take in air. *Don't move. Only another second,* she told herself. Another second to hold back the greasy rush of gelatinous soup into her lungs.

Then her attacker shoved her deeper, until the top of her head hit the bottom of the pot. The panic that followed broke her. *He's going to make sure I'm dead.* Sam opened her mouth to scream, to breath.

Her mouth filled with murky liquid. Then her throat. Her windpipe protested, trying to fight her lungs in their demand for air. Her chest spasmed in a coughing fit, and the soup rushed in.

No longer faking it, Sam's feet went still, kicking no more.

✇ Chapter 22 ☙
Greg

Greg lay flat on the floor in a puddle of his own blood, poison coursing through his veins. A man in a grimy army coat had attacked him and poured poison down his throat. Greg began coughing up blood, his stomach twisting like a wrung out dishrag.

A steady alarm tingled through his body. Sam was in danger. Vivid images hit him like flashes of light. Her blue sneakers kicking helplessly. Her hair floating in murky water. Her panic, her tremendous panic, coursing through her veins the same way poison was coursing through his.

Greg clamped his teeth over his lower lip, ignoring the pain and concentrating on the small vibration starting in his chest. Sam was in mortal danger. His magic was awakening in response. His body trembled as his latent energy came to life. Greg felt it spread down into his stomach, up his throat, through his veins, following the path of the poison and neutralizing it.

The slashing pain in his gut lessened and quickly became nothing but a phantom ache. Greg's eyes sprang open. He stared into a puddle of his own blood. Staggering to his feet, he left the storage room where he'd been attacked. The soles of his sneakers were slick with blood. He slipped a few times, but caught himself—each step stronger than the last, until he was running across the dining hall toward Sam.

The kitchen door swung open and Army Coat rushed out. When he saw Greg, his jaw dropped open and his gray eyes doubled in size.

"Sorcerer," the man spat the word like an accusation. He cowered close to the wall as he ran toward the exit.

Greg had an impulse to follow him and snap his neck, but Sam was his priority. He couldn't sense her! He had to make sure she was alright, as much as he'd like to see that bastard dead. He slammed into the swinging door, shoulder first.

Sam lay limp on the floor, her hair matted to her face, a reddish stain spreading across her t-shirt. Panic galvanized him for a moment until he looked closer. *Not blood. It's not blood.* The large pot sat on a stool, dripping reddish liquid down the sides and onto the floor. *She's covered in soup?!*

Greg crashed to his knees at her side. Sweeping hair off her face, he checked for breath. Nothing.

Oh, God!

He checked her pulse next. It was faint but there. Frantically, Greg turned her on her stomach and pounded her back. When nothing happened, he slid his arms under her midsection, placed his fist at the top of her stomach and squeezed violently, pulling her up into him.

Please, please, please.

He was about to squeeze a second time when Sam went stiff, then convulsed forward, coughing, spewing muck from her mouth, pawing at her neck as if to push the nasty, intruding liquid out of her body. Greg helped her to her knees. She retched, trembling, one hand to her throat, the other one to her stomach.

When the sickness passed, she sat back, crying, shoulders shaking. She held her head between pale hands and rocked back and forth. Greg wrapped an arm around her back and pulled her close, rocking with her, feeling all her terror, confusion, frustration and relief in waves—the same way she felt them.

He simply held her, wishing there was something he could say, something he could do to erase the horror she'd lived in the last minutes. And wanting very fervently to make someone pay.

ℬ Chapter 23 ℭ
Ashby

Perry shook his head. "You're asking too much of me. I can't take you back to Indiana."

"I know I am," Ashby said, "but nobody will find out this time." He had to convince him. After only a few days since seeing Sam at the mall, the urge to see her again had become unbearable. Not to mention how useless and underestimated his mother made him feel. Perry liked breaking the rules. He'd magically transported Ashby to her before. Of course he could do it again. Ashby refused to believe that his mentor, Portos, and Regent Danata had scared him into being a good boy.

Perry crossed his arms. "Is that so? And how do you plan to avoid detection?"

"We'll do it from outside the castle. From the old Derby cottage. It's abandoned and no one ever goes there. No spells to warn anyone there, since it's well outside of the castle's perimeter."

"How do you plan to get out without your bodyguards? God, it'd be so much easier if I could just make them forget," Perry complained, not for the first time. All guards at Rothblade Castle carried amulets that defended them against minor spells such as memory modifications.

"C'mon, I have my means." Ashby looked at the young sorcerer, a cocky smile on his lips.

"Of course, you have your means." Perry rolled his eyes.

Ashby had exited the castle a few times without a bodyguard, even though his mother strictly forbade it. One time he had used a disguise, another time, the help of an obliging gardener (long dead now). He had many tricks to get a bit of adventure away from the stifling watch of his mother and her guards. "All right," Perry said after thinking about it for a moment. "I'll do it with one condition."

"And that would be . . .?"

"I want to come, too."

"Oh, no. What if something goes wrong with the spell or with something else? No one will know what happened to us."

"Please, show a little respect, my lord," Perry said with a wry smile. "Nothing went wrong with my first transfer spell. Nothing will go wrong with the second. As far as something else going wrong? I doubt it. Hardly anyone knows who you are over *here*, much less in some obscure town in Indiana. If anything, you'll be safer there. Besides, why your mother fusses so much over protecting your Regent bottom is beyond me. I don't see people lining up to murder you. But maybe she knows something we don't." Perry winked mischievously. "At any rate, would it be so bad if we got stuck there and no one knew?"

"I guess not." The idea was actually tempting.

"Do we have a deal, then?"

"I suppose." He thought about it a little longer. Maybe it would be good to have someone with him. "Fine . . . deal," he said, extending his hand. Perry shook it firmly.

"It'll be fun." Perry grinned.

"No funny business, okay?"

"Not from me." Perry took a hand to his chest, looking comically injured.

"I'll meet you at 10 P.M. by the south tower. Don't be late."

Perry seemed about to protest, but stopped when Ashby narrowed his eyes at him. It didn't matter if the Sorcerer found the time difference between continents inconvenient, missed his beauty sleep, or what have you. He wasn't about to scare Sam by visiting at an ungodly hour.

*　*　*

At 10:15 P.M., Ashby was waiting hidden in the shadows of a massive stone column. He was dressed in a black suit and tie, and felt much more presentable and confident than the last time he'd seen Sam. But where the devil was Perry?

Just when his impatience started to simmer, Perry walked out through the service door. He looked around surreptitiously, holding his head down, casting a dim shadow under the moon. He wore dark jeans with a few fashionable holes and a simple black shirt.

"Over here," Ashby whispered.

Perry gave no sign of having heard, but walked casually in his direction.

"It's about time," Ashby chided.

"Couldn't help it. Xasdia was late delivering my dinner," Perry said with an impish smile on his lips.

"Stuff it! I don't want to hear it."

Perry looked him up and down. "Looking a bit . . . *stiff,* are we?"

"I want to make a better impression," Ashby said defensively.

"You'll stand out like a sore thumb, more likely."

"Just shut up, Perry. Take this." He picked up a burlap cloth from the ground and pushed it at the Sorcerer's stomach. Perry grabbed it and squinted at it, trying to figure out what it was.

"What's this?

"A cloak," Ashby said sarcastically.

"A cloak?"

"Yes, they're the latest fashion, didn't you know? Just shut up and follow me."

They walked toward the garages. All was quiet at this hour, which was a far cry from the hubbub that was common during the day. Only the padding of their shoes against a stone pathway disturbed the calm. The luscious lawns and flowerbeds filled the air with the scent of cut grass and manure. Next morning, a battalion of gardeners would be out, tending every blade of grass on the expansive grounds, every leaf on the towering bushes and topiary sculptures.

When they reached the prodigious building they called the garage, Ashby led Perry around the corner. Behind the structure, a delivery van sat, idling—no one at the wheel. Ashby's black Bentley was parked a few yards away.

"This is it," Ashby said.

Perry kept walking toward the Bentley. "What? You finally found a bribable guard? 'Bout time."

Ashby had tried to bribe a few of the guards in the past, but none of them had ever let him leave the castle without Danata's permission. They were trained *and* paid too well to risk losing their jobs.

"No, not my car. The van." Ashby walked quickly to the back of the delivery vehicle, where he found the back hatch open. Several burlap sacks lay on the ground, waiting to be loaded. In one leap, Ashby climbed in. The cargo area was only half-full. Perry followed, without a comment, for once.

Ashby sat and got as close as he could to one of the sacks toward the back. An earthy odor filled the space. Gathering his legs and arms in a tight bundle, he tucked his burlap blanket around his body, concealing himself as best as he could.

"I can still tell you're not a sack," Perry pointed out.

"Just do the same, Perry" he said tiredly

"They always check whatever goes in or out."

As if Ashby didn't know that. "You're a pain in the arse, you know?"

Biting his tongue, Perry positioned himself next to Ashby. "I feel like a huge potato," he said.

"Shh, it's time."

Someone was approaching. They ducked and covered their heads. A man, whistling a tune, loaded more sacks onto the van until Ashby and Perry were surrounded by them. His name was Higgs. Ashby had paid him handsomely to sneak them out of the castle and had promised not to mention their deal if they got caught. Soon the van was in motion, lurching back and forth none-too-gently.

"Quite a means of transport you've found," Perry whispered.

Ashby ignored him. The van came to a stop at the back gate, the checkpoint for all service vehicles.

"What do you have this time, Higgs?" A guard asked.

"Turnips," the driver responded, his voice a little shaky.

"This late?"

"Lord Bernard was late finishing his harvest," Higgs said.

"Bernard's a fool," sneered the guard. "Why does he even bother keeping a garden?"

Ashby tightened his fists. The guard deserved a punch in the gut. Uncle Bernard loved working on his vegetables. He was a Sower and could grow just about anything to perfection. It was the only thing the poor soul could still enjoy and do well.

"You shouldn't say that! Lord Bernard is generous to donate his harvest. It's well-appreciated at the soup kitchens in town," Higgs defended. "His are excellent turnips."

"Sure, sure," the guard said. "Well, let me have a look."

"O-okay."

Steps sounded outside as the two men made their way to the back of the van. The doors opened with a groan of hinges. Ashby waited for a beat, hoping to give the guard at least one small glimpse of the van's interior, then he pressed the panic button on the keyless entry remote of his Bentley. The car's anti-theft alarm began to wail, blaring through the still night.

"What the hell . . . ?" the guard said.

"What's happening?" A second voice called out. There were always two guards manning the booth at the back gate.

"I'll go check," the first guard said. "That damn thing's going to wake everyone up." Heavy steps moved away.

"What about Higgs?" the second guard asked.

"Let him go. It's just turnips." The first guard's voice was now distant as he made his way back to the garage.

"Off to the soup kitchen," Higgs said happily. Ashby exhaled a sigh of relief.

Once they were well outside of the castle's perimeter, Higgs stopped and let them off. Ashby thanked him. Higgs gave him a broad smile and said they could count on him anytime. A vineyard lay nearby, and the scent of fermented grapes filled the air.

"How far from here?" Perry dusted himself off. He smelled his shirt. "Ugh, I stink like a musty cellar."

"One mile, at most." Ashby started walking in the opposite direction of the vineyard. He sniffed the sleeve of his jacket and wrinkled his nose. Perry was right. They smelled bad. Hopefully, a brisk walk through open country would get rid of the musty odor.

"What?! I don't feel like walking. Let's do it here," Perry crossed his arms over his chest.

"Don't be lazy. A walk will do you good. Besides, doing magic in plain view isn't the best idea." Ashby removed his jacket, picked off a few strands of burlap, and slung it over his shoulder. Perry huffed, but followed. Humans around these parts already spread rumors about Rothblade Castle residents. They didn't need proof of their supernatural abilities.

In spite of Perry's initial grumbling, he caught up and began to clearly enjoy the walk over the rocky terrain. He stopped to poke a huge toad with a stick and bounded over the rocks like a happy goat, making Ashby remember the playful summers they'd spent together as children. As they neared a patch of woods, tall grass swayed at their feet, teased by a chilly wind.

Twenty minutes later, they walked into the woods and soon arrived at a small cottage overrun by weeds. The windows were dusty and broken, the door closed and uninviting.

"What's the rush?" Perry snickered when Ashby hurried to the crumbling gate.

Ashby ignored him, wishing his friend weren't so impertinent all the time. Yes, he wanted to see Sam as soon as possible. What was the shame in that? But of course, a Singular like Perry would never understand the strong needs for one's Companion. Ashby took a deep breath and, instead of letting his temper get the best of him, decided to feel sorry for Perry. The poor devil would never know true love.

While the young Sorcerer took his time surveying the place, Ashby approached the cottage. It appeared deserted, but he was cautious nonetheless. After looking through one of the broken windows into the dark confines of the small structure, he confirmed it was empty. Shoving with one shoulder, he forced the door open. It scraped loudly against the cobblestone floor.

"Great! Now everyone knows we've arrived." Perry walked past Ashby and entered the cottage first. "Nice," he said sarcastically when he saw the interior.

There were cobwebs, dust and broken furniture in every corner. A small fireplace, black with soot, stood in the center of the room as a forlorn reminder of warm, home cooked stew on long-ago winter nights.

"I think it's perfect," Ashby said, ignoring Perry's attempts to goad him.

"Maybe you and your lovebird can fix the place up and move in."

"Just get to work."

"Yes, *your Highness.*" Perry's tone was sardonic, but he closed the door and set to work.

It was dark inside, but they could see well enough. The young Sorcerer knelt in the middle of the room and pulled a scarlet handkerchief from his pants pocket. He unfurled the bundle and placed it gently on the floor. A small, corked vial filled with green liquid sparkled, casting a glow onto Perry's hands. Ashby gagged, remembering the brew's awful taste.

Perry cradled the tiny vessel and deposited it in Ashby's hand. "You know what to do."

"Why does it have to taste like liquefied snot? How about figs? Or pomegranate?"

"Look, does it work? Or not?"

Ashby huffed. He would drink a barrel of the foul stuff if it meant he could see Sam again. Ashby uncorked the bottle. Perry drew a thick chain from around his collar. A silver talisman slid from under his shirt. He set it on the palm of his hand. The edge of the amulet was adorned by two serpents eating each other in a vicious circle. Any silver disc would have worked, but Perry had a weakness for "wicked-looking" accessories. It helped collect Perry's powers until he was ready to release the strong conjuration.

For his part, Ashby needed the potion to absorb the spell. Without it, the magic would have no effect on him, and only transport Perry. Ashby's every molecule would remain tied to the elements that surrounded him. At least, that was how Ashby understood it. Perry was right about one thing, he thought: as long as it all worked, the details were incidental.

In one gulp, the green concoction washed down his throat, leaving behind glittering particles inside the vial. He winced in disgust, the taste of something like rotten eggs flooding his mouth. Perry watched, amused.

"Well? What are you waiting for?" Ashby asked.

Perry stopped grinning and started reciting a spell under his breath. Ashby waited impatiently, wishing the young sorcerer had more practice. After a few minutes, the same tingling sensation he'd experienced the first time spread over his body. He closed his eyes tightly as a wave of nausea hit the pit of his stomach. This was the worst part, but it was a small price to pay, considering what awaited him on the other side.

There was a loud pop as he felt transported. It has something to do with breaking the time and space barrier. He wobbled, but steadied himself quickly when he opened his eyes. He looked around, disoriented. Something was wrong.

Perry stood in front of him, staring up at a bright, green streetlight. "What in bloody hell?!" His exclamation was followed by a terrible screeching of tires.

"Hey, are you nuts?" someone yelled. A deafening car horn blared behind them.

They turned and found themselves face to face with the grill of a large truck. The driver stuck his head out the window and glared at them.

"The light's green, you morons. Get off the street," the man yelled when they just stared back, bewildered.

Ashby grabbed Perry's arm and dragged him out of the way onto the sidewalk. Traffic started flowing again. Ashby looked around at the different signs over the buildings. He spotted a couple of fast food restaurants and a pharmacy, but no Sam.

"Where is she?" Last time, he'd spotted her right away. But now, he couldn't sense her nearby.

"Well, it was a little harder than I expected. I think we got off course, just a touch."

"Damn it!" Ashby exclaimed.

"Now see here, my lord," Perry said sarcastically. "See how dangerous that was? We could have ended up in the middle of the Atlantic. This should be the last time we come here." Perry waved a mocking finger in Ashby's face. As Sorcerer adviser to the future Regent, Perry was supposed to impart counsel whenever appropriate. "Just practicing . . . for the future, you know."

"Yeah, sure. Now, let me concentrate." Ashby closed his eyes and let the need for Sam take hold of him. It was hard keeping it in the back of his mind, but extremely easy to let it flood him. Her pull became stronger, like a rope around his spinal column, tugging him. He felt her with all his being, and knew exactly where to find her.

"This way." He walked toward a large apartment complex. He wished she could sense him too, wished she knew he was coming, wished she'd meet him halfway and run straight into his arms. But he could be patient, because sooner or later, she would morph. It was inevitable.

℘ Chapter 24 ℃
Sam

"Your move," Sam said.

Greg's thick eyebrows bunched in concentration over the chessboard. He looked very handsome under the dim sunlight filtering through the overhead trees, his ebony hair lustrous and silky. Oh, how she wanted to reach out and touch it. She thought his well-proportioned, perfect features served as proof of what he claimed to be. He was like an anime character with his big, sparkling blue eyes, chiseled lips and to-die-for hair. *And don't even get me started on his body.* She held her breath and stared at the trees overhead to take her mind off the way he was biting his lower lip. They sat at a picnic table outside of James's apartment, after finishing their trig tutoring session.

"Check," Greg said.

She looked down at the board to find that he'd played right into her hands. Two more moves, and she would have him. Unable to keep the smugness off her face, she smiled and moved the rook to block the threat.

"Your turn," she taunted.

He tilted his head to one side, looking oh so cute. Sam twisted clammy hands in her lap, stealing glances from the board back to his face. Over the last few days, they had spent a lot of time together. She'd showed him around town after their lessons, and Greg had stayed over for dinner each night. The story was that Greg's dad traveled a lot and his mother did shift work at a hospital. Rose and James were satisfied with the explanation, and extended him a permanent dinner invitation. Sam had been grateful to them, glad to be able to spend time with Greg. She felt the safest when he was around and didn't get tired of ogling him. It was a guilty pleasure.

"I'm screwed," he said, seeing Sam's trap for the first time.

"Yes, you are."

"Well, don't get too smug. I was never good at chess." Greg put an index finger on his king and tipped it over. "You win," he conceded.

"Let's play again." She started rearranging the pieces, knowing she could go on for hours staring at his handsome face—what better than a quiet game of chess to help her indulge?

"No, thanks. I don't enjoy torture," he said.

"I can't help it if you don't like a good challenge . . ."

Greg sighed and stood. He looked around the picnic area. They were the only ones there. "Things have been really quiet." He sniffed the air like a hound dog.

Sam said nothing, instead she dropped the chess pieces inside a smooth velvet bag, folded the board and set it aside. She didn't want the conversation to steer Greg's way. She was still processing the whole Morphid story and both attempts on her life.

The magic she'd witnessed at the gas station couldn't be denied. Someone had almost killed her with red lighting. Days later, someone had almost drowned her in a pot of red soup—not magical, but pretty freakin' *funnyhorrific* or *funnyrrific*. She hadn't decided which. *Death by soup.* Yeah, hilarious. Her mouth flooded with the taste of sour soup—a food she'd never, ever, eat again, even if Le Cordon Bleu flunked her in L'histoire de la Soupe or whatever.

Greg said the man had force-fed him some foul poison that made him cough up blood. And it was true enough. She'd helped clean it, even when he objected. But they had needed to hide all the evidence before the other workers showed up and started asking questions. The next volunteer came in from the back just minutes after they picked up the last mushy vegetable, and had given her plenty of grief about "spilling" so much soup on her shirt. Greg was sure Veridan had paid the man to disable him before attacking Sam. He figured that the Sorcerer circumvented Greg's Keeper instincts by hiding the details about Sam until the last minute. Army Coat, as Greg called the attacker, had pulled an envelope from his pocket after disabling Greg, with the rest of his instructions. Clearly, this subterfuge and maybe even magic had been involved in concealing the plan from Greg's Keeper abilities.

None of it had been a dream, as much as Sam wished it were. Seeing was believing, right? Except the believing part got harder when Greg started saying she was a Morphid, too. That's when her brain slammed on the brakes.

"Avoiding the topic won't change anything," Greg said, snapping her out of her thoughts.

How does he always know what I'm thinking?

Sam was getting tired of this whole Morphid affair, but Greg brought it up every chance he got. She was frustrated at the lack of real answers to her questions. All Greg had were conjectures. Like yesterday, when she told him that Barbara and James weren't her biological parents, and he wasted no time speculating about her Morphid parents, their castes and the reason why they might have abandoned her. It was hard enough not to know who her real parents were. Didn't he realize that saying they weren't even human made things harder? If she couldn't have something concrete, she'd rather pretend none of it was true. Besides, what was wrong with the here and now? The new feeling of belonging, the novel awareness of the opposite sex, the giddy sensation in the pit of her stomach when she first saw Greg every morning.

"Would you like a snack? Rose and I baked peanut butter cookies," she said, making her avoidance blatant.

Greg twisted his mouth at a disapproving angle, but relented. "Are you sure James and Rose don't mind me hanging around so much?"

"I'm sure. They're too busy making googly eyes at each other to notice anything else."

"Maybe I should ease off, anyway."

"Come on. What would you do at your place?"

"I can read, study, I don't know . . . something."

"What about dinner?" She really didn't want him to go.

"I bought some cereal, and I know how to fry an egg and make toast. I'm not completely inept, you know?"

"I was going to help Rose make some linguine, and I—I want you to stay," Sam added tentatively.

Since they met, Greg had alternated between intensely close and strangely distant. Some days, she could swear he liked her, but others he pulled away for no apparent reason. She was afraid to put herself out there and run the risk of rejection. This was her first crush *ever,* and she didn't want it to end. Self-consciously, she rubbed the velvety chess bag with the tips of her fingers.

"You do?" he asked, sitting back down.

She nodded sheepishly, avoiding his gaze. He seemed to be on one of his warmer-than-lukewarm moods. Her heart thudded.

"Why?" he pressed.

It was unfair for him to put her on the spot, considering his fickle attitude toward her. She almost gave him a casual, noncommittal answer, but refrained, not wanting his mood to turn cool. Instead, she looked into his eyes with a meaning she hoped he'd understand.

"Sam . . ." His voice was but a whisper. She shivered at the intensity with which he pronounced the one syllable that was her name.

He reached for her hand. When he'd almost made contact, he stopped and seemed to think better of it. Disappointment swept through her, and she couldn't help but frown. Yet her dissatisfaction seemed to encourage him.

He reached out again. With an electrifying tingle, their hands met.

"It's . . . wrong," he said.

"What? What's wrong?"

"This," he caressed her hand, sliding a thumb over her knuckles. A current of tantalizing energy passed between them, making a wild shiver run through her. How was it possible for such a simple touch to feel this way? It was as if his fingers held the secret code to every nerve in her body. She tingled everywhere.

"W-why? It doesn't feel wrong to me." His touch was too good to be wrong—no matter what else she was feeling. In a daring move, she interlaced her fingers with his.

Greg inhaled sharply. He'd been fighting it all along, she realized with pleasure. Trying not to scare him, she stood and stepped closer, still holding his hand. He averted his gaze, looking nervous and conflicted.

"What are you thinking?" she asked.

"Wondering how soon I'll regret this." He stood and took his free hand to her face. First, he let it rest on her cheek, soft as a breeze. Then, he slid it down her neck, making her body scream with new, vast sensations. He lowered his mouth until they were only an inch apart. His sweet breath teased her half-opened mouth. He was going to kiss her, and there was nothing she wanted more. Her first kiss. Seconds stretched like hours as he got closer.

"WHAT IN BLOODY HELL?!" An irate voice yelled.

In one swift motion, Greg whirled and stood in front of Sam protectively.

"Sam!" Her name, a reproach on a faintly familiar, accented voice. "*Who* is this?!"

"Calm down, Ashby," a second voice said.

"Ashby?" Sam said in whisper. She peeked around Greg.

"Stay back," Greg ordered her, putting an arm out and holding her back.

"Take your hands off her," Ashby commanded.

"Don't take another step. Stay right where you are." A strange hum filled the air as Greg vibrated with some strange energy. "That's a warning."

Sam peeked from under his arm and saw two figures standing ten paces away. She recognized Ashby immediately, in spite of his slicked back hair and black suit. A guy with brown hair, in jeans and a t-shirt held Ashby back, and—if beauty was the biggest giveaway—they were both Morphids. *Crap.* She'd been so immersed in things with Greg that she'd forgotten about Ashby, and their off-the-wall conversation at the mall.

"Let go, Perry. Repel him. That's an order," Ashby said.

"But . . ." The guy named Perry started to protest.

"Just do it."

Perry shrugged and whirled his hands. An iridescent cloud appeared between his fingers. Sam shrieked and hid behind Greg, right before a dazzling beam of light shot in their direction.

"Greg," she yelped, clinging to his shirt.

The magic hit Greg square in the chest, dissipating and raining to the ground like harmless fireworks.

"Blast it!" Perry exclaimed.

"What did you do wrong?" Ashby demanded.

"Nothing. He should be on the ground," Perry defended himself. "He's . . . he's immune or something. But how . . ." he trailed off.

"What are you?" Ashby demanded, pointing at Greg. "Answer me."

"I've had enough of this," Greg rumbled. Over his shoulder, he whispered, "Stay here. I'll take care of them," and started in their direction.

"Wait," Perry yelled, extending his hand in a defensive pose. "You . . . you're a Morphid, right? I've only read of one caste that can do that . . . *Keepers*," he finished in a whisper.

Greg stopped short, swaying in indecision. "What do you want?"

"A Keeper?" Ashby repeated in a perplexed echo. "I've never heard—"

"It's a rare caste. A myth, I thought. A servile caste." Perry didn't sound very sure about his guess.

"Maybe he's just a Sorcerer. Clearly, one better than you," Ashby said.

"No Sorcerer's immune to magic."

Greg clenched his fists into trembling balls as he took a step toward them once more. Patience wasn't one of his virtues. Though he was probably thinking of Veridan's tricks at the gas station.

"Greg!" She grabbed his arm. "I—I know him."

Perry stepped in front of Ashby and spoke, quickly and reasonably. "If you're a Keeper, you must know we mean her no harm. Ashby's her Integral, for God's sake. He would never hurt her."

Greg's arm stiffened under Sam's hold.

"Sam, order your . . . *Keeper* to stand down," Ashby said as if Greg was a dog.

Sam bristled. *What? How . . . infuriating!* Greg wasn't some servant to be bossed around, by her or by Ashby. All fear gone, she stepped next to Greg and interlaced her fingers with his. Ashby's face disfigured into a mask of incredulity and pain. His reaction made her hesitate, but she forced the words out.

"Who do you think you are?" She really wasn't looking for answers. She just wanted to put Ashby in his place. Standing like a rag doll, Ashby babbled something unintelligible.

Serves him right. He had some nerve if he thought he could show up and order them around.

Perry came to his friend's rescue. "Please, forgive us." He bowed slightly.

She scoffed at the ridiculous gesture.

Perry continued. "Ashby and I are sorry for our sudden and unannounced appearance. We didn't mean to disrespect or . . . interrupt anything. We're here for a simple and harmless visit. We regret the unfortunate misunderstanding."

A bit over the top, but at least he was making sense. Ashby, on the other hand, was still babbling nonsense. "I . . . I don't think or expect . . ."

Perry began rapidly whispering in his friend's ear.

Greg growled under his breath, "So you actually know these guys?"

"One of them. It's a long story. Tell you later," Sam whispered back.

"But he . . ." Ashby started to protest. However, Perry intervened again. After closing his eyes and taking a deep breath, Ashby seemed to heed whatever advice his friend gave him. He took a step forward and bowed, just a bit.

"Perry's right. Please, forgive my . . . behavior," Ashby croaked. The words weren't coming on easily. "Sam, I wanted simply to *visit you.* I came expecting something different. Not this."

"What do you want with me?" Sam asked, finding it hard to maintain a harsh tone.

Ashby took another step forward and when Greg blocked his path, he did his best to ignore him.

"I came to talk to you, Sam," he said gently. He looked into her eyes so intensely that it made her falter.

She lowered her eyes. "W-what for?"

"Look. I think you should leave," Greg said. "You're upsetting her."

Ashby turned to Greg, black eyes flashing with hatred. "I don't understand why you don't know your place. You're standing between two Integrals . . . *Keeper*. I'm sure you know there's no way you'll get away with this for long."

To Sam's surprise, Greg lowered his head, abashed. She looked from one to the other even more confused than before.

Ashby turned to face her again. "I presume you now know what you are? What I came to warn you about before?"

Sam nodded. It was all too incredible, but as much as she wanted everything to be a big misunderstanding, denial wouldn't change anything—just as Greg had said.

"Then you know you'll morph soon." Ashby smiled, apparently happy at the idea of her changing into something she didn't want to be.

Sam shook her head, panic filling her chest.

"You mustn't worry," Ashby tried to calm her. "It's quite natural. Everything will be clear then. You'll know who you truly are meant to be, and I'll be the happiest Morphid alive. You're just confused, right now." He smiled pityingly, and Sam knew in her heart that he told the truth. Still, his words of reassurance just filled her with more doubt and fear.

"I'm your Integral, Sam. Do you know what that means?"

Sam shook her head. Not in answer to his question, but to the idea of being mindlessly attracted and devoted to someone she hardly knew, like a dumb puppy struck with instinctual lust.

"It means that . . ."

"I know what it means," Sam snapped. "And it's creepy and wrong."

Ashby looked as if he'd been stabbed in the heart. She stepped closer to Greg, but not without effort. She felt conflicted and knew that what she'd said was hurtful. Holding her breath, she tried very hard not to care.

"Maybe we should leave, Ashby," Perry interjected.

"No!" Ashby raised his voice.

"Uh, is something wrong?"

Everyone turned to find Rose standing off to the side, watching them warily. No one answered.

"Are these your friends, Sam? . . . Greg?" she added after Sam shook her head.

"They were just leaving," Greg said.

"Sure," Rose said with skepticism. "Um, what's with the suit?" Rose asked, looking at Ashby up and down. "Have a meeting or something?"

Ashby winced, and Perry smirked for some reason. The comment seemed to be the last straw for Ashby. An expression of deep shame colored his face, making him appear on the verge of either tears or a killing spree—Sam couldn't decide which. He looked so lost and out of place that she suddenly felt sorry for him.

"We *were* just leaving," Ashby managed somehow. He turned to look at Sam, and his eyes wavered with the most pained gaze she'd ever seen. His lips parted as if to say something, but instead a sad, little smile stretched his lips, making her want to evaporate.

When he turned to leave, Sam's mouth opened and uttered his name quite involuntarily. "Ashby," she said. The yearning in her own voice made her shudder. He faced her again, expectant, as if his life depended on it. At the same time, Greg took hold of her hand. Ashby shot him a murderous glare, turned and left without a second glance. She fought the sudden urge to run after him, but it took so much to resist that she trembled like a butterfly wing.

"What was that all about?" Rose asked. She blinked when she got no response. "Well, I just came to see if you're ready to help with that linguine," she added.

"Greg's not staying," Sam said, pulling from his grasp. "Sandwiches would be fine by me."

Rose looked at Greg, picking up on his surprise at Sam's words.

"Everything . . . all right?" Rose asked.

"Yeah, sure," Sam said. "His mom called and said she'd be home early. That's all."

"Oh! In that case, I'm glad you'll get to spend the evening with your mother, Greg. You don't get to do that very much." Rose tried to sound cheerful, as if to brighten the bad news Sam had obviously just given him.

"I'll see you tomorrow," Sam said, walking away toward the apartment without a backward glance. The tearing sensation inside her chest almost bringing her to her knees.

ℬ Chapter 25 ℭℛ
Greg

After Ashby's unexpected visit, and the even more unexpected reaction from Sam, Greg asked for no explanations. Worse yet, she offered none. It was for the best, he thought to himself. He didn't need the painful confirmation in her words. It had been foolish to let himself get carried away by his attraction, to hope for a greater outcome. His Morphid side had seethed at his behavior, warred with him as he leaned down to kiss her. That part of him knew he couldn't hold onto her.

In the following days, things had changed. Sam grew distant, distrustful. And how could he blame her? All along, he'd seen the situation more clearly than she did, and yet he'd allowed things between them to get out of hand. Her resentment and caution shouldn't have come as a surprise.

They continued with their lessons, and his math skills improved considerably, if not his ability to control his feelings toward her. If anything, with every passing day his attraction and feelings grew a little bit more. So much that he feared he was falling in love, as impossible as that should be for a Singular.

Summer school finished, and—after passing his final exam— Greg enrolled in his new school as a junior. Everything was quiet, without attackers or Ashby to disturb the peace. This was his only comfort, although something told him it wouldn't last. Theories about Ashby and Veridan whirled in his mind all the time, and the more he thought about it, the more he believed there was a connection between them. They were both English, well dressed and arrogant. It was just too much of a coincidence.

"I think I should sign up for the same classes as you," Greg had told Sam a few days before registration.

"Okay," Sam said. No protest, but her indifference hurt even worse.

Although Rose maintained her open invitation to dinner, Greg had spent every night in his apartment since that day, eating TV dinners and all sorts of pre-packaged goods. He just sat on the carpet and stared at the bare walls, wondering why people liked to pretend that living alone was a wonderful thing. No one to do the chores. Nothing good to eat in the refrigerator. No one to talk to. It sucked. He'd learned that much in just a couple of months. By now he was so desperate, he kept wishing for the first day of school to hurry up and get there. At least during classes, he'd be able to see Sam almost every day.

Tonight, his latest pathetic excuse for a Friday night, he sat cross-legged on the beige carpet, eating cereal. He chewed with disinterest, spoon clinking against the bowl. He was on his last bite when his cell rang. Mechanically, he picked the phone up never taking his eyes off the spoon. His parents called him every day around this time. Greg was more than surprised when Sam's voice resonated on the other side.

"Hi, Greg."

"Hi," he said, swallowing his surprise.

"Um, are you busy? Is this a good time?" She was apologetic, as if she were talking to a stranger.

No, it's not a good time. I ordered pizza and have all my buddies over. "No, I'm not busy."

"My friend, Brooke, came back from New York today. There's a party tonight at our friend Reed's house. Would you . . . like to come?" Greg felt his heart swell until Sam added, "Brooke wants to meet you."

-Of course she's not asking you on a date, you dumbass. A surge of spiteful pride made him want to say he'd made other plans, but it quickly passed. He was tightly wrapped around Sam's little finger, and would always lose this battle.

"Sure. I'll come."

"Okay. We'll see you there at nine-thirty. Do you have a pen?"

After writing down directions, he hung up and looked at his watch. It was just past seven. For half an hour, he paced up and down, wearing out the already-battered carpet. When he couldn't take it anymore, he showered. After changing into a pair of clean jeans and gray button-down shirt, he checked his hair in the mirror. He looked damn good, and even the two-day stubble on his angular jaw added to his appeal. *So why do I feel like the ugly duckling?*

But he knew why. Ever since meeting Ashby he couldn't stop making comparisons, and he always came up short. The guy should have looked ridiculous in that over-the-top, tailored suit just to come see Sam and, although Rose had mocked him, it was clear Ashby belonged in those expensive clothes.

Cursing his bad luck and his watch for not moving fast enough, he left his apartment and drove to the party. After finding the house, he parked at the farthest corner and waited. Slowly, people started to arrive. As they stepped out of their cars, laughing and hopping in excitement, Greg focused his sharp eyes on every face, trying to find the only one he cared about. Both sides of the street filled up with cars before he spotted Sam walking across the lawn, arm in arm with a tall, slender girl.

He got out of his car and casually headed toward them. He stuffed his hands in his pockets, trying not to betray the butterflies in his gut. He hated being such a fool for her. He was so hopelessly lost he might as well have morphed into a Companion. If only his Keeper side were strong enough to make him feel nothing at all.

"Hi," he said when he was a few paces from them.

"Oh. Em. Gee!" Brooke exclaimed as soon as she laid eyes on him, her mascaraed eyes growing round and doe-like. Her dirty blond hair was fake, judging by the dark, fashionable roots showing through and her olive skin.

An elbow hit Brooke on the side.

"Ouch," Brooke complained, then added, "You're going to break my ribs, girl."

Sam spoke up before Brooke managed to embarrass her even more. "Greg, this is Brooke."

"Nice to meet you," Greg said, extending a hand.

Brooke shook it and said, "Total sugar coma of the eye."

Sam's elbow went into action again.

"Okay, okay, I'll behave," Brooke promised, putting her palms up in surrender. But Greg almost wished she wouldn't. Sam's chagrin was oddly satisfying.

"Let's not stand here all night. C'mon." Brooke pulled Sam along toward the party.

While she wasn't looking, Greg admired Sam. She was wearing a form-fitting black skirt and a backless red top that revealed her creamy, smooth skin. She looked gorgeous.

As they walked in, all eyes turned to them. Greg towered above everyone, which made the upturned faces pointing in his direction painfully apparent. Loud music muffled the greetings Brooke and Sam received. They worked their way past a crowded kitchen and into the dining room where they met Sam's friend, Reed. Immediately, Greg found a reason to dislike him.

"Samantha!" he exclaimed as they walked in. "So glad you could make it." He rubbed her bare arm, keeping his hand there a little too long while he plastered a fawning grin on his round face.

Greg cocked his head to one side and imagined bending his glasses out of shape and stuffing them down his mouth. Jealousy had been unknown to him until recently, but it was easy to see how it could turn someone into a caveman. He took a deep, calming breath. He couldn't blame the guy for liking her, after all. She was beautiful.

Sam shied away from Reed's touch and offered a meek smile in return.

"Good to see you, too, *Reedy*," Brooke said, pretending to feel slighted.

Greg liked Brooke more and more every minute.

"Hi, *Brooke*," Reed answered, barely letting his eyes stop on her before they settled on Greg. "Who's the . . . giant?"

Greg took another huge breath.

"Sam's boyfriend," Brooke announced. "His name's Greg."

Both Sam and Reed went pale. Reed looked to Sam for confirmation. Or, more likely, hoping for denial. To Greg's surprise, Sam simply shrugged and offered neither. Reed swiftly turned toward the dining table, pretending to fool with a tray of sandwiches. He shifted it an inch over to the right. Then he left, murmuring something about more drinks.

"Is he all right?" Greg played innocent.

"Hey, anyone hungry?" Sam played avoidance. She picked up a small triangular sandwich that looked suspiciously like pimento cheese.

He wrinkled his nose. "No, thank you. I just ate."

"I'll eat some." Brooke snatched the morsel off Sam's hand and sat at the table. "I don't think Cody's here," she said with a pout, frowning as she chowed down on the sandwich and snatched another one. "Sam, get me a drink, will ya?" she mumbled, cheeks bulging with food.

Sam obeyed instantly, glad to get away. While she was gone, Brooke eyed Greg up and down like one of the little sandwiches she seemed to be enjoying.

"You're a sight for sore eyes," she said. "Once the initial blinding shock passes." She said with a chuckle. Greg hoped Cody showed up soon, whoever he was. "So, what's your story?"

"Um, story?"

"Yeah, you know . . . are you into her?"

Oh, that story. "I—"

Sam came back before he had to answer. She handed Brooke a juice box.

"What the hell is this?" Brooke looked at the tiny box as if it were a dirty diaper.

"It's all they have. Reed's parents have the situation *under control.*" Sam made air quotes.

"How lame." Still, Brooke peeled away the accompanying straw, viciously speared the box and sucked on it until it made gurgling sounds.

Walking around the table, Sam sat in the chair opposite Brooke's and started bobbing her head to the music, doing her best to ignore Greg. A couple was making out in a corner of the room, partially hidden by a large china cabinet.

"Don't want them to think I'm staring," Greg said, taking the chair next to Sam's and turning his back on the face snatchers. It was a convenient excuse to be close to her. As he sat, their arms brushed. Her inviting warmth instantly reminded him how lonely he'd felt lately. The touch wasn't lost on Sam. She shrank away and—even in the semidarkness—he could swear she seemed to be blushing.

"Oh, gross. Those two need to get a room." Brooke swiveled on her chair and faced away from the oblivious couple. "Cody *said* he'd be here. I bet you anything his idiot kid brother has something to do with this. If I could get my hands around his chubby little neck. Do you know what he did the other day when I called Cody from New York?" She didn't wait for an answer, or even take a breath. "Well, he picked up the phone and told me that Cody had been checked into rehab. He said his parents found drugs in his room and . . ." For the next fifteen minutes, Brooke ran her mouth about Cody, New York and all the boys she'd ever dated or would like to date. Greg and Sam grunted and nodded at the right moments. Meanwhile, he stole glances at Sam, wondering what was going through her mind. She didn't seem to be paying too much attention to Brooke's monologue, either.

"Sooo," Brooke said, once she seemed to run out of things to talk about. "*Are* you guys dating or what?" A mischievous glint sparkled in her eyes, accompanied by a raised eyebrow and an upturned smirk.

"Brooke!" Sam used her name as if it was an expletive.

"'Cause you totally should be," Brooke said, without missing a beat.

Sam crossed her arms and gave her friend a silent, murderous look. Sensing waves of discomfort and confusion flowing from his Integral, Greg squirmed as if his seat were red-hot.

"Awk-ward," Brooke said splitting the word in two and rolling her eyes in a big, distracted circle. "Uh, I've got to use the restroom. Be right back."

For a second, it looked as if Sam would reach out and beg her to stay, but instead she sighed in frustration and stared up at the ceiling.

"Something interesting up there?" Greg asked, looking up. He followed his question with what he hoped was his most charming smile.

"I'm sorry about Brooke. She's very . . . *crazy*."

"Yeah." Greg couldn't think of a better adjective either.

They were silent for a moment.

"Sam." She held her breath as he crooned her name. "I'm sorry."

"You don't have to—"

"Please, let me say what I have to say." This was the first time in several weeks when there hadn't been a trigonometry textbook between them. Sam had kept her guard very high to avoid this very conversation, but it was time he had his say. She agreed with a feeble nod.

"I screwed up, Sam. I should've been more honest with you about the turn our relationship was taking. I should've told you there's something wrong with me, that somehow I'm broken, that the part of my nature making me . . . *feel* for you is defective. I was selfish. I shouldn't have listened to that half of me. I should've listened to my Keeper side, 'cause it was screaming, telling me I'm not supposed to like you this way."

He stopped, waiting from her to slap him or something, but she just stared, hanging on his every word. Encouraged, he continued.

"I should be incapable of . . . of . . ." he couldn't finish.

"Of what?" she asked in whisper.

Greg squeezed his eyes shut for a second and tried to muster the courage to tell her how he felt. When he blinked his eyes open, he saw Sam's beautiful face twisted into a plea. She wanted to know. Her eyes were practically begging him to finish. His stupid heart started thudding out of control. Slowly, he leaned toward Sam, hypnotized by her moist, parted lips. He inched closer, allowing her ample time to back away. She didn't.

Her breath caught. Their lips met.

Greg's heart was suddenly locked in a vise grip of dread. The feeling was so absolute, so overwhelming that their kiss became nothing but a slight, fleeting caress. With a gasp, he recoiled.

Damn his Keeper side. It'd stolen their kiss.

He must have looked sick, because Sam looked worried. "Are you all right?"

He struggled to catch his breath and couldn't respond.

"Answer me," she said, throwing her arm around him and pulling him into a shy but desperate embrace. "What's wrong?"

"I'm fine," he breathed out, wrapping his own arms around her waist and pulling her closer.

"Greg," she exhaled in his ear. "I don't want to change. I'm so confused."

"I know, I know." Her hair smelled like some forgotten, blissful dream. His limbs went weak.

"It would be like . . . being possessed."

He nodded, burying his face deeper into her hair. Heat rose in his veins as he found his way to her warm, pulsating neck. In spite of himself, he brushed her skin with his lips. She yielded, and he had to fight to restrain himself.

She pulled away one short inch at a time, her arms clinging. "What do we do?"

In that moment, he suspected Sam might agree to whatever he dared suggest, but he knew it would be wrong to speak his heart. His senses were full of her scent, her taste, her touch. He couldn't think of anything honorable.

"I—I don't know," he managed, wanting nothing more than to take her out of here. From the corner of his eye, Greg saw Brooke step into the dining room.

"Are you two done? 'Cause I'm sick of watching you *not* make out!" She was pretending to be irritated, but promptly switched her tone to a regretful one. "Okay, guys. Sorry for interrupting this heart-pounding love affair, but I have to get home. I didn't exactly ask for permission to stay out late, and I'm kind of grounded already. Anyway," she turned to Sam and added suggestively, "Greg can give you a ride home, if you want to stay."

As he exchanged glances with Sam, Greg was immediately struck by the eagerness and fire in her expression. She definitely wanted to stay.

-Bad idea! Bad idea! A siren went off inside his brain. "Um, I think maybe she should . . ." Greg started.

"Actually," Sam cut him short. "I think I'd better go with you, Brooke."

Greg wasn't sure whether he'd hurt her feelings, or if—in the last moment—she'd realized what could happen if they left together *and* what a bad idea *that* particular step would be. All he hoped was that she didn't go back to giving him the cold shoulder. For her part, Brooke looked at them as if they'd just grown donkey ears. Clearly, she had no qualms about taking relationships to the next step.

They said their goodbyes outside. More than ever, parting from Sam felt like trying to pry two chain links apart. More than once, Greg bit back the urge to offer her a ride. He knew in his gut Sam would go with him if he asked her. They could go back to his apartment and . . .

. . . and when she morphs, she'll hate you forever for taking advantage of this moment!

More than anything in the world, this thought frightened him. He couldn't afford to lose her trust again. One more failure and he knew the hope of ever being together would die. And he would do anything to save it. Even if it died the day she came of age, at least he'd have her friendship.

❧ Chapter 26 ☙
Greg

Late after the party, Greg was in his apartment, brushing his teeth, staring dreamily into the mirror when there was a knock at the door. He rinsed his mouth and went to the front, wondering who it could be. He hadn't gotten a single visitor since he had moved in. He looked through the peephole and was surprised to see Sam standing there.

Looking around as if he needed to straighten up the place, he blinked, remembering there was little that could be out of order. His apartment still had an absolute minimum of furniture. He wiped sweaty hands on his jeans and opened the door.

"Hi," Sam said with a shy smile.

"Hey."

She suddenly looked like someone who wanted to be far, far away. "I think . . ." she cast a glance toward the stairs, ready to bolt, "Maybe I shouldn't be here. I don't know what came over me. I—I should leave."

Sam turned as if to go, but Greg snatched her wrist and pulled her inside. In one quick motion, he closed the door, pressed Sam's back against it, and seized her lips in his. Her response was immediate. She wrapped eager hands around him and returned his kiss with the same body-swaying passion he felt. Forgetting himself, he lifted her up, pinning her with his body against the door. Sam wrapped her legs around his waist and dug her fingers into his hair, making him groan deep in his throat.

His mouth left hers and began tracing a path along her jaw. She clung to his neck and whispered his name, eyes pointing to the ceiling as she stretched her neck, inviting him to sample the sweet taste of her collarbone. He obliged, tasting her, making her sigh.

Drunk with passion, they staggered to the floor, Greg falling on top of her as he continued to kiss her.

ℰ Chapter 27 ℘
Sam

Sam couldn't believe she was here, couldn't believe she'd actually borrowed Rose's car to drive here, walked up the steps, knocked on his door. Then he had pulled her inside, and what little rational thought she still had went out the window.

Now she lay under that strong body of his, squirming under his insistent and passionate kisses. Oh, his lips felt like heaven on her heated skin. She slid her hands under his shirt and made him shiver, made him call her name and kiss her harder. She traced the muscles on his back in awe of how wonderful he felt to the touch. His hands also found their way under her top, to her abdomen.

How was it possible to feel *so much*? Had her body been in a numb slumber all her life? It was like he had awakened a part of her nervous system that had been dormant up until now. How else could his touch, that simple caress on her stomach, feel as if the universe had converged there?

She fumbled with his shirt buttons, clumsily getting them undone. She couldn't believe her own nerve. When she tugged on his shirt, trying to peel it away from his shoulders, Greg paused and pulled away, his eyes wide, his lips parted and trembling.

Sam felt her cheeks burn with shame. What would he think of her now? That she was an easy girl who went looking for boys in their own houses to seduce them? Well, she couldn't blame him, could she? That's what she'd become after one simple half-kiss. She turned away, feeling terribly embarrassed.

Greg straightened, knees on either side of her wide hips. She thought he was going to get up, ask her to leave, but instead he removed his shirt very slowly and threw it to the side. Sam's eyes faltered, making their way down his beautiful torso. His chiseled muscles seemed to glow with the light from a lonely lamp. He offered her a hand. She took it, and he helped her sit up. Swinging one leg to the side, he sat with his back against the wall and pulled her into a tight embrace.

She pressed her cheek to his warm, hard chest and listened to his heartbeat and rapid breathing. After a moment, when his inhales and exhales slowed, his voice rumbled deep in his chest.

"I'm glad you came," he said. "I'm sorry I got carried away."

He got carried away? She was the one who'd come, hoping for what had just happened . . . and more. She knew she should show restraint, but wasn't it natural? Weren't her primal instincts wired for this? Why did it have to feel wrong, immoral? Why had society turned such pure feelings into something dirty? Still, she was grateful to Greg for stopping, for bringing some sense into this torrent of emotions.

"I won't lie to you," Greg said. "It's taking all I've got to keep my hands to myself right now." He chuckled sadly and made tight fists.

Sam grabbed one of his hands, pried it open and interlaced her fingers with his. They both sighed when the seal was complete.

He lifted their interlocked hands and kissed the back of her fingers, his lips lingering, lingering, lingering. Her eyes fluttered closed.

"I want it all," he said, his hot breath on her hand.

"Me too," she said shamelessly. And she did. Nothing else mattered, not the fact that she was only sixteen, that she might be fated for another. Right now, she chose Greg, and right now felt like it could carry her into forever.

"Maybe it's wrong. Maybe—" His tone was reluctant, as if these were the last words he wanted to say, but he had to say them.

"Don't," she cut him off. "Nothing has ever felt more right in my life. I feel whole, part of something real, for the first time ever. Don't cheapen this by saying it's wrong."

"I don't want it to be," he said fervently, his muscular arm pulling her harder against him. She kissed his chest and flushed. She shouldn't be pressed against him this way. He was shirtless and glorious, an unearthly temptation that made her blood surge. She took a deep breath and turned her face away from his intoxicating scent.

"You feel just right in my arms," he added. "I feel like I'm part of you, and you part of me. *We* are not wrong, could never be."

And she knew he was right. They belonged together. She could feel the connection, like something tangible, physically real. She could almost see it, touch it.

"But—" he started.

She put a finger over his lips, feeling the fleshy moisture, the latent promise of another kiss. "I said *don't*. Not now. Maybe tomorrow. Today no *buts*. Just you and I, like this." She slung a leg over his lap, faced him and took his beautiful face between her hands.

Slowly, she brought her mouth to his and caught his lower lip between hers. He kissed her back hungrily, sliding his hands around her back. They began exploring each other deliberately and gently, memorizing their taste, their scent, and the exquisite perfection of their togetherness.

❧ Chapter 28 ❧
Greg

Greg spent the rest of the weekend getting ready for school. He went to the store and bought school supplies: Notebooks, a backpack, and a pair of sneakers. On Monday, he was the first one in his classroom. He sat at the last desk of the last row, waiting for Sam.

Slowly, the classroom filled up. Try as he might, he was unable to be inconspicuous. Nobody seemed able to take their eyes off him. The girls for reasons that embarrassed him, and the guys for ones that made him clench his fists.

Where is Sam? Maybe looking into her honey-colored eyes would dispel his urge to flee. But when a familiar gaze finally crossed the threshold, it belonged to the last person he ever thought to find here.

Ashby!

The only good thing that could be said about that jackass' presence was that all the attention that had been directed at Greg immediately went away. With a regal and confident air, he stepped in, practically radiating light from his blond highlights. Greg had only seen him once, but he immediately noticed the difference in his aspect. Not that he had needed one before, but he looked as if he'd been through a make-over, aided by Calvin Klein himself.

The fancy, board-of-directors suit was gone, replaced by a pair of high end gray jeans and a navy blue button-up shirt rolled up to his elbows. His hair had been cut, replacing the long style with a messy, spiked one. He wore a wicked-looking watch with a wide, leather strap that even matched his boots. Everything about him exuded coolness and wealth, making Greg feel inferior in his stone-washed jeans and Pacers t-shirt.

Upheaval was a mild word for the reaction in the room. While Greg had wanted to hide under the desk, Ashby thrived in the spotlight. He walked in and immediately started introducing himself to everyone, male and female alike.

Greg seethed. Obviously, the guy was used to being the center of attention. Meanwhile, Greg's pre-morphing baggage still made him feel and act like the same gawky, nondescript kid he used to be—even if he looked nothing like that anymore.

Ashby was busy shaking hands and making chit-chat when Sam walked in the room. Without missing a beat, he spun around to face her, making full use of his built-in *Sam Radar*. Shocked, she froze in her tracks and gaped. Taking advantage of her dumbfounded state, Ashby took her hand and planted an honest-to-god kiss on it. Greg clenched the edge of his desk, full of impotent fury.

"It's so good to see you again," Ashby said, playing a completely different game than the last time they'd seen him.

A nervous half-smile graced Sam's lips. Greg felt his stomach twist in disgust, as well as something that felt like inevitable defeat. Everybody stared wide-eyed. Sam pulled away and pressed her books to her chest. Her eyes flew around the room looking for help. Greg wasted no time. He stood and waved, towering over the other students.

"Um, good to see you, too," she said with a meek smile as she circumvented Ashby, headed in Greg's direction.

A flash of anger passed Ashby's features, but he hid his frustration almost instantly, replacing it with a pleasant grin.

"What is *he* doing here?" Sam asked in a whisper, taking the seat in front of Greg and turning to look at him.

He shrugged uncertainly, but he knew the answer all too well.

"Are you okay?" Greg asked.

Sam looked pale, conflicted, sick to her stomach. She nodded, taking a deep breath and blinking slowly to regain her cool. Exuding confidence, Ashby took the seat next to Sam. He sat facing her, beaming a charming smile her way. Sam stubbornly faced the front of the classroom. Greg stared into the back of her head, but trying to ignore the guy was like ignoring a blister on your eyeball.

"Hello, Greg," Ashby said with strained cordiality.

Greg gave a curt nod.

"Brooke," Sam yelped, getting up and practically running toward her friend who'd just walked in the door.

"You realize you're making things harder on her, I'm sure," Ashby said as they watched Sam's escape.

Greg couldn't argue with that. He looked around, hoping no one could hear them in the commotion of the classroom.

Ashby's mouth quirked to one side. "Harder on yourself, too. What are you going to do when she morphs and *starts seeing you as she should?*" he said the last bit as if he were referring to vermin.

"And what is that?" Greg asked between clenched teeth, unable to stay quiet any longer.

"Her *Keeper*. Nothing else. I've read up on your caste. You are truly mixed up."

"Are you sure that's all I am to her?"

Ashby's eyes tightened. So he had considered the possibility that Sam's feelings for Greg might not change after her transformation? Still, he said, "I'm positive."

"Yeah? Then how do you explain *me*? What if the same happens to her?" Something had gone wrong with Greg's metamorphosis. All his hopes were riding on the same thing happening to Sam.

"You're an aberration, a freak of nature. The chances of that are one in a million."

Greg's nostrils flared. He had to make a conscious effort not to beat the guy to a pulp on the first day of school. Instead he cracked his neck and went for a little venom.

"So if she isn't like me, how come she's . . . reciprocating?"

"She's just confused and you're taking advantage of that. Nothing else," Ashby said, going red in the face, his voice edging close to anger. "It's not the Morphid way. Not the right way."

"The right way? I personally like the idea of having free will and not a single-track mind driven by mindless instincts."

"But of course you do. You grew up mostly among *Humans*," he spat the word out. "You probably don't even know that the divorce rate for Morphids is zero, that children grow up with loving parents who are always around, that husbands and wives don't cheat, that there are no crimes of passion . . ."

Greg felt like the guy could go on and on listing reasons why Morphids, with their perfectly mapped out destinies, were better than humans. All Greg knew, though, was that if Ashby kept spewing words in that irritating English accent, Greg would be the one committing a crime of passion—one on which prissy, metro boys got their head ripped off clean.

"Yeah, like perfect, little trained monkeys," Greg snapped. "Spare me the lecture, okay? Look, man. I wish I wasn't . . . broken or whatever. You're right, things would be a lot easier for me, but it is what it is. If it makes you feel any better, I'm . . ." He searched for Sam, who was now trying to keep Brooke from walking their way. "I'm sorry."

Ashby nodded slowly, seeming to reappraise him. "Fair enough," he said. "We'll just have to wait and see."

"Well, well," Brooke said, looking from Greg to Ashby. "Aren't you a lucky girl, Sammy?"

Sam stood behind Brooke, pulling her by the arm and wincing.

"But much too selfish, I should say," Brooke continued undeterred. She turned to Sam. "You have got to tell me where you find them."

Sam turned a new shade of red and muttered a curse under her breath, one Brooke had no trouble ignoring.

Greg smiled, a light bulb coming to life in his head. "Sam, where are your manners?" Yes, he'd just apologized to the guy, but this was war, after all. "Brooke, let me introduce you to Ashby. He's . . . British, quite the worldly man. Seems to know everything about fashion and hair salons . . . apparently."

Ashby self-consciously took a hand to his newly cropped hair. It was obvious someone had gotten to work on his appearance, and with a vengeance. In Greg's opinion, the look was too much for any self-respecting guy, but it was obvious the female population appreciated it. For a second, even Sam seemed to cast an indulgent look his way. Greg swallowed through the bile burning his throat.

Brooke sat down at the desk in front of Ashby. She batted her eyelashes. "Nice to meet you, Ashby."

Eyes like daggers shot in Greg's direction. He shrugged. If Ashby could play games, he could, too. Although he had the terrible feeling that in this match, he was the underdog.

ఇ Chapter 29 ಲ
Sam

On the second week of school, Sam barely managed to pull her cold feet out of bed. Halfheartedly, her toes searched the floor for her bunny slippers and found them. She tried to slip her feet inside, but they slid away. A curse brewed in her throat, but didn't come out. Her exhaustion was too much, even for a simple four-letter word. She'd had a terrible night, lying awake until midnight, uttering oaths against Ashby, Greg, Brooke and . . . herself. School had been awful since the very first day, when Ashby showed up like a knight in shining Armani.

His presence sickened her. Not in a simple nauseating kind of way, but in a heart wrenching and confounding-emotional-roller-coaster one. She couldn't stand the way he looked at her, or how he always tried to find excuses to get close and talk—no matter how much she pushed him away.

I wish he'd never come along.

It was a common thought for her, but one that never failed to produce a strange void in her chest. She put a hand to her breastbone and growled in frustration as the unwanted emotion assaulted her. She liked Greg, not Ashby! The moment Greg kissed her at the party, she'd made up her mind. The way she felt every time she remembered his lips on hers was too strong and real to deny.

Ashby only made her feel guilty and powerless and mean. The business with him was different, a compulsion that at times felt normal, but for the most part felt absolutely wrong on principle. She hated how it altered her moods and feelings, like she had split personality disorder. Lunacy was a mild term to describe her state of mind, and it was all Ashby's fault. All of it. At least now, Greg's initial hot-cold behavior made sense. Clearly, he'd been battling the same demons.

"Damn it!" She punched her pillow. Cursing and hitting stuff had become a common way to release her frustration. She wanted to clear her head, run away to some frigid land where frostbite, and not all this mess, was the only concern on her mind. And to top it all off, today she felt sick.

Great. Just great!

With unsteady steps, she walked out of her room toward the only bathroom in the small two-bedroom apartment. But no matter how small the place, she was glad James and Rose let her stay after summer break ended. Relieved to find the bathroom empty, she closed the door and pressed her back against it, hand fumbling with the lock. She felt as if she'd just crossed the English Channel—not just the narrow hall. How was she going to get through the day if she felt this bad already?

The second half of her night had consisted of intermittent dreams of light, troubled sleep, and groggy wakefulness. Aches and pains made the bed feel as comfy as a bumpy stretch of highway. With her eyes shut, she inhaled deeply and wished for the flu. *It has to be the flu,* she thought, denying the growing suspicion in the back of her mind.

Sam could almost hear her eyelids slide open when she cast a frightful gaze toward the mirror on the medicine cabinet. She didn't want to look at herself, afraid to find the reflection of a stranger.

That's stupid. That's not the way it works.

Greg had said she would feel sick at first, and once it started, the process would take two weeks or so. Still, she was scared to look. She wasn't ready for that. She never would be.

"'Morning, Sam," Rose said from the other side of the door.

Sam jumped. *What am I gonna do?* How was she going to hide this from James and especially Rose, who never missed a thing. Greg had been trying to explain a plan of his, but she'd been living in denial, shutting him down as soon as he mentioned it.

"Are you all right in there?" Rose asked when Sam didn't answer.

"I'm fine," Sam croaked. She cleared her throat. "I think I may be coming down with something," she added.

"Oh no! A summer cold?"

"Maybe . . ."

"Do you need me to call the school so you have an excuse?"

"No, no! Uh, I have a quiz and a paper to turn in. I'll see how I feel in a little bit." There was no way she could go through this without Greg. She desperately needed to talk to him.

"Your call. Look in the medicine cabinet. There's some cold stuff in there," Rose said, walking away.

Inhaling again, Sam approached the medicine cabinet and warily scanned her face on the mirror. She looked terrible. Nothing like the Malibu Barbie Greg kept talking about. *More like Little Orphan Annie after a week of sleeping under a bridge.* Sam huffed.

Tentatively, she took her hand to the back of her neck. She hesitated, then ran her fingers down her cranium. Brushing her skin lightly, she traced the path of her spine. Her hand froze, and her eyes went wide with horror, pupils shrinking to a pin prick.

No. She shook her head, grasping the sink with both hands, leaning into it with a nauseating pressure in the pit of her stomach.

It's true. It's all *true.* She couldn't pretend any longer. Greg and Ashby weren't crazy, no one had conceived an evil plot against her, and no *Punk'd* crew was lurking around ready to jump out and tell her it was all a joke. There was something on her back. Some kind of . . . bump. Right where Greg said it would be. She didn't dare turn to look at it. How much time did she have before . . . ? She couldn't remember what Greg had said, not as confusion smothered her thoughts like a thick layer of gauze.

Well, she couldn't sit around and wait until her antennae grew. She had to get out of here before someone found out what was happening, and she ended up in a research lab like some rare mutant insect. Hiding was her only option. She had to find Greg. After she morphed, she would . . . she would what? No one would recognize her. James and Rose would think she'd gone missing.

Without showering or even brushing her teeth, she left the bathroom. Robe wrapped tightly around her, Sam tiptoed across the hall. Only Wassily noticed her and tried to lick her ankles as she passed by. "Good doggie." She held a hand in front of his face to stop him from entering her bedroom. She donned a pair of faded jeans, a white top, and a pair of black leather flats. Once she was ready, she tried to sneak through the front door, but Rose caught her.

"What about breakfast?" she asked.

"Not hungry." Sam looked up only for a brief instant and continued her escape plan.

She was halfway out the door when Rose appeared and grabbed her arm. "Sam," she said in a tone that seemed to say, "You don't fool me." Sam turned reluctantly. Rose examined her face, pursing her lips, then released her arm. "What's the matter?"

"Nothing, I'm fine." Her answer was rushed and unconvincing.

"You don't look well at all. I think you should stay home."

"I'm okay."

"Feeling any . . . *nausea*?" Rose asked, raising one eyebrow.

It took Sam a few seconds to realize what Rose was actually asking. "Oh God, no," she said horrified, once Rose's meaning became clear. "I've never even . . . forget it."

She had just recently kissed a boy for the first time in her life, and that had been complicated enough. Going further had certainly been an option, but luckily, Greg was a gentleman. If he wasn't, she'd have had a nervous breakdown by now. Her conflicting emotions toward Ashby combined with the stress of taking *that* step would have been too much to bear.

"You know you can trust me, right?" Rose added with more maternal love in her voice than Barbara had ever mustered in all Sam's life.

"I know. It's nothing like that. I just didn't sleep well, and . . . maybe I caught a virus that's been making its rounds at school. I'll sign out of class if I don't feel well later."

"Promise?"

"Promise."

Feeling the nausea that she had so adamantly denied, Sam made it to school in Rose's car. As soon as she parked, she spotted Greg waiting for her. He looked anxious, and hurried to open her door.

"Is everything all right?" he asked as Sam stepped out. "Oh," Greg exclaimed as soon as he took a good look at her. "I sensed something was up, but I didn't think . . ."

She pulled her hair and shirt to one side to show him her neck. Greg understood her silent question.

He squeezed her hand. "Yeah, it's starting."

Sam swallowed. "What do we do? How long do we have? What do we tell everyone?" She had a million questions, things she should have been discussing with Greg all along, instead of pretending it would all go away.

"Well, I've been thinking about it. We have a few choices. We could tell Rose and James what's happening and—"

"Are you crazy?!" Sam interrupted. "I can't tell them. They won't understand. They'll . . . they'll flip out and send me to a military research facility or something. No, no way."

"Okay, we could drive to my parents' house in New Orleans. They wouldn't freak out or hand you to the government," Greg joked with a meek smile.

"What do we tell Rose and James?"

"Nothing," Greg said.

"You mean just run away?"

"Yes. I seriously doubt they'd let you go on a road trip with me. I can call them and at least tell them you're all right. Unless you can think of some excuse that would convince them to let you go."

They would probably lock her up if she even hinted at it. She shook her head hopelessly. "If we just run away, they'll look for us, Greg. Your parents will be the first ones they'll ask."

"They would lie, of course. They can say they haven't seen us."

"I don't know, Greg. What if we get them in trouble? Kidnapping is a federal crime. Have you thought about that?"

He nodded. "All I know is they'd take that risk for us. They'd help us no matter what."

"No. It's too much to ask of them. What else can we do?" Sam felt a sudden twist in her gut that almost dropped her to the pavement. Sweat ran down her neck, and her eyelids felt as if they'd been glued to her eyeballs.

"I—I don't know."

Sam coughed. "What if we find a hotel somewhere and crash there until it's over?

"I doubt anyone would rent us a room . . . being minors and all."

"What about hiding in your car?" Sam's desperation mounted.

"For two weeks? With our faces plastered all over the news? No. Someone could spot us. I can't take that risk. Not with you being in such a . . . vulnerable state."

Sam grabbed her head and squeezed. The pounding made it hard to concentrate, but even through the haze she could see none of the options were solid.

"It's no good," she moaned. "Even if we pull it off, what will we do afterward? I'll be . . . unrecognizable . . . right?"

"There's another option," a voice said behind them.

Sam peered over Greg's shoulder. Ashby stood there, looking calm and collected. Her gaze snapped back to Greg, who was standing close enough to reveal the sunburst patterns in his blue eyes. He blinked slowly and looked down in defeat. It was as if he'd been expecting this.

"We don't need your help, Ashby," Sam said in a scratchy voice. She leaned forward and took Greg's hand for support.

Ashby pursed his lips and stuffed a hand in his pocket. "I wouldn't be so quick to turn me down. There are no risks in my option. No one will look for you, and no one will question why you've changed so much, once it's over." He coolly took a few steps forward and sat on the hood of Sam's car.

"You're lying," Sam said, but she wasn't so sure.

"Am I?" Ashby asked, almost indifferently. He looked up at the sky and inhaled as if enjoying the morning. The school bell rang, announcing their first class. He looked back and examined Sam's face, black eyes sparkling with something like victory. "Your transformation is imminent. I can tell." Ashby's tone switched into a caring, gentle one. "You don't have very long before it starts, Sam. You shouldn't even be here. Please, let me help you."

"Greg?" Sam searched his gaze, but there was only pain there—not the answer she was hoping for.

"Tell her, Greg. You're doing her a disservice—always seems that way, as a matter of fact."

A chill traveled like a wave from Sam's head down to her toes, making her every bone and muscle ache, like she was at the brink of shattering into a billion pieces. She staggered, but Greg held her steady.

"We'll figure something out on our own." Sam squeezed Greg's hand weakly. Standing firm, physically and mentally, took every drop of resolve she had, but she'd made her decision. "Let's go." She tugged Greg's hand, but he didn't budge. "What's wrong?" She didn't need him making things any harder for her.

"I think we should . . . listen to his offer," Greg mumbled.

"What?!" Sam couldn't believe it.

He blinked his eyes closed as the painful words came out. "I don't know how to keep you safe, Sam." His voice was hoarse. He was giving her up, letting her go for her own sake.

"Greg!" She threw her arms around his neck, nearly losing her balance in the process. He hugged her, holding her up against his hard, heaving chest.

He was being selfless, entirely pure. He loved her. Of his own free will, against his Morphid nature. Not because of a sick obligation he couldn't overcome. What if she wasn't able to do the same once she morphed? The thought was searing, like a hot poker to her heart.

Sam was dimly aware of Ashby sliding off the car, but she couldn't care less. Why didn't he just go away? She held Greg tighter and shut the rest of the world out.

Greg's warm breath brushed her ear as he begged, "It's for the best."

She shook her feverish head, cheek brushing against the cool skin of Greg's neck.

"No," she whimpered. This couldn't be the end of the immense passion brimming inside her chest. She didn't want to let it go. She couldn't.

Greg gently grabbed her by the shoulders and pushed away, pain in his wavering eyes. "You have to."

Sam shook her head more vigorously now, causing her vision to blur and ears to ring. Her temples were pounding.

"If you . . . if you feel the same way I . . ." He couldn't finish. "Do it for me, please." His voice was but a whisper.

"It's not fair."

"I know." It was least fair for Greg.

"I—I can't." Tears rolled down her cheeks, cool against her flushed skin.

Greg smiled weakly and cupped her face in his big hands, running both thumbs across her cheeks to wipe away the tears. Suddenly, the tender look in his eyes changed to one of panic.

"You're burning up," he said, noticing for the first time.

He turned his searching eyes in Ashby's direction, but he wasn't there anymore. "Where did he go?"

Greg looked around, eyes frantic. "Hey!" he yelled when he spotted Ashby walking away. "Wait here. We'll go to my place, and we'll hear his idea."

Without waiting for an answer, Greg ran, calling out Ashby's name. When he reached him, Ashby ignored him and kept walking. Sam watched from a distance, feeling worse by the second. Greg put a hand on Ashby's shoulders and tried to stop him. Ashby turned abruptly, placed both hands on Greg's chest and shoved hard. Greg stumbled backward, at the same time that another wave of nausea hit Sam in the pit of her stomach. She choked, bile rising to her mouth.

Through hazy eyes, she saw Greg and Ashby arguing. She wanted to call out for them to stop, but her voice was gone. Unsteadily, she turned around and slumped against the car, head swimming. The sky overhead, or actually the whole world, lost its color. Everything went very pale, then gray, and finally dark. She knew she was still standing, and not falling through a black hole, because she could feel herself wobbling and knew the pitted surface of the asphalt under her feet was waiting to smash her face.

"Greg," she managed in a choppy breath. Then the ground rushed up to meet her. Or maybe it was the other way around.

෨ Chapter 30 ෬
Greg

In a flash, Greg was there and caught Sam before she hit the ground. He cradled her neck in the crook of his arm and caressed her face.

"Sam, Sam!" His first instinct was to pull out his cell phone to call 911, but that wasn't an option. Looking around desperately, he found Ashby standing behind him. He didn't look worried at all. Quite the contrary. He seemed to be almost salivating, a grin stretched from ear to ear like a kid waiting for his favorite cookies to finish baking.

Without letting go of Sam, Greg pulled the car keys out of her pants pocket. He craned his neck to peek over the hood and make sure no one had noticed her fainting.

"Here, drive," Greg said.

Ashby looked at the keys as if they were a Chinese puzzle. "I, uh . . ."

Greg grew impatient. "Okay, open the back door then."

"You'd better start the car. Someone's coming," Ashby said, quickly opening the door.

"Take her!" Greg let Ashby slide an arm under her limp neck.

They exchanged a quick, hostile stare, then Ashby lifted Sam into the back seat, while Greg got behind the wheel. He cranked the engine and spared a backward glance. Ashby had laid Sam across the seat, her head resting on his lap. He gently brushed away matted hair from her forehead. Jealousy ripped at Greg's soul, but there was no time for that. They had to get away.

Greg shifted into gear and looked around, wondering who had spotted them, but no one was in sight. He clenched the wheel, making the leather creak, and shot an accusing glance into the rearview mirror. Ashby smirked. White-knuckled hands turned the wheel and drove them out of there.

When they arrived at Greg's place, they managed to unload Sam without being seen.

"Which way?" Ashby asked as they walked into the empty living room. He cradled Sam in his arms as he would a treasure.

Greg slammed the front door shut and ran ahead of Ashby. "Over here." He led them into his bedroom. "Lay her on the bed. I'll call my mom."

"Fine . . . if you never intend to lie on it again," Ashby mumbled.

Greg fumed. Did Ashby think he gave a damn about the stupid bed? He dialed his mom's cell phone, and it began to ring. If he didn't like Ashby's plan, he'd drive Sam to New Orleans. He couldn't risk anyone finding them here. It would be the first place they'd look, once they realized they were both missing.

"Is everything all right?" Mom asked without saying hello. It was unusual for him to call during school hours.

"Mom, she's morphing . . ."

"And what's your mum going to do?" Ashby added sarcastically. "Stop it?"

Greg seethed silently as Ashby sat next to Sam and held her hand. "We brought her to my place."

"We? Who's we?" Mom asked.

"Ashby's here."

"Oh." Greg had told his parents about Ashby, and although he hadn't mentioned anything about his feelings for Sam, they had at least figured he hated Ashby.

"Mom would it—" Ashby had his hands on Sam. "Hey! What are you doing?"

Ashby didn't flinch and continued unbuttoning Sam's delicate white top. "We have to undress her." Ashby rolled his eyes.

"Don't touch her, you perv!" He felt a burning indignation rising from his neck up to his face.

"Greg, what's the matter? What's going on?" Mom asked.

"Mom, I just want to ask you something. If I can't figure out a way to keep her safe, can I bring her to New Orleans?"

Ashby's hands stopped on the second button, turning disapproving eyes on Greg.

"Of course you can, honey. You didn't even have to ask. We'd do anything for you."

"Thank you, Mom. I have to go now, but I'll call you later." He hung up.

Ashby turned his attention to Sam's shirt once more.

"Stop right there." Greg pulled Ashby away from Sam.

Yes, they needed to undress her, maybe put her in the tub—morphing was a messy business, not that he knew from experience—but they weren't doing any of that until Ashby explained his plan.

"What's your plan?" Greg demanded.

"Oh, yes. The plan. Like I said, it will be easy. Perry will take care of everything."

"Who?"

"Perry, my . . . friend. You met him," Ashby said the last sentence with some difficulty.

Greg wondered why Ashby had hesitated on the term *friend.* Suspicion rose in him, and his first thought was of Veridan. Was that who he was referring to? Then, noticing Ashby's chagrined expression, Greg remembered the other guy on the day of his would-be first kiss with Sam.

"Oh, the guy that was with you the day of your executive board meeting."

Ashby's upper lip curled up, making the comment worthwhile. He didn't respond.

Bring it on, thought Greg. Sam wasn't here to save him from a beating. After a moment, Ashby exhaled and simply left the room. Greg followed him out.

"So what about this *friend?*" Greg's patience was dissolving quickly. "What's he going to do?"

Ashby faced him again. "*Perry* can prepare an incantation for Sam's family. They'll simply forget about her until he casts a counter spell."

For a moment, Greg wanted to laugh, but Ashby appeared quite serious. Greg cleared his throat. "Is that possible?" He had to admit, he had no idea what a Morphid sorcerer could do.

"Quite so. None of the humans in her life wear protective charms, so there's nothing to stop Perry's magic. How do you think I was able to become a student here? Who needs transfer papers when you can use magic to alter people's minds?"

Greg scowled as he considered the lack of scruples it would take to mess with somebody's brain. He wondered, not for the first time, who Ashby really was. From what Greg's parents had told him about Sorcerers, most of them stuck to themselves and rendered their magical services only for a high price. Greg had no doubt Ashby had the money to afford paying someone to do his dirty work, but the way he'd said *friend* seemed to indicate some deeper secret. He pushed these thoughts aside and concentrated on the priority: Sam.

"Could he make her dad call the school to tell them Sam has the measles, or is on a family trip or something?" Greg didn't want Sam to miss the school year for truancy. She would be very upset if she had to delay going to culinary school one more year.

"Sure."

"Good. And when it's all over, he can . . . cast another spell so people can recognize her?"

"I suppose."

"Can he put a spell on the whole school?"

"What for?"

"For when she goes back." *You idiot!*

Ashby laughed a weak little laugh and looked at Greg with irritating condescension. "She won't need to go back. She'll come with me then."

"That's a huge assumption you're making."

"Is it?" His smile grew wider and more satisfied.

Greg felt his whole body quake on the spot. He wanted to erase the little bastard's self-assured grin. He wanted to punch him until the brat's ears bled. But the jerk was right. If Sam's metamorphosis went off without a hitch, she would do just what Ashby had said. He, himself, had gotten out of New Orleans like a madman to find his Integral, hadn't he? Of course, Sam would follow hers, whether she wanted to or not. And if she left . . . what would he do?

His Morphid side gave him the answer right away. "If that's the case, I'm coming with her," Greg said resolutely.

"Oh, but you haven't been invited."

"She needs me to keep her safe."

"I can do that myself," Ashby said arrogantly.

"Can you?" One thing Greg knew was that no one could keep Sam safer than he could. Defending her from harm was now his sole purpose in life. "I'm her Keeper. I know when she's in danger. I've saved her life twice. Where were *you* when she needed help?"

Ashby's face twisted in shock. He frowned, eyes wandering over the carpet as if he could find the thread of his thoughts there. His next words took Greg by surprise.

"You're a worthy Keeper then, and I thank you. I would very much like to hear what happened and how you saved her." Ashby gave a slight head bow, increasing the awkwardness of the moment twofold.

Greg was speechless. The guy was such an oddball.

"If you don't mind, of course," Ashby added when Greg didn't respond.

"I can tell you about the first instance," Greg finally said, realizing he might learn something about his suspicions of Ashby. "I'll leave it up to her to tell you about the second."

Drawing his eyebrows together, Ashby regarded Greg suspiciously. "Why is that?" he asked.

"Because . . ." Ashby could think whatever he wanted. Hopefully, he would imagine something torturous.

Relenting, Ashby held up his hands. "All right, share what you will."

Greg measured his words and watched Ashby's face for the smallest reaction. "Someone tried to kill her. I was there and managed to prevent it."

Ashby staggered back in disbelief. "What?! Kill her?! I thought you were referring to an accident or something."

To Greg, Ashby seemed genuinely surprised, but considering what little he knew of him, his suspicion stood.

"Who would have something against her?" Ashby's surprise left his face, which tightened in concentration, as if he were considering a known possibility.

Greg didn't like his expression at all. "Yeah, I thought you might know something about it."

Ashby looked up at him, defensive. "Why? What makes you think I would?"

"I don't know. Kinda makes sense."

Ashby said nothing.

"It was a Sorcerer, and he wasn't shy about using his magic in plain view. He said he wanted Sam dead. He said his name was Veridan. Heard of him?"

"Veridan?" The name escaped Ashby's mouth like an involuntary hiss.

"Ah, so he *is* from your neck of the woods. Maybe even a *friend* of yours?"

Instead of answering, Ashby started pacing. His breathing sped up, making him look more anxious than an expectant father. "That can't be."

"Who is he? Tell me!" Greg demanded, but Ashby was lost in his own thoughts, thoughts that seemed to race across his forehead like bullet trains. Ashby knew who Veridan was, but this was also an unexpected development.

"I should go." Ashby suddenly walked to the door.

"Whoa, whoa, stop right there, man." Greg blocked his path. "You're not leaving until you tell me what the hell is going on."

"We don't have time for this. I need to find Perry, so he can get to work on Sam's parents."

"I'm not stupid, dude. Something's going on. You know this Veridan guy, don't deny it. If you want to help me protect her, you need to tell me now."

"You're mistaken. I don't know this person."

"Bull crap," Greg sneered.

"We're wasting time," Ashby said emphatically. "Perry needs to set to work. You should put Sam in the tub, and I need to . . ."

"You're holding back," Greg accused him. "You know what? Never mind. Deal's off. Clearly, there's something you care more about than Sam. Suit yourself." He stepped away from the door. "I can take care of her without holding *anything* back. I guess we can't say the same thing about you."

Hesitating with his hand on the door knob, Ashby stared at the floor. Greg watched him intently, sensing the internal struggle, watching his hands shake. After a deep breath, Ashby turned the knob and left without a word.

Greg locked the door, wishing he could shut the entire world away. He went back into the bedroom and stared at Sam. Her skin was covered in a thin, transparent sheen. Her face was losing shape under a coat of the viscous material that coated her entire body. Her chest wasn't moving, and her utter stillness almost sent him into a panic. Determined to stay calm, he set to work. Kneeling in front of the bed, he undressed her carefully, peeling off her shirt, pants and everything else. The clothes came off with a wet sound, pulling gooey strands away from her skin. When he started to pick her up, the sheet clung to her back. He peeled it away and threw it on the floor. He carried her into the bathroom and carefully set her down inside the tub.

The sight of her pale, naked body against the cold surface was just too much. She looked so helpless, like a newborn thrown into a strange new world. He wanted to get a blanket to cover her, but this was what she needed. Gently, he stroked her hair.

"Sam," he whispered. Even through her hair, she felt impossibly hot.

Two weeks were going to be a very long time. The uncertainty would kill him. What if she woke up a stranger to the feelings they'd shared? He looked at her bare body without emotion, purely as a protective Keeper. He understood that—from now on, if he planned to survive—that's the way it should be. He would still see her, but as if from the corner of his eye, trying to spare his heart the agony of her unavailability, of her love for someone else. Maybe it was time to embrace his Morphid side. Sam might not be the same person in a couple of weeks. If he didn't brace himself, it would tear him apart.

But what if she was the same? What if she still cared for him? He shook his head. He was fooling himself. For a moment, he wished he could kill the hope that nestled deep in his soul. Still, his passion took a stronger hold. He didn't understand how he could feel so deeply when half of his heart kept screaming it was wrong to love her? How much bigger would his love be if he had a whole heart to love her?

The word *epic* came to mind.

ℬ Chapter 31 ℭ
Sam

At first, the sound was faint. *Rap, rap, rap*—maybe someone knocking on the door. The tapping gradually became a pounding. It seemed impossible no one could hear it.

Will someone answer the blasted door? It felt like a dream. Sam struggled to wake up. A furious voice finally helped her break through the gelatinous unconsciousness that weighed on her brain. *I know that voice.* Her eyes sprang open.

"What the hell's the matter with you? Do you want the neighbors to call the police?" It was Greg. Her Greg.

"What took you so long?" a different voice asked. "And what are you doing dressed like that?" Threat and suspicion brimmed in this question.

"I was taking a shower, you moron."

Sam looked around, taking in her unfamiliar surroundings. With a jolt, she sat up.

"Greg," she called out in alarm.

She jerked a hand to her throat. *My voice.* She sounded all femme fatale, smooth and mature. Panicked, she tried to stand, but stumbled on legs that felt as if they belonged to a stork. She started to fall and closed her eyes. *This is gonna hurt.* Then Greg was at her side, catching her, keeping her safe. Her eternal savior. He gently helped her sit on the bed.

"You're awake," he said, sitting next to her, an arm around her shoulder.

She sighed. It was such a relief to see those blue eyes. He looked at her anxiously as if asking a desperate question. The answer to what he wanted to know hung from her lips, but Sam was distracted, too baffled by the fact that she didn't have to look up at him anymore. *I must be six feet tall*, she thought incredulously.

Her eyes slid from Greg's face to his naked chest. It was smooth and muscular. She blinked. He was wearing nothing but a white towel around his waist.

"Sam, I asked you a question," someone barked from the doorway.

Reluctantly, she extricated her gaze from Greg's breathtaking torso and looked up at the source of the intruding voice. *Oh great, Ashby's here.* She frowned.

"Is your mark defined yet?" he demanded.

Her answer was another frown. *What the hell is he talking about?*

"No, it isn't," Greg snapped. "She just woke up . . . for the first time." He sounded disappointed and hopeful at the same time.

Ashby made no attempt to disguise his displeasure.

"I've changed?" Sam asked in a whisper. She was afraid to speak too loudly and be freaked out by her new voice again.

"Not completely," Ashby complained.

Sam scowled at Ashby. *What a pain in the ass. Clearly, morphing didn't make him seem likable. Good!*

"He means there's one final step left," Greg explained. "Remember? Your body changes first, then your mind." He finished the sentence with a wistful air.

"Oh," Sam said. So much had changed, yet nothing had changed. "When, then. . . ?"

"Any time, now." Ashby seemed to overflow with impatience.

What if she skipped the next part? Was that possible? It wouldn't be wrong if only her body changed and her mind remained her own, would it? Maybe that would be freaky or unheard of, but she felt fine the way she was, like she was still herself—at least her mind did.

"Is there a mirror?" she asked, suddenly eager to know just how unlike herself she had become.

"In the bathroom. Come with me." Greg stood up, keeping one hand around her shoulder and the other one on the towel at his waist.

"I'll take her," Ashby said. "Go put on some clothes."

For a moment, Greg looked as if he would object, but then removed his arm, leaving Sam with a feeling of loss and abandonment.

"I'd rather go with Greg," she blurted out. She spoke her mind, but her body protested with a pang in her chest. She dismissed the odd sensation.

Ashby patiently stepped aside. He was content to bide his time until the final battle. Fate was on his side. All he had to do was wait, right? If only she could defy fate. She wished it with all her heart.

She looked at Greg and made a point of feeling his arm around her, of memorizing his handsome profile from this exact angle. They walked together across the hall and into the bathroom. When she saw her image in the mirror, her mouth gaped.

"I told you," Greg said, leaning close to whisper into her ear. He stood behind her and only his closeness, his warmth along the length of her body, convinced her that the astonishing woman looking back was real. He was so near that not even the astounding image of her new self could distract her from this intimacy.

"Look at yourself." Greg lifted a hand and pushed back the hair that rested on her right shoulder.

Sam did as he said. Tracing her altered features with the tips of her fingers, she attempted to dispel her incredulity. This really was her. Her hair was longer and lustrous, and its once-flat brown color now burst with reddish highlights that no beauty salon would be able to recreate. The childlike roundness of her face was replaced by angular, yet feminine, features. Her eyes remained the same shade of honey, but now they appeared golden, even iridescent.

Engrossed by her face, Sam's hands subconsciously travelled downward. Her neck seemed to go on forever before she reached her chest. She wore an old black t-shirt with golden letters that read "New Orleans Saints NFC Champions." She smiled faintly, remembering that Greg wore it all the time. She wrapped her hands around herself, shrugged and smelled her shoulder. The fabric still carried his scent. As she hugged her torso tighter, she also discovered she wasn't the same flat-chested girl she had once been. She smiled, delighted and bashful at the same time. Letting her fingers travel further down, she discovered a narrow waist. All this, in a matter of days!

"Greg," she turned around, eyes wide. "How long did this take? What about Rose and James? And school? Oh my God!"

"Relax, relax. Everything's okay. Come, are you hungry? I can fix you a peanut butter sandwich while I explain everything. Go to the kitchen, I'll be right there."

She obeyed him without protest and found Ashby sitting on the countertop next to the stove. When she approached, he lifted his gaze from the floor and offered her a meek smile. Feeling awkward, Sam pulled the waistband of her pants up. They were sliding off. She may be as tall as Greg, but she certainly wasn't as wide. Blood rising to her face, she tried not to think of how she'd gotten dressed in those clothes.

"So, a peanut butter sandwich sounds good?" Greg asked. He was still getting dressed as he walked out of the bedroom. In one fluid motion, he stuffed his sinewy arms inside a black t-shirt and pulled it over his head. He was barefoot, wearing black jeans that were frayed at the bottom.

"Sure," Sam said.

"No problem."

Greg started making a sandwich.

Sam didn't wait to ask, "So how long was I out?"

"Sixteen days," Greg said as he opened the refrigerator and poured milk into a red disposable cup.

"What?!" Sam coughed, her throat feeling a little raw. "Sixteen days?"

"You have nothing to worry about," Ashby put in, hopping off the counter.

"I wouldn't say that." Greg frowned at Ashby as he handed her the food.

Sam took a gulp of the cold milk. It felt great sliding down into her empty stomach. "Why not?"

"Well," both Greg and Ashby started.

"One at a time, please." Sam looked back and forth between them.

"Go ahead, *Mr. Regent*," Greg said sarcastically.

Mr. Regent? Sam blinked, but said nothing.

Ashby gave him an acid once-over, then turned to Sam. "Rose, James and even Barbara received a visit from my friend Perry. He made all three of them forget that you even exist . . . temporarily, of course," he added when Sam seemed about to protest. "At school, everyone thinks you are in Europe with your father."

"So, I guess now we can tell everyone that the French have amazing plastic surgery techniques that work overnight," Sam joked sarcastically.

"That won't be necessary. I doubt you'll want to bother with anyone here, once your transformation is complete," Ashby said, conceit dripping from his voice.

Anger bubbled up inside Sam. She put the milk and sandwich down on the small peninsula that separated the empty breakfast nook from the kitchen. "Just so you know," she growled, walking toward Ashby and waving a long finger at him, "I hope you're wrong. The last thing I want to be is some mindless zombie. I like who I am, and I like making my own decisions." She was beyond caring if Ashby was hurt by her words. This might not be his fault, but she was sick of his smug, arrogant attitude.

"I'm sorry you feel that way," Ashby said calmly. "But it's your nature, and once your mind has fully matured, you will feel differently. Everything will be as it should."

"I wouldn't be so sure about that," Greg disagreed. Turning to Sam, he made things plain. "His plans are to take you away with him."

"What? No way. I'm not going anywhere with you." She went to stand next to Greg. Ashby simply shrugged.

"And not just that. He's hiding something," Greg added.

"I'm not hiding anything," Ashby protested.

"Well, something smells rotten. He knows the guy who attacked us, and he's denying it."

"The guy at the gas station?!" Sam exclaimed.

"Yes. Conveniently enough, the *future Regent* here also knows a Sorcerer who goes by the name 'Veridan.' Turns out he works for Ashby's mother, the current *Regent* no less. But his *mummy* says they had nothing to do with the attack, and this moron believes her. *I* don't. How common is the name *Veridan*?"

"Quite common among Morphids, actually," Ashby said. "The Regency is not in the business of hurting anyone. On the contrary, we help our kind. Besides, Veridan is under my mother's command and she has nothing against Sam. It would be absolutely ludicrous of you to think the Regency is involved. My mother—"

"Wait a minute. What's all this 'Regent' mess?" Sam interrupted.

Greg explained for her. "Regents are like Morphid royalty. They lead the governing council, make sure our existence remains a secret, keep historical archives and stuff like that."

"You mean you're the future . . . head of some Morphid council?" Sam felt really confused.

"Yes. My caste marks me as a Regent. I'll inherit the post from my mother, Regent Danata. As my wife, you'll be there to help me ensure the safety of our kind," Ashby proclaimed with pride.

A fit of roaring laughter came over her. This was too much. "Me? Your wife?" Sam managed to say between choppy breaths.

Greg grinned, though it didn't reach his eyes.

Ashby, for his part, looked less than amused. "Why is that so funny?" he asked, looking half mad and half embarrassed.

"There must be some mistake," Sam said, trying to regain her composure. "If you're like Morphid royalty, shouldn't you be pestering some exotic princess somewhere? Won't your mother be disappointed all you got is a *plebeian*?"

For the shortest instant, Ashby looked taken aback, as if he'd never considered this. "You . . . you don't even know who you are, who your real parents are. It's quite possible your lineage is as good as mine."

Greg blew his cheeks in mockery. "Well, I guess he doesn't do *plebeian*."

Missing the jibe altogether, Ashby went on. "There have been a few occasions throughout history where even the Regent was of common descent. Fate decides what is best for our kind and what is best for us as individuals. The marks spell our jobs out *clearly*." He gave Greg a pointed look.

"Common descent, huh?" Sam shook her head, unable to believe the guy's brazen comments. The worst part was, he was clueless about what he was doing.

"It happened at times when great change was needed. Regent Vessey's Integral turned out to be a peasant girl, she later gave birth to the most powerful and revolutionary Regent Morphids have ever known."

"What are you trying to say?" Sam asked in disgust. "That you need me so I can pop out a snotty heir for you?"

"No, you're distorting my words. That was just an example. But still, forgive me if I fail to see how that's a bad fate for someone of low stature."

In two quick steps, Sam covered the distance to Ashby and slapped him across the face. Her hand throbbed as if from a thousand ant bites. Ashby didn't move, just stared at her, looking shocked and injured. His black eyes were too much to bear. Suddenly, she started trembling all over. She clasped the wrist of her itching hand and controlled herself. *No.* She wasn't going to apologize. Her pride wouldn't suffer at the hands of some rotten, half-baked instinct. He deserved it.

"Before I turn into a puppet," she said with slow measured words, "you should know that no matter who the hell you are, I hate the idea of suffering from some sick infatuation for an arrogant jerk like you. I want to be free to decide my own path, where to go, what to do with my life, and who to love. And if I make a mistake, so be it, because being led by some instinct like a lamb to the slaughter house is a curse far greater than choosing my own death."

Rage and frustration shook Sam from head to toe. Suddenly, Ashby and the walls behind him stretched far, far away, as if the whole apartment was being pulled from opposite ends. She blinked in slow motion to clear her mind, but when her eyes opened, the room was revolving and she was falling fast. She fought to stay awake, but the weight upon her consciousness was oppressive. A tortured scream escaped her throat. As she drifted away, fear took hold of her heart. She was losing herself, losing Greg, and there was nothing she could do to prevent it.

*   *   *

The compulsion was immediate. It was there the very instant Sam awoke. Even before she opened her eyes, she knew where he would be standing as if she was a compass and he was her magnetic north. She pretended to be asleep for a few moments. There were comings and goings elsewhere in the apartment, like someone pacing impatiently. However, the person who served as her north star was holding vigil in that very room.

Sam let her eyelids slide open slowly. Through her eyelashes, she saw two white tendrils of light extending away from her. Taken aback, she shut her eyes again and held her breath. Was she dreaming? Was it a trick her new eyes were playing on her? Before trying again, she squeezed her eyes tightly shut, then let them spring open all at once. The room came into focus. Nothing strange wafted around her, just the pale brightness of a common, bare light bulb.

"Hello," said an approaching voice. The tone was hesitant and hopeful at the same time.

Sam propped herself up on one elbow and smiled. It was an involuntary gesture which felt genuine in its spontaneity.

"Did you sleep well?"

She nodded and sat up. "How long did I . . . ?" She didn't finish her question. It felt as if she'd been out for days.

"About six hours since the last time you awoke." Ashby sat next to her at the edge of the bed, so close that Sam could feel the exposed skin on her arm tingle from his proximity.

Tentatively, he reached for her hand. As it approached, Sam's heart thudded expectantly. When their fingers intertwined a gasp of satisfaction escaped Ashby's lips. Still as a statue, Sam watched their hands meld into one. An ardent, unnatural heat burned between their skins, and she had to look away.

She stared at the off-white wall in front of her, and for some reason its starkness overwhelmed her. She closed her eyes, and a single tear rolled down her face. It was inexplicable and incongruous with her overwhelming happiness. Gradually, she opened her eyes again, fearing the onslaught of more tears. The faint threads of light were there again. This time she jerked her eyes open, looking around for the source of the luminescence, but they had vanished. It must have been just her imagination, or a momentary side effect of her transformation.

A tall shadow entered her peripheral vision. She tightened her lips, unwilling to look toward the door, unable to face the one who'd come to stand at the threshold.

She stood one inch at a time, untangling her hand from Ashby's. Greg remained still, looking in from the hall. His features were concealed in shadow and by the mass of jet black hair over his forehead. He took a step forward, allowing the light in the bedroom to illuminate his face.

Sam wanted to say something, but there were no words that could make everything right. They looked at each other for only a moment, but it was enough for Sam to know she'd never seen or known pain like the one in his gaze. Without a word, Greg whirled and started to walk away.

"Greg," Sam called out.

He stopped, his back toward her, right hand gripping the door frame. The wood groaned under the pressure of his powerful hand. His arm trembled with tension.

"I wish you two the best," he said in a steady voice that still couldn't hide his heartbreak. And with those words, he left, slamming the front door so hard that the whole apartment rattled.

"Wait!" She took a step forward, but Ashby gripped her wrist.

"Let him go. He'll come to understand." He stood and held her gaze. They looked at each other for several heartbeats. Then, he smiled, eyes glinting with delight.

"You're beautiful," he said, taking a hand to her face, his thumb traveling up from the corner of her mouth to her hairline.

Her legs went weak. Her heart raced. A sharp breath escaped Sam's half-opened mouth. The touch electrified her, making her body quiver, while part of her mind tried to deny the effects. Ashby leaned in, aiming for a kiss. Sam's eyelids slid downward, closing, readying for the moment when their lips would meet. Yet, a small part of her still fought, causing her lashes to flutter with indecision.

In a subtle evasive maneuver, she turned around and blurted out the first thing that came to mind. "I want to look at my mark."

She didn't look at Ashby as she headed for the bathroom. His reaction was easy to imagine, but she wanted no painful confirmation.

"Is it a gray wolf?" she asked, disguising her reluctance with false curiosity.

"Of course, it isn't a gray wolf," Ashby said with irritation. "You're *my* Integral and will rule the Regency with me. Your mark will be a staff to complete my crown."

In front of the medicine cabinet, Sam looked over her shoulder and bared her back. Yes, there was a staff, but . . .

Ashby stopped short at the sight of her mark reflected on the mirror. He narrowed his eyes, grabbed Sam by the shoulders and turned her around.

"W-what . . . ?" he said in a shaky breath.

"What is it?" Anxiety began to mount in Sam's chest.

"You . . . you're a *Dual*." He said the last word as if it were something mythical.

"What does that mean?"

"It means you have two castes. There's a staff," he put a finger on the spot, sending a cold chill across her shoulders. "But the staff is small. The rest is more predominant."

"What is the rest?" She had seen it, but hadn't liked it at all. She wanted him to say it, to tell her what it meant.

"A spider and its web," he said in a shaky tone, only intensifying her fears.

"But what does it mean?"

Ashby removed his finger from her mark and took a step away. She covered her back and skirted around Ashby to exit the claustrophobic bathroom.

He followed into the living room, shaking his head. "I—I don't know what it means." He sounded truly bewildered.

"What do you mean you don't know?"

"I've . . . never seen that mark before."

Frustration bubbled in Sam's chest, threatening to rise. "Never?!"

Ashby searched her face. "You aren't mad at me, are you?" It wasn't even a question. His voice was tender and playful, making light of the strange moment. He seemed unable to believe she could ever be upset with him. "Portos will know. It's nothing to worry about."

Put out like a candle under a snuffer, her tiny flare of anger extinguished and a smile stretched over her lips.

Ashby took her hands in his and squeezed them gently. "Oh, Sam. Now you see what I meant. Do you feel it?"

Her head bobbed up and down of its own accord.

"I knew it would be so. I was foolish to ever think your nature was damaged, that you'd . . . oh never mind. I am *so* happy!"

Before that feeble voice inside her head could prevent it, her lips locked with Ashby's in a smoldering kiss. A passionate moan rose from his throat as he slid his hands under her shirt and up her back. Possessed with minds of their own, her fingers raked through Ashby's hair and pulled him closer with wild, mindless lust.

What are you doing? Stop!

But her body was drunk and deaf to that infinitesimal side of her. The lust was too big to control, too primal to deny. Sam squeezed her eyes and quashed the unsettling thoughts. Ashby pushed, leading her as they kissed. Her back collided with the wall, and she was deliciously trapped between the cold surface and the scorching passion of her pre-destined Integral.

Stop, stop, stop. You don't want this!

Oh, but she did want it. Fervently. The feeling was sublime. Her body tingled with emotion. Why should some small voice in her mind interfere? Why should reason ever come into play when her body knew so well what it wanted?

Ashby buried his face in her neck, tracing random shapes with insistent lips. Giving in completely, Sam slid her hands under

Ashby's shirt. His abdomen tightened at her touch, even as it contracted and expanded with short, agitated breaths. She searched for his lips, kissing from his earlobe down the contour of his jaw. Sam opened her eyes, ready to give her all. He withdrew for a second, catching his breath.

And in that moment, it was Greg's cerulean gaze that she saw, bringing the sweltering emotions to a screeching halt.

Sam retreated, pressing harder into the wall and shutting her eyes again. Ashby didn't miss a beat and went back to kissing her neck, still lost in the throngs of passion, oblivious to Sam's now-tense, unresponsive limbs. Greg's image burned in her memory, the way he had looked when they kissed so passionately in this very place, just a few weeks ago—when *all* of her mind had been as exuberant as her body was now.

This is wrong!

Feeble corners of her brain cried out, but she had to strain to hear them. How could she do this to Greg? He didn't deserve this. All he'd ever done was protect her, help her, care for her.

"What's the matter?" Ashby's caresses had stopped.

"I . . . I was thinking . . ."

"Yes?" His gaze grew dark.

"We should leave." She rushed the words out. If she stayed, she'd only hurt Greg. It wasn't fair to him. Not when her compulsion for Ashby had been so complete, so immediate. She'd lost herself, and whatever part of her still cared for Greg was too small, too easy to ignore. It would soon fade into nothingness.

A twinkle of joy returned to his gaze. "And go where?"

"England."

Ashby laughed, throwing his head back, overjoyed by her decision. He picked her up, whooping as he twirled her around. "She's coming with me! My Sam, my bride, my all."

As the room whirled, involuntary laughter reverberated in her throat. Sam's head spun, dizzy with the movement, but even more so, with the biting realization that her mind was no longer her own. The truth was . . .

She hadn't meant to laugh.

๛ Chapter 32 ๛
Greg

Greg drove around aimlessly to escape the pain, but it stayed with him, like an unbreakable chain tugging on his heart the farther he went. Sam was with Ashby. She had morphed, and that was that. Her feelings for Greg were dead. He squeezed the steering wheel until his hands hurt.

Twice he drove across the Wabash River, from West Lafayette to Lafayette. Finally, he found himself on the Purdue campus, and parked in front of Ross-Ade stadium. The Boilermakers had played a game against Notre Dame, and a few stragglers were still exiting the sports complex.

He got out of the car and leaned against it, arms crossed. It was a clear, cool night, and the stadium lights still shone brightly against the dark September sky. The night was mockingly beautiful.

A car drove by, music blaring from giant speakers. Over the loud rap song, the occupants' excited cheers pierced the air. A hand emerged from one window, madly waving a "Fighting Irish" flag.

"Jerks," a girl called out. She was walking in Greg's direction, drunk and hanging from a friend's shoulder. Her hand went up in the air, gesturing obscenely at the retreating car.

A pang of regret hit Greg. He would never live this life of homecoming parties and drunken euphoria over an inconsequential football game. His life would never be normal.

"We were robbed," the girl yelled, tripping over unsteady feet.

"Shh, be quiet, Jen. You're gonna get us killed," the other girl protested, holding her friend upright.

"I take it we lost?" Greg asked the girls as they passed in front of his car. He was a LSU Tigers fan when it came to college football, but since Sam rooted for the Boilermakers he did too. He hated his unswerving loyalty to her, even in something like football. The sober girl squeaked in alarm. She hadn't noticed Greg, dressed all in black, resting against his equally dark car.

"Yes, we lost," the drunken girl pouted. Without missing a beat, she whirled and walked toward Greg.

"Jen," her friend objected, pulling her by the arm and staring dubiously at Greg.

"Ooh, he's a hottie," Jen said when she took a good look at Greg. "How come I haven't seen you around? I would never forget such a handsome face and awesome bod." She took a hand to Greg's bicep and squeezed.

"I'm sorry," Jen's friend apologized. "She's really drunk." She grabbed Jen by the waist and pulled her away.

Greg shrugged with a weary half-smile.

"C'mon, Jen. Give the guy a break. It's late. We need to get back to the dorm."

"Aw, you're always such a bore, Samantha," Jen complained.

Greg winced. That was the last name he wanted to be reminded of. He looked at the girl who shared Sam's namesake and tried to find a resemblance in her features. Maybe it was his imagination, but her shy, light brown eyes looked like Sam's had before she . . . another painful spasm twisted his insides. How many things had he lost? How many things would never be the same again?

"I can help you get her in the car . . . I mean, if you'd like," Greg offered.

"Oh no, thank you. We're fine," Samantha categorically refused.

Smart girl, thought Greg, unlike her drunk, babbling friend.

"C'mon, Jen." She tugged and Jen lost her already precarious balance. The girl went sprawling, and hit the pavement with a thud.

She pouted and whined like a toddler, while her friend stared in exasperation. At a different time, Greg would have laughed, but no cheerfulness was left in him now.

Without asking again for permission, he crouched and picked up the girl. The moaning quickly switched to cooing. "Oh, how strong you are," she said. "Just the way I like."

Greg headed toward the only other car left in the parking area. "Open the door," he directed Samantha.

Wariness registered in her eyes. She clicked her remote anyway. The locks popped as she walked toward the driver's door. Jen clung to his neck like a baby monkey, and he had no difficulty opening the door for himself. He deposited her into the seat and peeled her arms off his neck, over her giggling protests. He pressed the door shut against her octopus arms, but Jen was apparently too wasted to mastermind an escape.

"Make sure you buckle her up," he advised, circling to Samantha's side. "You're a good friend if you can put up with that."

"She doesn't do it all the time," she said, sounding a little less anxious. "Her boyfriend left with his fraternity brothers after half time. She was just . . ." Samantha trailed off.

Greg ran a hand over the smooth surface of the vehicle. "Nice car," he said. He yearned for an ordinary life where his girlfriend left with her sorority sisters for some girl bonding and not with the rich, future Regent of all *Morphidkind*.

"Are you all right?" she asked.

Wistfully, Greg looked at the girl who oozed normalcy out of each and every pore. For a second, he imagined she was Sam, and they'd just finished watching a football game. Their team had lost, but with four years of college ahead of them, a chance to watch them win would come again.

"Yeah, I'm fine," he answered. "It's just that you remind me of somebody. That's all. Have a good night," he said, walking away.

"Wait. What's your name?"

"Greg," he answered over his shoulder.

"Thank you, Greg. Maybe I'll see you around campus someday," she said, sounding hopeful.

"Yeah," Greg said simply. It was nice to pretend life could be that easy.

The tail lights of Samantha's SUV disappeared as she exited the parking lot. Now empty, but for Greg. Everyone had gone home, or to a bar to drown the blues of the loss in booze. Vaguely, he wondered if alcohol could help *him* drown *his* blues, but it wasn't worth the trouble. He was a minor in this willful Human world, and it wouldn't help. Not in the long run.

Lying on the hood of his car, Greg looked up at the sky. He closed his eyes and heard thunder rumble in the distance. The hair on the back of his arms stood on end, as if electrified by the faraway storm. His eyes sprang open with a familiar dread. A cold finger crept down the back of his neck.

"Sam!" He sat up as if someone had pricked him with a needle. It seemed like he'd only been gone a few minutes, and danger already loomed near her. It approached, unraveling around her like yarn between the claws of a vicious cat.

Struggling with the urge to hop into the car, he bit his lip and clenched his fists. There was as much Human in him as there was Morphid. He could fight this. He could let her go into whatever dangers she chose. Ashby would have an army at his disposal to protect her.

At first, he'd have been willing to follow her to the depths of hell. Even if she felt nothing for him, he thought he'd be happy just keeping her safe and being by her side. But when he saw them together, when he saw her holding Ashby's hand, Greg understood it wouldn't be that easy. The pain was almost crippling. What good was free will when it let you love the wrong person? He would be better off as a true Morphid, a slave to his instincts with no room for love in his heart. Love was too vicious; it had fangs and claws that tore the tenderest parts of you. He wanted to feel nothing.

He slid off the hood and crouched next to the car, resting his back against the tire. The compulsion to find her was growing rapidly, throbbing in his ears with violence. He wrapped his hands behind his head and covered his ears with his arms, pressing as hard as he could. He hummed and rocked back and forth like a child in need of comfort, but the desire to run to Sam was excruciating. His insides were being pulled apart—every cell in his body diving into either denial or the need to find her.

He whined like an injured cat, the sound growing at the back of his throat. He was exploding inside. A big bang. He wondered if he'd be able to remain in one piece without detonating and expanding into eternity, if he could live without staying in this fetal position forever.

Maybe if his Human side didn't crave her just as much as his Keeper nature did, he could have resisted. Maybe if his Human half weren't splitting in two as well: One part wishing to be near her, and the other one refusing to be a third wheel. How could he let her go when only one fourth of him was putting up a fight?

Impossible.

He was torn between his own choices and the choices of Blind Fate. He had chosen wrongly, had fallen for her. And this freedom to love of his own accord caused him so much pain that he sometimes wished to be a true Keeper.

Free will hurt . . . free will tore his heart in two . . .

Free will was a lie.

Shaking, Greg stood and climbed into the car. He drove instinctively through empty, unknown streets. He could have found the place with a blindfold. After a short drive, he arrived at a hotel. It was a narrow, six-story building, nice but unimpressive. Sam wasn't here yet. He could feel her absence in his blood like a missing piece on a chess board. Still, he knew she'd be here soon. He was getting better at this.

It was safe to assume Ashby was staying here, using one of its rooms as a portal to go back and forth, traveling through his exclusive, magical means. No doubt by now, he'd talked Sam into leaving. The thought pained him. If she only knew her decision was taking her straight to danger.

She sure didn't take much convincing, he thought bitterly. How quickly she'd stopped giving a damn about him. How easy and convenient for her. In spite of that, here he was, ready once again to stop her from walking into the predator's mouth. Only this time, he might have to do so against her will.

Sam's arrival was imminent, indicated by a pulsating urgency in the back of his brain. He stepped out of the car and walked into the lobby through sliding doors. The large reception counter was empty. *Good.* He didn't want anyone asking questions. He hurried and found the elevators. To one side, a metal door read, "Stairs." He opened the door and stepped into the stairwell. Wedging the door open with his sneaker, Greg waited, peering through a tiny crack. He had a clear view of the elevators.

Only a minute passed before he heard steps and then he saw them. Ashby had an arm around Sam's shoulder, and she accompanied him willingly. He pressed the elevator button and kissed her on the forehead, smiling like an idiot. She smiled back, but it seemed reluctant.

Greg had no time to wonder about Sam's slack demeanor or whether he was imagining it. The elevator doors opened with a *ding* and the love-struck puppies stepped inside. After the doors slid shut, he watched the numbers above the elevator door light up, one at a time. They stopped moving on the fourth floor.

Running at full pelt, he climbed the stairs three, even four at a time. When he reached the fourth floor, he pulled the door open, stuck his head out and looked both ways. He spotted them just as Ashby opened the door, ushering Sam inside.

The hall was long. The door to the room was already shutting as Greg ran toward it. At the last possible moment, he stuck a hand through the narrowing crack and prevented the door from closing. He slid in the room quietly and unnoticed. The door shut behind him with a click.

"You can sit while I summon Perry," Ashby said, reaching for an object that rested on the night table.

Sam walked to the window. Dim streetlights were visible through the sheer, white curtains. She lifted her hand to draw them aside, her hand feeble, her attitude detached. The curve of her now long neck bowed as she lowered her eyes to the floor. Greg wanted to reach out, touch her shoulder and reassure her. He mentally kicked himself for his stupidity. She didn't need any comforting. This had to be heaven on earth to her.

Greg snapped his attention to Ashby. He was turning away from the night table, holding something that looked like an empty picture frame. When he caught sight of Greg, he startled and dropped the object to the ground.

"What are *you* doing here?" The anger in his voice was undeniable.

Sam whirled, scared at first, but—when her eyes met Greg's—her face lit up, giving hope to his stupid heart.

"Greg," she said, but there was only relief in her tone. Part of him had hoped for more.

Ashby went to stand next to Sam. "What do you want now? I thought you'd finally understood."

"I came to warn Sam." Greg walked farther into the room. A single, undisturbed king-size bed occupied most of the space. There was a dresser and a desk, standing on opposite corners. Red accent pillows atop a white comforter, a painting of crimson roses on the wall, and red valances gave the room that stylish-yet-generic look of hotel rooms everywhere.

"She only needs to be warned about you," Ashby said.

Greg bristled with fury. Sam would never have to worry about her well-being with Greg. "If I've guessed right," he talked to Sam, ignoring Ashby, "you've decided to go to England with him."

"Of course, she has," Ashby said arrogantly. "That's where she belongs . . . with me," he added in triumph.

"I'm not talking to you," Greg said icily. "Sam, when you made that decision, all kinds of red flags went up in my head. If you go, you're stepping right into danger."

"That's ridiculous. No one means her harm in my home. No one even knows her," Ashby said.

"Are you sure about that?" Greg asked.

"Of course, I'm sure. And even if I'm wrong, I'll be perfectly capable of protecting my bride."

Greg looked at Sam searchingly, hoping for some argument from the Sam he knew, some sarcastic quip. Instead, she lowered her gaze, and Greg almost staggered from the blow of her quiet acquiescence. His Sam was gone. Ashby beamed with unbound gratification.

"I have to go," Sam spoke at last. "Even if you're right. You know I have to, Greg. For the same reason you're here right now."

Had she tried to fight it too? Had she tried and failed just as miserably as he had?

"What about your family, your friends, school?" Greg had to try something. She obviously didn't care about her safety or leaving *him* behind, but she may care about Rose and Brooke.

"I'll be able to visit them. Ashby promised."

"And what if he can't protect you? What then?"

"I trust him when he says I have nothing to worry about."

Greg shook his head. "What about me? Do you trust me? My instincts have never failed me. Even he can't deny that if I know you're in danger, that means you're in danger. Isn't that right, Ashby?"

Ashby stared at his shoes.

"Not even *he,* for all his . . . feelings for you, can protect you like I can. He'll have no forewarning and he can't be with you every second of the day."

"I guess I'll have to take my chances," Sam said simply.

"Take your chances?!" Greg couldn't believe she was saying that. "Are you insane? You'll be walking into a death trap if you leave. I guarantee it. How many guys do you know that go by the name *Veridan?* It isn't a coincidence, Sam. That guy works for the Regent."

"Fine! I've already told you my mother wouldn't hurt Sam, but fine. Come with us, then" Ashby choked out, surprising both Greg and Sam. He looked gray with repugnance, loathing the idea. Ashby continued, "I won't risk your safety for one moment, Sam. Even if it means carting this... person along."

"No!" Sam snapped. She rushed and stood in front of Greg, a desperate fire burning in her eyes. She shook her head over and over. "I can't ask this of you," she said in a hoarse whisper. "It's not fair."

"Fair has nothing to do with it, clearly," Greg said bitterly. He took a step back—her proximity more than he could stand. "I can't stay behind. Believe me, I've already tried."

Sam said nothing. Instead, she sat limply on the corner of the bed.

"I have no other choice." Greg sat on the chair by the desk.

Looking on, almost to remind them that he was still in the room, Ashby chimed in, "Very well," and moved to his bedside table.

Back to square one, Greg realized. *Just where I'd always known I'd end up.* Why had he even bothered trying to resist? Armoring himself with indifference was his only choice. He had to be an impervious statue, one whose job was to watch and protect, not feel. A slave, just as Mom had feared.

Knowing they'd reached an unspoken consensus, Ashby crouched and picked up the object he'd dropped earlier. He held the frame up and looked into it as if it was a mirror. It made Greg think of people in tourist traps, sticking their heads through cutouts of historical figures for silly photos. He might have laughed, in a near past.

"What is that?" Greg asked distrustfully.

Ashby lowered the frame, looking aggravated. "Something that allows me to communicate with Perry."

"How does it work?"

"How am I supposed to know? I'm not a Sorcerer." Ashby seemed insulted.

"I didn't invent the cell phone, but I still know it has microchips inside and it receives signal over radio link," Greg said, trying to sound as obnoxious as possible.

"He put a spell on it and it works." Ashby turned away from Greg and started gazing into the frame as if a movie played inside it. He murmured something Greg couldn't decipher, then set the frame down. "Perry should be here in an hour or so."

"Speedier than air travel, just not *that* speedy, huh?" Greg said sarcastically.

"We can't transfer into the castle without alerting everyone. Perry must go somewhere else to cast his magic."

"You mean the future Regent has to sneak out without permission," Greg said, injecting his tone with as much derision as he possibly could.

Ashby's lip curled up in anger. He looked like he was having second thoughts about agreeing to take Greg along.

"Well, I'm hungry." Greg kicked back and propped his feet on the bed, giving Sam a crooked grin. "If it'll take an hour, we may as well order some pizza." His voice was cool with a generous edge of I-don't-give-a-damn in it. He wanted to show Sam he didn't care, so he shifted his attention as far away from her as he could. Food was the first thing that occurred to him.

"Pizza?" Ashby said puzzled at the random idea.

Sam looked up at Greg surprised, and her expression seemed to say "How can you think of food at a moment like this?"

Mission accomplished.

"Yeah, pizza. Some version of Italian food, *your highness,*" Greg said, feeling the bitterness grow inside of him with every passing minute, despite his outward cockiness. Maybe he'd be good at this game. Greg looked for a phone book inside the drawers of the night tables. "Coke would be good. Oh, and cheesy bread, too." He sounded positively chipper. "For all we know it will be the last time we'll have a chance to enjoy some fine American food. No offense, but English cuisine . . . well . . . not such a thing." He laughed without amusement.

Sam frowned, looking a bit disappointed at the prospect. Well, if she hadn't thought about all the things she was abandoning, however trivial, Greg would make it his job to remind her. Then her eyes softened a little, and they exchanged a nostalgic glance from which Ashby was excluded. They had so much in common that Ashby would never be able to understand, but what difference did it make? Greg broke eye contact and stiffened.

"I only have five bucks," Greg stared at the contents of his wallet. "Oh wait! I have my parents' credit card. They said I could use it for emergencies. I think this qualifies."

Thirty minutes later, Greg sat, licking his fingers and gulping Coca-Cola with exaggerated delight. Ashby tried the pizza at Sam's insistence and found it only "acceptable." The Coke he dismissed as the foulest tasting brew ever invented by man, saying he much preferred tea. At which point, Sam lost her appetite.

"Good. More for me," Greg said before devouring five thick slices and drinking more than half a liter. Patting his belly, he forced the last bit of Coke down his throat. He was coarsely burping the alphabet when the air crackled and an almost imperceptible shimmer appeared by the window. Sam jumped off the bed as the empty space was abruptly occupied by Perry.

"Did you call, *My Regent*?" Perry said with a mocking flourish.

Greg grinned. Maybe he would like this Perry guy, after all.

ℰ *Chapter 33* ℛ
Ashby

"Transportation?" Ashby asked Perry as soon as they transferred back into the old cottage and stepped outside.

"Around the corner," Perry said, already walking off to one side of the decrepit house.

"Nice castle," Greg quipped, making Ashby wish he'd been able to avoid bringing this impertinent fool along.

Ashby acknowledged the comment with a poisonous glance, then turned to Sam and offered his hand. "We must ride for a few miles, and then we'll be home." He'd explained that much to Sam already, but she still seemed taken aback by the decrepit surroundings.

"Okay." Sam took his outstretched hand in an automatic gesture that was, to Ashby's disappointment, almost detached.

Patience, Ashby told himself. He refused to think of Morphid feelings as mere compulsions. There was more to it than that. He could feel it in his own heart every time he looked into her eyes, and he was sure she'd felt it, as well. It was just too fresh for her mind to process all the changes.

He followed Perry, guiding Sam. It was dark outside, and when his eyes adjusted, he saw two ATVs parked under a tree.

"ATVs, seriously?" Ashby asked.

"Hey, that was the only thing your contact had available on such short notice. I had to tow the smallest one, so don't complain. Besides, they're the smartest thing on this terrain."

"I guess you're right. You can ride with me," Ashby told Sam as he sat astride the first ATV.

Sam turned and looked around. "What about Greg?"

"He can ride with Perry."

"What?" Perry asked from atop his ATV. He didn't sound pleased with the idea, which made it an excellent way to get back at both of their impertinent asses. "I think he can walk," Perry added, turning the key to start the engine.

"*Perry*," Ashby admonished.

"Oh, all right. Get back there," Perry told Greg.

Greg stared at Perry and the ATV with a sideways glance. "I think I'd rather walk."

"Suit yourself," Perry revved the engine.

"Greg, please," Sam pleaded.

"Let him walk," Ashby intervened. "It'll do him some good after pigging out on cheap, greasy pizza." He winced internally at his own comment. Lately, it had been very hard to keep from gloating and sounding arrogant. Greg seemed to bring out the worst in him.

Sam mounted behind Ashby, wrapped her arms around him and said, "We can't stand here all night. Do what you want." The comment brought Greg's posturing to an end. Begrudgingly, Greg mounted behind Perry. Ashby smiled.

First, they traveled for a mile down a bone-jarring hill until they reached the main road. The narrow, steep road led all the way to Rothblade Castle, atop its craggy mountain. At this early hour, they encountered no one. The countryside slept peacefully, not a flicker of light anywhere.

With the wind blowing his hair and Sam's arms around his waist, Ashby felt as if he could fly. Things were almost perfect. If only he could get rid of Greg. Yet as much as he hated to admit it, a small part of him was still worried about Sam's safety, and Greg's admonishments had struck a chord with him.

Although his mother had denied any involvement, a part of him felt wary and unsatisfied with her emphatic denial. He'd turned the events over and over in his mind, trying to convince himself that Veridan had nothing to do with the attempts on Sam's life, that it was just an unfortunate coincidence. But he couldn't be 100% certain, and Greg was the only insurance he had if there was foul play. If Veridan was involved, he had to be acting on his own. For some reason, the noxious black cloud in the Sorcerer's alcove flashed before Ashby's eyes. The man was evil, no doubt, but Ashby tried to tell himself Veridan had nothing against the Regency.

Since transferring back and forth between worlds would no longer be necessary, Ashby decided it was time to stop sneaking into the castle. He had to confront his mother. Sam had morphed. The Regent could forbid him no longer.

"We'll use the main entrance," he yelled over the roar of the ATVs.

"At this hour?" Perry asked. "That may cause some trouble. I think we should—"

"No, Perry," he cut him off, "I'm sick of hiding."

So instead of trying to slip in their regular means, Ashby rode to the main gate and punched in his high-level access code.

"Sir?" asked a surprised guard, standing at attention as they rode past when the gate open. "I wasn't informed you were expected tonight." The guard looked at the group dubiously. "Is everything . . . all right?" he asked.

"Nothing to worry about," Ashby said. "Some unexpected guests."

"This is a bit irregular. Please allow me to consult my superior, sir." He nodded to three guards who stood behind him. They immediately took positions blocking their path.

"That won't be necessary," Ashby tried to argue.

"Just following procedure, sir. My apologies," the guard said as he disappeared inside the control booth.

"Sounds like you're just a figurehead foiled by procedure, your highness," Greg piped in.

Ashby squeezed the ATVs handles, wishing he could crush something. However, he managed to rise above once more, and remained silent. The guard's *superior* also found the situation "out of the ordinary," and wanted them to wait until he arrived. Frustrated, Ashby ordered the guard to fetch Portos while he was at it. The Sorcerer would set things right.

* * *

They all stood in the entrance hall, waiting. Logs burned on a large fireplace at the center of the imposing room. Tall tapestries depicting colorful spring fields hung to either side of the hearth. Majestic stone columns and marble floors adorned the otherwise-empty room. Ashby squeezed Sam's hand for reassurance.

"Portos will clear things up," he whispered in her ear.

The High Sorcerer, wearing a silk robe and rubbing sleep out of his eyes, looked disapprovingly on the whole group. He shuffled into the room, looking less than dignified and quite annoyed.

"What is the meaning of this?" he asked. "What in God's name were you doing out there at this time of night? Or should I say dawn? Have you lost your mind?"

"I did what was necessary, Portos," Ashby explained. "My mother forbade me to—"

"That's exactly right," Portos interrupted, his raised voice echoing across the hall. "The *Regent* forbade you to try anything on your own, and for very good reason."

"It was perfectly safe," Ashby shot back defiantly, sick of being treated like a child. "And as you can see, I managed just fine."

Shaking his head with irritation, Portos looked at Sam and Greg. They were too taken in by their surroundings to fully follow the conversation.

"So she has finally morphed," Portos observed, looking at Sam up and down.

Put off by the old man's attention, Sam inched closer to Greg, looking like a scared mouse.

"It's okay," Greg told her. "No red flags yet," Ashby heard him whisper.

A pang of jealousy hit Ashby in the chest. He tugged her hand, irritated that she should look to the Keeper for comfort.

"And who is this?" asked Portos, looking at Greg.

"He is—" started Ashby.

"I'm her Keeper," Greg cut him off, pronouncing each syllable as to leave no room for interpretations.

Ashby shook his head. *The brute has no manners.*

"Keeper?!" exclaimed Portos. "She has a Keeper? But that means she must be . . ." He stopped. His mind seemed to suddenly go in a thousand directions.

"She must be what?" Ashby asked. He didn't like the trepidation in Portos's tone.

"This is most grievous! Your mother must know."

"What's wrong?" Greg demanded.

"We should see the Regent, right away!" Portos turned to leave.

"Now? But she'll be furious," Ashby said.

"I told you we should sneak in, but you wanted to waltz in like a hero," Perry put in under his breath.

"You had better keep your mouth shut, Perry." Portos shot an angry eye at his apprentice. "Your disobedience will not go unpunished this time."

Ashby peered at Perry and imperceptibly shook his head, trying to tell him he wouldn't let him be punished. Perry cocked an eyebrow and scoffed. He didn't have any confidence in Ashby's ability to keep him out of the hot cauldron this time. While Portos walked ahead, Ashby took the chance to lean into Perry and whisper in his ear.

"Let's get you out of here," he said, trying to prove he could keep him from the Regent's rage. "Why don't you go back and work those spells on Sam's family and everyone else? Make sure they don't think she's been missing these past two weeks. She can call them and explain everything later."

"Yes, boss. That sounds great!" Perry said, making a military salute. "I'd rather not see your mother turn blue again." And with that, he stepped into a side passageway, leaving Ashby behind with a half-smile.

They followed Portos down the winding, stone corridor, and soon found themselves in the Regent's grand hall, waiting for her to appear. The high arched ceilings and marble columns flanking every wall made the hall seem cold, in spite of the warm lighting. Moon light broke through the stain glass window above the dais and six white marble statues watched over them, three at each side. Ashby felt ill to his stomach, and halfway wished he had listened to Perry. However, this was inevitable, and the sooner everything was out in the open, the sooner he could marry Sam.

"Regent . . ."

"Mother . . ."

Portos and Ashby spoke at the same time as Regent Danata entered the hall through a side door. She looked none-too-pleased to be disturbed at such hour. She held a silencing hand out as she climbed onto the dais and took a seat on a large, solitary chair. Her robes were as red as the velvet upholstery on which she grumpily settled herself, making her blend almost perfectly with the chair and appear like a floating head. Ashby hated that she chose to conduct business from such an elevated place, as if she were some sort of ancient queen. When he became Regent, he would do away with the stupid, throne-like set up.

His mother icily surveyed each of the people before her. When she came to Ashby, her severe gaze descended down his arm until she found his hand interlaced with Sam's. Her eyes moved up again, this time following Sam's arm up to her pale and anxious face. There, her attention lingered, and an expression of surprise softened her features. She quickly blinked, as if to disguise her scrutiny of the foreign girl, and set her disapproving gaze back on her son.

"I think I can guess what is happening here." She looked to the accompanying guard. "Please leave us." The men did as ordered. "I don't understand," she scoffed, looking at Portos, "why you have deemed it necessary to disturb my sleep for such a trifling matter."

"It may appear so, but I would not have disturbed you if it wasn't important," Portos paused, waiting for the Regent to say something. When she didn't, the High Sorcerer continued. "Ashby blatantly disobeyed your orders and took it in his own hands to retrieve his Integral, disregarding any risk to his person."

"I can deduce that for myself, Portos. He will be suitably reprimanded for his disobedience, but it can certainly wait until tomorrow."

"Indeed," Portos answered with a slight bow. "However, as you can see, his Integral is not the only one he brought back with him."

His mother's attention moved to Greg. She examined him as if she beheld a dirty farm animal. His jaw firmly set, Greg held the Regent's gaze with defiance. Ashby had gotten to know Greg, if only a bit, and at that moment, his countenance revealed more than just the stubbornness of not admitting his proper station. Fear, distrust and a righteous anger also clouded his features.

As Ashby had seen his mother do repeatedly, she inspected Greg through half-lidded eyes. When she was done, she frowned quizzically, as if her examination had revealed something unexpected.

"I assume you speak of this lad?" the Regent disdainfully remarked.

Accustomed to Greg's emotional declarations, Ashby expected him to say something rude, like pointing out he was the most amazing Keeper to ever walk the earth. However, Greg remained silent, hovering near Sam, never taking his eyes off the Regent. Ashby didn't like this one bit.

"Yes, the lad claims to be the girl's *Keeper*," Portos said, looking glad to finally deliver the news that had compelled him to bother the Regent at the break of dawn.

Revealing absolutely no emotion, Danata regarded Portos with a measure of contempt. "Indeed he is," she said, unsurprised.

Stirring uncomfortably on the spot, Greg stepped impossibly close to Sam.

"Can someone please explain the crux of the matter?" Ashby asked irritated. "So Greg is Sam's Keeper. I read he's supposed to protect Sam from danger, but what other significance is there?"

Portos shook his head. "The ignorance of today's youth is appalling."

"We need to get out of here," Greg whispered out of the corner of his mouth, leaning his head toward Sam's until they almost touched.

Sam shuddered. Her eyes shifted questioningly to Ashby's. He tried to appear reassuring, even though he, himself, was feeling more and more uncertain. He smiled and winked nonchalantly.

Portos donned his scholarly voice, as he had countless times before. "Very few people throughout history have ever required a Keeper. Perhaps you'll remember statesman Benofoix, who fought for the momentous reform that spelled the end of the totalitarian Regency that had ruled Morphids for centuries. He personally rallied many of the cause's strongest supporters, finally overcoming harsh opposition. It is to him we owe our current form of leadership. However, he couldn't have done it without his Keeper, who saved him from assassination attempts innumerable times.

"There was also Derfrine Rovenspear who, as a Keeper, was more famous than the person she protected. She sacrificed her life in a duel in order to defend General Mujehn against the High Sorcerer of the old . . ."

"Enough," snapped Danata. "Let us not jump to any conclusions about these two . . . outsiders. We know absolutely nothing about them."

Ashby's mind was reeling, trying to understand what Portos had said. He didn't remember any of the people the old man had mentioned, except for Derfrine Rovenspear. Everyone knew she traveled disguised as a man, hiding her fiery curls and smooth features under a heavy helm just to remain by Captain Mujehn's side. But Ashby had always heard that Derfrine was the General's lover. Nothing more. What was the old man trying to say?

Ashby had to ask. "Portos, are you implying that something momentous lies in Sam's future, that she might be fated to do something that will change the course of our history?"

"Yes, the likelihood is—" started Portos.

"I said enough," Danata repeated, striking the arm of her chair and rising to her feet. "These conjectures are of no use at this moment. Summon Veridan and two of the guards," the Regent ordered a young attendant who stood quietly in a corner. He jumped to attention and hurried out without making a sound.

Sam's grip on Ashby's hand tightened. Her eyes darted around the room, as if looking for some hidden exit. Greg moved to stand in front of her and looked around, too.

"Why must you summon them?" Ashby was puzzled.

"Keep quiet, Ashby. I'm terribly disappointed in you."

From experience, Ashby knew that, at moments such as this, arguing with his mother was useless. However, he'd dragged Sam into this situation, whatever it may be. He couldn't just stand idly by.

"Mother, I don't understand. This is my Integral, for God's sake. My future wife! Please, I—"

"Such insolence from my own flesh and blood," boomed Danata. Her face was now red with fury. She seethed, and was about to launch into a tirade when the two summoned guards walked in.

"Did you call?" Simeon asked. He was accompanied by Omar, who looked small next to Simeon's gigantic frame. Both wore dark suits and sour expressions on their faces.

"Take these two to the southernmost guest room and keep them there until you receive further instruction," the Regent said.

Without a moment's hesitation, the guards walked toward Sam and Greg. Ashby blocked their path. In the past, he had commanded both these man in training exercises. Now, he tried to defy them with the same mastery. The men stopped and looked hesitantly back at the Regent.

"Mother, this is ridiculous. They are my guests. Must you treat them so . . . callously?" Ashby protested.

"Would you rather I sent them to a cell?" The Regent's voice was full of barely-restrained venom.

The southern guest rooms were windowless and austere, reserved for minor visitors, but they were certainly better than the musty dungeon. Ashby hesitated, unsure of what to say or do.

"Do as I said," the Regent commanded the guards. Her harsh tone erased all hesitation. They brushed Ashby aside and none-too-gently took hold of Sam and Greg's arms, ushering them toward the exit.

At a loss for words, Ashby decided that the least he could do was keep them company. He started to follow.

"You stay here," his mother ordered.

Ashby stood torn between showing solidarity and finding out exactly what was happening. Finally he opted for staying, desperate to understand his mother's behavior. Knowing Danata, she might even take it out on Sam if he stepped out of line, just to teach him a lesson. With one last glance at Sam's long brown hair, he swallowed his impotence and chose to play the Regent's game.

ℰ Chapter 34 ℰ
Sam

Sam clutched Greg's arm with apprehension as they were herded down semi-dark corridors. After exiting the great hall, the guards released their grip and allowed them to walk in the front, barking directions when they needed to turn down certain passageways. The palace was a strange combination of medieval and modern-looking touches, unlike anything she'd ever seen. Ancient oil paintings hung on the walls, interspersed with colored photographs. Strange sconces, glowing dimly like night lights, barely beat back the darkness of the empty halls.

"Take a left," the giant of a guard barked as the corridor forked in two.

When they reached the intersection, a dark figure appeared in their path.

"Who goes there?" the same guard asked, jumping to the forefront. The figure didn't respond, but stood watching from beneath the hood of a heavy cloak, face concealed in shadows.

Almost climbing up Greg's arm with fear, Sam peered into the black hole under the hood, certain she would find Veridan's piercing black eyes. For his part, Greg remained calm, as if he knew this person posed no threat at all.

Slowly, the figure peeled the hood back. As he uncovered himself, the guards relaxed. Sam didn't understand why they'd expected trouble within the castle. Maybe the presence of two strange Morphids and the Regent's behavior had set them on edge.

"It's just Bernard," the smaller guard said. "What are you doing roaming the halls at this hour, you crazy, old fool?"

"Watch yourself," the burly guard warned. "He's still the Regent's brother-in-law, even if he's not quite . . ." he trailed off, twirling an index finger next to his temple.

"Roanna," the strange man said, looking straight at Sam. "Roanna, is that you?"

Sam and Greg exchanged inquisitive glances. Like a ghost, the old man floated toward Sam, extending a shaky hand. "Is that you, my darling?" he asked, with an edge of terrible desperation in his voice. Abashed, Sam hid behind Greg, thinking the man must be truly bonkers.

"Easy, old man." The burly guard placed a hand on Bernard's chest.

"Who's Roanna?" the other guard asked.

"His dead wife, the poor fool. He thinks she's still alive and he roams around, scaring the boots off everybody," he explained, as if the old man wasn't there.

A surge of pity enveloped Sam. *Poor old man.* She stepped away from Greg's side to get a better look. Examining his face, she found that he wasn't old after all, maybe just middle age, like James. Nonetheless, the weariness of many years was etched across his face. A soulful tear rolled down the man's cheek, making Sam's throat tighten in pity. She wanted to reach out and touch him, overwhelmed by the strange urge to console him, to somehow make his worries disappear.

"Bernard, old fellow, why don't you go in the kitchen to see if they've baked the yeast rolls?" the burly guard offered.

At the mention of yeast rolls, Bernard seemed to forget his sadness. "Yes, yes," he smiled. "I will bring you some back," he added, looking at Sam. "You've always liked them."

Bernard ran along, looking back at Sam with a big grin on his face. She was reminded of a child's enthusiasm at the mention of candy. Her pity for Bernard intensified.

"Poor man," she whispered as she watched him disappear at the end of the hall.

"Come along." The burly guard pointed the way. "We're almost there."

After a couple more left turns, they were deposited into a crude, windowless room, furnished only by a small bed and armoire.

"The lavatory is through there," the large guard said, pointing at a narrow door at the far corner, then closed the heavy wooden doors with a loud *clunk*.

Expecting an immediate, "I told you so," Sam peered up at Greg. He didn't say anything. Instead, he walked to the bed, sat at its edge, and stared at the wall, face strained as if a million ideas were flying behind his eyes.

"How bad is it?" Sam finally asked, sitting next to him.

He shook his head. "As bad as it gets," he said, getting up and walking as far from her as the cramped room allowed.

"What does that woman have against me?" she asked to no one in particular.

"She hates you," Greg said.

"Hates me? But that's insane! She's never met me."

"Oh, she hates you, all right. Have no doubt about it. And it's not 'cause of your *lowly pedigree*. There's something else. I can sense it," he said.

"How can you be so certain?"

"I just know, all right? Makes my hair stand on end. It's no idle hatred, either. She means you harm. The killing kind. Maybe not now, but soon."

"I guess . . . I should've listened to you." Sam said, clasping her head.

Greg averted his eyes. Obviously, he didn't want the conversation to go in that direction. He started pacing the room, examining it carefully. He opened the armoire, searched under the pillow and under the bed, and looked in the bathroom. As he went around, it became clear more occupied his mind than just the objects he examined. He stopped in the middle of the room and pinched his eyebrows together. "What's your mark?"

"What?" she mumbled unable to follow his train of thought.

"Your mark, on your back, what is it?"

"Oh, it's a . . . I don't know, a spider and a staff."

"You mean you're a . . . *Dual*?"

Sam nodded, feeling lost. "Yeah, that's what Ashby said. What does that mean?"

Greg ran a hand through his dark hair. "Can I see it?"

Getting to her feet, Sam pulled her hair to one side. Greg hesitated for a moment, then approached her. He gently pulled down the collar of her t-shirt. She was still wearing his clothes. With a feathery touch, he traced the mark, sending a chill down her back.

"The staff means you're destined to be part of the council, but it's small. The spider's the most prevalent one, and . . . the web." He traced the web patterns that radiated from the center of the mark. Sam hugged herself, trying to contain the shudders his touch incited deep within her. "Some of the strands are broken." His voice was eerie and distant.

Unable to resist it any longer, Sam stepped aside, trying to control the nauseous feeling in the pit of her stomach.

"What does it mean, though? Do you have any idea what caste?" she asked.

Sam faced Greg, but not before gathering herself. Somewhere Ashby, her Companion, held her soul, her essence. Whatever feelings remained were unnatural, a delusion that could never be.

"I don't know."

"Ashby didn't know, either," her voice was calm, showing none of her inner turmoil. "The staff matches his mark," she added, scrutinizing Greg's features for a reaction. Nothing. She, on the other hand, had to look away not to reveal the conflict raging inside her. "He didn't know about the spider either. He said Portos would know. I hate it," she blurted out. "I don't want that ugly spider on me." She knew she sounded like a child, but the mark was hideous.

"It isn't ugly," Greg said coldly. "Besides that should be the last of your worries. You should be more concerned about its meaning, what ability comes with it or what it'll make you do."

Sam frowned.

"Have you had any urges or experienced anything out of the ordinary?"

She raised an eyebrow. "Seriously? The entire summer has been out of the ordinary—not to mention the past few hours. It would be hard to notice some extra little . . . " Sam trailed off suddenly reminded of something.

"What?" Greg asked.

For some reason, the image of the Regent examining them through semi-closed eyes popped back into Sam's mind. At the time, Danata's careful scrutiny had seemed strange, as if by squinting at them the woman could see beyond the physical. Compelled by that, and the memory of what she'd seen when she first awoke as this new, strange being, she narrowed her eyes at Greg.

"Are you okay? What's wrong with your eyes?"

When she didn't respond, he took a step in her direction. "Don't move," she ordered him.

It took a moment to unfocus her eyes enough to finally see what—just hours ago—she'd thought was a trick of the light. Sprouting from Greg's head, a tendril of light radiated upward, bright as a white laser beam. With some effort, she traced its path upwards. She lost sight of it twice and had to retrace her steps to find it again. The ribbon of light rose four feet above Greg's head, before it arched down again. As she tried to follow the luminous cord in its descent, it got brighter and brighter, as if a flashlight shone directly into her eyes.

"Ouch," she yelped, shying away from the light, hands on her face.

"What is it?" Greg took her by the arms and drove her toward the bed. "Sit. Please, answer me. Are you all right?"

"I think so," she said, rubbing her eyes while multicolored spots danced before her. After a few moments, she looked around the room, relieved to find she could see just fine.

"What were you doing? You're freaking me out."

"I think . . . I think I know what my ability is."

Greg frowned, looking skeptical. "Do you?"

"Is there a mirror in here?" she said, looking around.

"Yeah, over here." Greg went to the armoire and opened one of its heavy doors.

She walked up to the mirror and was startled by her own image. She shook her head. It would take a long time before she got used to her new self. "Stand right behind me where I can see you," she told Greg.

Obediently, he took his place two paces away from her. She looked into his deep blue gaze in the mirror and smiled sheepishly. Greg returned her smile, but no cheer emanated from his eyes. His demeanor was icy and unyielding.

He's cutting me off, she thought. And how could she blame him?

"So, what are we doing?" he asked, sounding a bit irritated.

"Testing a theory," she said, unfocusing her eyes, doubtful whether the strange light would reflect on the mirror.

But it did. She held her breath and stared at the aura that surrounded her. Two tendrils sprung out of her, like snakes on Medusa's head. Following one of them—first on the mirror and then on its true trajectory—she discovered that the smooth light disappeared right through the ceiling, piercing it like sunshine would water. Guessing where that ribbon led, she traced the second one, and—confirming her suspicions—its trail led her straight to Greg's aloof features. Blinking away the patterns still glowing on her retinas, she closed the armoire and faced Greg.

"Okay . . . well . . . assuming I'm right, I think I can see the links between us."

Greg's eyes narrowed.

"The links between . . . Morphids. I guess. It's like looking at one of those 3D puzzles. When I unfocus my eyes, I can see these . . . shafts of light. There's one connecting you and I. There's a second one that goes beyond this room, and I think it . . ."

". . . connects you to Ashby." Greg's lip twitched as he finished her sentence.

"Yes."

"O-kay." Greg said, pronouncing the word deliberately. "And how does that help us?"

"I . . . I don't know. I guess it doesn't."

"No, I guess not." He sighed. "What made you think of screwing with your eyes like that?"

"Oh, it was that woman. You saw the way she was squinting at us, like bugs under a microscope."

"Yeah . . . I noticed that. I thought it was weird."

"Also, when I woke up in your apartment yesterday I thought I saw something as I was opening my eyes. I thought it was a trick of the light or something. It kind of freaked me out."

"I guess anything we can learn at this point can become useful. The more we know, the better."

Sam nodded in agreement.

"Ashby mention anything else that could help?"

"Not really. I think he's in the dark as much as we are."

They remained silent for several minutes, Greg pacing the room and Sam sitting on the bed, playing with her hair. It was awkward. She wanted to say something to cut through the cold veil that seemed to be building around them. Mainly, she wanted to thank Greg for being there. She didn't even want to think how frightened she would be if he wasn't here. But she bit her tongue and said nothing. It wasn't as if he'd had a choice. And, judging by his manner, this was the last place he wanted to be.

"Why don't you sleep some? Who knows how long they'll keep us here." Greg's tone was suggestive, as if he'd had enough of her company.

"I don't think I would be able to," she said, wishing she could at least offer Greg the pleasure of unconscious company.

"I think I can," he said approaching the bed.

Sam didn't understand how Greg could even think about sleep in their current situation. She glowered at him. In turn, Greg offered her an exacting expression that seemed to say "stop hogging the bed." She stood and watched him stretch luxuriously on the small bed. He closed his eyes, and in no time, his breathing became heavy and rhythmic.

"I can't believe this," she mumbled under her breath, looking around for a place to sit. There were no chairs, so she sat on the floor with her back against the cold wall.

Maybe Greg was trying to punish her for getting him into this mess and for other things that—at the moment—she didn't have the heart to think about. All she knew was that things wouldn't work out if they remained this way. Something had to change, or their lives would devolve into a constant struggle, with her stuck between two bitter combatants. Still, she loathed the idea of what some of those changes could be. Some of the possibilities—like being away from Greg—were too agonizing to consider.

Greg's chest went up and down peacefully. Tracing his perfect profile, Sam thought of how different things had seemed just yesterday. She'd known what she wanted with so much certainty. Now, her conviction was turned inside out, transformed into perfect chaos. Her logic fought with the new passions and desires that whirled inside her. And while her reason told her that love couldn't be discarded or turned off like a light switch, her feelings of yesterday seemed dim and distant, their memory causing only nausea and anguish when she tried to bring them to the forefront. Greg stirred and his lips moved as if uttering silent words. Something in Sam's chest fluttered when, in his dreams, he said her name.

No, she thought, *there's no light switch.*

-*Maybe a thermostat*, another part of her said. Maybe the temperature can be lowered a few degrees at a time until the memory of love is no more real than the memory of a fiery summer long ago.

Perhaps this coldness Greg had wedged between them would help them endure what was to come. It seemed, at least, that this was the realization he'd come to. She could already feel the frigid walls rising around him. A shiver ran down her spine, and she hugged her knees. Tears filled her eyes, rising from the remnants of yesterday's feeling. Oh, how she wished there was another way.

ಲ Chapter 35 ಲ
Greg

Greg sprang to a sitting position, his instincts jolting him back to the moment. He'd been lying on the bed, pretending to sleep (mostly) and worrying over Sam's safety and the dark mass of hostility that vile woman harbored.

Sam looked up from where she was, huddled against the wall hugging her knees. "What is it?" She looked so lonely and sad that Greg felt his self-imposed coldness melt a little.

"Someone's coming," he said, jumping to his feet, "and they don't mean well." He stared at the door, poised for anything to walk in through the door, even the devil.

Sam stood, wringing her hands, looking terrified. "I'm scared, Greg." She stepped right behind him.

She didn't need to tell him how she felt. He could sense her apprehension. "You shouldn't be," Greg said, looking back over his shoulder. His fingers came to the brink of touching her hand, offering a reassuring touch. But as he came within millimeters of her, he refrained.

"I won't let anything happen to you, okay?" he said, pulling back. His tone was confident enough, but it didn't carry the warmth she needed, the warmth he couldn't give her. *Not* my *job anymore,* he told himself, compressing his lips into a harsh line of grim determination.

Steps echoed outside. They waited, eyes glued to the door. The large lock clicked, and Sam gasped in fear. The same two guards who'd brought them to the room walked in.

"Come. The Regent is ready for you," Beefy Dude said, looking over Greg's shoulder at Sam.

Sam and Greg stood motionless for a moment, processing the guard's words, waiting for some further explanation.

Finally, Greg exhaled. Things weren't going to get any better if they just stood there. Best get the suspense over with. "Let's go, then," he said, taking a step forward.

"Not you," Beefy Dude said, pointing a finger at Greg. "You stay here, mate . . . as an *honored* guest." He smirked.

"She's not going anywhere without me," Greg said.

"So full of himself, this lad. Maybe we should teach him a lesson, Simeon," the smaller guard said, taking a threatening step forward. He wrapped one closed fist with his other hand and made his knuckles crack.

"Careful, Omar," Beefy Dude Simeon admonished. "Portos and Veridan said to be careful."

Veridan. That name again. Did Sam need any more proof? Ashby was an idiot for trusting his mother. She'd wanted Sam dead all along.

"Careful? Of this snotty whelp? What could he do?" Omar asked, sounding just a little less sure of himself.

Greg clenched his fists. "Why don't you ask Veridan? He can give you a full account. Come to think of it, why don't you ask him to come get us instead?"

Simeon narrowed his eyes, sizing Greg up.

Omar took a step back. "The lad's a Sorcerer, then?" he said, eyes wide with distrust. "Why wouldn't the Regent send Portos or Veridan to fetch him? They always deal with their own kind."

Simeon shook his head. "No, not a Sorcerer. A Keeper, they called him."

"A Keeper? And what in bloody hell is that?"

Simeon shrugged his massive shoulders. "Doesn't matter." He gave Sam a pointed look. "You, girl . . . get moving."

Sam stayed put behind Greg.

"Don't make it harder on everyone." Simeon took two steps forward, eyes switching to Greg's. "I don't want trouble, mate." Simeon's hands bobbed up and down in a pacifying gesture. "Just let me get the girl. The Regent promised not to harm her."

"Yeah, right. I know better." Greg tapped his temple. He could sense the guards were only following orders, but something sinister waited beyond the labyrinth of corridors.

Simeon took another step and, with a scowl, tried shoving Greg out of the way as he went for Sam. That telltale vibration coursed through Greg's body, and he crackled with energy. He took hold of the man's arm and discharged the power that had quickly accumulated in his chest. Simeon shrank back with a scream and bent over at the waist, cradling his arm. The scent of broiled flesh filled the room. The man made a pained, surprised gurgle.

"Shit, what happened?!" Omar asked. He looked ready to flee back through the doorway.

"I'm all right," Simeon hissed as he straightened. The fiery, red imprint of Greg's fingers encircled the man's forearm. Blisters bubbled up on the surface. "No matter," Simeon said, letting his hand drop to one side. His face became a mask that betrayed no pain. "They said you could come if you proved . . . troublesome."

"Aw, I guess you could've saved yourself all that *trouble*." Greg looked at Simeon's arm with mock regret.

The guards led them through the door, making sure to stand several feet away from Greg. They walked the same corridors again, except this time, there were a few people moving about—mainly maids, judging by their black and white uniforms. They appeared busy, hurrying out one door and into another, completely ignoring the teen couple, who looked strangely out of place in their casual, American clothes.

Greg searched for a window that would reveal the time of day, but there were none in the stone-lined corridors. Artificial light still illuminated the areas they traveled, but Greg felt certain it must be daytime. He looked at the ostentatious paintings, rugs, and tapestries with disdain. It all gave him a nauseous feeling in the pit of his stomach.

Peering into one of the long corridors branching off the main hallway, Greg recognized a shape hiding behind a dark, twisted sculpture. He was more than a little wary of hooded shapes lurking in the dark, but his Keeper mind raised no alarm. On the contrary, his instincts showed him an aura of goodwill surrounding the shadow. Greg frowned, remembering the old man the guards had called Bernard. It had to be him. As they continued, Greg could sense the presence trailing behind them, but he pressed forward without looking back or giving away their shadowy follower.

When they reached the tall, arched doors to the grand hall, alarms went off inside Greg's head, each one louder than the other. He felt the mounting urge to take Sam and run as fast as they could .

. . but where to? The same Keeper instincts that urged him to escape, also told him they wouldn't get far. There was strong magic in this place, spells upon spells blocking their way out, spells that had been there earlier, as well as some new, stronger ones. The walls practically shimmered with latent energy. Greg tried to imagine how to break through it all, but his Keeper instincts were at a loss against that kind of power. He cursed under his breath, and Sam's already apprehensive eyes looked up with mounting anxiety. Without warning or ceremony, the guards pushed them inside.

Dim morning light seeped through the stain glass window, but it didn't manage to make the hall any more inviting. Greg eyed the marble statues with disgust, finding they resembled Danata somehow.

Ashby was still there, standing rigidly at attention in front of the Regent, his eyes glued to the floor. He looked more troubled than before. Sam searched his eyes, and—although he seemed to struggle to meet her gaze—he was unable to do so.

Greg seethed. *Of course. He's too ashamed to even look her in the eye. This was all the idiot's fault. Mother or not, how could he have ever trusted this evil woman?*

The man named Portos was still there too, wearing the same night robes and looking twice as conflicted. He exchanged a quick glance with Greg, one that felt like a dire warning. Greg switched his attention to the Regent. She sat on her tall chair, someone new at her side. It was a hooded figure, but not one that gave Greg any sort of good feeling—quite the contrary.

Even under the heavy cloak, Greg could tell it was a man. He thought it must be Veridan with his evil dark eyes and cruel features—if not, why conceal his identity? Whatever the case, he didn't need to see his face to know his intentions. An aura of danger emanated from him, every bit as tangible as the one Greg sensed from the Regent.

"Ashby?" Sam whispered as they came to stand next to him. Shaking visibly, he managed to look up. "What's going on?"

"Samantha, dear," the Regent said before Ashby could get a word out. "I want to apologize for my reaction early today. I was roused out of bed quite suddenly, and my nerves aren't what they used to be. I could hardly form a coherent thought." The Regent's tone was conciliatory and overly cordial. Its phoniness set Greg's teeth on edge. He only hoped Sam could see through it as well as he could.

"I trust you will forgive my . . . rudeness," the Regent added, raising her eyebrows. For a few seconds, she waited for an answer, but Sam gave none. The Regent's mouth twisted in displeasure for only an instant. She continued undeterred. "I also hope you'll understand if my wariness hasn't been relieved, even after talking to Ashby. I still have many questions about your . . . background. As a mother, his well-being is my biggest concern. Furthermore, it is my duty to look after the welfare of our kind. Given that my son is the future Regent, there's much I need to understand before I can *allow* a match to take place."

Greg cast a glance toward Ashby, wondering how the guy could just stand there without a protest. It wasn't as if there were a choice in the matter. Sam was Ashby's Integral. Fate had decided that. Danata couldn't change that even if she wanted to. But maybe things were different here. Maybe the Regent or her Sorcerers had the power to alter Morphid fate. Suddenly, Greg found himself wishing Sam didn't meet the Regent's lofty standards.

Sam's head swiveled back and forth between Ashby and his mother. Clearly, she was also wondering why her beloved Companion didn't say something to help. Ashby managed a glance in her direction. His face was red, his mouth trembling. It looked as if he was burning to speak up . . . but couldn't?

"Well . . . ?" the Regent said, noticeably put out by Sam's lack of response. "Are you at all able to speak . . . *girl*?"

Greg was about to come to her defense when Sam took a step forward. To his surprise, she no longer appeared frightened. Instead, her face was darkened in a cloud of anger and injury.

"I don't know what you expect me to say," she spoke through clenched teeth. "I have no interest in your tribulations as a mother or as Regent. I'm only here because I have no choice."

It was Ashby's turn to look injured, and he gaped at Sam in quiet disbelief at her words. Sam gazed up at the Regent, unblinking and unabashed. The Regent, in turn, regarded Sam with curiosity, as if she were a rare specimen never encountered before.

"I see," Regent Danata said after a moment. "Choice isn't something *most* among our kind have the luxury to enjoy, or even consider. I suppose you grew up believing you possessed free will, but alas." The Regent laughed disdainfully and exchanged a conspiratorial glance with the hooded man at her side. "Be that as it may, this doesn't change our current dilemma, does it, my dear?"

Regent Danata stood, smoothed her robe and stepped down from the dais. She walked toward Sam, wearing a sly smile. "I wish for nothing more than my son's happiness. Sadly, he won't be able to attain it if he cannot be with his Integral."

A strangled grunt escaped Ashby's throat. He was sweating profusely and shaking on the spot, as if waging an internal battle.

Greg then realized that Ashby had been magically gagged. The Regent ignored her son's muffled protest and continued.

"For that reason, I will ask a favor of you," the Regent continued in her most beguiling tone. "It's a simple thing that won't harm you in the least."

Greg knew a lie when he heard one. "No," he snapped. "She's lying, Sam. Whatever it is, don't believe her."

A grin containing zero amusement curved the Regent's lips. "Just a little white lie, perhaps," she admitted. "Let me explain. You see, I wish for my Succeeding Sorcerer to divine you. That means," she continued, noting the look of puzzlement on Sam's face, "he shall look into your mind to try to find out who you truly are, and whether you're . . . fit to enter our family. People who live in exile, as you have, do so to escape from justice, to escape for their crimes. I can't be taken in by allowing you to become part of the Rothblade family without knowing if there's something in your past that may taint our name."

"Don't do it, Sam," Greg said between clenched teeth.

The Regent's eyes wandered over the hall, never alighting on Greg. She sure was going out of her way to pretend he was invisible. Jutting her chin up in the air, she said, "Divination can sometimes cause . . . harm, but it's rare. I assure you. Problems occur only when the mind has been tampered with. I doubt, however, this is the case with you. According to my son, you've lived in exile since you were quite young. So I doubt anyone tampered with those early memories."

"I see you have no problem putting her in danger," Greg pointed out.

"Quiet," the Regent said angrily, finally looking at Greg, eyelids at half-mast. She held a shaky hand up as if ready to strike him. Her hand trembled in midair, as if she were reaching for something. To Greg's surprise, the simple gesture gave him an overwhelming sense of dread. He took a step back, expecting his magic to surface, but . . . the Regent wasn't threatening Sam, was she? A feeling of doom and despair enshrouded him. After a moment, Danata's hand lowered, and she opened her eyes to their normal size. The hair on the back of Greg's arms stood on end. How could the threat of a simple slap make him feel as if everything precious to him would be lost?

After a deep inhale, Danata said, "I really hope you can make your own decisions, my dear Samantha." Danata's voice shook. "Otherwise, you'll make a lousy council member. Try to remember, he's just . . . *a servant*."

"Okay. I'll do it," Sam replied, surprising everyone in the room.

"Excellent." The Regent smiled with satisfaction and walked back to the dais.

"No, Sam. Are you crazy?" Greg said.

She turned to face him and spoke in a barely audible whisper. "I don't really have a choice, do I? They'll do it anyway if I refuse."

Greg knew she was right.

"This is where *Fate* has brought me. I couldn't stay away, even if I tried," she said, with an odd mixture of passion and resignation. "And who knows? Maybe they can help me figure out who I am." She smiled sadly.

"What if they fry your brain? Have you thought about that?"

Sam shrugged. She looked so despondent, so given over to this Fate crap. He opened his mouth to protest, but Sam placed a finger on his lips. "Please, Greg. It'll be best for all of us if we go along."

"No, that's—"

"I've made up my mind." Her tone was harsh and final. At that moment, he could still hear Danata's voice echoing the word, "*servant*" in his mind. "Fine!" Greg said angrily, resenting her decision and her ability to cut him out so easily.

Sam whirled and took two steps toward the dais. "I'm ready," she said.

The Regent smiled and nodded at the man at her side. The hooded figure stepped down from the dais, striding toward Sam.

"Remove your hood. I want to see your face," Sam demanded.

Slowly, the man lowered his hood, revealing unkempt, blond hair and green eyes. Greg and Sam exchanged a quick glance. Not the same Veridan, after all. Disappointment and confusion mingled in Greg's mind. He'd been so sure!

"What are you—?" Portos began, but was abruptly cut short by the Regent.

"Portos! My son doesn't look well. Can you please take him to his room and make sure he is cared for?"

The old man shifted his attention to Ashby and—finding the boy close to collapse—he promptly put an arm around the young man's shoulders. Ashby struggled weakly, eyes swiveling desperately, shooting an admonishing glance at Sam.

"What's wrong with him?" Sam asked, concerned.

"Perhaps all that *travel* has affected his nerves," the Regent suggested with mock concern.

Sam walked up to Ashby and whispered something in his ear. He went very still at her words. After a moment, Sam said, "I want him to stay. He's the reason I'm here, and if he goes, I don't see why I should comply with your demands."

Regent Danata shrugged. "It makes no difference to me."

As if Ashby were a child, Sam brushed hair off his forehead and kissed him lightly on one cheek. The gesture was tender and oddly private. Greg bit his tongue and looked away. His eyes stumbled into the Regent's, who smirked knowingly, making Greg feel like an open book, like she knew exactly how he felt for Sam.

Sam returned to Veridan and looked him in the eye.

"Whenever you're ready," she said.

ᔆ Chapter 36 ᘖ
Sam

As Veridan approached, Sam's whole body went rigid. The aura of hatred emanating from the Sorcerer was tangible, and his presence felt strangely and hazardously familiar. She looked to Ashby, who stood there tongue-tied. They had done something to keep him from talking. She was certain of it. If they could do that, what could they do to her while they sifted through her mind? What could they do to Greg if she didn't agree to go along with it?

Tight-lipped, Veridan stood before her. "This won't take long."

"Just get it over with," she said, feeling her resolve slipping away quickly.

"Very well. Stand right here." The sorcerer pointed at a pentagram on the floor.

Sam hadn't noticed the inlay of a five-pointed star etched into the marble floor. Black obsidian, she guessed, artfully outlined the pentagram's contour in flawless lines. It must have taken countless hours of carving and chiseling to make such a perfect design. The surface of the pentagram was smooth, as if generations of feet had polished it into its glossy state. She tried not to think of how many people had stood there and for what purpose, every single one of them just as scared as she was, as she stepped inside.

Without preamble, Veridan stepped inside the pentagram with her. The outer lines were big enough to accommodate two people, but not enough to stop Sam from shuddering at the violation of her personal space by this menacing man.

You have to do this, Sam, she told herself. *You couldn't live without him even if you tried.* She looked at Ashby. *His world. His rules. You have to learn to live by them.* How horribly helpless it was to be a Morphid. How robbed of her own essence she felt, and how full to overflowing at the same time.

"Close your eyes," Veridan said. She did, shutting Ashby, Greg and everyone else away.

A puff of breath from Veridan's sudden incantation reached her nostrils. It smelled of mint candy and something else that was also pleasant, totally incongruous with the unkempt man. Sam shuddered. The Sorcerer's words were gibberish, yet they seeped through her mind like sand through an hour glass, filtering through the cracks of her subconscious. There was a gentle pressure against her thoughts that felt kind and reassuring. After a moment, Veridan's words, although still foreign, started making sense.

Relax, he said inside her mind. *Let me in.*

Sam's limbs became heavy and warm. It was oddly comfortable. She was in a safe place, dark and moist. *A cocoon*, she realized. A moment later, she was fainting by her car in the school parking lot, aching with the realization that she would lose Greg. As if from a distance, she felt her body quake with the intensity of her feelings of loss. Suddenly, she was yanked from the parking lot, and she was kissing Greg at his apartment, her body flush with passion.

Her heart quickened. She was there with him. It was real. Desperately, she tried to hold on to that moment, but things were speeding up, falling through the dark pit of the past. This time, she was transported to her school library. She shook Greg's hand. An abrupt jolt of electricity ran up her arm. Next, she was naked in her bathroom, answering the phone call that saved her life.

Greg, Greg, Greg. It was all Greg and their feelings for each other. The images sped up, like the pages of a book being thumbed through by an expert librarian. There were only flashes now, some of which didn't even seem familiar—a pink bike, a skinned knee, mean words and loneliness. Sam trembled, feeling cold, abandoned, unloved, so unlike her most recent memories.

Unexpectedly, the warmth from earlier returned, and the onslaught of images gradually slowed down. There was something of interest here, something unforeseen. She felt happy, loved once more and treasured beyond words. Bouncy curls and chubby cheeks on a small ornate mirror that someone held in front of her face. She lifted a hand to grab the beautiful object, but it was taken away. She started crying, but the mirror was replaced by a face that made her forget her disappointment.

She giggled, and with pudgy arms, reached out to touch the beautiful features that glowed with immense tenderness and pride. *Mama*, she babbled. Loving arms picked her up and hugged her. *Isn't she precious?* Her mother asked to no one in particular. Yet an answer came, *More precious than all the jewels in this world and any others*. A man stepped into Sam's field of vision and wrapped his arms around her and her mother.

Wait, Sam thought. *Let me see your face!* The man was too close to distinguish more than a few strands of his long hair. She felt his warmth, smelled his sweet scent and felt his scruffy beard rubbing against her baby skin. She yearned to see his face.

Who are you? She screamed desperately, trying to lift her arms to push the man's face away from hers. But these arms belonged to the past, and would only hug her father tighter and tighter. She had to see his face. Yet she couldn't.

Forget, a voice gently suggested.

No.

Forget, came the voice once more. This time it was an order, but she refused it again.

You will *forget*. There was terrible force in the command. It came on like a ramrod against the fragile constructs of her mind, tearing and ripping through the precious memories, through her reason, threatening to tear her sanity apart.

No. No. No. Her lament echoed as if through a cavern, while she desperately tried to hold on to the shreds of happiness she'd glimpsed. But they were torn like shreds of brittle paper, while she fell down a black hole of oblivion. Her thoughts scattered, leaves in a violent, cold wind.

Could she ever gather them together again?

* * *

"Sam, please wake up." It was Greg's voice.

"If she doesn't wake up, I'll make you pay." This time it was Ashby. He sounded terrified and irate at the same time.

"That's a bit melodramatic," Sam heard Regent Danata reply.

"She's fine," Greg said. "I stopped him as soon I sensed he was trying to hurt her. She's fine. She's got to be fine." He caressed her temple. "I think she's coming around."

As soon as Sam became aware of her surroundings, she curled up into a fetal position. She felt cold and desolate, as if there was no happiness left in the world any longer.

"What happened? Why are you crying?" Ashby asked, almost hysterical, pulling her hands away from her face. "Sam, what did he do to you?"

But she couldn't speak. Even if she could, she couldn't answer his question. All she felt was a ravaged void where there had been . . . something, something that she'd owned for only a few precious seconds. Ashby stepped away, and his face was replaced by Greg's.

"Did you find out what you wanted?" Ashby was screaming at the top of his lungs, making Sam pull her legs tighter into her chest. "Answer me, you bastard! Why do you look this way?"

"That's quite enough, son," Danata said. "Behave yourself, or I'll have you—"

"Or what?" Ashby sounded on the verge of madness. "You'll render me mute again? Cripple me beyond repair, so I can't get in your way?" There was a short pause. The tension in the room crackled. "Isn't that . . . isn't that what you did to Akerman and Uncle Bernard and—"

"Enough insolence," the Regent snapped. "The girl's fine. Look at her. She's getting to her feet, now."

Greg had silently pulled Sam erect. She was so cold, and his arms were so warm and inviting. Her knees wobbled, but Greg held her up and pressed her tight against his body.

"It's okay," he assured her. "You're okay."

"Ashby," Sam murmured. He was walking in her direction, arms outstretched, ready to receive her. Reluctantly, Greg let her go.

She fell into Ashby's arms with more zeal than she believed possible. Was her link with Ashby strengthening? They embraced almost desperately.

"Sam, I'm sorry," Ashby said, squeezing her so hard that she could hardly breathe. "I didn't condone any of this. I didn't know they would . . . we shouldn't have come."

"It's okay. I know it's not your fault." It felt good to be in his arms, just as good or better than being with Greg. Tears were still spilling down her cheeks, but she forced herself to breathe and tried to look around through hazy eyes. She gave a little gasp when two ribbons of light floated in front of her. Remembering her gift, she desperately followed one of the links and confirmed it was attached to Ashby as she'd guessed. She scrutinized the others in the room, but no one else seemed to be linked as she was. She wondered if her gift was limited to seeing herself and her Integrals.

Just when she was almost convinced her talent was useless, Sam noticed a luminous ribbon floating indolently by the door. It rose from behind heavy drapes and ended abruptly in a ragged tip. A feeling of despair and utter sadness washed over her at the sight of it. Something was wrong, but what? She stared, feeling weak with anguish.

There was a bulge behind the drapes. It squirmed, as if it could sense her watching. Out of the corner of her eye, Sam noticed the Regent stand from her chair. Sam whispered in Ashby's ear, "I think there's someone hiding behind the drapes."

Regent Danata followed Sam's gaze. "Bernard!" she cried in anger.

The shape behind the drapes quaked. And who wouldn't? Sam trembled every time the harpy just looked her way.

"You two," she ordered the guards, "get that fool out of here." Simeon and his partner headed for the drapes without hesitation.

"Who is he, Ashby?" Sam asked.

"My uncle," Ashby said sadly.

The guards dragged the man away from the wall. He cried out in protest, kicking his feet wildly. Sam saw his face and realized it was the same man they'd ran into in the halls.

"Don't treat him like that," Sam said weakly, narrowing her eyes and seeing the jagged-tipped ribbon of light once more. Her soul shrank to half its size. Yes, something was wrong, terribly wrong! The whole room started spinning as a spasm of nausea gripped her insides. What had been done to that ribbon was an abomination. Something more perverse than murder.

Ashby held her by the waist to stop her from crumpling to the floor. "Sam!"

"What . . . what's wrong with him?" she sobbed.

"Nothing. Uncle Bernard is just . . . a little unbalanced. He's been like that for a long time. You mustn't let him worry you."

Bernard threw himself on the floor and kicked wildly at the guards. They lost their hold of him.

"Roanna," he cried, "don't take me away from my Roanna!"

"Take that demented man out of here, you incompetent buffoons," the Regent yelled at the guards.

"No." Sam protested, taking a step toward Bernard. "Let him be."

"They won't hurt him, Sam," Ashby said, holding her back.

Sam put her hand out and reached for the errant ribbon of light. *I can fix it*, she thought. *I can mend this horrible crime.*

"Let go of me, Ashby."

The grand hall was thrown into commotion. Something powerful was taking over her, a formidable instinct turning her into a force of nature. Whatever had been taken from this man, she could restore it. Doing nothing, standing idle would be the most terrible evil. Ashby released her arm. She took another step toward Bernard. Her hand reached desperately. The ribbon of light, which had been wafting aimlessly, swayed in her direction, like a snake beckoned by a charmer. A weak jolt of energy made her fingers tingle.

"What is she doing, Veridan?" the Regent demanded. For the first time, Danata sounded uncertain, even a little scared. There was no answer from the Sorcerer. "What is her mark?!"

The guards took hold of Bernard's arms and dragged him toward the door. He thrashed, trying to pull free. Sam had to reach him before they took him away. In her logical mind she was baffled by her own actions, but there was no questioning the clarity of her instincts; she had to get to him. The ribbon of light floated above her. She stretched her hand upward, fingers twitching frantically, but it was too far. To grab it, she had to go to its source. Sam staggered weakly toward Bernard, her legs still numb and cold.

"Stop her," the Regent commanded. Veridan moved to intercept Sam while the Regent yelled another order. "Tell me what her mark is, Ashby."

Greg stepped in Veridan's path. "Oh no, you don't."

The Sorcerer stopped and considered Greg warily.

"Danata, this is madness," Portos said, speaking for the first time.

"Stay out of this." Danata left the dais and approached Ashby. "Tell me what she is. *Now!*"

"I don't know, Mother. I've never seen a mark like hers."

"What does it look like?"

"Why is that so important right now?" Ashby asked.

Sam took two more steps toward Bernard. The link was within reach now. Seeing her close, the man fought more forcefully. She put out a hand, ready to take hold of the dangling, broken strand. She almost had it when Simeon let go of Bernard, grabbed Sam's arm and twisted it behind her back. Sam cried out in pain.

"No! Take your hands off her!" Ashby tried to rush to Sam's aid, but his mother dug her nails into his arm and held him back.

"Somebody fetch more guards," the Regent ordered, but there was no one to follow her order. "Veridan, you good for nothing, do something!" But Veridan remained oddly impassive, merely staring Greg down, as if he feared the teenager more than the Regent.

"Let go of her, you bastard," Greg shouted past the Sorcerer, ready to fight.

Simeon twisted Sam's arm to a breaking point, driving her up onto her tip-toes, then planted a hand on her head and shoved her into Greg's arms.

He caught her and wrapped her in a protective embrace. "Are you all right?"

She didn't answer. Instead, she disentangled herself and headed back toward Bernard. The second guard, Omar, was still struggling with him, an arm wound tightly around his neck. Simeon stepped up to them. "Stubborn old fool," he said, and knocked Bernard out cold with a hook to the jaw.

Greg caught her by the arm, pulling her away. "No," she protested. "I have to help him."

"Okay." Greg sighed. "Let me take care of these two assholes first." He stepped in front of Sam and faced the guards.

The Regent howled in frustration. "Must I do everything myself?"

Suddenly sensing greater danger from the Regent's direction, Greg whirled and shielded Sam with his body.

"Don't move, Sam," Greg ordered, his protective arms corded with tension. "I don't know how, but she's dangerous."

Regent Danata laughed wickedly, and said, "You're right to be afraid." She stalked menacingly. "You won't cause me any more problems, *little Keeper*." She extended her hands above her head and mimed a beckoning motion with her fingers.

"Let's get out of here." Greg snatched Sam's wrist and pulled her toward the door. The guards blocked the exit, but he didn't hesitate.

Sam looked back at Regent Danata, standing there with her beckoning fingers and half-lidded eyes. Following her instinct once more, she squinted and located the two links that joined her to Ashby and Greg. To her astonishment, she saw one of the links descending into the Regent's long fingers; it was the one that connected her to Greg.

"No," she screamed. "Don't do it! Stop, please," she begged, the edge of desolation cutting right through her core.

In answer to Sam's despairing call, Ashby stepped behind his mother and slid an arm around her neck. "I don't know what you're doing, but I won't let you." He seemed shocked to find himself in that situation, but angry enough to act on his instincts. Sam's plea had erased any hesitancy he had left.

Oblivious to what was happening behind him, Greg pressed forward toward the door.

"Enough of these kids' games," Simeon said, pulling a pistol from his hip holster. Omar did the same. "Stand down."

Greg's body shimmered and crackled. He flicked his hands and snapped out two bolts of lightning. Deafening thunder filled the hall as the guards' guns went flying up in the air. The weapons hit the marble floor and slid out of reach. Simeon and Omar clutched their singed hands in shock. Looking warily at Greg, they put their hands up in surrender. In one swift motion, Greg pulled the burly guard into a headlock. The man groaned and cursed as he fought, furiously punching Greg's sides. Soon, his voice became a choked gasp, and he fell unconscious to the floor. Greg let go just as Omar reached him. The guard swung a meaty fist at him, but Greg ducked with uncanny speed and retaliated with an uppercut to Omar's stomach. When the guard doubled over, Greg caught Omar with a knee to the forehead and sent him sprawling next to his fallen comrade.

"Let's get out of here!" Greg pulled Sam's arm, but she dug in her heels. She couldn't leave. Not without Ashby.

"Damn you, Ashby," his mother cursed in a strangled voice, scratching at his arm. "Let me go!" She stepped to the side, trying to free herself from his steadfast grip. Her face was red, her eyes all but glowing with rage. "Let. Me. Go!" she repeated once more.

"No, Mother. This has gone too far. You need to stop."

"Take your hands off me, or you'll regret it. You're no son of mine if you dare go against me. Don't make me hurt you."

"I'd let her go, if I were you," Veridan said, looking as calm as if he were strolling through the park.

"Ashby, Danata, please," Portos said, dancing around them like a headless hen.

Danata slammed an elbow into her son's stomach. Ashby grunted and tightened his hold around her neck. The Regent's face went crimson and her body shook with anger and impotence. A growl, like an animal's, broke through her throat. Trembling, she thrust her hands above Ashby's head.

"No!" Sam lurched forward.

Danata's hands clasped together and gripped what might have been an invisible tree branch. Twisting her grip viciously, she jerked her hands apart in a brutal ripping motion. Instantly, Sam felt a wrenching tug in her very entrails. Like a rag doll, she crumpled to her knees. Hands spasming at her sides, she watched the luminous lifeline that had connected her to Ashby flailing like a fish out of water. She pitched forward and shook on all fours.

"Ashby!" Her voice was nothing but a weak whine of agony. Her Integral lay motionless at Danata's feet. She reached out a trembling hand in his direction. "Ashby." She tried to crawl toward him, but she felt devoid of energy. Lifeless. With a thud, she collapsed on her face. Cold tears ran down her cheek and seeped between the cracks of the marble tiles beneath her.

The room went utterly silent. In the back of her dimming mind, she knew no one there would understand what had happened. In a way, she had known all along but her mind had been too slow to grasp it. Her instincts had told her what was wrong with Bernard. Not just that, they'd also told her she could fix it—she'd had the power to mend what the Regent's devilry must have done, only now it was too late. Her life was slipping away.

A vast chasm of emptiness opened and grew inside her, quickly engulfing her soul, threatening to swallow her forever. Her body, her mind, her whole being floated aimlessly. But she didn't care. Ashby had slipped away, and she had nothing else to fight for. He had been swallowed as soon as his mother severed the lifeline between them. Her love was gone, dead. No gift, no magic could bring him back. She would follow him now. Without him, going on living was impossible.

ℰ Chapter 37 ℛ
Greg

The moment Regent Danata reached for the ceiling, Greg sensed the looming danger, his Keeper senses blaring louder than ever. But her decision was so swift, her gesture so weird, he had no time to understand, much less react to what she was doing. Ashby collapsed to the floor, then Sam a moment later. Portos gaped and stood speechless. The Regent's gesturing to the heavens had done something, but Greg had no idea what. Only that it was ripping his world apart.

Wavering, he approached Sam and knelt by her side. Tears streamed from her open, vacant eyes. With a tremulous hand, he removed a strand of hair from her face and felt his own eyes sting with despair. After Veridan had looked into her mind and Sam crumpled to the floor, Greg had known she was fine. Now confusion and agony descended on him, chilling his very soul. She was breathing, but her face was ashen. Other than that, she might have been sleeping or . . . No! She would be fine. She would come to.

"It serves you right, you impudent lass," the Regent said, rubbing her neck and looking down at Sam with contempt.

"Ashby?" Portos's hesitant voice. The High Sorcerer knelt by him. Greg watched him impassively, waiting for the same strange fate to strike him down at any instant.

Portos rose to his feet unsteadily and backed away from Ashby. His face was contorted in horror. "What have you done?" he asked the Regent. "What sort of dark gift have you been hiding from us?"

The Regent laughed maniacally and turned to Portos. "A powerful one, Portos. A unique gift that a simple-minded, spineless Sorcerer would never understand." Danata lowered her gaze and, for the first time, looked at her son.

"But how could you? Your own son . . ." Portos shook his head incredulously, pointing at Ashby's prone figure.

"He brought it upon himself with his witless audacity." Her words were harsh, but regret colored her voice. "Nobody raises their hand against me. I would rather have a lame son than such a rebellious, disrespectful one."

"A dead one, you mean?" Portos said, his wrinkled face spelling the pain he felt for the boy that lay immobile at his feet.

Dead?! Greg's eyes flickered down to Ashby, whose face was visible between the Regent's feet. His features were ashen, distorted in a grimace of pain, but he appeared as if he would wake up any second. There was still color in his cheeks. He looked like . . .

Sam! Greg snapped from his trance. He put a hand over her chest. *Oh God, did she stop breathing?* Her chest didn't seem to be rising up and down anymore. He pressed an ear to her chest and listened. Her heartbeat was faint, but still there. *What do I do?* He felt impotent. This wasn't like at the soup kitchen, where he'd known exactly how to save her. Here, she'd just collapsed for no apparent reason.

"Dead?" the Regent asked dumbly. "What do you mean, dead? He's not dead . . . he's just . . ." Danata took a step back, away from Ashby's lifeless body. "Veridan, Veridan!"

The Sorcerer walked reluctantly toward Ashby and knelt. With a blank and unfeeling expression, he got back up and shook his head.

"No, no," Danata cried, shaking her head. "He can't be dead. They never die."

In a sudden dash, Danata rushed to Ashby's side and shook him. "You're not dead," she yelled. "Wake up!" She grabbed his shoulders and shook him violently. "Wake up, wake up, wake up," she repeated with each thrust of her arms. She fell into a frenzy, wailing and shaking his inert body.

Greg watched in a stupor, feeling his own life slipping away while Sam's face grew paler and paler. *This is it*, Greg thought with a detached calm. She was slipping away, and he couldn't stop it. All he could hope for was a similar fate. Except somehow he knew he wouldn't share it. She was going to leave him behind. Death would not come for him now. It only felt that way because the thought of losing her was unbearable, because life without her would be senseless.

"Somebody help her," Greg demanded suddenly. He couldn't let her die if she wasn't going to take him along.

No one came to their aid. No one said a word. The only sound in the huge hall was the Regent's with her shrieks of denial, her hysterical laments for the son she had unknowingly murdered.

"That's quite enough, Danata," said a new voice.

Listlessly, Greg looked to see who had spoken. In shock, he realized it was Veridan. Not the blond, disheveled man who had prodded inside of Sam's mind, but the fastidious Sorcerer with manicured nails and perfectly cropped hair, the man who had tried to kill her at the gas station. So it had been him all along, concealing his true identity through an illusion—a trick that was no longer needed, now that Ashby was dead, and Sam dying.

"Stop, Danata," Veridan said, but the Regent carried on in despair. "Have you gone mad?"

All the commotion had attracted an audience. At every doorway leading into the hall, heads peered in, though no one dared to enter. Seeing Ashby's body near the dais, many gasped in horror, and commotion grew outside.

"You, Xasdia," Veridan said, pointing a finger at one of the peering heads. She stepped in shyly and exchanged a few quiet words with the Sorcerer.

Portos shuffled toward Greg, looking dazed and twice as old.

Greg looked up helplessly. "Please, help her."

The High Sorcerer looked down at Sam's motionless, crumpled body and shook his head. "I'm sorry, lad. This magic is unknown to me."

The desire to stand and shake the old man flitted past him. Greg had no passion left in him. There was nothing left, only despair. He picked Sam up and cradled her to his chest.

"I'm sorry," he whispered in her ear. "I'm so sorry I couldn't keep them from hurting you. I failed you."

Sam's clouded eyes looked to his. There was the barest hint of life left in them. Yet they seemed to tell him it wasn't his fault. That she didn't blame him for anything.

Oh, but it was his fault. He could have prevented this. He knew from the beginning that they shouldn't have come here, but he'd been too busy building walls around himself—his pain making all the decisions for him. Being discarded so quickly and so absolutely had been too much, so he'd done the only thing he could to survive the blow. And in the process, he'd stopped fighting for Sam. Now it was too late to fight for her. The only thing he had left was to drop the pretense. He owed her at least that much.

Greg looked into Sam's cloudy eyes and slowly lowered his lips to hers. He brushed them lightly and was shocked by how cold and lifeless they felt. He pulled back and searched her features. There was no reaction. Again, he lowered his mouth to hers, but stopped right before their lips met.

"I love you," he whispered. He wished he'd said it before. He wished he'd been honest.

He touched his mouth to hers once more, pouring his entire being into the kiss. They would never be this close again. They would never feel the indescribable surge of their bodies melding into one. He lifted his face. He wiped his eyes angrily. She had just morphed. She'd had her entire life ahead of her. This wasn't fair.

Someone has to pay for this, he thought. He couldn't just sit there, crying like a helpless child. He had to avenge her. He looked past Danata, already ruined with grief. Past Portos, talking to her in hushed whispers. He looked at the first one who had put Sam in danger, the one who had reached into her mind and done God knows what. The one who had stood by, smirking while she was murdered, who had strolled about while Danata murdered her only son. The one whose arrogant, knowing gaze said plenty.

Veridan.

Greg kissed Sam's forehead, set her down gently, and stood. He wouldn't be a Keeper much longer. Whatever powers he still had would disappear when his link to Sam was gone. He had to do something with the remnants of his gift. He had to fight. Maybe even go down fighting, to follow Sam wherever she was going.

He spotted him in the back of the room, issuing orders to the witnessing crowd. In Greg's mind, the Sorcerer still posed a threat to Sam, which was enough to let him wield his Keeper powers against the bastard. With suicidal determination, he charged in Veridan's direction. Those talking to the Sorcerer retreated in panic.

Alerted, Veridan whirled to face Greg, reached inside his shirt and pulled out a thick chain. From it hung an amulet crisscrossed by intricate lines and set with a dark rock at its center. Veridan mouthed a spell and the necklace began to glow.

Greg faltered, wondering if his powers would hold, then remembered that it didn't matter. Self-destruction was the goal. If he bloodied up the Sorcerer in the process . . . so much the better.

Gathering what was left of himself, Greg attacked. A burst of energy erupted through his fingertips, shooting across the room in a jagged lightning bolt. As the surge erupted from his core, he felt his limbs weaken. He staggered, fighting to keep his balance, and watched his magic hit Veridan square in the chest. The Sorcerer staggered, but recovered almost immediately. A smile of surprise and satisfaction stretched his thin mouth.

Greg inhaled, focusing all his attention on his enemy. More energy collected in his hands and he let it strike again. With a quick gesture, Veridan drew a circle around himself. Greg's magical force sizzled through the air, hit an invisible barrier mere inches from its target, then rolled off to the floor like rainwater on a clear umbrella. Veridan smirked with satisfaction once more.

"I'll kill you," Greg shouted, storming forward.

Veridan flinched and moved back a step.

Just like his magic, Greg slammed against an unseen barrier. He bounced back, dazed. Veridan straightened from his cowering posture and laughed. Leaving one hand outstretched to hold the shield in place, the Sorcerer launched a counterattack with the other. After an inaudible whisper, a red blast struck Greg's face. Blistering heat licked his skin. He should have been immune, but weakened as he was, he felt every nerve ending scream.

Greg shrieked, blinded, and covered his face with both hands. Distorted shapes rose in front of him. He ignored them and stubbornly plowed ahead, seeing little more than the Sorcerer's outline. Veridan was a breath's length from his reach, but Greg's hands flailed against the barrier, unable to take hold of him.

"Not so strong anymore, are we?" Veridan's smug voice.

Greg growled in frustration, pushing against the Sorcerer's invisible wall.

"I guess your little pet's slipping away," the Sorcerer sneered.

How dare he even think of Sam, the filthy bastard? His mocking and dismissive tone made Greg's blood boil. Worst of all, it was true. Sam was slipping away. His dwindling strength was proof. But she wasn't gone yet was she? Which meant *he* wasn't gone.

Determined to die, Greg shut his eyes and focused all that remained of his power. His body vibrated with the effort. Sweat dripped down his back as he emptied each and every one of his cells, seeping their life force and condensing it in his right hand. For a few more seconds, he pretended to struggle, smashing against Veridan's shield. When his fingertips felt like blazing claws, Greg drew his arm back and released it. The glowing mass of his fist hit Veridan's barrier with a strident pop that almost burst his eardrums. Ignoring the pain, he pushed harder.

Greg's knife-like fingertips cut through the barrier with a sizzle. Veridan jumped back, shocked, but not before Greg took hold of the chain around the Sorcerer's neck, squeezed his hand around it and pulled, trying to rip it off. The remnants of energy left in his fingers crackled against the coarse metal, fusing the chain into a lumpy mass.

Veridan looked down in panic. Greg yanked the chain. The Sorcerer stumbled forward and crashed into Greg. Losing their balance, Keeper and Sorcerer tumbled to the floor. In the tussle, Veridan rolled on top of Greg and clamped his hands over the young man's throat. Air flow to Greg's lungs stopped immediately, blocked by Veridan's strength as much as his magic. Blood began pounding in his ears. Greg tried to push the Sorcerer off, but his body had gone as rigid as the marble floor. He shut his eyes, hoping to find some magic left in him, but he was spent. This was it. He had failed her even in his revenge.

Sam. He sent his mind in search of her familiar presence, the presence that had been with him ever since he morphed. She wasn't there.

I love you, Sam.

As his vision darkened, he finally managed to picture her beautiful honey-colored eyes—the part of her that the metamorphosis had altered the least. As quickly as it came, the image blurred and began to fade, melding into the ominous shadows that crept around the edges of his consciousness.

If only he'd been able to tell her he loved her, he would have one less regret.

Gradually, the darkness engulfed his vision until only a tiny circle of light was left, much like a lonely star against a black, lifeless universe.

Goodbye.

The tiny circle suddenly flashed, expanding at the speed of light, eradicating the darkness like a supernova. The light was as blinding as the blackness had been.

It held him in place.

℘ *Chapter 38* ℭ
Sam

Drifting.

Like a hollow log in a river, Sam sailed on an invisible current. It was gentle and slow, yet powerful. Floating adrift in this tranquil and painless abandon was easy.

For what felt like a lifetime, she glided without resistance. It didn't even occur to her to go against the flow. Something beckoned her downstream, and she was loyal to her instincts, just as she had ever since she morphed. It was too late to learn from her mistakes.

From a million miles away, a pleading cry reached her. It brushed her numb consciousness like a feather's touch. It almost made no impression, yet the plea was fierce and sincere. Something in her soul stirred. The calm flow that had set her adrift changed, and Sam now felt herself being tugged by another, opposite current. At first, the draw was weak, but before long its intensity became impossible to ignore.

She listened, and thought she recognized the call. It was . . . hope. Even though it was harder, much harder, to heed this new plea, she opened her mind and her heart. As abruptly as the call began, it stopped. Sam struggled to find the lifeline cast into her river of abandonment, but every time she thought she'd taken hold of something, it slipped away.

Goodbye?

Sam fought harder. Hope awaited on the other end. It couldn't be *goodbye*. Giving up no longer seemed a good idea. Like a drowning victim kicking desperately to get her head above water, she struggled against the relentless current that promised only oblivion.

With all her might, she reached toward a pinprick of light through which her lifeline retreated at an alarming speed, an anchor being pulled up by a departing ship. Her redemption was sliding up and away. If she let this one chance go, there wouldn't be another. And not just for her. She needed to save herself if she wanted to save him. She couldn't allow Greg to perish. Wouldn't.

But how? How could she make a choice when her nature didn't allow her? She searched her heart for an answer. The despair of her loss stared her in the face. Pain was the only thing pulling her down and away from life. There was nothing else. What had held her back before had been severed.

There is choice, now. There is *a choice!*

Realizing this, Sam fought. Her own heart and mind, not something alien, drove her to act. Her desire was rooted on free will, not blind obedience to her Morphid nature.

I'm free, free to choose.

Suddenly, her vision exploded into a kaleidoscope of blinding light. With a jolt, she sat up and gasped for air, calling out the one name that burned in her mind and in her throat. But her voice was weak, and didn't carry. She looked madly around the hall. She saw Danata first, kneeling on the floor, and ignored the bundle by her side. She couldn't look at it. She *wouldn't* look at it, or she'd be lost again.

"No," she gasped when she saw Greg across the stone floor, pinned beneath Veridan, his face slack and red. "Greg!" Her hand reached out to him, fingers trembling.

Blood coursed through her veins, making her limbs tingle, giving back her strength in spurts. She staggered to her feet, even as the hall seemed to tip over to one side. He needed help. She teetered weakly toward them.

As she approached, she could see Veridan's face contorted in rage and vicious pleasure as he throttled him.

"Greg," Sam called out again, fearing it was already too late.

At the sound of her voice, Greg's eyelashes fluttered and his hands lifted from the floor. Veridan's mouth dropped open in shock. His victim was coming back from the brink of death, and started fighting back. Greg's eyes sprang open, and Sam's blood flowed faster, flooding her with warmth and coordination. She was like a tree relishing the sun after a long winter.

Sam realized what was happening. Their link was growing stronger, and that was all Greg needed to regain his power. Sam halted and felt Greg's power surge. A terrible, raw cry of agony broke through the hall as Greg threw Veridan to one side, the Sorcerer's face contorted in an awful grimace. Greg rolled over and straddled the Sorcerer, face intent on murder. His eyes were dark, huge pupils blotting away the cerulean of his irises.

Veridan's shrieks were reduced to a strangled groan as Greg squeezed his throat with one hand, his other fist raised over his head. A sizzling sound that made Sam's insides churn hissed through the hall. The Sorcerer's legs kicked under Greg's weight.

Veridan's raspy pleas were reduced to no more than an annoying bee's buzz. Greg slammed his fist into the Sorcerer's face and growled savagely.

"Greg?" Sam said hesitantly.

He stopped and turned to look at her. He was breathing heavily, chest pumping, eyes full of despair. He sat stock-still, staring at her without a shred of comprehension, pupils still wide, expression savage. He showed no signs of recognizing her.

A jolt of fear went through Sam. "Greg. It's me. Sam."

He stood. Veridan cowered at his feet, not making a sound.

Hands shaking, Greg hesitantly approached Sam. His expression cleared. A few paces away from her, he stopped. His lips parted and his eyes wavered. A breath caught in his throat while different emotions colored his features.

"Sam," he said in a husky breath of incredulity. For a short instant, their eyes held fast.

After a too-short moment, Greg turned, glaring at the few who remained. The intensity in his stance was such that several took a step back. They knew what he was capable of. No one dared challenge him.

"Perry!" Greg shouted, "Someone bring me Perry or I'll make you regret it."

Sam's skin crawled at the ferocity of Greg's threat. In spite of that, no one moved even an inch. Making good on his threat, he started toward a group of people in the back, looking ready to tear them down.

"Wait!"

Portos—the tired, old Sorcerer—hobbled forward, looking stricken with grief and shame. His eyes were red, and his hand shook as he gestured toward the door. "Please, come with me."

Without a second thought, Greg took Sam by the wrist and pulled her along. She looked back and saw Veridan squirming on the floor, each jerk of his body accompanied by an agonizing groan. As she passed by the Regent, now weakly keening by her son, Sam shut her eyes. A world of pain lay at her back. If she looked, she'd never be able to leave it behind.

As they stepped into the corridor, they found it blocked. Greg bristled.

"Move out of the way," Portos ordered.

"Y-yes, Sir." It was Simeon, who was pulling Bernard's unconscious body, probably feeling guilty for having punched him out and trying to get him some help. A fearful eye toward Greg, Simeon yanked on poor Bernard, dragging his limp body into an adjacent hall.

"Wait." Sam pulled her hand free from Greg's grip. "I have to help him."

"No." Greg took her by the shoulders. "Sam, we have to get outta here."

"I have to, Greg. He's in such pain. I felt that agony today. So did you. He's lived with it for years." Sam struggled in Greg's arms, while Portos and Simeon regarded her warily. "Now let go of me!" She pushed him aside and calmly stepped to Bernard's side. Simeon took a step forward, trying to stop her.

"Don't interfere," Portos ordered in a stern tone that was also full of curiosity.

The guard backed away, muttering something under his breath.

Sam knelt next to Bernard and stared into his careworn face. His nose bled from the punch he had taken earlier. All his features spoke of pain and misery, but physical injury was not the cause. It was something much deeper, something Sam now knew from experience.

Closing her eyes almost completely, Sam let her instincts take control. After a moment, her hand reached upward. Her fingers moved in a beckoning motion, coaxing the ribbon of light to her. As it brushed her fingers, she made a fist and caught it. Feeling its weak energy blundering, searching, Sam shut her eyes and lowered her face as if in prayer. In her mind's eye, a ribbon of energy oscillated in a gentle and aimless search for its other half.

She reached with her free hand to the heavens, lips moving in a litany of unknown words, like a priestess beseeching her god. For a few seconds, nothing happened. Greg's shoes scuffed against the floor, making her aware of his restlessness.

Before Sam realized her actions were having a visible effect, she heard the surprised gasps of those around her. She saw a warm, orange light through her shut eyelids. Her eyes sprang open. The hall was shining under a dazzling light, as if the sun had broken through the castle's stone walls. Everyone shielded their faces from the luminosity that descended from above. Simeon took several steps back, abandoning all pretenses of courage. Portos stood immobile, in complete awe, barely shielding his eyes from the blinding light.

Sam beckoned to the light. She didn't know how she was calling it, or why it obeyed, but it descended until the tips of her outstretched fingers felt the smoldering heat emanating from it. She flinched, but it was a human instinct, like a child shying away from a candle flame. The brilliance retreated, but she gently commanded its return. It fell upon her, reaching her hand, traveling down the length of her body until it engulfed her. Brilliance embraced her. Sam's arms tingled with energy, and she felt something barely tangible slip between her fingers.

Her heart swelled, and a tantalizing sensation filled her being. She reveled in the sweet, blissful feeling. A cry of victory rose to her throat. She felt like a goddess, a being capable of restoring life. A glorious shiver ran down her spine, while in her hands, two pieces of a broken puzzle yearned to be reunited.

She marveled at the existence of such powerful connections between two people, and at the audacity and heartlessness of the one who'd severed them. Such an evil, twisted soul.

In awe of her own gift, Sam brought her hands together and watched as every strand of the severed strip extended to find its missing thread. Each tiny filament joined its match and rejoiced, exploding into a million colors that Sam never knew existed. Absolute joy washed over her in waves.

She carefully let go of the repaired connection, confirming that it would remain whole. The burst of light that had blinded them all gradually diminished. At last, all that was left was a floating ribbon of light that seemed to pulsate with rapture —a union that only Sam could see. It lifted up and disappeared through the stone ceiling. Sam imagined it lead to Bernard's Roanna, but where was she? Where had she been all this time?

A sharp cry of something between pain and deliverance pulled Sam out of her state of amazement. Bernard sat up with a jerk, panting like a man who'd just been saved from drowning. He looked at Sam as if he'd never seen her before. The man looked from one unfamiliar face to the next, trying to make sense of his situation. His eyes were clear and attentive. At last, they settled on the High Sorcerer.

"Portos?" He said, his voice full of uncertainty and bewilderment.

"Bernard?" Portos's voice echoed the same wonderment.

"You . . . look different," Bernard said, trying to stand. Sam offered him a hand. He took it, and wobbled to his feet. "What happened? Who's this lovely young lady?"

Portos was at a loss for words. "I . . . well . . . she's . . ."

"Where is Roanna?" Bernard asked, forgetting his previous question.

The High Sorcerer shook his head and averted his eyes. Bernard looked to the others for an answer, his anxiety growing with every second of silence.

"Is she all right? And the baby?" Bernard demanded. "Has something happened? Where is Danata?" He asked this last question with dread. When he received only blank faces in answer, he burst into action. "I'll find Roanna and Celestine myself." He scurried past the guard and disappeared into the long corridor.

With Bernard's parting words, Sam felt all her happiness disappear. Confusion filled her instead.

"Simeon," Portos said, "follow him and inform me of his whereabouts." As the guard left to obey his orders, the old Sorcerer turned to Sam.

His inquisitive eyes made her squirm. To divert his attention, she asked, "Who's Celestine?"

Portos didn't answer, but continued to scrutinize her. "What are you?" he asked after an interminable moment.

"I . . . I don't . . . know."

"Sam, we've stayed long enough. We need to find Perry. He can send us back." He wasn't pleading anymore. His tone was now commanding.

Portos stepped forward. "You don't need Perry. I'll help you get back, lad. You two have had your fill of Castle Rothblade's hospitality, I'm sure. Follow me."

Greg gave the old man a dissecting once-over, then said, "Yeah, he's safe."

They followed the High Sorcerer, hurrying down a different set of corridors.

"We need the potion. I've got it in my room," Portos said, "They took my talisman away. I couldn't do anything to help you. I'm so sorry."

Greg's eyes swiveled all around, checking every corner for danger. He was much more interested in speed than apologies.

"Bernard's *vinculum* must have been broken. You repaired it, did you not?" Portos asked Sam.

"Yes," said Sam, assuming *vinculum* was the proper Morphid name for the wafting tendrils of light, the links her kind shared.

"And Danata . . . she . . ."

"She's a monster," Sam blurted out.

"A *Ripper*," Portos whispered. "Something I thought was only a myth."

"Yes, a Ripper." It was the perfect name for her.

"I never suspected it . . ." Portos said with shame as they turned another corner.

"Nobody around here seems to know much of anything," Greg said.

"You don't understand, boy. Your kind and . . . her kind have only ever existed in the distant past. For many, only in fairy tales and nursery rhymes."

"Perry!" Greg exclaimed as he spotted the young sorcerer walking away from them down a grand stairway.

Perry stopped and climbed back to the top of the steps. "Hey, I just got back from undoing all the spells on Sam's family. Where's Ashby?"

Sam closed her eyes at the mention of the name. Something inside her twisted in agony, and she held onto Greg's arm for support.

"He . . ." Greg started, but after looking at Sam, he was unable to utter the words.

"His mother, she . . ." Portos started, but he was unable to finish, too. "Not now, Perry. Later. I need to help them get back home."

Perry looked back uncertain. "And Ashby's good with that?"

"Everyone's okay with it," Greg said, hoping to avoid the impending fallout. "Let's go, old man."

"Nah, wait a minute." Perry stepped in front of Greg to block the way. "Portos, Ashby can't be okay with this."

"Ashby's dead," Greg blurted out.

Portos went pale. Sam choked back a sob as Perry gaped and turned to Portos with a questioning glance. The old man gave him a grief-stricken nod as his only response.

"No," Perry shook his head. "He can't be dead. He was just . . ." Perry stopped.

"There they are," someone shouted from the bottom of the stairs.

"Go!" Greg gave the old man an encouraging shove on the shoulder.

Portos started up the hall again. Greg ushered Sam forward. Perry stayed on the spot, staring blankly at the floor. After a moment, he turned sharply and ran toward the Regent's hall.

In an instant, the sound of boots against the stone floors filled the halls. Portos lumbered, going as fast as his old legs seemed to allow. After a few more turns down the labyrinth, Greg and Sam entered a large room filled with bookshelves, long working tables and a small, austere bed. Portos shut the door and locked it, just as something heavy thudded against it on the other side.

"Open the door," someone shouted, followed by several loud knocks on the heavy oak.

The High Sorcerer hurried to a large, wooden cabinet and threw the doors open. Its shelves were stacked with row upon row of vials filled with luminescent potions, half-spent candles, jars with yellowed labels stuffed with herbs and small white things that suspiciously resembled teeth.

Something heavy crashed against the door. Sam jumped and yelped. Portos slid a drawer open, pulled out a sun-shaped, silver amulet and slipped it over his neck. He grabbed two small vials of green, iridescent liquid and turned around to face them.

"Drink this!" he ordered, handing each a small bottle.

They uncapped the containers and gulped the nasty brew.

Outside, one of their pursuers barked an order, "Back away from the door!" Seconds later, the metallic *click* of a gun cocking was followed by a loud bang. Splinters flew as the heavy lock twisted in the wooden door.

"Do it. Send us back. Now!" Greg shouted.

Portos squeezed his amulet between old, nubby fingers and quickly began muttering an incantation. A tingling feeling began in Sam's lips and spread downward, traveling all the way down to her toes. She shut her eyes as her stomach dropped like she was riding a roller coaster. There was a cracking sound, as if the world were breaking in half. She lurched, but Greg was there, one arm around her waist.

Then everything went still. Sam opened her eyes and found herself staring into grease-stained pizza boxes. They were back in the hotel room that they'd left only hours ago. Portos wasn't with them. It was only Sam and Greg.

No one else.

She pressed her face to Greg's chest, her body exhausted with both relief and dread. He held her tight and whispered reassuring words in her ear. They were home, but she didn't feel safer—no matter how many times Greg said it would be all right.

ℰ Chapter 39 ℭ
Sam

"So how was Europe? You have got to show me some pictures!" Brooke exclaimed, giving Sam a tight hug that felt different since she was now taller. "I missed you." As Brooke released her, Sam looked carefully for any hint of skepticism in her features, but her friend showed no sign that she'd noticed anything different—even if Sam didn't look anything like her old self anymore. Not even the fact that Sam was now taller seemed to make an impression.

What a mind job!

Apparently, Perry was quick at following orders, and everyone, including James and Rose, showed no awareness of the physical changes Sam had undergone or the time she'd been missing.

"I missed you, too," Sam admitted, giving Brooke another tight hug that made the girl blink in surprise.

"You okay?" Brooke asked.

"I'm fine." Sam fought the tears that suddenly filled her eyes.

She'd missed the normalcy, even the boredom. She'd wanted her life to change, but not like this.

For now, it was good to be back in school. They had stayed away for two weeks after their return from England, afraid that an army of Morphids, headed by Regent Danata herself, would come after them. But nothing had happened, and Greg's instincts had remained quiet, though alert. The possibility of having to run, if and when Greg sensed danger, loomed over their heads.

Fearful and gloomy thoughts occupied Sam's mind most of the time. She found herself staring off into space, the feeling of emptiness heavy on her heart. Sleep eluded her most nights and when it came, nightmares made real rest impossible. She dreamed about being *ripped* from Greg, the way she'd been separated from Ashby.

Most disturbing of all was the sudden recollection of the memories Veridan had unlocked. The woman she had now come to believe was her mother, and the unseen face of the man who must have been her father. Her need to learn their identities made her restless and taunted her, driving her mind to tragic explanations for her adoption.

With all of that, school was a much needed distraction. She had to have a purpose and *weaving* people back together was not a profession that would ever put food on the table. As elated as she'd been after helping Bernard, she wanted to feel normal and human, even if she was a Morphid. She didn't have the slightest idea how to be comfortable in this new skin. After all the trials, she didn't even know her caste. What if there were more mental changes she wasn't even aware of?

Greg kept insisting it would take time, but she doubted it would ever be all right. What they'd gone through with Danata and Veridan made her despise her own kind. They were also part of her nightmares, lurking in every shadow.

Bernard came to her, too, with his sad, lost eyes. She always thought of him with longing, and the crazy hope that he and his Roanna had something to do with her past—that they might even be her parents. Why else would Bernard have kept calling her by his wife's name? Why else would Danata hate Sam so much? There had to be some sordid history there. So many questions, and no answers.

"You didn't have to take both of them, you know," Brooke said as they walked toward class. "School's been dull without those two hotties. Did you bring them back?"

She hadn't stopped to consider how obvious it was that they all disappeared at the same time. It was best to avoid this question altogether. "So what did I miss?"

"What did *you* miss? Are you serious? You're *not* going to get away with that so easily. I have to see pictures, hear about what you did—"

"That's the thing. Uh, my . . . camera phone broke."

"What? What kind of lame excuse is that? You could have bought another one, bought a disposable, something!"

"Um . . . no, it broke *after* the trip. Some TSA guy dropped it at the airport. I lost all my pictures."

Brooke narrowed her eyes and pursed her lips. "You're kidding, right? Sam, I'm your best friend, and you didn't even send me one miserable email or text. What's going on?"

"Nothing's going on."

"Sure." Brooke rolled her eyes. "Well, well, well. If it isn't another of our most talked about missing persons. We were about to issue an Amber alert," she added, looking at Greg who was headed in their direction. "What did you guys do with the other one, kill him?"

Sam felt her knees buckle, then Greg was right beside her, holding her by the waist at just the right time.

"Hello, Brooke. How are you? It's good to see you, too," Greg said.

"I guess neither one of you is going to answer my questions. Fine, be mysterious for all I care." Brooke stomped away without a backward glance.

"Brooke," Sam called after her.

"Let her go. She'll get over it."

"I hope so."

"How are you today?"

"Glad to be back . . . I guess."

Greg smiled and shyly took her hand. "Things will settle down."

"I'm counting on that, or I won't be able to stay sane. I don't know how you . . . ?"

As always, Greg understood. "You don't know how I . . . deal with it?"

She nodded. Since their return home, her conversations with Greg had been circumspect. She didn't like discussing what had happened, reliving the agony. So many faces haunted her dreams. But today, she felt as ready as she'd probably ever be. She met Greg's gaze and nodded.

"I take it one day at a time, one minute at a time. Do you . . ." he paused, allowing her a chance to dismiss the conversation, "feel different, now that . . . you're only linked to me?"

She took a deep breath. "Yes." The word came out as a breath of exhaustion.

Greg stared at the floor and shifted his weight from one foot to another. She let go of his hand and hugged herself.

"But each day, the emptiness gets a bit smaller. Sometimes I manage not to think about it all. Other times . . . well, it's not so easy. I guess time will make it all okay . . . eventually."

"Good . . ." Greg's lips stayed parted as if he wanted to add more, but then he pressed them back together. What else was there to say? Nothing.

"Any . . . alarms?" she asked.

"Nothing." Greg tried to smile reassuringly, but it fell short of its goal.

They had left things in an upheaval at Rothblade Castle. It might take the Regent some time to get it together again, but they had no doubt she would recover, and once she did . . .

"She's crazy," Greg said. "She'll want revenge, even if it's all her fault, even if she was the one who . . ."

"Who killed Ashby," Sam finished for him. "You can say it. I can handle it now." She tried to tell herself that at least once a day. It still hurt like hell, but at least she could say it out loud.

"Yeah well, we won't be safe indefinitely. I'm sure of that. If only I'd killed that bastard," Greg expressed his regret yet again, but he wasn't a killer.

Sam sighed. "Veridan's just one of our problems."

"I know what you mean. The Regent's the one. I'm afraid she might try to . . ." He didn't finish.

"I know. I've been thinking about it a lot." Her head wasn't stuck in the sand, even if it seemed that way. Her link to Greg was their only weapon. If Danata had managed to sever that, they might die or, in the least, Greg would lose his powers.

"We'll be okay, Sam. That's my job, and I won't let anything happen to you. I'm getting more used to my powers every day."

"She's an awful woman," Sam continued. "What she did to that poor man, Bernard. Only a monster could do that. I wonder how many others she's hurt that way."

"Don't worry about that, Sam. You'll drive yourself crazy."

"Every day, I try to tell myself that I shouldn't worry about it, that it's not my problem, but what if it is? What if that's the reason I'm here?"

The bell rang, announcing their next class. Sam was relieved. Her mood always turned sour when she considered the possibility that weaving broken, lost souls was a moral duty she must fulfill.

"Ugh, calculus next," Greg complained, bringing her back to a much easier reality, a reality she wished to be part of wholeheartedly. "You're going to have to help me catch up."

She smiled. "How do you do that?"

"Do what?"

"Always know what I need?"

He shrugged and smiled, his eyes twinkling. "One of the perks."

They exchanged an awkward, meaningful glance. "Don't worry, I'll help you with math. You'll be fine."

Greg tenderly brushed her cheek with the back of his hand. "I know." It was the first time since they returned that he'd touched her this way. A chill ran down Sam's spine, leaving her with a pleasant thrill. A small part of her resented the reaction, but that half was growing quieter every day.

"Let's talk after class," Greg said, inclining his head toward their classroom.

* * *

Later, in Spanish class, Sam found her regular seat empty. As she sat, reassured by Greg's presence in the back of the room, Brooke ignored her by pretending to doodle in the back of her notebook.

"Brooke," Sam whispered. "Brooke!"

"What?" Brooke turned around, looking peeved.

"I'll tell you everything."

Brooke's face lit up and her eyes widened with expectation. "So . . . ?" she nagged when Sam remained quiet.

"I just can't right now . . . not for some time."

"Oh, what a load of . . ."

"Buenos días," Profesora Garza said, walking in at her customary brisk pace.

"It's not good, and . . . it wouldn't be easy right now. It's too soon," Sam whispered.

Brooke must have seen the pain on Sam's face, because her expression became sheepish. "Yo comprendo," she said in her best Spanish accent. "But don't think I'll let you forget." Brooke waved a warning finger in front of Sam's face.

"I know you won't. Don't worry. I'll tell you, even if you'll think I'm crazy."

"I won't," Brooke said, sounding hurt by the accusation.

"We'll see about that."

After a *very* normal day of classes, Sam met Greg by the lockers. He was putting his books and basketball inside. His last period—the only one they didn't share—was gym, so he wore shorts, a Pacers jersey, and wet hair.

"Cool tattoo, dude. Can I look at it?" Matt Canden said as he noticed part of Greg's mark peeking out from behind his collar. Whether from secrecy or embarrassment, Sam couldn't tell which, Greg pulled his jersey back up.

"Sorry, man!" Matt looked chagrined. "I just wanted to see what it was, but that's cool. I'd love to get one, but my folks won't have it."

Greg smiled apologetically. "No problem, man. Good game," he told Matt, trying to smooth things over a bit. Matt seemed unaffected, and waved goodbye without a second thought.

"Hey, there you are," Greg said as he noticed Sam, standing off to the side.

"I hide mine, too. We should research how they do scarification, so we can explain when somebody asks the inevitable questions."

"I can tell you how. I've already looked into it," Greg said with a rueful smile.

Sam couldn't help but be amused by his innocent expression. For all his heroic bravery and good looks he was still the same shy Greg she'd met in the beginning. Her lips stretched into what must have looked like a sad smirk. Her life had been so bleak lately, it felt as if a hard shell of grief was breaking off her face. As she smiled, Greg's eyes sparkled with satisfaction. Once more, she was amazed by how well he knew her, by how in-tune to the smallest details, including the exact words she needed at a given time, or whether a mere smile or shrug would be better.

In a sudden spur of relief and gratitude, she threw herself at Greg and wrapped her arms around him. He stumbled a little, then returned the embrace. His scent was masculine, and his strong arms felt good around her. Greg held her tight for a long moment, then muttered something so low that she couldn't catch it.

"What did you say?" Sam asked.

"Uh, nothing." He shook his head and avoided her searching eyes.

"You said something."

"It's nothing. I'll tell you later."

"I want to know now."

Greg stared at the lockers as if what he'd said was written on one of the metal doors. He seemed very nervous. "You . . . you know already."

She searched his face, trying to make eye contact. Greg's gaze shifted, and with azure intensity met hers, reaching into the deepest corners of her being. Suddenly, she was glad he hadn't spoken the words loud enough for her to hear. What he'd said to her was plain to see in the fervor of his gaze. Once again, he seemed to understand it wasn't time for her to hear him out.

She shook herself and changed the subject. "Are . . . are you planning to stay and do your homework at the library?" Sam asked. After what had crossed between them, it seemed like the most callous thing to ask, but Greg replied casually enough.

"Nah."

"Oh." She was disappointed.

"What if we go to my place and study there? I mean . . . if you want."

Sam felt her breath snag like a piece of silk on splintered wood. The idea of being alone with Greg was exhilarating and scary at the same time.

"I better not," she managed.

"But you will, right? Someday?"

Sam didn't know what to say, but the heat gathering in her cheeks answered the question. An irksome smile of triumph stretched on his lips. It wasn't malicious or conceited, but her womanly pride told her to show her displeasure at such audacity. She shoved Greg as hard as she could. He barely moved and his expression only grew more satisfied.

He laughed wholeheartedly, and Sam almost wanted to punch his teeth out. Instead, she giggled like a four-year-old. Slowly, their laughter died away. Greg leaned in, and she froze. His lips parted just a little as he got closer. He was giving her a chance to turn away, to step back, to run away. But Sam had turned to stone, petrified by desire and apprehension.

Gently, so very gently, Greg's moist lips reached hers. It was a glorious and terrifying moment. She closed her eyes and dared to think of nothing else but that moment. Much too quickly, he pulled away, taking away the bliss that had banished her doubt and pain. The disparity between reality and the dreamlike quality of his tenderness was startling, and made her long for absolute abandonment.

"Maybe I'd like to go back to your place after all," Sam suggested, forgetting all decorum.

Greg's eyes glinted devilishly for a split second, then he bit his lower lip. "Very tempting," he said, lowering his head to rest his forehead on hers. "But . . ." he let the word hang in the air.

"I know." Sam nodded. It wasn't time yet. She still had so much healing to do.

"Soon, I hope."

Sam nodded and their foreheads rubbed together.

He sighed and took his leave. Sam resisted calling out, clenching her fists to contain the yearning his absence left behind. He trotted away. Before he disappeared from sight, Sam squinted and saw that their *vinculum* was bright and strong. She smiled, knowing that a link existed between them and they would always be able to find one another. No matter the distance.

ACKNOWLEDGMENTS

The first book I ever wrote was a young adult fantasy novel. Since, this has been the genre I hold dearest to my heart. I love writing speculative fiction and I'm delighted to finally be able to share my first young adult fantasy novel with all my wonderful readers. Thank you so much for reading *KEEPER* and for your amazing support. You are a huge part of this passionate dream of mine. Keep finding me on Twitter and Facebook. I love connecting with everyone.

As always, I need to thank Michael, Ella, Isabella and Alexander. You cheer for me relentlessly, never letting me give up, no matter what.

Thanks go to my beta reader Bret Williams for always being willing to read and discuss projects with me. To my editor, Luke Anthony, for all the hard work and help. This was a hard project and needed lots of attention to detail. Luke kept a keen eye every step of the way.

To Billie and Subu, always along for the ride.

For news on releases, giveaways and more, visit

WWW.INGRIDSEYMOUR.COM